Aaru

By

David Meredith

ISBN 978-0-9910311-3-9

Acknowledgements

To anyone who has ever wondered; "What's next and what if?"

*

Thanks to Jymmi Davis of White Tree Photography for supplying his amazing pictures for the cover art. You can find more of his expert images on Instagram: @lenslifebyjymmi and on Facebook at https://www.facebook.com/whitetreephoto

*

To Drew Alexandra Hill, the beautiful model whose participation in this project was instrumental in producing the striking cover image

*

Much gratitude to Sean Marmon for his brilliant cover design.

*

Special appreciation to the troubled genius Friedrich Nietzsche, whose words, works, and ideas are liberally referenced throughout this text, as well as numerous other philosophical and religious thinkers and texts – all quotes and references of course, from well before 1923.

"...Death and the stillness of death are the only things certain and common to all in this future......"

Friedrich Nietzsche

TABLE OF CONTENTS

Other Titles Available from David Meredith

The Reflections of Queen Snow White Available NOW on Amazon!

Aaru: Halls of Hel Coming Soon!

Chapter 1

Before…

It was both quiet and not. There was no human sound certainly – no comforting hum of low conversing voices; no occasional chuckle, gasp or cheerful exclamation that might have indicated the warmth of another charitable soul nearby; no whoops or shrieks of joyful children at jubilant play. Quiet reigned, but not like a lullaby her grandmother might have sung at bedtime or a calm summer dusk on the back porch with fireflies winking and flashing in the failing light of perishing day. Rather, it was a silence born of sterility and cold. The only noises were the soft yet incessant beeping of the heart monitor, the dull, low roar of the HVAC unit as it switched itself on and off, and the occasional shrill ejaculation of incomprehensible medical jargon over the intercom.

The whole building is soulless, Rose thought in disgust.

The place was starved for color. There was virtually nothing that was not white or metallic. Much like the silence, the white was not the comforting sort either, like say, gently billowing linens on the clothesline in the back yard on a warm spring day or the sparkling kind like morning sunlight on a virgin snow that kept one home from school. It was a nothing white, a void white – pallid and sickly.

God, I hate hospitals.

Rose tried to lift her hand, but even that slight movement exhausted her. The appendage was covered with bandages and bristled plastic hoses, tubes, sensors, and wires as if they were sprouting from her ailing body - burgeoning from the wasted limb like so many fungi to engulf and devour her like a mass of toadstools might consume some rotted log. It felt as if they had catheterized her soul, bleeding away her life into some indiscernible, whirring machine of a great and fathomless factory – a factory that sucked in the living and spit out the dead or the half dead… if you were lucky.

Rose was not lucky. She was sure of that. If every detective, policeman, and investigative reporter in the world did a search, if they banged on every door and sniffed out every nook and cranny in every far-flung country, distant city, or lonely little town to find the unluckiest possible person, Rose could not imagine that it would not be her own oncology unit door that would be thrown wide with a triumphant "Ah ha!"

A nurse had just left after cleaning her, changing the IV bag, and filling Rose with pills and needles that left her stomach roiling, her head hurting, and her body weak, so very weak. That was the part she hated the most. She hated feeling weak.

Rose detested wanting to throw up all the time but knowing she didn't have the energy to drag herself out of bed and get to the toilet, or even grab for the bed pan on a nearby tray table. Her arm flopped back down to the white sheets in ignominious defeat. She could not even hold up her own skeletal hand.

Things had been this way for so long… She barely remembered anything anymore but hospitals, doctors, needles, and surgeries. There *had* been a time when things were different, she recalled – a time of jumping, playing, and rolling down hills, kicking soccer balls and leaping off of diving boards in the hot summer sun. She remembered dancing and singing and laughing! Albeit vaguely… So long ago, now… Another life… They felt almost like the memories of a different person.

There was a soft knock on the door, and Rose turned her head towards it. A fit and attractive blonde woman came in. Her eyes were downcast, exposing the crown of her head and a good inch of brown roots where she parted her otherwise yellow hair. She was wearing tight khaki pants, a green, collared sports-shirt, and a plastic nametag that read "Gypsie". She smelled strongly of old fry oil.

"Hey sweetie," Rose's mother began softly. "How you feeling, sugar? Any better?"

She sidled past the bed and sat down on a nearby chair.

No! Rose wanted to say, she wanted to *scream.* No! She wasn't better. She would never be better. There *was* no better! There was always just more "treatment" – more pricks and pokes, pills and procedures – things that would keep her alive, but wishing for death.

"No worse," Rose croaked instead. It was not a lie, at least - not today anyway.

"Well, that's a blessing," her mother replied. "Nobody ever has enough good days that we should forget to thank Jesus for 'em…"

Rose groaned inwardly.

Sure, she thought bitterly. *Thanks so much God that I haven't thrown up or crapped myself yet today…*

Mom struggled to say something more, but could not come up with anything. She stared at her folded hands instead. Silence stretched between them.

"Do you wanna watch TV?" her mother ventured at last. "The Triumph Network always has some good singing on... That might make you feel better..."

Rose shook her head weakly, but emphatically no. The last thing she wanted to hear right now was some spackle haired television pastor with his fake, toothpaste smile tell her that if she just prayed hard enough, God would give her whatever she asked for. What a lie...

"Well," her mother tried again. "I think one of your shows might be on. What's that cartoon channel you always watch? Eighty-one, isn't it? I could look..." She half stood, but Rose once more shook her head.

She had no interest in television. There was nothing on TV but healthy, happy people going about their spectacular lives - Lives *not* spent in hospital beds staring up at dim fluorescent lights and cold white ceilings - lives spent envisioning a radiant future that Rose knew would never come... not for her at least. She wanted no part of them. Mother sank back into the chair.

"Alright, sweetie," she fidgeted a few moments more, and then ventured again. "Your doctors seem real excited about this new medication they've put you on. It'll take a day or two before we know for sure of course, but you might be up and around again before you know it! All things are possible in Christ, after all..."

Rose looked at her mother's helpless, ashen face. They both knew her words were hollow. She was not lying really, but Rose did not think her mother believed what she was saying either.

"Sure," Rose replied noncommittally. "I hope so."

The uncomfortable silence enveloped them again. The monitor beeped. Somewhere far off down the hallway they heard hard-soled footsteps crack against linoleum flooring, and then fade away into the distance.

"You know," her mother tried again after several more awkward moments. "Your sister's gonna come by this afternoon to see you when school lets out. She really misses you, and she's really looking forward to seeing you again. That'll be nice, won't it?"

Rose arched an eyebrow.

"Really?" she asked. "I thought you said no one under fourteen was allowed up here?"

Her mother got up and began pacing, wringing her hands.

"Well," she replied nervously. "It's been a real long time, hasn't it? And Koren really wants to see you before..." She stopped herself and started again. "Well, she's begged and begged actually... Every day! So the doctors finally said yes... They thought it'd be alright for a little while, at least..."

Before.

Rose stared at her mother. Her throat was suddenly tight and her mouth dry. She felt her heart flutter in her chest. *Before what?!* She wanted to ask, to *demand*, but dared not put voice to the question. Rose was too afraid that she knew the answer already, had always known.

"When will she come?" Rose asked faintly instead.

"Koren gets outta school at three," Her mother answered, forcing her face to smile. "So she'll probably get here by about four or four thirty, you know, with traffic and all..."

"Okay," Rose said.

They stared at each other. What was left to say?

Her mother stood and leaned over the bed. She kissed Rose on her smooth, pale head and hugged her tight. She made as if to go, but then abruptly stopped.

"Oh! I almost forgot! I brought you something," she exclaimed, before riffling around in her purse. She pulled out a small wrapped bundle and laid it on her daughter's lap.

Rose lifted her hand and poked at the amorphous package. It was about the size of a soccer ball and wrapped in blue paper with yellow roses. She could not quite make her fingers grasp it.

"Let me help you, sweetie..." her mother offered, before reaching down to unwrap the gift.

Rose's initial impulse was to be angry, but it wasn't really at her mother. It wasn't *her* fault that Rose's stupid hands wouldn't work. It wasn't *her* fault that her daughter was so broken and weak. Rose was mad at herself, she realized - furious with her treacherous, sickly body. She let her hand fall back to the bed sheet and watched as her mother opened the present.

The colorful paper parted to reveal a black and white lump. It was a panda, Rose realized - a stuffed one wearing a red *kimono*. The panda held a red folding fan and wore tiny wooden sandals. On her face was a happy grin. She was quite cute, and Rose ghosted a smile in spite of herself.

"Do you like it?" her mother asked as she noted her daughter's pleased expression. "I knew that you were into all that Japanese cartoon stuff, so I thought you might. I found this cute, little thing at that comic book store you always went to before..."

Mother trailed off.

Before.

Yes, there was that word again. Rose did not like that word anymore. It implied both that everything good was well past and that nothing more of value was to come. She had had interests once, dreams even, but all of those were *before* - Before she was sick, before she had ever heard the word "leukemia", before the sum of her existence had turned into a revolving door of monotonous boredom interspersed with periods of crippling pain - Before her whole life had simply stopped.

"Thanks, mom," Rose breathed. "She's really cute."

"I'm glad you like her, Rose," her mother replied. "She can keep you company 'til your sister gets here. I have to go back into the restaurant this afternoon. Charlie's been trying to give me a few more hours here and there, you know... but I'll be back over as soon as I get off!" Her eyes pleaded for understanding and forgiveness.

"Yeah," Rose sighed.

She was not pleased at being left alone, but it was probably for the best. Her family needed the money after all. Rose's medical bills were ruining them, she knew – knew and hated herself for it. Besides, whenever her mother was around these days, she always acted all nervous and weird, making them both uncomfortable.

"I'll see you when you get back then."

"All right, sweetie." Her mother kissed her on the cheek. "Do you need anything?"

"Nah, I'm okay."

"I'll just put your button here." Gypsie paused, set the panda doll in the crook of her daughter's bandaged left arm, and laid the call button in Rose's right hand.

"Just push it if you want anything. Try to rest a little. It'll make you feel better... And don't forget to pray! The Lord will give comfort to them who ask..."

"Okay," Rose answered with another poorly suppressed grimace.

Her mother still seemed reluctant to be on her way, but neither of them could think of anything more to say. At last her mom waved awkwardly, turned, and walked from the room leaving the door open, but Rose was otherwise alone - alone with the single, terrifying question.

Before what? Koren wants to come before what?!

Rose did not want to think about it. She tried to put it out of her mind and just focus her attention on the face of her new, smiling panda princess with her red paper fan, but the question was still there, echoing through her brain over and over again in the silence of the hospital oncology ward.

Before... the end?

*

Rose tried to rest, but couldn't. The time seemed to drag. It always did. So when she finally heard the indistinct murmur of hushed voices coming down the hallway, she perked her ears and looked toward the open doorway eagerly.

She was expecting Koren, so she was disappointed to see it was only her father accompanied by a middle aged man in a white lab coat. He was clearly yet another doctor, but she didn't recognize him. Rose deflated a little in her bed.

"Hey, munchkin."

Her father whispered her affectionate childhood nickname as he came into the room. He was wearing a short-sleeved, button-down blue shirt that was splattered and splotched with vivid, black oil-stains, and his face was smudged with grease. A patch on his left breast pocket read simply, "Bill" in thick, block letters. He must have just come from work.

"How you feeling, girl?"

Rose shrugged, not wanting to waste her shallow breath answering the inane question.

"Koren?" she ventured instead.

"Soon, sweetie, soon," her father promised. "She's in the waiting room now. You know, they only let two people in at a time, and I wanted you to meet someone - someone who I think can help you!"

Yep, Rose thought unenthusiastically. *Definitely another doctor.*

"It's nice to meet you, Rose," the middle aged man said as if by talking too loudly, he might break her somehow. How she wished people would just speak to her like a human being again! "I'm sorry this has happened to you."

His was not a bad voice really. It was low and gentle like the nighttime broadcaster on the easy listening station her mother tuned into before bed. His grey eyes were kind and he was neatly pressed wearing a sensible tie, the top of which was just visible at the neck of his long white coat. His grey hair was implacably gelled and coifed. It glistened faintly beneath the dim fluorescent lights.

Rose sniffed. "Me too…"

The corners of the man's mouth turned ever so slightly upwards.

"I'm sure," he said. "I'm here to help you Rose."

Rose rolled her eyes.

"I'm tired of doctors," she said.

The man did legitimately smile at that. "I'm sure of that too, Rose, so it should relieve you to know that I am most certainly *not* a doctor. At least… not in the sense that you are used to…"

"Just listen, Rose," her father pleaded. "This isn't more medicine or chemo this time. It's… It's different…"

"Very different," the man added. "And it won't hurt at all. If you let me, I can save you Rose."

If she let him? Since when had anyone asked what *she* thought about more treatment, more medicine, more procedures, different hospitals, or new research facilities? Why did anyone suddenly care about what *she* wanted?

Then she thought; *Koren is coming.* The sooner she let this guy finish whatever it was he had to say, the sooner she could see her sister. She sighed in resignation.

"They all want to save me," Rose croaked with a slight sneer. "It's worked so far, I guess. I'm alive, but I feel like I'm fading… Like every day a little more of me is gone - gone into all of these stupid machines they have plugged me into, but they make my body keep chugging along a little while longer… It'll probably keep going after I'm gone all together…" She met the man's eyes gravely. "I'm getting tired of being 'saved'."

"I know it, Rose," the man replied intensely. He knelt at her bedside and took her cold, thin hand in his own. "Trust me, I do. I know *exactly* what you mean, but I think you misunderstand me. I don't just want to save your life. I want to save *you*, all of you, the *essence* of you – I want to save who you are at your soul so that it will live forever!"

Rose sighed.

Okay, she thought. *So not a doctor then... He must be a pastor or priest or something.* She'd seen almost as many of them as doctors.

"I already '*believe*'," Rose wearily answered. "I said the prayer and everything. I don't need to hear the spiel again. I think as far as that goes I'm as 'saved' as I'm going to get."

"I still don't think you quite understand what I mean," the man replied with a small frown, "but please, don't dismiss what I offer lightly. I come to offer you *hope*, Rose."

He walked across the room and picked up a framed photograph that was lying face down on the dresser. He looked down at it a moment then turned it over and held it up so Rose could see it. It depicted two smiling girls wearing shiny pink jerseys and soccer cleats. They each had a companionable arm wrapped around the shoulders of the other. The taller of the two had waist-length curly brown hair and a happy face flushed with health and high spirits. The shorter was very attractive and sported a blonde bob of a haircut. She held up her middle and index fingers in a peace sign as she bit her lower lip with a defiant jut of her pretty chin. Rose noted Koren's sassy expression and smiled in spite of herself.

The man pointed to the long-haired girl on the left. "I want to save *her*, Rose."

"I don't understand..."

"I know you don't," the doctor-priest soothed. "Not yet, but you *will*. Wouldn't you like to run and jump and play again? Wouldn't you like to lace up your cleats and run out onto the pitch one more time? Wouldn't you like to be *this* Rose again?" He again pointed at the picture. "I believe I can give that to you... If you let me."

Rose stared at him. She was suddenly suspicious and more than a little angry. What he was suggesting... Well, it was simply impossible. It wasn't fair to get her hopes up. It wasn't fair to tease! *Of course*, that's what she wanted!

That's what she saw every night when she closed her eyes and drifted off to sleep. In her dreams she was still healthy and strong. Her erstwhile, kinky brown hair, with which she had always taken such care, still whipped and tossed in the blustery wind. In her dreams she could run or even fly if she chose, but that was all they were – dreams. She turned her gaze away in unshrouded disgust.

"If a hundred, hundred doctors can't manage that after four years," she replied bitterly. "What makes you any different? I already told you. I'm tired of doctors. I'm tired of 'new treatments' and 'new medicine' I... I'm... I'm just tired! So... So just... leave me alone and let me *die* already!"

It was the first time she had said the words out loud.

Her father gasped.

"You don't mean that!" He exclaimed. "Just hear the man out, Rose. What'll it hurt? It might actually help you!"

"Do you know how many times I've heard that before, daddy?" Rose asked dispiritedly. "Maybe *this* will help. Maybe *that* will help. This new drug, that new chemo regimen... I'm over it! I just... I just wanna see Koren before... Before..."

"I understand, Rose." The man stood, put a restraining hand on her father's shoulder. He gave Rose a sympathetic smile. "Really I do, and I *will* leave you alone if you so choose. It's your right, but just think on this; There won't be any needles or pills or surgeries. For it to work, all you have to do is to concentrate on things that make you happy. That's all. Just leave the rest to me. All you have to do is recall your favorite things, and friends, and what your best days were like. All you have to do is think happy thoughts. Even if it doesn't do any good at all, wouldn't that be better than moping about, dwelling on all the sadness that so surrounds you of late?"

"What are you going to do?" rejoined Rose acidly. "Sprinkle me with pixie dust?"

"Perhaps," the man in the white lab coat chuckled. A much broader smile spread across his face. "In a manner of speaking, I suppose I just may at that! I might go so far as to say I'll send you to Never-Never Land!" He laughed. "That wouldn't be so bad, would it? Seriously though, it's up to you, Rose. You can refuse if you want, but I hope you'll give it a try..."

"Come on, Rose," her father interjected again. "What'll it hurt? It never hurts to try."

"Dad," Rose countered as she recalled the last four years of on-again, off-again chemotherapy, radiation treatments, and bone marrow transplants with a shudder. "Yes it does. Sometimes, daddy, it *does* hurt to try."

"I promise you, Rose," the man knelt at her bedside. "This will not. It will not hurt at all. In fact, if what I propose is successful, you'll never hurt ever again. I hope you'll think about it at least. This is most likely your only chance. Just *think* about it. I'll come again tomorrow…"

He stood, shook her father's hand and left. Dad looked at her, frustration and helplessness clearly scrawled across his haggard face.

"Please, Rose. Just give it a try for me. Please? For all of us… Don't lose hope…"

"Can I see Koren now please, daddy?" Rose asked, voice quavering. She didn't want any more hopes. She couldn't handle her heart breaking again as they were dashed. "Please?"

Her father sighed in defeat and looked at the floor. "Of course, munchkin… I'll go get her…"

*

Rose did her best to compose herself while her father was out getting her little sister. She felt responsible somehow – obligated to show Koren a brave face. How she missed the other girl! They had shared a room since infancy and used to spend nearly every day together.

They had most of the same friends and played together on nearly all of the same sports teams growing up. It had always been Rose's job to take care of Koren. Whether kissing away bad dreams when their parents were still asleep or fighting off bullies in the school yard, Rose had always taken it upon herself to protect the smaller girl. She tried to sit a little straighter as her sister hesitantly entered the room.

"Rose," her father called softly from the doorway. "Your sister's here… I'll just… I'll just leave you two alone for a few minutes."

For a long moment the two simply looked at each other. Rose noted that Koren had grown her hair out. It now reached just past her shoulders. She was wearing make-up too – a little blush, purple eye shadow and lip gloss. She looked almost grown up and Rose smiled.

"You look pretty, Koren," she said at last. "I like your hair."

"Thanks…" replied her sister, touching her golden tresses. "You look… You…" She bit her lower lip as it began to quiver, her voice to shake. She averted her gaze "How are you feeling?"

"Tired," sighed Rose, "very, very tired… but today's a pretty good day. I haven't thrown up, and I've had a lot of visitors… makes the time go faster. Thanks for coming to see me…"

Koren nodded. "I've wanted to come *forever*. Texting just isn't cutting it… It has been *awful* not seeing you. It's a stupid rule about having to be fourteen. I mean, come on! Thirteen, fourteen, what's the difference?! I just… I just really needed to see you…"

"Before," Rose finished for her.

Koren gave a loud sob and threw her arms around her sister's neck. She crushed Rose's head to her chest.

"I'm scared, Rose!" she sobbed. "They didn't say why, but they don't break the rules for *anybody*! They've always been super strict, and the only reason they'd break them now and let me come up here… The only reason I can see you must be… I'm scared, Rose!"

Rose felt her own throat grow tight, but did her best to maintain her composure. She tried to smile.

"Come on, now" she chided gently. "Cut that out! I haven't left you yet, have I? Keep it down, or one of those Nazi nurses will come in here and make you leave!"

It took Koren a moment, but she quieted her tears and wiped her eyes.

"I'm sorry, Rose," she apologized. "I'm not trying to upset you… I just… I'm… I'm sorry. In fact, I brought you something!"

She began digging in the gym bag she had slung over one shoulder. After a moment, she removed a large, white orb scrawled all over in black Sharpie.

"The girls wanted to send you the game ball from regionals," she laid the soccer ball in Rose's lap next to her panda doll. "Everyone signed it."

Rose looked down. 'Region III Champions' was boldly emblazoned in gold along with the date and then surrounded by nearly two dozen signatures and short messages: Get well soon! We miss you! Look forward to seeing you on the pitch again! - among many, many others.

Rose felt tears welling in her eyes.

"That's great, Koren," she murmured. "I wish I coulda been there…"

Neither spoke. They just looked down at the soccer ball in silence.

"Rose," Koren ventured at last. "Are you... Are you scared?"

"Yes," she answered truthfully. "A little. I'm a little scared, but more than that Koren, more than being scared, I'm just *tired*! I'm tired of being sick. I'm tired of everyone coming in here feeling sorry for me. I'm tired of being stuck in bed all the time. I'm tired of missing *everything*!" She batted at the championship ball in frustration. "Maybe... Maybe I'm just... Just ready for it to be over with, Koren. Maybe it's just time..."

"You don't believe that, do you?" Koren interrupted, eyes wide. "Don't talk like that, Rose. It'll get better. You'll see! Like, daddy was telling me in the car on the way over here about a new treatment or something he wanted them to try. I know there's been a ton, but they'll get the right one eventually! I just know they will! He said you'd be able to run again!"

"Damn it, Koren!" Spat Rose angrily. "Don't you start in on me too! Dad was just in here with that doctor... pastor... whatever the Hell he was... guy saying all the same crap as you! I'm sick of hoping, Koren! I'm sick of getting my hopes up and then everything falling apart! I..."

She stopped. Koren was biting her lower lip nearly hard enough to draw blood. Her bright blue eyes were swimming with tears. Rose deflated, and the anger bled out of her all at once. She did not want to upset her sister, especially when she saw her so seldom. She didn't really have the energy to be mad anyway, and this wasn't the other girl's fault.

"I'm sorry, Koren, I..." Rose began softly, but she stopped when the younger girl threw her arms around her neck once more.

"I don't want you to die, Rose!" she cried into the other girl's shoulder. "I don't want you to go away. Please don't leave me! You have to fight! Remember what you promised me? Remember what you said?"

Rose did her best to drape her infirmly weak arms around her sister. She felt her own tears coming.

"I remember..." she breathed. Then she met her sister's eyes. "I don't want to die either, Koren," she whimpered. "I don't want to die! I want to *live*! But not like this... not spending every day in bed alone, staring at the ceiling too weak to do anything, even move! Not throwing up all the time and having to be cleaned and fed by strangers like some big baby! I even... I even have to wear diapers now, Koren, *diapers*! I can't take it! No more! I just don't want any more! I want it to end, Koren! I'm so tired of hurting! I'm so, so tired…"

They spoke no more after that. They just held each other. When their father returned, Koren was reluctant to leave. Rose could tell her sister was afraid this was the last time they would see each other. She was a little afraid of that herself.

Koren lingered until nearly thirty five minutes after visitation hours ended, but at last allowed herself to be escorted away by a sympathetic nurse. As her father followed them out he turned back to Rose, his own eyes red with ruthlessly suppressed tears.

"Please, Rose," he begged. "Come on. Just one more try… Just one try - one more for Koren. Please?"

He flipped the light switch off and left.

Rose closed her eyes and let out a shuddering sob. She wouldn't allow herself to be betrayed again. She could not bring herself to hope. Rose had been let down far too many times already, but neither could she bring herself to steal the last shreds of it from Koren.

Alright, she thought in defeat as she slipped into sleep. *One more try for Koren. One last try… then finally… rest.*

*

The man in the lab coat showed up early the next morning with a big cart load of equipment. He asked if Rose had changed her mind, and all she could do in response was nod unenthusiastically. He gave his tiny smile again as if that was just what he had expected all along. Then he got to work setting up what must have been a heaping ton of unidentifiable wires, dials and electronic devices.

He introduced himself finally as 'Adams' as he leaned her bed back. Then, from the bottom compartment of his cart, he produced what looked to be a large, white plastic cube with one side cut out – something like a boxing helmet. It was covered with hundreds of blinking lights. He pressed a button and the box beeped. All of the lights turned yellow.

"Now Rose," Mr. Adams began as he settled himself on the chair next to her bed and plugged a wire from the rolling cart into the device. "I need you to lay back and relax. Try not to move too much. I am just going to put this over your head and then maybe I'll have a better idea of just what we've got to work with…"

Rose really had no idea what Mr. Adams was talking about, but was far too weak to protest. She offered no resistance as he laid the contraption over her head. Mr. Adams stared fixedly at a screen on his cart, and after a few seconds the box began to buzz and whir. It flashed with pulses of blinding light.

"Good girl," murmured Mr. Adams as he manipulated the controls with an intensely concentrating look on his face. "Don't move. Not a bit… Stay completely still and this will just take a few minutes more…"

She must have lain like that for a half an hour or better, but at last there was a loud beep, and Mr. Adams switched off the machine. He raised her bed up.

"Now, that wasn't so bad, was it?" he quipped. "All done … with that part at least."

"What was that?" asked Rose.

"I was getting a scan of your brain," Mr. Adams explained. "Like I said, just to kind of see what's what. You see, we need to map the structure of…"

"Like an MRI?" Rose offered.

Mr. Adams halted at her interruption, seeming to consider.

"Sort of… but not exactly. I guess that's close enough though. It's similar I suppose."

"Are we done?" Rose asked hopefully.

"Almost," said Mr. Adams as he began digging in his cart again. "Just a couple more little things, then I'll leave you alone, but the hard part's all finished with."

Mr. Adams pulled a small black box from a different cabinet near the middle of the cart, and placed it on the bedside table. He began plugging into it a veritable spider's web of twisted and tangled wires. He flipped a switch, and the box lit up, covered in lights of red, green and yellow.

"There we go." He nodded in satisfaction. "I'll just need to stick these right here…" He reached toward Rose's head, and she recoiled, but he only chuckled. "Remember what I promised? This won't hurt a bit. Just relax."

He began affixing some kind of sensors all over her smooth, hairless head. When he finished, there was barely an inch of exposed scalp remaining.

"This will help me?" Rose asked suspiciously. She did not care for all the wires and machines she had been connected to before. Now it looked as if Mr. Adams had tripled them at least. She was sure she must look ridiculous.

"I hope so," answered Mr. Adams. "We'll just have to wait and see, but that will really depend on you, you know…"

Rose furrowed her brow. "What do you mean?"

"Well, first of all, don't fiddle with the wires," he instructed sternly. "They have to stay put to do their job. Next," this time he smiled. "It's time to start doing what I told you yesterday. I need you to get started on all of those happy thoughts!"

Rose made a dubious scowl. "Seriously?"

"I'm always serious," answered Mr. Adams with a bland expression, but there was a mischievous glint in his eye. "So yes, but we'll give you some help."

He walked around to the other side of the cart and started removing more boxes.

"I've taken the liberty of talking to your friends and family about the sorts of things you like to do," he said as he continued to pull containers from inside the cart. Rose could not see well, but it appeared to be board games, video games, and stacks of *manga* graphic novels. "You'll be having quite a few visitors as well" he continued. "I've cleared everything with the hospital already."

Mr. Adams paused in what he was doing to meet Rose's gaze seriously.

"Now," he stated. "I cannot emphasize enough how important it is for you try to enjoy yourself as much as possible…"

Rose regarded him with a bemused half smile. "You are seriously serious?"

"I am," he replied. "I won't get into all the boring details, but believe me when I tell you that your emotional state will drastically affect the outcome. The happier you are, the better."

Rose chuckled at the irony. Here she was, confined to bed, too weak to even move, and bristling with more wires than a power plant substation.

Happy. Sure. Easy. She thought.

"I'll try," Rose agreed acidly.

"That's all I ask, Rose," replied Mr. Adams.

Contrary to her expectations, what followed was perhaps the nicest week Rose had spent in months if not years. Her parents both took off work and made a special effort to insure that someone was with her all the time. Her mother even brought some things from her

room back home – an *Inuyasha The Movie* poster she had bought on
E-bay, a Japanese tapestry she found at a second hand store a few
years ago that depicted a castle on a high hill covered with trees and
waterfalls, and (even though her mother had never really approved
of it) a pin-up poster of Ronaldo Casillas, her favorite soccer player.
He bore a fierce expression with his Real Madrid jersey off, clutched
in his victorious fist, sculpted abs and pecs glistening with sweat
beneath hot stadium lights.

Koren came three more times, and Rose even got a surprise
visit from her whole soccer team (a huge hospital rules violation).
They looked at family pictures, listened to music, played games, and
watched movies on Netflix constantly for six days. In particular, she
enjoyed *Bend it Like Beckham, Frozen,* and *Summer Wars* - a
dubbed over Japanese *anime*. Even though she still felt decidedly
sick and weak through it all, she could swallow her discomfort and
put it out of her mind most of the time. All in all, it was the closest
she had come to feeling happy in a very long while.

A nice way to end things, she thought.

*

Two days later, they moved her to the ICU – something
about a 'staph infection', whatever that was. Apparently, whatever it
was that Mr. Adams had attempted was not working, and Rose
steeled herself, awaiting the inevitable.

At least I tried for Koren, she thought. Maybe that would be
something her sister could hold on to. The idea gave Rose a measure
of peace.

She fell asleep a little after noon that day and dreamed of
kicking the winning goal in the District Three Championship game.
Her long, brown hair blew and fluttered in the wind as her
teammates hoisted her onto their shoulders and screamed her name
while she held aloft a golden trophy. In the bleachers, the princess
panda her mother had given her danced in enthusiastic celebration,
and the Japanese school girl from *Summer Wars* clapped and clapped
next to a fiercely cheering and shirtless Ronaldo Casillas.

When Rose awoke, it was very late. Or perhaps it was very
early. The hospital was never really dark, of course. There were
always those horrid fluorescent tubes glowing in the hallways and a
steady if intermittent stream of doctors and nurses wandering the

halls as they silently executed their duties. However, there was something more subdued about the wee hours of the morning, as if the near constant silence was even more muted somehow. Rose knew immediately that something was wrong.

The first thing she became aware of was a sensation of frightful cold. Her body shivered violently. As usual she was infirmly weak. However, this time she felt nearly paralyzed, barely able even to draw air into to her lungs. She was dizzy too, as if she stood at the edge of a precipitous cliff. Her chest hurt.

An alarm went off, shrill and blaring and suddenly her still and quiet room was filled with frantic people in light blue scrubs. Everything seemed like it was happening in slow motion - the nurses' movements, the droning, unexcited voices calling out incomprehensible medical gibberish to each other. It was as if Rose witnessed the scene from under water, everything wavering and surreal and she strangely disconnected.

"She's crashing," someone stated with not nearly the degree of excitement Rose felt the dire situation merited. "We've got a Code Blue. BP 81 over 47 and falling."

"I've got a temp reading of 103.4." said someone else.

"Could you please wait in the hallway, sir," came an overly sweet, female voice.

"What's going on?!" Rose recognized her father's frantic cries. "What's the matter?!"

"Sir, I really need you to..."

"BP 73 over 39" came the first voice again. "Lean her back. Elevate her legs."

Black spots danced in Rose's field of vision. Her body started to spasm and jerk. Her stomach heaved, and she vomited. Bile and blood quickly soaked the front of her thin hospital gown.

"I need a fresh saline bag on her IV now, please," stated an older male voice. "And a 500 parts concentration of dobutamine on drip as well."

Another buzzer went off.

"She's flat-lined. No pulse, I've got no pulse."

"Prepare to defib on my mark," came the older male voice again. "Three, two, one, clear!"

Rose's body convulsed as the shock was delivered.

"BP, stat."

"No pulse, doctor."

"Let's give her another one. Ready… Clear."

The electrical charge shot through her again, and the room seemed to go silent. She could still see the doctor and the nurses moving about her ICU bed in their slow, but purposeful way. Their mouths moved, but she could no longer hear any words that made sense. She caught sight of her reflection in the stainless steel surface of a nearby machine.

Could that really be me? So gaunt and pale and skeletal…

The doctor delivered another shock and it felt like she was jerked back to reality again staring up into the blinding light of the overhead examination lamp.

"I've got a pulse. BP 69 over 31…" The neutral voice trailed off. "No… Wait… No good. It's falling again…"

Again the alarm sounded.

"Alright, let's get ready to defibrillate again," came the doctor's voice. "On my… What's all of this garbage she's got stuck to her head?" the voice muttered in annoyance. "This isn't our equipment. Get it off now! It's in the way!"

Rose felt someone grasp the wires attached to the sensors on her head. There was a tug, and then everything went dark like a suddenly unplugged TV set.

Chapter 2

An Empty Swing

Koren sat alone in the backyard swing behind her house. It was well dusk and full dark would be coming soon. The temperature had already fallen quite a bit since she had come outside. Her skin prickled with goose bumps, but she made no move to warm herself. Koren sat staring at her folded hands, swinging slowly back and forth. She concentrated on the rhythmic creak of the long disused playground equipment and drew little circles in the dust at her feet with the toe of her shoe.

She remembered when her father had put the swings up on a broad branch in the ancient tree. Koren had been quite small – four or five perhaps, but even now as a young teenager, she vividly recalled the initial delight when it had been revealed one autumn morning for her birthday. What made it especially exciting was that daddy had made two seats - one hung low for her and one higher for Rose. She had been positively giddy with the idea that they would be able to swing together.

Koren sighed and glanced at the empty swing beside her. Her own slow movement made it sway back and forth a little as if perhaps Rose's spirit was right there, swinging next to her one last time. She swallowed a sob and clenched her suddenly moist eyes tightly closed. Tears rolled down her cheeks to drip from her chin and make tiny, dark spots on her white dress and upon the dusty ground.

Oh, Rose... She thought miserably. *Why?*

Rose was right. Koren had been foolish to hope. The whole grueling ordeal had all been so unfair; As if one day her sister had been perfectly healthy and active – running and playing with her, watching out for her, sometimes fighting with her. Then the next everything had changed.

In a matter of weeks her sister's long, brown hair was gone. In a matter of months her developing body was reduced to a skeleton, pale skin drawn far too tightly over stark angular bones. And in a matter of years? Koren looked at the empty swing beside her, put her face in her hands, and wept.

Why did it have to be poor, sweet Rose? Why couldn't it have happened to some rapist or murderer, or terrorist, a steady stream of whom paraded across the nightly newscasts in a never-ending procession each night? Why not some robber or thief? She had no answers for any of those questions, and the Receiving of Friends she had just returned from had provided no greater illumination either.

The minister had thought of a great deal to say, of course. They always did. Long, rambling platitudes about how God had a plan, and perhaps we could just not see it yet. Rose had been put on this Earth for a purpose, and now that purpose was complete. They should all be happy about it. They should *celebrate* that Rose had moved on to everlasting glory!

The words felt hollow. Koren could not even begin conceiving how she might feel any joy that her sister was dead. It felt disloyal to even consider it, regardless of what the pastor said.

Of course, seeing her sister so weak and miserable had been horrible. However, perhaps because of her own youthful naivety, Koren had never considered the idea that her sister would not one day get better. In her mind, nothing seemed possible but that Rose would eventually get up out of bed to run and play again just like she always had before.

That's the way it's supposed *to work!* Koren howled in her brain all through the somber service at the funeral home. *You get sick. You go to the hospital. They give you some medicine, and in a few days you're all better again!*

It had been surreal, the funeral. Watching her sister lie there in that polished, pillowed box, eyes closed as if sleeping. The last time Koren talked to Rose, her sister had been bald, pale and skeletally thin. In the open coffin her face had been painted and her nails done. They had even found a fairly realistic wig somewhere that almost matched the way she remembered her sister's hair from before. Rose had looked healthier dead than alive, and the idea deeply unsettled Koren.

She stolidly endured through most of the service. The petty, insufficient words from a series of grim and doleful speakers entered through one ear and out the other – worthy neither of note nor recollection. She bit her lower lip and held back her tears all the way until the speaking finally stopped, and two elderly gentlemen from the funeral home came in to close the lid of Rose's coffin.

There was something final in that closing – more so than a car door or front door or window - and the irrevocability of it tore at

Koren's soul. In that moment, with the soft, but irreversible click of the coffin latch, she realized fully that she would never see her sister again. Rose was gone forever.

Koren had wept then, long and hard until she felt she must surely have no tears left, but they did not stop even as her father coaxed her into the waiting car and drove her home. Now, hours later, all she felt was empty as she stared off over the horizon watching the apricot sun sink slowly behind the distant hills. The wind blew, rustling the leaves over her head.

"Koren?"

The deep, hesitant voice floated to her from behind, and she closed her eyes. Why did he have to bother her now? She was tired of words.

"It's getting kinda cold out here don'cha think?"

"I'm fine, dad," she replied, not looking back.

"You should probably come in…"

There was no force behind his words. Her father recited them like the lyrics of a song he had memorized but did not really want to sing – something he was obligated to say, but felt no conviction about.

"We've got the graveside service early tomorrow. You should eat something and go to bed, sweetie…"

Koren's chin sunk to her chest.

"I'm not hungry," she murmured.

"Koren…" her father began, but did not say anything more.

He wanted to say more, she could tell. The silence was pregnant, the emptiness begging to be filled. She even wanted him to say the words, she realized – words of comfort, words of healing, something to make the pain in her heart less somehow. Only, he did not have any.

He felt the same as she, Koren realized - empty and helpless. He wished he had the words, but simply did not, and she could not fault him for it. What would they have been anyway? Instead, he simply sighed.

"Well… come in soon," her father said. Then he turned and went back into the house.

Koren continued to sit and stare off into the distance, as if maybe, just maybe, she could glimpse some portion of the somewhere Rose had gone off to. The sky steadily changed from orange, to red, to purple until fading finally to the velvety sable of night. The stars appeared like diamonds cast one by one upon a stygian blanket – beacons glimmering from beyond the infinite, but still Koren could catch no view of what she sought. The onyx firmament above gave no answer to the nagging question echoing through her brain over and over again.

Why, God? Why?!

*

The next day was even worse. They had to get to the funeral home early, and line up the cars in preparation for the most perverse sort of parade that Koren had ever witnessed. The hearse took the lead – a vehicle that seemed specifically designed to look extra especially forlorn.

Then the suited gentlemen from the evening before passed out the party favors. That was how Koren thought of them in her morose cynicism anyway. Decorations with which to adorn their vehicles - gold letters on black plastic with magnets on the bottom - were attached to every roof. They grandly proclaimed "FUNERAL".

When everything was in readiness a couple of motorcycle policemen flipped on their lights and led the somber vehicle carrying her sister's remains out of the parking lot. Another pulled in behind the last car. Her father's car, in which she rode along with her mother, followed the hearse closely. It positively crept down the road as if trying to drag the whole miserable ordeal out as long as possible. Traffic on both sides of the street pulled to the shoulder and stopped, gawking at Koren's misery, it felt like.

When at last they reached the cemetery, the procession seemed to grow even more onerous, as if the hearse driver wanted to force everyone to take a good, long gander at the inevitable mortality awaiting them all. Orderly rows of marble markers and monuments filled Koren's vision. There was a tree here and a mausoleum there, of course, but the endless columns of bleached, angular stones were otherwise unbroken, stretching to the limits of the horizon as if the whole world was nothing but row upon row of neat, buried corpses.

When they finally stopped, it was on a little hill near a large ash tree, straight and tall. It shaded a specially demarcated section of the cemetery, surrounded by a low iron fence. Koren thought it was the saddest place she had ever seen.

Unlike the stern, staid pillars of alabaster she had glimpsed on her way up to this low, grassy hillock, each of these markers and statues bore an element of whimsy that seemed horridly perverse here. One gravestone was decorated with colorful laminate balloons and puppies. A bleached, stone statue depicted a little boy with his thumb in his mouth holding a teddy bear. A third monument she noticed was decorated with pink ballerina slippers and a glass encased photograph of a smiling little girl in piggy tales who could not have been more than six. At the gate, the mourners were greeted by a serene statue of Jesus; palms spread wide, nail wounds vivid. At its base were carved the words: "Let the little children come unto Me."

Koren looked away.

They got to Rose's spot in short order. A fresh, deep gouge in the cold, loamy earth stretched at their feet. It was surrounded by thick, green plastic, but there was no disguising the scraggly roots jutting from the sides of the precisely squared hole like so many exposed nerves. It reminded Koren of wriggling worms. She shuddered; not at all interested in where that line of thinking might take her dark imaginings.

A large brass rack was stuffed with what must have been hundreds if not thousands of meticulously arranged and fragrant flowers. However, even that vivid splash of color could not begin to counter the ashen gloom of the heavily overcast day. The display sat to the left of a hard, gray block of stone, the name "Rose Johnson" a vivid scar on its otherwise glassy surface.

Koren's father, his brother, and four of her older cousins slowly pulled the brown lacquered box from the rear of the hearse and gently set it on the contrivance of pulleys and straps that would lower it into the pit. Dozens of family and friends disembarked their vehicles. Some Koren knew. Others she did not. They seated themselves in rows of folding chairs under a green pavilion struck just over the grave.

More words were said. *Would the words never end?* She recalled not a syllable of them later. Instead, Koren remembered the quietude, broken only by the groaning wind, the chirping birds, and the occasional sniffle or poorly stifled sob. Then, when at last the long loquacious display was concluded, they all piled back into their cars and went home.

That was that.

It felt strange to just leave Rose there – like abandonment. Her sister should come home with them, Koren thought. Wouldn't she be lonely? Wouldn't she be cold? It was a ridiculous idea, she knew, but she could not help thinking it anyway.

When they arrived at the house, her mother went to the kitchen to begin preparing dinner, and her father went outside to sit on the back porch. No one spoke. Koren went upstairs to the room she had shared with Rose her entire life, not bothering to flip on the lights. The half-light of mid-afternoon still illuminated the bedroom dimly through a single window.

Rose had not slept here for months of course, but it felt especially empty now. Rose's side of the room looked entirely too neat and clean, but for the slightly darker squares on the wall where her poster and tapestry had hung. Koren had no idea what to do next, so she just sat on her sister's bed and stared at her hands. Gradually, the sun fell behind the distant hills, and the room grew dark. Still Koren sat.

She thought nothing. She felt nothing. All she knew was she had been wounded. Koren was hurt, perhaps mortally so, and she had no idea how to heal it. At the moment, she could not even really summon the motivation to try.

"Oh, Rose…" she breathed into the darkness.

Then she stopped herself, not wanting to voice the question she knew would come – that always came. It was the one for which Koren knew she would never receive adequate answer.

Why?!

***

Koren looked at herself in the mirror, detesting what she saw, but too stubborn to change it either. A poster of her favorite singer, a shirtless Jonas Perry, hung on the wall over her bed. It was the one she had fought her mother so hard to put up and match Rose's Ronaldo Casillas poster, but it brought her no comfort. His inviting grin seemed to be mocking her, and Koren could not help resenting it.

She was angry. She was always angry these days, and her parents drove her crazy about it. They were constantly nagging, ever asking what was wrong, and Koren could never tell them. Asking and asking and *asking*! How the Hell was *she* supposed to know what was wrong?! It just was.

Her parents were not the only ones either. It had gotten to the point that she avoided all of her old friends. She didn't play soccer anymore. Her golden hair was now dyed an unnaturally dark shade of black and matched her equally sable lipstick and fingernail polish.

Screw 'em all! She thought belligerently. *Who are they to tell me how to feel anyway?!*

The six weeks since Rose's funeral had been miserable. Koren did not really understand why they had been so miserable. No one had been mean to her. In fact, her friends and teachers had gone out of their way to be nice. Nothing else particularly tragic had occurred, but for some reason all of the old things that everyone expected her to do – sports, school, church, friends – they all seemed just a huge and pointless bother!

She sighed, hating the way she felt. Rose would have known how to make her feel better. *She* could have cheered her up. It was not right that she wasn't here. Why wasn't she? What had Rose ever done to deserve the living Hell she and the family had gone through over the past four years?

If someone had broken into her house and stolen her sister away, if he had tortured her for four years then murdered her, that person would go to jail forever! That person might even be *killed* for what he had done!

The problem is, Koren reflected bitterly, *there is no one to blame.*

There was no one to hate. There was no one to put in jail or strap down to a table to receive a lethal injection in return for having stolen her sister from her. There was no one to punish, and so she was expected to simply move on with her life, forgetting the whole thing had ever happened.

That made her the angriest of all.

There had been councilors, of course – perhaps a half dozen. There had also been some therapists, several pastors and a well-meaning next door neighbor. All of them had counseled her to try and let go, to move on with her young life. What happened to Rose had been terrible, it had been unfair, but there was nothing to be done about it now. Then of course the pastors always concluded with "God has a plan" or some other similar, unhelpful rubbish.

So God had wanted Rose dead? He had wanted her to suffer and waste away for years before she died?! Well, if that was true then God was a *bastard*. He was a mean-spirited jerk and Koren didn't want any part of Him. What purpose could there have possibly been in what Rose had been forced to go through? How could Koren get over something so horrible?

There was a tentative knock at her bedroom door, but Koren did not react. After a few moments, it inched open.

"It's time to go, Koren," came her mother's low, nervous voice. "If you don't leave now you'll miss the bus..."

"So what?" responded Koren tersely.

Why go at all? She'd just sit through class after class, hour after hour of garbage, tormented by her jumbled and tortuous thoughts until it was time to go home again. She'd just be forced to interact with dozens of oblivious, ignorant people too stupid to understand how hopeless life was, blithely chittering and chattering about whatever inane nonsense was going on in their nice, neat, happy little lives - Never realizing that at any moment it could all be cruelly snatched away. None of them had the slightest clue or concern about what Koren was trying to deal with. Better just to stay here, at home in the dark.

"You have to go to school, Koren" her mother's voice hardened. She came fully into the room and flipped on the lights.

"Why?" Koren shot back squinting at the sudden brightness and shading her eyes with her hand. "What's the point? All they do is make you read about stupid, boring stuff that doesn't matter. Then in between classes all everyone does is talk about stupid crap that doesn't matter, so that eventually you can graduate, work yourself to death for forty years and die. It's all the same in the end anyway, isn't it? I don't want to go! I don't like the people there. All they do is piss me off!"

"Look Koren, your father and I are doing our best to be understanding," her mother growled. "But this is getting ridiculous. You're failing every class, and all of your teachers say that you aren't putting forth the slightest bit of effort. You used to make straight A's! You can't keep going on this way! It isn't healthy and you're gonna sabotage your future! Everyone was sad when your sister died. I know it's hard to understand God's plan sometimes, but you're doing Rose no favors by blowing up your own life. Do you think she would be proud of the way you're carrying on? Do you think she would approve of your Morticia Adams wardrobe and lousy attitude?"

"Shut up!" screamed Koren, leaping from her bed and rounding on her mother in a fury. "Screw *'God's plan'*! What do you know about it anyways? You and dad go on like nothing's wrong. Maybe *you* can forget all about Rose like she never existed, but I can't! I won't! I'm not going to be all nice and good and kiss everybody's ass like there's nothing wrong! It's total bullsh..."

A loud crack echoed through the room and Koren clutched at her suddenly stinging cheek.

"I will not be talked to like that, young lady!" Her mother shouted, grapping Koren's shirt by the collar and thrusting her toward the open door. "Get downstairs right now, and get to the bus stop! You're going to school, and you are going to lose the attitude or... or... or you'll never see the outside of this room ever again!"

Koren just stared at her mother, her face throbbing. Hate burned in her eyes. How could the woman be so damned stupid? Why didn't she get it?

"Fuck you!" she screamed, before spinning on her heel to sprint down the stairs and out the front door of her house. She did not go to the bus stop, however. When her feet hit the sidewalk, she kept going.

Faintly she heard her mother calling her name from the front steps, but she didn't care. Koren sobbed as she ran, choking on her tears and clutching her stinging face. Why didn't any of them get it? Why couldn't they see how much she was hurting? Why did no one but her feel this way?

Koren cut through several yards and jumped a couple of fences. She didn't stop until she staggered panting to a halt in front of the Methodist Church. She climbed over the fence to the playground and collapsed beneath a large, wooden play set. Then she drew her knees up under her chin and cried.

She was not sure how long she sat there, but it was quite a long while. It was long enough that the foggy mist of morning was burned away, and the air beneath the playset began to feel sticky and hot. Koren did not know what to do. She honestly felt bad about how she had screamed at her mother, but the idea that everyone around her was so oblivious to the pain that constantly felt like it was trying to twist her inside out made her absolutely furious.

The crunch of gravel made her look up. There beside the play set was a pair of large battered work boots. They were familiar to Koren, and she swallowed before speaking.

"How did you find me?" she asked neutrally.

"Well," her father began, kneeling down beside the low wooden structure. "I just kinda guessed. I used to bring you and Rose over here to play a lot when you were little. It was the third place I checked..."

Koren had already prepared herself for a scolding. She already had a snide rejoinder ready on the tip of her tongue, but she never said it. Contrary to her expectation, her father didn't sound angry. He sounded exhausted.

"What happened?" He asked wearily. "Your mother called me at work. She said you were pretty upset. You know, you really scared her running off like that..."

Koren did not know what to say. She wasn't even quite sure what *had* made her so angry... Well, being slapped certainly didn't help, but she had been on the verge of a fit well before her mother said anything at all. She did not answer.

Her father sat down on the pea gravel beside her and crossed his legs.

"Your mother didn't do this, Koren," he murmured gently. "Rose died because she got sick. Your mother didn't make her sick. I didn't make her sick. *You* didn't make her sick. Why are you so angry at us? Don't you know that we're struggling with this just as much as you are?"

"Then how..." Koren began, voice cracking. "Then how do you just go on every day like nothing's the matter? How do you just go to work and come home and eat your dinner and go to bed like everything is normal? Rose is *dead*!" she wailed though frustrated tears. "How will that ever be alright and '*normal*'? How can that ever be *fixed*?"

"We go on every day, sweetie," her father replied softly. "We go on because we have to. The bills won't pay themselves. Human beings have to eat to survive. You can't get your work done without sleep. If we didn't go on, what would that mean? Who would make the house payment? Who would pay all the medical bills we racked up? Who would take care of *you,* Koren? We cope. We take each day one at a time and get through them the best we can, but that doesn't mean we don't care.

"You know, Koren," he ventured hesitantly. "You know that your sister loved you, don't you?"

He waited so long that Koren felt compelled to reply. She still did not want to give up on her anger so easily, didn't want to cede any advantage, but she also knew there was only one answer to that question. They both knew. She nodded.

"I know she did," her father went on. "I also know that she wouldn't want you to go on like this. You know, that last week, all she could talk about was looking forward to seeing you again. She could barely wait 'til you got out of school every day. She wanted to know every detail of your soccer tournament. She worried about you and wanted you to be happy.

"I know it's hard, but you really have to try. Try for Rose. You can't just give up on your own life because Rose lost hers. She wouldn't want that. What you're doing... It doesn't help. It doesn't help anything or anybody – not you and certainly not Rose. Why don't you come on out of there? Let's go home. You can wash your face, and then I'll take you to school. *You* didn't die, Koren. You've got a life – a life I'm sure Rose would love to have. You disrespect her by not living it."

Koren did not respond. She understood what her father was saying – understood it in her brain if not in her heart. If she was willing to be rational for a moment she knew that what he said made sense, but it just wasn't that easy. Some stubborn part of her soul, deep, deep down simply couldn't let her sister go.

Still, she got up, brushed herself off, and climbed into her father's big blue pick-up truck, but it was more out of defeat than agreement. Koren cleaned her face at home and let him drive her to school. She immediately went to the bathroom and reapplied her sable make-up. Then she went to class, laid her head on her desk, and did not move again until the bell rang signaling the end of the day.

*

When she got home that night, Koren barely looked at her mother, and Gypsie for her own part seemed content to stare at her plate, offering only the minimum of necessary communication. Koren felt ashamed at having yelled and run off, but could not quite summon an apology. The sense of stubborn resentment was still too strong.

She only picked at her dinner. Then she went back upstairs to her room, turned off the light, and closed the door behind her. She sat on her bed and stared into the darkness – stared into the void that used to be Rose's side of the room. Koren closed her eyes.

"Please, God," she prayed with her eyes tightly clenched. "Please help me to understand! If you're so good… If you've got some amazing plan in all of this, please help me understand what it is! I need to understand why you took her away from me! Please help me let her go! Please take the hurting away! Please take it away! I don't want to be sad anymore. I don't want to hurt. Please take it away! Please… *Please*!!!"

She rolled to her side and lay sobbing on her bed for a long while, just repeating that last word over and over again in her head – *Please*… but the hoped for divine revelation and respite were not forthcoming, and Koren eventually cried herself to fitful sleep.

Chapter 3

Elysian Industries

The next day was Saturday, so there was no battle over going to school. Koren awoke early, still wearing her sable clothing from the day before. She was awake because she couldn't sleep, but did not really want to do anything either. So she just sat in the swivel chair at her desk, stared out her bedroom window, and watched the light slowly grow from grey dimness to blinding brilliance as the sun rose outside.

At about nine thirty there was a gentle knock on her door. She ignored it, but the knocker was insistent. This was a little unusual. Most of the time her parents just barged right on in whether she invited them or not. Maybe her fit yesterday had spooked them. The knock came again.

"What?!" she screamed, voice quavering. "What the Hell do you want? Why don't you just... just leave me alone and... and go away!"

The door cracked open.

"If you really are not in a mood to talk, Koren," a low gentle voice replied. "I will of course respect your wishes, but I've come to speak to you about something... inform you, really... I truly think that this is something you are going to want to hear, however..."

Koren furrowed her brow. She didn't recognize the carefully correct voice and looked up quizzically. A middle aged man in a white coat stood at the doorway. He seemed sort of familiar to her, but she was not immediately sure who it could be.

"What do you want?" asked Koren tersely.

"What do I want?" the man repeated slowly. "I think I'd rather ask you. What do *you* want?"

"Are you like some kind of counselor or therapist or something?" Koren shot back. "If my parents sent you up here to talk about my *feelings* then I'm not in the mood."

"Oh," replied the man with a chuckle, "nothing like that. Although I do think I can make you feel a great deal better."

"I doubt that," spat Koren. She turned away with a deep scowl and resumed staring out the bedroom window.

"What if I told you I had saved your sister?" The man asked standing straighter and folding his hands behind his back. "I've saved her, Koren, and I've come to take you to her…"

"You're a liar!" Koren screamed, suddenly roused to fury. She leapt out of her chair. "Rose is dead! I saw her dead in a coffin and buried in the ground! What is this? Are you trying to play some kind of sick joke on me? It's not funny! I don't know what the Hell you think you're doing, but it's not fucking funny!"

"My… Your mother did say you had developed quite a mouth," the man stated with a small displeased scowl. "But I suppose it's understandable under the circumstances. Yes, Koren, you saw your sister's dead body. You saw that mortal shell returned to the Earth from whence it came, but I did not say that I saved her body. I said that I saved *her*.

"It is the business of medicine," he continued, "to heal the body; to maintain that fleshly husk that ties our souls to the living world, but I do not practice medicine. I offer something completely different. This is something altogether new, and you are lucky enough to be among the first beneficiaries."

"I don't know what you're talking about," Koren muttered, still not the least bit mollified. "What are you, some kind of pastor or something then? Yeah, thank God for me so much for sending my sister to Heaven. Now get the Hell out!"

"I am not clergy either," the man responded evenly. "My name is Adams, and I am a neuroscientist. Do you know anything about neuroscience, Koren?"

Koren blinked in confusion. She was not at all sure what this was about. What was this strange man saying?

"No…" she murmured at last.

"Well then," Mr. Adams replied, seating himself on the edge of her bed. "You don't mind if I sit, do you?"

Koren shook her head.

"So," he continued. "Let me illuminate you, if you would be willing. Neuroscience is the study of the human brain, how it works, how it's put together. We study all sorts of things, really - The function and structure of the brain itself, how the pieces all fit together, how that causes people to act a certain way. Why do some people react another? What causes problematic behaviors like neurosis, schizophrenia and other mental diseases and dysfunctions?

"However," he lowered his voice and leaned in more closely.

Koren recoiled.

"What I've always been *really* interested in, what I have always found the *most* interesting in fact, is that essential question of human existence - What in the brain causes us to be *us*?"

He smiled in a knowing sort of way, eyes practically daring her to ask the next question. Still not at all sure where any of this was going and not the least bit less annoyed than she had been a few minutes earlier, Koren still found the urge to ask it irresistible.

"What does any of that do with 'saving' my sister?"

"Ah," he replied with a satisfied smirk. "Now we come to it, but I would much rather you try to answer my question first. What makes you, you? What made Rose, Rose? What is it that makes any of us who we are?"

"I don't understand what you mean," protested Koren shaking her ebony-dyed head. "Lots of stuff, I guess... The stuff we like... The stuff we do every day... How we're raised, but I still don't under..."

"Now, think about what you just said," Mr. Adams interrupted. "Those are all characteristics of our person, certainly, but is that really *who we are*? I mean," he spread his hands wide. "Say you play soccer. You think of yourself as a 'soccer player'. It's a way you identify yourself, but then one day, you can't play soccer anymore. Maybe you get sick or hurt. Do you suddenly cease to be the same person? Is that really who you are at your core? The *essence* of you?"

"You mean, like Rose?" Koren looked up sharply. "You mean like how she got sick and couldn't play soccer anymore?"

"Yes, exactly!" agreed Mr. Adams. "So, let me ask you this. Did Rose suddenly stop being Rose just because her body let her down? Surely there was more to her than her long hair and soccer jersey, wasn't there?"

"She was sadder," Koren conceded. "She was more frustrated, but no. She was still Rose, but I still don't get..."

"Just so - She was *still* Rose," Mr. Adams cut in passionately, coming to his feet and walking over to Koren's chair. He put his hand on her shoulder and met her uncertain blue eyes. "It was all right up here." He tapped his index finger against Koren's temple. "That is what we saved."

"What are you saying?" asked Koren in confusion. "How would you..."

"Do you know how the brain works, Koren?" Mr. Adams interrupted again. "Your brain is a physical structure. It's made out of tissue, just like your heart, or your lungs, or your kidneys, but it is specialized tissue. Really, you could describe your brain as a big chemical battery. It uses electrical signals to form your thoughts and store your memories just like a computer does with its microprocessor and hard drive. It chemically encodes the information in your brain cells and then connects all the different pieces together in a way that makes sense.

"That's why, for example," he continued pedantically, "if you smell something down in the kitchen one morning, a distinctive smell, it might make you think of bacon. That is because the synapses in your brain fire off and connect those two pieces of information – the smell and the image of bacon in your mind. This is something that we have known for quite some time, however."

"I still don't get what you're trying to say," protested Koren shaking her head in confusion. "What does this have to do with Rose?"

"I already said that the brain is like a big battery, right?" Mr. Adams asked her patiently. "And it uses electrical current just like your smart phone or television set. However, just like a computer must have a key to interpret the information saved on a hard drive - for example if you try to run Mac software on a PC, the computer won't understand it - to unlock the information stored in the brain we must have the key to unlock it. That is a key we have been lacking... Until now.

"About two weeks before your sister's body died, I went to her hospital room and made a scan of her brain," Mr. Adams went on. "It's what we call electroencephalography, or EEC, but using our specialized equipment we were able to get the most detailed and accurate three dimensional image ever produced! This was, of course, in order to have a record of the physical structure of Rose's brain, which we reconstructed in virtual form on our mainframe. Then if you recall, we placed a number of sensors on her head."

Koren nodded.

"Well," Mr. Adams continued. "Those were put in place to keep a careful record of just how her synapses fired - Where exactly the current flowed, what parts of the brain were involved when thinking about certain things or experiencing different emotions, which cells were connected to which other cells and how, what chemical reactions occurred and where, etc., etc. We took all that information and applied it to the virtual model we had made before. In this way we were able to save *everything* about Rose that made her Rose – all her thoughts, her feelings, her memories. We saved *all* of that. Then we uploaded the data to our mainframe where Rose can continue her life however she wants! In a way, Koren, I did send your sister to Heaven."

"Whoa, whoa, whoa," interjected Koren raising her hands in front of her. "Are you telling me you've downloaded my sister's brain? You put her soul on a computer hard drive somewhere?"

"Yes, Koren," Mr. Adams answered levelly. "That is exactly what I'm saying."

Koren stared at him for a long moment. What he claimed was nonsense. It was clearly impossible. She narrowed her eyes.

"You're a liar," she growled dangerously. "What exactly are you trying to pull?! How much money did you scam out of my father in exchange for this load of bullshit?! How dare you come in here and…"

"Nothing," stated Mr. Adams simply.

"What?!"

"I charged him nothing," Mr. Adams repeated. "The company I work for covered all the expenses, and once the system goes live with the general public, you and your family will have unlimited, free access forever. In fact, we paid him over two hundred thousand dollars for Rose to participate in the beta test of our final product."

He sighed.

"I know it's difficult to accept," Mr. Adams murmured. "And I certainly don't expect you to accept it on faith alone. I *am* going to prove it to you though… Prove it to you today actually, but you *will* believe in the end. Death no longer exists, Koren. That is what we've accomplished! Our bodies will die, but our consciousness, our creativity, our intellectual capacity? All of that can now continue on forever!

"Just think about it," he continued. "What if we could have saved the genius of Einstein, the creativity of Michelangelo, the wisdom of Gandhi? If we could have kept the truly great and exemplary minds of our civilization alive for centuries after their bodily deaths, what miracles and innovations would we have seen? What secrets that died with them might have been salvaged? This is what we've achieved, Koren, and your family, *your sister*, is a very, very important part of it…"

Koren was silent. She just stared at her hands. She found it impossible to process what the man beside her was saying.

"I… d… don't believe you," she stammered at last, tears leaking from the corners of her eyes. "I don't believe any of this…"

"And you shouldn't," Mr. Adams responded quickly. "Not yet…"

He stood.

"I'm a scientist, Koren," he stated matter-of-factly. "And you're a smart girl. I don't believe anything without evidence, and I would expect nothing less from you. However, if you will indulge me this morning, I will take you and your family someplace where you will receive all the proof that you require. We've invested a lot of money in this," he concluded. Then he smiled "If all this was not so, I would have told you."

Koren was still unconvinced. What Mr. Adams claimed was absurd, but still… still… Though she consciously tried to repress it, in the back of her mind she could not help feeling the stirrings of an emotion she had thought long dead – an emotion that died with Rose.

She felt hope.

"Alright," she sighed at last. "I'll play along. It's not like I've got anything else planned for today…"

Mr. Adams' answering smile was glowing.

"Wonderful!" he exclaimed. "Then let's go! There's no reason to delay, and trust me, Koren. *Trust* me! You will experience *joy* today. Today you will witness the end of death as we know it!"

He rushed to open the door for her and led her down the stairs. Koren and her parents were quickly ushered outside and into the back seat of a waiting, black limousine. As soon as they were settled it roared away from the curb and into the rising brilliance of a beautiful new day.

*

Koren had never ridden in a limo before and was a little overwhelmed by the experience. Neither of her parents, sitting next to her, perched on a seat that was bigger than their living room couch, looked to be any more comfortable with the opulent conveyance either. Her father accepted an imported German beer with an unpronounceable label, but sat staring at it uncertainly. Her mother sipped nervously at a bottle of Perrier.

Koren had flatly refused the offer of a Diet Coke. She didn't want anything from this man – still certain that he was lying to her, but what could his game possibly be? Why would he pay so much money to her father to go through some long, elaborate charade? She did not want to allow herself to hope, knowing with certainty that the very idea of Rose being sucked inside a computer was ridiculous, but doubt gnawed at her. What on Earth was this Mr. Adams playing at?

She barely noticed the city as it rolled by outside the heavily tinted windows. Likewise, she hardly noted the lavish interior of the limousine – mini chandelier, mini fridge, wet bar, satellite TV, surround sound *karaoke* set… She perceived it all only peripherally.

Koren's mind was in a sort of limbo. She was quite oblivious to what was going on around her, so wrapped up was she in what was playing through her own head. At the same time however, she could not seem to string any of her many random thoughts together in any way that made sense. *Nothing* happening today made any sense. All she knew was that her stomach was a knotted mess.

After quite some time, the houses and businesses of town became fewer and farther between. Walmarts, McDonald's, and gas stations gave way to fields and pastures. Koren was not at all certain how long they drove, but it had to have been at least an hour or more. At last, the long black car turned down a narrow access road. That soon gave way to twisting gravel, and even the premium shocks on the decadent vehicle could not disguise the poor condition of the road.

"We have found privacy advantageous to our work," stated Mr. Adams apologetically. Perhaps it was in response to some dubious expression or quizzical glance from one of her parents, but it was certainly in response to what all of them were thinking: *Where the Hell are we going?*

"Don't worry," he soothed. "We're almost there."

The gate seemed to pop up right in front of them, right out of the woods. It was about ten feet high with razor wire on the top. A single security guard waved at the limo driver. Then he leaned into a tiny guard box, and the heavy electric portal stirred into motion. The long black car slowly rolled through, and the gate closed behind them.

On the other side of the fence was an enormous if nondescript rectangular building covered in white aluminum siding. It looked like it might be a warehouse or something, but Koren couldn't tell because there was no sign or labeling to declare its appointed purpose. They passed what appeared to be a small employee parking lot – very small for a building of this size, Koren thought – on their right and continued on around to the other side of the structure where they stopped at what must have been the front door.

"All right," called out Mr. Adams with a wide smile. "We're here!"

The driver got out and came around to open the door for them. Then Mr. Adams led them out of the vehicle and up the front steps. As soon as Koren walked through the glass double doors, she was reminded forcibly of the hospital. Everything in the entrance hall was white and sterile to the point of uncomfortable cleanliness.

At the end of the hallway was a single desk with a well turned out and smiling middle-aged woman behind it. On the front of the desk was the first indication of where it was exactly they now found themselves. In big silver letters were written the words "Elysian Industries".

"Hello, Cathy!" Mr. Adams called out cheerfully. "Would you tell Mr. Ashe that our guests have arrived and that they are ready for the demonstration?"

"Of course, Mr. Adams," replied Cathy in a syrupy sweet voice. She pushed the intercom button. "Mr. Ashe, the Johnsons are here."

Just a few moments later, on a section of wall behind the receptionist a door that Koren had not noticed before shifted and rolled upwards into the ceiling with a mechanical whir and hydraulic hiss. A youngish man in perhaps his mid-thirties or so came out with a wide smile and arms spread. Compared to the immaculate Mr. Adams, he looked positively scruffy.

His short-sleeved dress shirt was untucked and he wore no tie. He sported a thick pair of hipster glasses and his auburn hair was disheveled and spiky. He wiped his hand on his shirt before extending it to Koren's father.

"Great to see you again, Mr. Johnson!" He ejaculated affably as he gave Bill Johnson's hand a hearty shake. "I am so looking forward to da demonstration today! I think you're gonna be really happy. I know we all are. It turned out better dan we expected actually. Follow me, please..."

He went back through the door he had just exited and gestured casually for the Johnson's to follow. The three stood looking at each other curiously for a moment before rushing to catch up with the excited young man.

"I... I'm sorry, Mr. Ashe," Mr. Johnson began uncertainly. "I'm still not exactly sure what this is all about. We understood that the... the attempt didn't work... I mean... Rose died..."

"Call me Askr," replied Mr. Ashe with another broad smile flashed casually over his left shoulder, but he slowed not at all. As he said his name, Koren thought she detected a faint accent of some sort, but could not immediately identify it.

"Mr. Ashe makes me sound so old!" he complained good-naturedly. "Dat's my father after all!" He laughed. "I rather wish Cathy would stop using it, but I suppose we have to put up with at least some of da basic business conventions and practices if we are going to go public with dis thing, won't we?"

Mr. Johnson opened his mouth to voice, judging by his expression, a reiteration of his still unanswered question, but Askr Ashe barreled on.

"But no indeed, it was very, *very* successful!" he turned to face them but kept walking backwards. "I can't wait to show you! I think you'll be really excited!"

There was something Swedish-Cheffy about the very slight rising, falling quality of his voice, Koren decided. It was barely perceivable, his excellent English obviously well-schooled, but the more excited he got, the more apparent it became. Perhaps Norway? Finland? She wasn't sure why she was fixating on the detail so much. Maybe it was in self-defense. Perhaps it was because in her mind, she still expected this whole strange trip to prove an enormous waste of time. She was still waiting for the catch and refused to let herself get too excited.

Mr. Ashe turned back to face the front, and his pace quickened. They took a couple of turns down identical, sterile white hallways before walking into what appeared to be a large conference room. It was largely empty except for a single massive screen at the far end of the room. Mr. Ashe finally slowed his frenetic pace and approached the flat screen monitor with a demeanor akin to reverence.

"Well," he stated slowly. "Here it is… Dis is what all da fuss is about. I'd like to introduce you to Aaru."

He spread his hands wide before taking a deep breath and pushing a red button in the bottom right corner.

"Enter login information," came a musical if unexcited female voice.

"Admin1," stated Mr. Ashe loudly.

"Password please."

"Ǫnd gaf Óðinn," he replied.

The screen flashed, and a symphonic fanfare played over surround-sound speakers. The silhouette of a great tree appeared and there was a flash of lightening. The words 'Elysian Industries' materialized above and below the tree in bold, Grecian letters, which quickly faded to reveal a dazzling blue sky. Fluffy, white clouds billowed here and there across the screen.

"Access granted," the female voice replied. "Good morning, Askr,"

Several touchscreen buttons appeared on the bottom of the monitor with a soft whooshing sound effect. They read 'connect,' 'user settings,' and 'help'.

"All right," said Mr. Ashe. He turned toward Koren. "Would you like to try it out, young lady?"

"What *is* this?" asked Koren in irritation. "Is it like some kind of new social media site? I don't understand why you've drug us all out here for this. And why won't anybody explain anything? What is your *deal*?! What does any of this have to do with my sister?!"

Askr's mouth tightened, and he furrowed his brow at Koren's heated exclamation. He did not reply, but instead touched the button marked 'connect'. He cast his focused gaze upon Koren as the screen once again flashed.

The sky scene shifted to twilight shades and the female voice called out. "Connection ready. Input user please."

"Call her," Mr. Ashe stated simply.

"Call who?" snapped Koren, already more than a little bit creeped out.

"Call your sister," he replied. "Call Rose."

"Now, Mr. Ashe," protested Koren's mother. "I don't know what all of this is about, but I don't think it's funny. I…"

"Do you really think, Koren," Askr interrupted, still looking pointedly at the teenage girl and ignoring her mother. "Dat we would build all of dis, pay your father thousands of dollars, and den drag you out here just to upset you? I wish I had so much free time... Trust me, Koren. What we have accomplished is something dat will change your life - Change da world even! I'm not trying to trick you or mock you, but merely to show you. Let me show you something *wonderful*. Say your sister's name, first and last."

"Input user please," repeated the female computer voice.

Koren looked down at her black leather boots and bit her lower lip. What did she have to lose? The sooner she humored this jerk, the sooner she could get the Hell out of here. She huffed and looked up at the screen.

"Rose Johnson," she growled.

The twilight scene swirled into a radiant rainbow tunnel.

"Establishing connection," stated the computer voice. "Please wait."

After a few seconds, a crystalline ping rang out from the speakers.

"Access granted. Rose Johnson connection established," the computer said. "Configuring video feed."

The first thing Koren saw was a hand pressed against the screen, as if someone was leaning against the other side of a window pane. Then she caught her breath.

A smiling brown-eyed face looked back. The figure's long, kinky chestnut hair was arranged on her head in a complicated hair-style. She was also clad in a beautiful kimono, the like of which Koren had certainly never seen her sister wear before, but there was no mistaking that face. The brown eyes focused on her at last.

"Oh!" exclaimed the girl in the monitor. "Koren! It's so good to see you! I've got so much to tell you! You won't even *believe* what's happened to me!"

Koren could only stare with her mouth open. There was no question she recognized face and voice both.

"R... Rose?" she gasped in disbelief.

Chapter 4

The New Place

It was an unsettling feeling to say the least. One second she was lying in the hospital bed surrounded by frantic medical professionals, and then suddenly she wasn't. In fact, Rose was not at all sure *what* she experienced.

Rose had understandably developed an interest in near-death experiences over the past year or so. She had watched a ton of documentaries on the subject before she got too weak to work the TV remote. Her mother had encouraged it, along with far too many hours of what Rose scornfully referred to as "Jesus TV". Gypsie Johnson had hoped this would reassure Rose, help her cope with what was happening to her, but it did not.

Usually, the shows just made her angry that she had to worry about such things at all. Still, she was well versed in the usual particulars of transitioning to the afterlife – the out of body experience, the long tunnel, the bright light, the dearly departed relatives to greet you in Heaven... That was not at all what she experienced now.

Is this it? She thought in confusion. *Am I dead?*

She waited. Then she waited some more for *something* to occur that felt... she wasn't sure... death-like? Nothing really appeared to happen, but Rose could not be positive, not at all certain what 'dead' was *supposed* to feel like.

"How long are you going to lie there?" a bemused female voice asked. "You've arrived, you know... Wouldn't you like get up and look around? I've been waiting for you."

Slowly, Rose cracked open her eyes. She saw earth and grass beneath her tightly clenched fingers. Hesitantly she lifted her head and caught her breath at what she beheld. Rose stood and slowly turned a wide circle in amazement.

A flaxen field of tall grass stretched away from her in every direction to disappear into the distant horizon. Birds chirped, insects buzzed, and she felt warm sunlight, golden on her face. The smell of fragrant flowers and greenery, heavy in the honeyed air, assailed her nostrils and permeated her deepest self to saturate her very essence with an abstruse sense of felicity and well-being. Then she caught sight of a figure, standing just a few feet away.

She was a very beautiful woman. Her dark-brown, luminous eyes were large, almond shaped, and sparkling. They glinted with amusement. Her hair was long, black, and silky, flowing nearly all the way to the red, wooden sandals on her tiny feet. It gracefully framed her pretty face. She was dressed in a gorgeous, bright pink kimono liberally embroidered with a swirling floral pattern of gold.

"Welcome," the woman greeted amiably with a low bow as she twirled a red, paper parasol slung casually over her left shoulder. Her genial voice floated across the bucolic plain. There was a quality about it that sparkled as brightly as the effulgent sun. "You are among the first to arrive."

Rose simply stared. A gentle breeze tousled her long brown hair, and she casually wiped a strand from her eyes. Then she froze. Her hair… She gave the errant strand a tug then gaped at the smiling woman in astonishment.

"Where am I?" she breathed. "Is this Heaven?"

The kimono wrapped woman laughed.

"Well," she began. "Perhaps it could be. *I* like it, certainly. I hope that you will too! I'm glad that you've chosen my kingdom. You're actually my first."

"Kingdom? Chose? I don't…" Rose stuttered. Then she shook her head and took a deep breath before asking, "Who are you? Are you a… a queen or a… a… an angel or something?" Her voice softened to a murmur. "You're beautiful…"

The woman giggled girlishly, and her cheeks flushed pleasantly pink. The parasol flashed out of existence.

"Thank you," she murmured, fanning herself with a pink, silk folding fan that suddenly materialized in her right hand. "I *do* try. In any case, to answer your second question first, you may call me Hana. If I have to choose, I think I prefer to think of myself as a princess, but some of the others choose differently. And your name is… Rose?" A broad smile spread across Hana's face.

Rose nodded wordlessly.

"Rose!" Hana repeated with a musical giggle. Her eyes glittered, and her grin pleasantly dimpled her porcelain cheeks. She clapped her dainty hands together in delight. "Rose and Hana! What an apt pair! Well, I am quite delighted to meet you, Rose. I'm glad you are my Veda. I hope you will be happy here."

There was too much of the woman's speech that Rose did not understand - far too many questions to be asked. They seemed to flood her brain to bursting so that she could not fully articulate any of them. At last she picked the one that seemed simplest.

"Please, Princess" Rose entreated. "Where *is* here exactly?"

"Oh!" Princess Hana exclaimed. "I apologize! This place is called Aaru, and you now find yourself in my kingdom of Tenkoku. Aaru is a new place… Another place… Maybe, I could say… the next place?"

Her brow furrowed as she noted Rose's confused expression.

"I'm sorry," Hana apologized. "I don't really know how else to express it. If I told you simply that Aaru is a *good* place, could you accept that?"

Rose nodded uncertainly. Her head was spinning. Hana approached her and placed a soft, reassuring hand on her shoulder. She leaned forward to kiss Rose on the cheek. Her lips were soft and delicate, leaving a pleasant tingle in their wake. It made Rose blush with pleasure and embarrassment.

"First of all," Hana breathed gently into Rose's ear. "I *do* want you to understand something; You are my Veda, so you simply *must* call me Hana. I think we are going to be great friends! There is much I wish to show you. We have a great deal of work to do in preparing this place for Those-Who-Come-After. I will really need your help, Rose…"

"I…I'm sorry…" Rose stammered. "I don't understand any of this…"

Hana smiled. "I know you don't, but you will, given time, and that is something you are going to have in abundance! It's my fault really," she demurred. "I'm saying too much too fast, so I apologize. Forgive me." She bowed low once more. Then she met Rose's eyes with another dazzling smile.

"I'm just so happy you've finally come!" The folding fan disappeared up one of her voluminous sleeves, and she took both of Rose's hands in her own. "Let me show you our realm, but perhaps… Would you like to tend to your attire first? I want to *celebrate* with you! I'm sure you can come up with something more festive to wear."

Rose looked down at herself. Her mouth fell open in mortification as she realized that she was still clad in her vomit and blood-stained hospital gown.

"Now, now," chided Princess Hana good-naturedly. "No need to feel bad. No need ever again! We can fix it with a thought! What would you like to wear?

Rose considered a moment, and her clothing shifted and changed. First she was wearing a luxurious blue gown like she might have chosen for her Prom, then a sheik, grey pants-suit she remembered from an issue of Cosmo her mother had left on her hospital bedside table. That then quickly transformed into a scanty bikini like in a picture of a sexy model a boy with the locker next to hers at school had posted inside his door. She squeaked in embarrassment, and Hana laughed.

"Would you like me to help you, Rose? I think I know what will suit you." She waved her hand and the revealing swimwear was replaced with a kimono that was at least as beautiful as the one that Hana wore. "Better?"

Rose nodded.

"And let's see about your hair...." Hana pursed her lips in contemplation. "This perhaps?"

A mirror appeared in her hands. She held it up so Rose could behold herself.

Rose gasped. Her long brown kinks were suddenly tamed and arranged on her head with an impressive array of lacquer-wood cosmetic chopsticks and ivory combs. A beautiful jade crane ornament hung down at her left temple, and her face looked as though it had just been attended to by an expert makeup artist.

"How did you do that?" Rose breathed in amazement. Then she smiled. "I feel so pretty!"

"I'm glad you like it," Hana replied with another pleased grin. "We shall be princesses together, you and I, and so of course you must look the part! However, in truth Rose, I did very little. I simply accessed what was already within you and then set it in place. It's quite easy actually, and you'll learn to do it soon. Now..." her tone turned more business-like. "Let's get on to what's what.... What do you think of this place so far?"

Rose was a little taken aback by the directness of the question, but looked around again. She could smell the fresh, clean fragrance of leaves and blossoms on the warm breeze, and the high grasses played a gentle, swishing melody with the wind. White fluffy clouds rolled lazily across the bluest sky she had ever seen. It was as if the most perfect summer's day she had in her memory had been magnified a hundred-fold.

"It's beautiful..." she breathed. Then her brow furrowed.

"But?" ventured Hana expectantly.

"It's very... empty," noted Rose at last. "It... It... I don't know... It feels like.... It *wants* something."

Hana laughed in delight.

"Yes!" she cried. "Indeed it does! That is just *exactly* right. It's a big blank canvas waiting to be filled with whatever we decide we want to put here! We have nothing but space and time! So let us get to it!" She clapped her hands together and bit her lower lip in barely contained excitement. Her eyes sparkled. "So, where shall we start?"

"I don't know," began Rose helplessly.

How was she supposed to know? What could they do with all this space? What was something nice? She tried to think of something simple - something pleasant and beautiful.

"Maybe, some flowers or something?" she replied at last.

Hana squealed in glee and hugged herself.

"Perfect!" She exclaimed. *Of course*, we should start with flowers! *It's so perfect!* Something like this, perhaps?"

Princess Hana bent her knees as much as she could in her beautiful but restricting kimono. Her face hardened in concentration, and the muscles around her temples tightened as if she was reaching down to pick up something heavy. Then she slowly raised her arms over her head. As she did so, a tiny green shoot popped out of the ground at her feet. Then it grew, stretching up toward the bright sun and cerulean sky, branches springing forth and forking away from the steadily lengthening trunk until it had expanded into a tree of considerable size. The boughs were bare, and Rose cocked her head to the side quizzically.

Hana shot her a coy, sideways smile and winked, then wrapped her hands around the end of a low-hanging, naked branch. She breathed into the space made by her cupped palms which then glowed with a brilliant golden light. The limbs warped, and tiny knots appeared all over the tree. Then they burst open with thousands of intensely pink blossoms, the smell of which was nearly intoxicating. The beauty of the *sakura* tree in such spectacular array stole Rose's breath.

Hana turned toward her with a wide, pleased smile.

"Something like that, perhaps?" she said and Rose could only nod. "Why don't you give it a try?" Hana invited. "All you have to do is visualize what you want, and then focus your will upon where you want it to appear."

Rose was uneasy. What Hana had just done was amazing, magical even. Surely plain old Rose Johnson could never do something so incredible. Hana seemed to sense her reluctance. She glided behind Rose, and took both of her hands in her own with interlaced fingers.

"Just see what you want," Hana breathed into her ear. "See it with your heart and your mind, and I will help you bring it to be. Just believe that you have that power within you. I have granted you in this place the ability to change anything and everything as you see fit. You are a *Veda*. Do not be afraid to use that power. If you make something and find it displeasing, you can always create it anew. It will cost you nothing but time, and from this day forward, time shall be limitless. Create with me Rose."

Rose took a deep breath and fixed the image of Hana's beautiful flowering cherry tree in her mind. Then she closed her eyes. It might have been at the gentle nudging of Hana's consciousness against hers, but she reached out with her senses. She smelled the earth and grasses beneath her toes, tasted the fresh air, and felt the gentle caress of the wind. She reached into her mind and gently lifted her image of the cherry tree out to place it in the empty space at her feet, where it felt just right - where it was surely meant to go. It snapped into the world of the shimmering veldt like a puzzle piece clicking into place.

"Very good, Rose," whispered Hana in her ear. "Perfect even! But finish it now. Breathe into your creation. Breathe into it and give it life!"

Rose did as she was told. She drew breath deeply, but certainly not into her lungs. Rather, it seemed as if the honeyed air of the verdant plain was drawn directly into her heart and soul to mingle with her very essence. Then she exhaled and opened her eyes. As she did so, the cherry tree shimmered briefly in gilded hue before bursting into glorious bloom.

Hana released her hands to once again squeal in elation at Rose's accomplishment. She hopped up and down clapping her hands.

"There!" she exclaimed happily. "You see? Easy-peasy!" She hugged Rose tightly, then beamed into her wonderstruck face. "Let's do more!" She begged. "Let's do *everything*! Let's make this place *live*!"

Hana took her hand, and it seemed as if the ground fell away beneath them. They flew up and up until the two blooming cherry trees were tiny dots below. As they climbed higher and higher, Rose noted that a wide sparkling river ran through the middle of the grassy plain. Like everything else here, it was beautiful. The clear water sparkled and shimmered in the sun, bright as crystal. It stretched off into the distance in both directions - off into forever.

"What to do next... hmm..." Hana pursed her lips together, index finger resting thoughtfully thereon as she scanned the plains below. The wind tousled her clothes which billowed all around her grandly, but it did not seem to touch her perfectly styled hair. "I know! Where will you live, Rose? You choose! What shall be our first mansion?"

"Mansion?" Rose asked, more than a little apprehensive about the ground being so far below her bare, dangling feet. "Do we need something so grand?

"Of course!" cried Hana. "It is a magnificent kingdom we are charged to build! In our Kingdom, Rose, shall be many mansions. We go to prepare a place for Those-Who-Come-After. Choose the first mansion!"

Rose was about to demur. This was all too much too fast, but unbidden an image flashed into her mind. It was the picture from the Japanese tapestry in her bedroom. The one she had asked her mother to bring to the hospital depicting the white castle on the steep, green mountain all covered with waterfalls and trees and a cool mist down in the valleys.

"A wonderful idea, Rose!" cried Hana, seeming to know her thoughts. "How about right down there?!"

She pointed to a spot on the seemingly limitless field below them just on the banks of the great river. The ground quickly rushed up towards them, but they did not crash. Rather it was as if the rolling lea rose to meet their feet with a touch as soft as a flitting butterfly wing.

"This will take both of us, Rose," Hana said seriously. "We'll have to do it together and put all our effort into it. I've never made a mountain before... Now step back," she directed. "When I say so, reach down with your feelings – deep, deep down, down into the bones of this place. Then lift it up with me. Lift it with all of your might! Ready? Now!"

Rose did just as she was told. She closed her eyes and reached down. She could not say with which part of herself she reached, but it was as undeniable a portion of her whole as her arm or foot or head. As she did so, something awakened within her – a connection to this place that was undeniable and comforting. She belonged here, she realized. Aaru was a part of her now even as she was a part of it. She could bend it to her will, but then it too impacted her on a spiritual level. The old Rose would have never tried to move a mountain. The old Rose never would have thought it possible, but...

"I tell you the truth, Rose," Hana murmured, her soft soothing voice not at all diminished by their increased distance. "If you have faith as small as a mustard seed you can say to this mountain remove to the sea and it will be so... Lift with me Rose! Now!"

Rose felt something then, deep down in the most remote depths of Aaru. Far below the surface of what she could see with her eyes. It was strong, hard, and cool. She grasped it, then lifted with all of her strength.

The something was slow to awaken, but Rose did not cease in her striving. Gradually it began to stir to motion, to rise up and take on a physical form. Beneath her feet, rock exploded from the plain. It lifted her up into the sky. Then upon those naked, craggy slopes, she brought forth trees, hundreds of them, just like the flowering cherries they had created earlier. Rose breathed life into her creations. She called up waters from the depths beneath the mountain and sent them cascading down over rocks and boulders, gurgling and murmuring until they joined the great river far below. Then she turned her attention to a flat spot, on the very pinnacle of her peak.

Again, she reached down and lifted. A great palace all of seamless white marble exploded from the earth to perch majestically upon the craggy summit. Its gently sloping, tiled roof towered above her, ornately carved carp at the eves. Then in the front of her creation she set a mighty gate of polished ebony wood.

Rose's heart soared, her feet frozen to the spot in awe of what she had done. Hana came around behind her to encircle her shoulders with a fierce embrace.

"Do you see, Rose?!" she whispered excitedly, practically dancing in her glee. "Do you see what you are capable of? What you have within you? What we will be able to achieve together? This is but the smallest portion! We shall make Aaru a magnificent place! It shall be a perfect world without pain or death or sadness, and the others will help us too, when they arrive. It is a great and wonderful thing we do, Rose. Thank you for sharing it with me. It is good to have a friend."

"Hana," Rose asked with abrupt sobriety, as the implication of what her new friend said struck her. "Are we the only two people here? Are we all alone?"

Hana stilled her dancing, and her face became thoughtful.

"Not really *all* alone," Hana replied slowly. "*Mostly* alone though. In Aaru there are ten kingdoms that know no bounds - not height, not width, not depth, and in each of them there are two rulers – a lord and his lady. My lord dwells across the river there." She pointed off into the distance. "His name is Mikoto and he is good and kind, but *very* serious. He constantly ponders the creation, planning and worrying and quite frankly making a colossal bore of himself. Whereas I... I would rather *do* than plan. I would rather wander until I find a spot that pleases me and call up a *sakura* as we did earlier, or summon a garden, or place a cooling lotus pond. You are like me, Rose. You want to *do*. That is why you were sent to me, and I am *so* happy to see you! Only a few of us have Vedas yet."

"Do you never go and see him? – This Mikoto..." Rose asked curiously. "You said he is your lord, so isn't that like your husband or boyfriend or something? Have you been alone a long time? And what's that word you keep using? What's a Veda?"

"My, you *are* full of questions!" Hana exclaimed with another giggle. "Of course, I suppose that is to be expected. So, you want to know about Mikoto? He's not my *boyfriend* certainly." She made a face and stuck out her tongue in distaste. "He drives me too crazy. Hmmm..." Hana thought a moment

"I think it more correct to describe Mikoto as my 'partner'." She said at last. "We work well together, I suppose. After all, he wants to plan everything and do nothing, and I am just the opposite, so I suppose that makes for a good balance. That is probably why the

Makers put us together. I'll introduce you eventually, but frankly, I'm afraid he'll want to interrogate you for an age once he meets you, and I am determined to enjoy your company for the present."

She smiled.

"Now, you also asked what a Veda is…" Hana became serious. "It is a very special thing, Rose. You are among the first Residents. The Vedas will help us to perfect the Creation before all the others arrive in numbers beyond count. It is a blessed thing Rose, and you must be quite special to have been chosen…"

Hana gazed at her intensely and Rose was beginning to feel a bit uncomfortable. Maybe there had been some mistake? She was a sick teenager who liked Japanese anime and was passing fair at soccer. She certainly did not feel like she was "chosen". It sounded far too grand.

Hana must have picked up on Rose's nervousness. She touched Rose's cheek and smiled.

"Fear not, Rose," she murmured earnestly. "There is no mistake. You are just exactly where you are supposed to be."

Hana's hand dropped back to her side before she reached into the folds of her voluminous kimono sleeve to withdraw the pink, silk fan again. She fanned herself with it lazily.

"Anyway, you also asked me how long *I've* been here by myself?" she pursed her lips and lay an index finger against them, as she seemed to be wont to do. "I think it's been a long time – longer than I've liked certainly, but I'm not really sure. Time… well, we have so much of it that we don't really bother to count it here." She brightened. "But do not think on that too deeply. The past is irretrievably gone and it is *never* the future. Only now *is*."

Rose cocked her head to the side, and Hana giggled in her merry, girlish way. "What I mean to say, Rose, is that now, *right* now, I am with you. I am no longer alone, and I am happy. That is all that matters." She smiled sweetly. "Would you care to show me the mansion you have built?"

Rose answered with a glowing smile of her own. Yes, she had done this great and beautiful thing – her and only her! She was not sick anymore. She was not weak. She was happy and healthy and had made a new friend. She could think on what all of this strangeness might mean later. For now, Rose decided, it was good just to *be*. Hana was right. Today was a good day, and that was all that mattered.

She nodded and shyly took Hana's hand. The Flower Princess squeezed it affectionately. Then together they walked through the tall black gate and onto the grounds of the shining palace Rose had wrought.

*

Sometime later, Rose sat beneath a canopy of brilliantly pink cherry blossoms. Hana sat next to her on the mossy ground holding a cup and an intricately decorated teapot. *Sakura* petals fell gently around them like warm pink snow. Hana poured a little of the piping beverage for Rose and then for herself before sipping it daintily. Rose quickly followed suit.

As good as it smelled it tasted even better. The aromatic bouquet of the steaming liquid in her cup filled Rose's senses. It left her with a profound sense of peace and wellbeing. It was very nearly indescribable but filled Rose's mind with images of flowers and greenery and sunny summer days.

"Do you like it?" Hana smiled noting Rose's euphoric expression.

"Oh yes," sighed Rose. "It's very good, thank you."

She paused a moment to watch a couple of diminutive panda bears wrestle and play just off to her left. The one on top flapped tiny gossamer wings to rise up briefly before mischievously dive-bombing his companion. They were only about six inches in length and were the absolute cutest things she had ever dreamed up. Rose was actually rather proud of them. She took another sip.

"So," Rose began. "We've done an awful lot of building."

And they *had* – mountains and valleys, rolling plains and misty hills, gleaming castles and nonpareil gardens - all different, all beautiful, all perfect.

"Indeed," replied Hana, taking another small sip herself. "I am quite impressed actually. You have done very well, Rose."

"Thank you," Rose blushed at the praise. She could still scarcely believe that this peerlessly beautiful woman was her friend and felt almost ridiculously pleased any time she complimented her.

"But" Rose continued seriously. "You keep talking about others – 'Those-Who-Come-After' – when do you think they will begin to arrive?"

"Are you lonely, Rose?" Hana asked with mischievous smile over the rim of her teacup. "Am I not companion enough for you?"

"No, no, no!" Rose protested. "Please don't think that! I... I love you! You are the best friend I could ever have – I mean you're so nice and pretty and you like everything I like... I guess I'm just a little anxious. I feel like we've been working so hard, I just can't wait for someone else to see it!"

"I'm just teasing you, Rose," Hana giggled. "I am quite taken with you as well, and please understand that I feel much the same way. I've just been waiting much longer than you, so perhaps I've tempered my anticipation. I understand your impatience, but there's simply no rushing it. Those-Who-Come-After will arrive when the Makers will it, and not a moment before. Actually, I really believe..."

Hana said something else. Her mouth kept moving, but Rose could no longer hear her. Instead a loud, deep voice echoed through her brain.

"Rose," it rumbled. "Come here, Rose."

Rose shook her head to clear it, and Hana's mouth stopped moving. She put a concerned hand on Rose's shoulder.

"Come here, Rose," the voice echoed again.

She looked at her friend helplessly. Hana's eyes widened in comprehension. Then she placed both hands on Rose's shoulders.

It's okay, Hana mouthed, though Rose could still not hear her. *You are being called. Do not fear. Go to the window!* She pointed up through the pink canopy above.

"Come here, Rose," the voice called again.

Don't worry! Hana again mouthed. She smiled reassuringly. *Go to the window!*

Rose nodded and launched herself upward. She flew above the trees, above the fertile plains and into the azure sky. Then she saw it – a dark black rectangle in the otherwise cerulean firmament. It beckoned her, impossible to ignore. She rocketed towards it.

"Come here, Rose," the voice repeated, and she complied, soaring up to the strange black window. Rose placed her hand against the smooth, dark surface and looked inside.

Chapter 5

Our Thomas

Koren had no words. All she could do was stare with her mouth open. What she was seeing was impossible. The intricate kimono the girl on the monitor wore was not familiar, but the kinky brown hair and sparkling chestnut eyes were unmistakable.

"Koren?" Rose cocked her head to the side and wrinkled her nose, looking hard at her sister. "Is that you? What on Earth did you do to your hair?!"

Koren could only continue staring. Her mouth worked, but no sound came out.

The girl on the screen regarded Koren curiously.

"Are you alright, Koren?" she asked "You look as green as when I dared you drink the strawberry scented shampoo that time. You remember? You swore it must really taste like strawberries if it smelled like that…"

Koren's knees felt weak. She sat backwards heavily where another Elysian Industries worker – an Indian man of about 35 or 40 in a white lab coat – had already rolled up a chair to catch her. She barely noticed him. It *was* impossible, she knew. It must be some kind of joke, but it looked *so* like her.

"Rose?" Koren whispered at last.

"Well yes," replied Rose. "Of course it is! Who else would it be?!"

"That *can't* be Rose," protested Koren's mother.

"It must be… some kind… some kind of simulation or something!" stuttered her father, "like a… a… a hologram!"

"Ask her something," cut in Mr. Adams calmly as he entered the room. He shut the door quietly behind him. "I know it defies belief, but I assure you that this is all quite real. Ask her something that only Rose would know – something we could never know. She will be able to tell you. It *is* her. This *is* Rose Johnson."

"Who's your favorite soccer player?" asked her father.

"Duh, dad," replied Rose. "Ronaldo Casillas. That's not like a secret or anything."

"What did I get you for your birthday last year?" asked her mother.

"An iPhone and socks," answered Rose sounding slightly annoyed. "They had frogs on them... I think you got me a t-shirt too. Why are you guys being so weird?"

"When we were little," Koren began softly. "When we were little and Skylar Michaels hit me with a rock, and my head got all bloody, you beat him up..."

Koren stared hard into Rose's eyes, her own brimming with tears.

"You wiped my face with your shirt," she went on and leaned forward in the office chair. "You promised me something, Rose. You made a promise, and you pinky swore. What did you promise?"

The image of Rose in the view screen seemed to deflate. She looked away sadly. Everyone in the room tensed.

"I..." Rose began. "I didn't..." she swallowed.

"What was it Rose?" Koren pressed, her anger swiftly returning. "What did you promise me? Can you tell me or not?!"

"I... I promised... I'm sorry..." Rose stammered quietly.

"Do you know or don't you?!" shouted Koren, leaping from the chair and taking a threatening step toward the monitor

"I promised," stated Rose with difficulty. "I promised that I would always take care of you. I promised I'd never leave you alone. I'm sorry, Koren... I guess I didn't keep my promise..."

Koren's face went white, and she sank back into the chair.

It had been a day more than five years ago, well before Rose got sick. The blistering, summer sun of early-afternoon had beaten down upon them as the two walked home from the Methodist Church playground. Their steps had been slow and plodding. The sky was blue, but the midday heat was such that she could see shimmering mirages contorting the air further down the street. A few dogs had barked at neighbors' houses as Koren sniveled into a bloody napkin, and her big sister held her close.

No one else had been around during that long walk home. It had been far too hot for most people to want to venture outside at that time of day. Even later they had never told another soul about the incident, afraid that Rose would get in trouble for fighting. They had actually told their parents Koren fell off the monkey bars. No one could have known about that.

Koren just stared at the image on the screen, stricken dumb by a combination of choking incredulity and a stubborn joy that wanted to bubble up and spill out all over the place in spite of her best efforts to suppress it.

"This… This isn't real," she stuttered at last. "This is a dream… I must be dreaming! I…" she stood and took an unsteady step toward the screen. The girl certainly *looked* like Rose.

"Who was my third grade teacher?" she demanded suddenly.

"Mrs. Wozniaki," replied Rose. "I had her too."

"Who asked you to the Spring Formal in seventh grade?"

"Ugh." Rose stuck her tongue out. "Kenny Treworgy… He always smelled like dill pickles.

"In fifth grade, what did you do when I tried to pierce my own ears?" Koren barked again as she took another few slow steps closer.

"I told you that you were retarded," Rose answered with a disapproving scowl. "I said Mom would kill you, and that they'd probably get all infected and fall off anyway. I still can't believe you tried that…"

"I'm dreaming…" Koren repeated, voice quavering. "This isn't possible! I saw your *body* Rose. I saw them put you in the *ground*!"

"I'm here now, Koren."

Koren came close enough to put both of her hands against the flat screen monitor. Rose matched her from the other side, pressing her palms against her sister's. Koren cocked her head to the side, utter disbelief plastered across her thunderstruck face. A tear leaked from the corner of her eye.

"Rose?" she breathed, dark eye make-up already starting to paint her cheeks in runnels "Is it really you?"

"It's me, Koren." She smiled brilliantly. "Oh, I wish you could see it here! It's *so* beautiful, and I've made a wonderful new friend. You'll like her! She's *gorgeous* and her name is Hana. We're getting this place ready for the others. She calls them Those-Who-Come-After. She says they'll start arriving soon…"

"I've missed you so much, Rose!" Koren sobbed. "It's been *terrible* at home without you! Our room just feels so… so *empty*!"

"Well, it won't ever again," murmured Mr. Adams coming up behind Koren and placing a comforting hand on her shoulder. "After today you'll be able to talk to Rose whenever you want. I'll send a couple of techs to your house to set it all up."

"See?!" exclaimed Mr. Ashe, practically dancing in his excitement. "Can you *believe* it?! When dis goes live it will change da world, Koren, Mr. and Mrs. Johnson! No one will ever need to fear death ever again! Over da course of human history, we've always struggled with da reality of our own mortality. We've invented surgeries and medicines to extend and improve our lives, but dere's always been dat dark specter hanging over our heads, dat inescapable knowledge in spite of all our achievements and advances we are doomed - doomed to die and ultimately be forgotten, but no more! We've finally beaten death! We have transcended our own flesh and discovered Da Fountain of Youth, Da Holy Grail, Da Pinyin Peaches, Ambrosia! Families like yours never need be torn apart again. Heart-broken parents never again need cry over a dead child's grave!"

The Johnsons did not really appear to hear Askr Ashe's progressively louder and more impassioned monologue. All three of them were beyond speechless. Koren continued to cry against the flat screen monitor, and Mrs. Johnson was not much better off, sobbing into a handkerchief that the Indian gentleman had thoughtfully provided. Mr. Johnson just sat heavily in one of the conference room chairs staring up at the screen in helpless shock.

"It *can't* be real!" gasped Mr. Johnson, staring wide-eyed into Mr. Adam's stoic yet clearly pleased face.

"That can't be my little Rose," added Mrs. Johnson tearfully. "Can it?"

"Bill, Gypsie," began Askr. "May I call you Bill and Gypsie?" He did not wait for an answer as he barreled on. "It is all very, very real, I assure you! And soon we will bring dis new reality to da whole world! And…" he quieted, meeting their eyes sincerely. "And we want your help to do it."

"What?" asked Mr. Johnson in confusion. "What could *we* possibly do?"

"I don't even *begin* to understand any of this," added Mrs. Johnson, and her husband nodded in agreement. "How on Earth could we…"

"What did you do?" Koren interrupted. "How did you do this?!"

"How about we take a step back," suggested Mr. Adams. "I'm sure all of this has been quite overwhelming for you. Why don't we take a few minutes to calm down, collect ourselves, and perhaps indulge in some refreshment? We will explain everything to you, and when we have finished I think it will all make a lot more sense." He turned to the monitor.

"Rose," he said. "Do you remember me?"

Rose looked at him for a moment. Then she smiled.

"Oh yes!" she exclaimed. "You're Mr. Adams! You visited me in the hospital and said you could help me." She spread her arms wide and turned in a circle. "You gave me all of this."

Mr. Adams ghosted a slight smile. "Quite right, Rose. Did I do all I promised? Are you happy?"

"Very, Mr. Adams," she answered with a giggle. "You did everything you said... Never-Never Land..."

"I'm glad, Rose." He shot the Johnsons a sideways glance. "I must apologize, but I'd like to borrow your family for a little while, if you don't mind. I'm sure you have scads to tell them, but this should only take a few hours. Then I'm certain you and Koren will have a great deal of catching up to do... Would that be alright?"

"Of course, Mr. Adams!" replied Rose quickly. "I can't wait!"

She turned to Koren, who was kneeling in the floor at the base of the huge screen, completely overcome.

"Talk to you soon?"

Koren nodded.

"Yeah," she replied affectedly. "Yeah... I... I... I missed you Rose..."

"I missed you too, Koren," Rose answered. "So it's a promise then!"

"It's a promise," Koren agreed.

"Goodbye, Rose," said Mr. Adams.

"Goodbye everyone," Rose called back. "And thank you!"

She waved enthusiastically. Then she faded from the monitor. The twilit sky scene brightened to midday blue once more.

"Session ended," droned the female computer voice.

The surround-sound speakers continued to hum with the gentle, rhythmic whooshing of a brisk wind. All Koren could do was stare at the empty screen. She was not at all sure what she just witnessed had really happened. A loud and persistent voice continued to scream through her brain that it couldn't possibly be real, that there had to be a catch somewhere.

The door at the back of the conference room opened with a soft click, and a pretty blonde woman in her early twenties stood smiling in the doorway.

"Dis is Amy," stated Askr. "She will take you to wash up and get a little lunch. When you're ready we'll meet back here, and all shall be revealed! I know it's overwhelming, but I do hope you'll regard today as a bit of a celebration. You are about to be a major part of da biggest discovery in human history! I do encourage you to enjoy it."

"Right this way, if you please," lilted Amy. She gestured towards the open door.

The Johnsons rose numbly from their seats. All of them bore slack expressions of extreme bewilderment. As they followed Amy out into the hallway, the question clearly showed in their dumbfounded faces.

What had they just witnessed? They still weren't entirely sure, but they *were* sure of one thing; That was Rose.

That was Rose.

*

Koren and her family could only pick at the sumptuous lunch, all lost in their own uncomfortable thoughts. None of them knew quite what to feel. The sudden reappearance of her dead sister should have made Koren positively ecstatic, she thought. How many nights had she dreamt of that very thing? Rolling over in her sleep to look across the room and see Rose in the bed opposite hers, snoring softly just as she had done every night for most of their lives… At the moment however, her predominating emotion was instead one of profound discombobulation.

Her parents seemed to feel the same. Mr. Johnson barely touched the rare angus steak in front of him, and Mrs. Johnson idly pushed peas from one side of her plate to the other with her fork, but did very little actual eating.

The unexpected events of the morning seemed like something out of a dream or hallucination. It left them all in a daze. When Amy came to get them about an hour later their plates were still mostly full.

The genial blonde frowned slightly as she noted their subdued demeanor, but said nothing as she lead them down yet another achromatic hallway – hard-soled shoes echoing against colorless linoleum tile. They passed not another person as they went, and all of the half dozen or so offices they passed on their way were empty and dark. The huge complex looked to be mostly deserted.

At last they stopped before a pair of polished, double doors. Amy put her hand on a large brass handle and pulled. Then she held the door wide and smiled sweetly.

"The Board will see you now," she lilted with a slight bow.

It was a large conference room, but not the same one as before. It contained a long table in its center, which looked far too small for the cavernous chamber. A large monitor hung on one wall. Other than that, the room was unadorned and sterile, much like everything else they had already seen here.

Around the table sat approximately two dozen men and women who looked up at the family expectantly as they entered. They all bore varying expressions of excitement and elation. Mr. Ashe and Mr. Adams, who were sitting near the middle of the table, stood.

"Ah! Bill, Gypsie, Koren!" greeted Mr. Ashe warmly. "I hope you had a nice lunch?"

Mr. Johnson muttered something that might have been yes, and Askr Ashe quickly continued in his customary bombastic style.

"I'm so glad!" He continued. "I have been *so* excited to share our achievement with you! Now we get to explain in detail just what it is we have managed to accomplish, but first," he took in the entire assembly with an all-encompassing gesture. "I would like to announce for dose of you who were not able to attend da trial dis morning dat it was an unmitigated success!"

All of suit and lab coat clad individuals around the table clapped. Here and there were even a few hoots and whistles.

"We tested the basic functionality of all retrieval and recall systems, and it was a hundred percent green across da board!"

There was more applause, hand shaking, and back slapping. Koren felt profoundly out of place. Askr Ashe made a good natured shushing gesture and the acclamation subsided.

"Thank you so much for your participation in dis trial." He clasped his hands sincerely. "We never could have done any of dis without your cooperation and da cooperation of da other Beta families."

More polite applause.

"I'm sorry, Mr. Ashe…" Koren's father began.

"Please, Bill, call me Askr."

"Alright, Askr then," retorted Mr. Johnson, a degree of irritation beginning to show through. "I believe you said you'd start explaining just what's going on around here. Well? We're ready. Start explaining!"

"Quite right," Askr answered contritely. "We have kept you waiting far too long. Please…" He gestured to three open chairs. "Have a seat and we shall begin."

The Johnsons seated themselves.

"Now," said Mr. Ashe. "I think dat Mr. Adams has already explained somewhat to you."

They nodded.

"Right." Mr. Ashe said. "So dere is little purpose in rehashing all dat. You know what we have done is scan Rose's brain and reconstruct a virtual copy of it on our system - A backup copy, if you will. In Aaru, which is what we have decided to call our mainframe, she will be able to continue her life much as it was before, but without any pain, sickness, violence insecurity or any other negative thing dat has, until now, been an inescapable part of da human condition. We have created Heaven on Earth! But unlike da usual Heaven, dis one you will be able to visit… Virtually of course…"

"Mr. Ashe," interjected Koren's mother, clearly aghast. "What you have done is amazing certainly… but… this…" she gestured helplessly. "This… It sounds like… like playing God!"

Askr Ashe shrugged.

"Perhaps it might sound so to some, Gypsie," he conceded. "I am reminded of my Voltaire – 'If God did not exist, it would be necessary to invent him'."

Koren's parents gasped, and perhaps sensing that he may have overstepped himself Mr. Ashe quickly made a placating gesture.

"Now, I'm not saying dat we *are* creating God here. We take no position on a deity one way or da other. Religion is a very personal decision I don't feel qualified to advise upon. What we *have* done however, is solve a very old human problem which is at its core – 'how do we preserve da past?'

"Previous generations of Man," he continued, "carved da words and wisdom of deir generations upon great stone tablets and monuments. Later, da knowledge of ages was preserved upon paper in printed books. Today, we save billions and billions of terabytes of information digitally upon computer hard drives, but always our preservation has been imperfect. It is perishable and incomplete.

"For example," he stood and began pacing, "only a fraction of da wisdom of ancient civilizations like Mesopotamia, da Indus Culture, and Ancient Egypt, has survived. Even in more modern days, we have da words and discoveries of brilliant minds like Currie, Galileo, Oppenheimer, Copernicus, and Keynes, but not deir vision… not deir *souls*.

"We now have da capacity to allow da truly great members of da human race to continue deir work of advancing mankind indefinitely!"

Mr. Ashe was becoming more and more impassioned as he spoke, but Koren's parents did not seem to be persuaded. What he was suggesting rankled their deepest sensibilities. It sounded blasphemous.

"And an added bonus," cut in Mr. Adams smoothly. "Is that in the process we have also found a way at last to save unfortunate children like yours from pain and misery and death. Surely," he reasoned passionately. "Surely, Rose did not deserve the fate that befell her – the weakness, the illness, the sadness, and despair – all just to end in her death? *Surely*, you do not believe that to be right or good or fair…"

This line of reasoning appeared to carry more weight. Both Mr. and Mrs. Johnson seemed to be at least partially mollified. Mr. Adams turned his intense gaze to Koren.

"Surely, Koren," he stated. "Surely, you are glad that your sister has been saved. If not for us and our discovery, she would be gone forever. Now she will *live* forever instead! How could that be bad?"

A great silence fell as the Johnsons considered. It all still struck Koren as strange and disquieting, but as she pondered Mr. Adams' words, she found them hard to dispute. Perhaps her misgivings were simply because she had failed to fully digest everything that had happened. Perhaps, it was simply because she had not yet internalized the truth – Rose was back. Her sister was alive again.

Koren met Mr. Adams' steady gaze. Her darkly painted eyes shimmered with tears.

"Thank you," she said. "Thank you for saving Rose…"
Koren found she could say no more.

Maybe this was how the family of Lazarus felt, she thought. *That turned out alright, didn't it?*

"Well…" murmured Gypsie in the smothering silence that ensued. "The Lord… Well… He does move in mysterious ways. Maybe…"

"I know it's a lot to process," spoke up a neatly pressed Asian woman sitting to Mr. Ashe's left. Her hair was tied back in a simple bun and her dark business suit and skirt were prim and conservative, but she was *very* pretty, Koren thought. "Please, do understand. We have all come together to realize this project with the purest of intensions. We seek to accomplish what countless others before us have tried – simply to make the world a better place." She smiled disarmingly, and Koren could not help but smile back.

"Thank you, Kiku," said Mr. Ashe gratefully. "Quite right."

"Indeed," agreed Mr. Adams. He gestured to the woman Mr. Ashe had referred to as Kiku. "Do think on what Miss Hanasaka says, because that is indeed the way we all feel." There was some supportive murmuring and a number of heads nodded in agreement. "But I think perhaps we have gotten ahead of ourselves. Let us start at the beginning and then tell our vision through to the end. I think that once we've laid it all out, you really will feel more…" he paused as he searched for an appropriate word. "…More… at ease about the whole thing.

"I think I shall let my colleague Dr. Kapoor begin," Mr. Adams gestured to the Indian man in the white lab coat whose thoughtfully provided chair had saved Koren from collapsing to the floor in a heap earlier. "He worked on many of our core systems right from the beginning."

"Right then," Dr. Kapoor stood and cleared his throat. Then he paused to shuffle nervously through a stack of papers he was holding. "I shall endeavor to do my best in illuminating all of this."

His voice bore the distinctive up and down cadence that Koren thought of as a typical Indian accent, but also contained a decidedly British flavor as well.

"In the beginning, this project was nothing nearly so grand as it has become," he said. "At the start, we were simply interested in producing a better, higher resolution imaging process for the brain.

Traditional EEGs… that's electroencephalographs… devices we use to record the electrical impulses produced by the brain, in conjunction with CT scans and MRIs could give us a three dimensional image of the brain and tell us where electrical activity was occurring, but not really tell us anything about the contents of that activity – how the thoughts and information were connecting up to fly about different hemispheres and such."

Koren was doing her best to follow what Dr. Kapoor was saying, but he was using an awful lot of big words that she did not quite understand. A glance at her mother and father's concentrating faces told her that they were not doing a great deal better themselves.

"We could see it working," he went on officiously, "and even *how* it worked to a degree, but the way the brain actually stores information is chemical. What we really wanted to see was that interaction between the electrical and the chemical, and then perhaps decode it. It was merely a first step, but we knew that if we could do it successfully the potential applications would be enormously important. For example, we thought we might be able to measure EPs and ERPs more accurately, which would then allow us more complex processing of individual stimuli as well as the interplay among simultaneous processes thereof…"

"Forgive the interruption, Vikram," interrupted Miss Hanasaka smoothly. "I apologize, but I fear some of the more technical details might prove… troublesome for those of us not so learned in neuroscience as yourself. Perhaps you could simplify it a little for lay persons like me?"

She flashed the scientist a glowing smile, and he blushed beneath his dark skin. There was some scattered chuckling, and Miss Hanasaka caught Koren's eye briefly to give her a wink.

"Sorry," Dr. Kapoor ran a sheepish hand through his thick black hair and ventured a nervous grin. "You've caught me talking shop, I'm afraid… but anyway…"

He quickly regained his composure and focused his gaze on Koren. "So, to make a very long, very boring story, very, very short, we enlisted the help of biologists and computer programmers and imaging experts and a whole host of very, very smart people so that eventually we got to what we'd been hoping for - A decoder key…"

"Yes," spoke up Mr. Adams, "and this key allows us to measure the chemical composition in various parts of the brain and all of the millions of reactions that occur every millisecond right through the skin. At the same time, we can analyze the electrical information with the advanced EEG we developed. We learned not only how to read the information stored on the brain, but how to record it also."

A fat man in a white lab coat with a balding head and several days' worth of scruffy looking beard raised his hand. Mr. Adams nodded, and the man struggled to his feet.

"Uh... Sorry," he began with a nervous stammer and a thick German accent, but much like Dr. Kapoor, he was clearly excited to speak. "Dr. Florian Heidler... Yah, we thought in za beginning zat we could use this information to treat mental illness. Our idea was to copy za information from za patient's brain and then modify it chemically to fix whatever might be causing za trouble. After which we would eh... how you say... update za patient's brain with za new, corrected information, but we could never perfect za process of... eh... I guess... editing and updating, so we were forced to try and think of other applications."

"So," cut in Askr Ashe. "We thought, we can save information directly from da brain, but not alter it." He smiled slyly. "Not yet, anyway... In any case, what we den came up with was simply a plan to save information from people and create a sort of bioelectrical library, but once we really got into da process, we realized we had done much more dan copy bland old information. Dis was not just a photocopy of our test subjects' brains. What we saved was *everything!*"

"The brain is very complex," added Mr. Adams. "When I think back on it now, I suppose we were silly to think we could just separate out all of the qualitative facts without also copying something of the person who supplied them. The way the brain organizes information into pathways that are useful is by building an almost infinite system of connections – like the bacon smell and image example I shared with you this morning. However, that is just an example. The real connections are vastly more complex and interconnected. What we ended up copying to our system then was not merely long lists of data provided by individuals, but rather the *whole* individual. Everything about the way they thought and felt and saw the world."

"So our next task," added Miss Hanasaka. "Was to take this information, as raw as it was, and come up with a kind of retrieval system, which we did but..."

"But," laughed Mr. Ashe, "it was very crude and we very naïve. We weren't just retrieving data. We were retrieving *whole people* and they were not very happy with us at all."

"They told us they were bored," continued the pretty Japanese woman. "And they refused to talk to us anymore until we gave them something to do."

"Thus," concluded Mr. Adams. "Aaru was born...

"Kiku here was heavily involved with designing da framework, although all of us have had a hand and added our touches," said Mr. Ashe. "And dat is because after da basic foundations are set up, Aaru is a user designed system. Once da content is uploaded, like we did with Rose, individuals have total control over da make-up dereof. Users can form da world however dey choose within certain parameters."

"For instance," added Miss Hanasaka, "even in bioelectric form, human beings are social creatures. We knew we wanted all of our users to be able to interact with each other, but with interaction invariably comes conflict. This we wanted to eliminate so, except for administrators and a few other protected classes of Residents, no user can modify anything established by another user without their authorization. Also, we decided very early on to include a 'Harm Failsafe'."

"Again," added Mr. Ashe, "We are dealing with people, and we wanted to insure dey would not somehow find a way to injure each other, so no change can be made in da system at all dat could possibly harm another user, again without an administrative override..."

"Which we would never use, of course," cut in Mr. Adams quickly.

"Right," agreed Miss Hanasaka. "So any user is free to build their world any way they like..."

"How many 'users' are we talking about here?" asked Mr. Johnson curiously. "You keep talking about 'changing mankind'. If you're trying to upload millions and millions of people, won't it eventually fill up? What will you do then?"

A very mousy looking blonde woman with thick coke-bottle glasses raised her hand hesitantly.

"Julie Warren," she stated softly. Koren had to strain to hear her. "I don't know how much you know about Quantum Computing, but because of the explosion in data collection over the past ten or

66

fifteen years or so, processor speeds as well as data storage methods have and continue to significantly advance. We more than double both our speed and our capacity roughly every two years, so we don't anticipate any problem with space for the foreseeable future."

"Also," cut in Askr Ashe. "Our facility here, ninety five percent of it or better, is nothing but hard drives and processors. We have literally a billion, billion, billion petabytes of storage space and, with constant updates as technology advances that capacity is only going to increase."

"How will you decide who gets in?" Koren's father asked again. "I sure know there's a whole bunch'a people I wouldn't want to spend all eternity with. How do you keep the rapists and murderers and psychos out?"

"We will definitely have a selection process," replied Miss Hanasaka. "We realize that there might be certain... undesirables let's say, who could create problems in the system. We certainly want to avoid that, but don't worry. That process is under development right now."

"This is all really impressive," noted Koren's mother with a perplexed expression, "but I still don't understand what any of this has to do with us."

"Yeah!" exclaimed Koren, some of her defiance returning. "What exactly *do* you want from us? You said you paid my dad two hundred thousand dollars. You brought us here in a limo... You have to want *something*. I don't believe that you're just being nice."

Mr. Adams chuckled, and Askr Ashe smiled.

"Like I said earlier this morning, Koren," replied Mr. Adams smoothly. "You are a very smart girl. We do indeed have a proposal for you, and when I say you, I mean *you*." He fixed his gaze on Koren.

"What do you mean, *me*?" she asked nervously.

"Well," he shrugged. "Your parents will have to agree to it of course, but frankly, we need... well... we need a spokes-model."

"What?" Koren asked in confusion.

"Dis has all been very expensive," explained Mr. Ashe. "Da research, da property, da building itself, da constant updating and maintenance we shall have to engage in once da system goes live – none of it is free. We have investors who want to recoup da money dey've lent us, so at least in da beginning we will have to charge for our service, but we hope to change dat eventually.

"Anyway," he went on. "Think about how skeptical you were just dis morning. You accused Mr. Adams of lying to you, and I have to think da public, when we come out with our discoveries, will be just as skeptical.

"You will be our 'Thomas'," added Mr. Adams, "The doubter who became a true believer!"

"You are very pretty, Koren," noted Miss Hanasaka matter-of-factly. "People will like you and your story. They will sympathize with you and with Rose. They will trust you."

"All we really want to ask you to do," said Mr. Ashe, "is to tell your story. Tell what happened here today. Explain how it changes your life, because I know it will. In exchange, like I mentioned before, you will have lifetime access to Aaru and can talk to Rose whenever you like. Furthermore, you and your parents and up to two hundred close friends or family you would like to nominate will be added to da system whenever you choose, *and,*" he finished grandly with a very broad, toothy grin. "We will pay you a whole lot of money – so much dat neither you nor your parents will ever have to worry about anything ever again."

Koren just stared at them, overwhelmed. She looked from Askr Ashe, to Mr. Adams, to Miss Hanasaka and back.

"You will also be quite famous," Miss Hanasaka added. "When people learn about what Elysian Industries can offer through Aaru, you will be our face. You will become a celebrity."

"Help us, Koren," added Mr. Adams. "Help us give others what we've given to you and your sister – given to your family. Help us give that to thousands... *millions* of other families just like yours."

"Come on, Koren," pressed Mr. Ashe. "Fame, fortune, immortality... and all we ask in return is for you to tell your story to da world!" He extended his hand.

Koren bit her lower lip uncertainly.

There must be a catch, she thought yet again. *There must be some downside I'm not seeing.*

Try as she might however, she could think of nothing. Why wouldn't she want to let people know how her sister had been saved? Why wouldn't she want to give that to the world?

After but a moment's hesitation, she firmly grasped Askr Ashe's hand, and everyone in the room cheered.

Chapter 6

A New Friend

Rose spun away from the window. She flew up toward the brilliant sun and then swooped down toward the verdant plain below. Her heart was full to bursting, and she simply *had* to find Hana to tell her about it.

She soared over the plain, long unbound hair whipping in the brisk wind, until she saw the great river. Then she followed it until she came upon her mountaintop castle. Hana stood at the front gate waving.

Rose plummeted towards her, hit the ground with a spectacular explosion, and then wrapped her friend up in a fierce embrace.

"I saw Koren! I saw Koren!" Rose squealed. "That was my sister up there in that black window thingy!"

Hana giggled at Rose's enthusiasm.

"I'm pleased to hear you so happy, Rose," she replied. "Actually, I have a bit of news myself as well. I think it will please you. Would you like to hear it?"

"Of course, Hana!" Rose exclaimed. How could this perfect day get any better? "What is it?"

"Mikoto just contacted me," she said. "Another Veda has arrived. Shall we go meet him?"

Rose took her happy squealing to an entirely new octave.

"Yes, yes, yes! Of course, yes!" she screamed. "I can't wait!"

Together they stepped into the sky and rocketed across the great river. Once they crossed it, Rose honestly could not tell any difference between that side and the place they had just left. Just like Hana's side of the river the vast empty space begged to be filled. The same unbroken, grassy plains seemed to stretch off into the infinite.

Not after too long however, Rose thought she detected something more distinct upon the horizon; something – though not much more than an inky blot when she noticed it – that looked more substantial. As they drew closer, Rose could see it was a large and impressive structure.

Much like her own mansion, it sat atop a tall and imposing hill. Unlike hers the walls were tall, black, forbidding, and topped with large obsidian thorns. There was no visible gate or entrance.

Hana descended on the western side of the structure, if the sun was any guide, and traced an indiscernible symbol upon the thick onyx walls with her finger.

"I just don't know why he goes to such trouble!" she muttered in obvious irritation.

Nothing happened for a moment or two, but then the golden outline of the character Hana had drawn glowed upon the stone, and the edges of a great door appeared. She held her face close and breathed a few words that Rose could not hear. There was a loud noise, like some great stone mechanism being stirred to life. Then the large, heavy door creaked open to reveal a broad and desolate courtyard.

Rose followed Hana nervously, but the Flower Princess did not seem at all perplexed. The emotion that her friend most clearly displayed was in fact one of decided annoyance. She kicked at the bare, parched ground to release a small cloud of dust. Hana grimaced.

"Not so much as a dandelion…" she grumbled. "I hope he has a halfway decent excuse cooked up for everything of his looking so barren." Then she turned to Rose with a flush to her cheeks. Hana bowed deeply. "I am sorry this place greets you in such disarray. As I mentioned before, Mikoto can be quite… difficult."

Rose was not quite sure what to say. She gaped at her friend's apologetic posture for a long moment before shaking her head and making some amorphous gesture that she hoped conveyed her forbearance. Hana seemed satisfied by the display and sighed.

"I do hope we can finish here quickly… Follow me, Rose."

Hana walked into the hushed compound, and Rose quickly joined her. They entered a large central building. The narrow path they took was steep and led sharply downward.

The hallway was dim, and the bare and unyielding stone, lent nothing to the eye, yet emitted a feeling of enormous, comforting strength. After they had continued down identical grey and gloomy passageways for what seemed like an eternity, they at last stopped at a massive iron door. It was heavily draped with chains, and there were no fewer than a dozen locks and bolts holding it closed. Hana gave Rose another long suffering look.

"Again, I apologize," she said.

Hana traced a series of symbols across the surface of the door. The path her delicate finger left glowed brilliantly yellow for a moment, then flashed brightly green.

"He's such a pain!" Hana complained as the locks and chains clattered to the hard, stone floor.

The heavy door moaned as it cumbrously stirred to motion. The room beyond was black, and Rose actually felt, for the first time since she had come to Aaru, a little bit apprehensive. Hana strode confidently into the darkness however, so Rose reluctantly followed.

It took a moment to adjust to the dimness, but when she did Rose was more than a little bit disappointed. The room was vast, but much like the rest of the fortress, it was also barren. The walls were unadorned and grey, and there was no furniture. A dim figure, stood on a very slightly raised platform scrawled all over with glowing symbols that Rose did not understand. His arms moved slowly, but deliberately as if he was conducting some onerous symphony orchestra. He stared fixedly into space.

He was not large or imposing – not at all what Rose had expected of the mighty Lord Mikoto. In fact, he appeared to be quite a small, bookish man, dressed haphazardly in mismatched blue T-shirt and garish, orange slacks. A thick, black-rimmed pair of hipster glasses sat atop his eagle-like nose. Hana stood next to him expectantly for a moment before clearing her throat. Then she growled. Still Mikoto did not appear to pay her any notice. She gave Rose yet another apologetic glance. Then she smacked her partner sharply in the back of the head.

"Gah!" He cried out and finally looked up at her. The symbols on the platform winked out.

"Dammit, Hana!" He shouted in irritation. "What is it? I'm busy!"

"Let me remind you, Mikoto, dear," Hana drawled icily. "That it was *you* who called *us*. Can you not pull yourself away from that thing for five seconds to greet our guest? And did you not say you had finally been sent a Veda yourself? Can you not be the least little bit cordial for a moment and converse with us in a halfway civil manner?"

"Dammit, Hana!" he exclaimed again. "Can't you see that I'm still working on the security measures?! They all have to be *perfect* before the first of our Residents start arriving!"

"If you didn't want to talk to me, Mikoto," Hana retorted in annoyance. "Then why did you summon me here?"

"Well, yes I wanted to talk to you…"Mikoto replied. He rubbed the back of his head, suddenly seeming less irritated and more embarrassed. "It's not like I don't *want* to… I just… Well… Anyway…" He took a deep breath. "Thank you for coming, Hana. Yes, I wanted to talk to you…"

"So what is it that you wanted?" she asked. "It's not like I don't have anything to do myself, especially with you locking yourself down here all the time getting absolutely nothing put together… Have you seen your courtyard?! It's *dreadful*!"

"Alright! I said I'm sorry, Hana," he interrupted, the annoyed tone creeping back into his voice.

"You most certainly did not," Hana cut in. "And frankly I'm getting tired of it. Are you ever going to actually *do* anything, or do I have to keep working on our kingdom alone? When exactly do you plan to..?"

"Okay, Hana, I'm sorry!" Mikoto exclaimed, cutting her off in a decidedly unapologetic fashion, but then he paused and murmured. "Trust me when I say that what I am doing is *very* important… In any case," he assumed a sudden assertive confidence. "Yes, I did ask you to come here, and I do indeed have a new Veda." He indicated a previously unnoticed, skulking figure off in a darkened corner of the chamber - little more than a pair of wide eyes in the shadows.

"And frankly," Mikoto growled reluctantly. "I just don't have the time to guide him right now. I wanted to ask you to look out for him for a bit, if you would be willing."

Hana drew in a clearly offended breath. Her dark eyes flashed.

"Do you realize how *long* I waited to get *my* Veda?" she hissed dangerously. "Do you understand how intensely I longed for that moment?! Guiding the Vedas is our primary function. It is our first and most vital charge! How can you so easily seek to cast off that responsibility?!"

"Perhaps that is *your* primary charge," Mikoto replied in a rather self-important manner, Rose thought. "But it is not mine. *Mine* is to protect this place. However," he went on." I do care enough about it to take time out of my busy schedule and ask you to spend a moment less on your flowers and a second more on helping me out…"

"You condescending…."

"Please, Hana?" Mikoto seemed to wilt as he sighed. "The Makers have told me that we will go live *very* shortly. I have *so* much to do, and it absolutely *must* all be finished… Please?"

Hana rolled her eyes, then sighed deeply herself.

"Very well," she growled.

She turned to the shadowy figure in the corner and made an effort at a pleasant smile.

"Come here, boy," she lilted. "Let me have a look at you…"

The huddled figure was reluctant. He retreated back into the shadows.

"There's nothing to be afraid of," said Rose. "Hana is really nice, and it's *beautiful* here! I'd love to show you around…"

The shape in the corner paused. It regarded Rose suspiciously.

"I'm not afraid!" insisted the thin, nervous voice, "but… Will you take me up out of the dark?"

"Of course we will," Hana answered and shot Mikoto a poisonous look. "*I* would show you how to be free here, and how to create and fly, not shut you away beneath the ground like some skulking rodent…"

"So I'm a rat," Mikoto replied disdainfully. "And you'll all be the safer for it… Thanks Hana…"

Hana sniffed contemptuously, but Rose smiled. The new boy intrigued her.

"Shall we go?" Hana asked..

"What's your name?" Rose asked the boy excitedly as the Flower Princess turned toward the exit.

"My name is Franco," he murmured, slightly rolling the R in his name.

Rose found it charming. She extended her hand.

"We can walk up together, Franco, if you want," she said shyly." Would you like to hold my hand?"

Franco said nothing for a moment, mistrustfully staring at Roses extended appendage. At last he thrust out his own brown fingers. His large hand grasped hers, and she was immediately taken by how warm and strong it felt. Rose inhaled sharply at the unexpected sensation. She had expected a child.

"I'll show you the way…" she reassured gently. "It's not so bad here, really…"

"I hope so," Franco replied uncertainly. "So far it has not been… what I was hoping…"

He trailed off, and Rose concentrated on the feel of his fingers. Despite his assertion that he was unafraid, he still gripped her hand awfully tightly. Hana led them steadily upwards, back to the desolate courtyard. When they once again glimpsed the clear light of day she turned to Rose.

"I couldn't wait to get out of there!" she exclaimed. "It's so dark and gloomy and *ick*! I am *so* sorry for making you go down there. I should have known that he still wouldn't have accomplished anything. Mikoto is *always* like that – too busy doing all of his oh-so-important nonsense to even be polite… I hope you don't hate me for taking you there…"

"Hate you?" Rose replied. "Certainly not! And we've met a new friend anyways!"

She held up Franco's hand to demonstrate.

"Well," sighed Hana. "That's good of you. Thank you, Rose, for being so understanding. In any case," Hana perked up and donned her customary sunny demeanor. "All of that's over now. Why don't we go and do something more pleasant? There is much that we must teach our new friend!"

"Could you tell us a little about yourself, Franco?" Though there was not much true resemblance, there was still something compelling in his dark face that reminded Rose forcibly of her Ronaldo Casillas poster. "Where are you from? How did you end up here?"

"I'm from Pomona," Franco answered.

Now that they were out in the sun he seemed already much improved. He was taller than her and looked as if he might be just a bit older. He wore a pair of dirty blue jeans and a torn and bloody t-shirt, but he stood straighter and his voice sounded stronger and more confident.

"That's in Cali near Los Angeles, but my dad is from Argentina, and my mom's from Guatemala. I don't know how I got here though… The last thing I remember was being in the hospital. This *gavacho* in a white coat was putting all kinds of wires on my head."

"Yeah," answered Rose nodding vigorously, "that Mr. Adams guy, I bet! It was the same with me. One minute I was laying on my back in the ICU, and then poof! I was here."

"All I remember was the truck…" Franco said with a shiver. "I was on my bike. I looked up, and it was like, bigger than a sky scraper! It was the only thing I could see, but I couldn't hear nothin'. Everything went quiet, and it felt like everything all slowed down, ya know? Like in slow motion kinda... Then BAM! Lights out… Nothin'… I woke up in the hospital, everything hurtin'… that guy, messing with my head… Mama crying… Then it just faded out, and I didn't hear nothin' again… I woke up in the dark…" His voice broke a little, but he grit his teeth, refusing to cry in front of a girl. "My mama was always… always on my case, ya know? About not going to church… not going to confession enough. I thought… I thought I'd died… and… and gone to… to…"

Rose couldn't help herself. The very idea of it broke her heart. She hugged him.

Franco started in surprise, but did not resist.

"You're not in Hell, Franco…" Rose murmured into his ear. There was a strong musky smell about him that was not at all unpleasant. She inhaled a little more deeply. "This is the farthest place from it…"

"Certainly not!" exclaimed Hana. Her cheeks flushed, and her eyes flashed in barely contained fury. "The very idea that one of our Vedas… One of our *honored guests and founders* could be greeted so at his arrival!" She was very nearly shouting and her anger took Rose more than a bit aback. Hana had always bordered on saccharine sweet before. Tiny thunder clouds formed right above her head, and lightening flashed about her shoulders.

"This is just too much!" She went on offendedly. "Mikoto *absolutely* must answer for this! I shall inform Lord Draugr! How dare he…!" Hana trailed off into helpless spluttering as she spun on her heel, apparently ready to march back into Mikoto's fortress and drag him out by his hair.

Rose lay a restraining hand on her arm.

"Hana," she began softly and the Flower Princess stopped, though her cross face was still vividly red. "Could we let it go for now? Could we perhaps show Franco something more fun?"

"I... I don't wanna go back down there," Franco murmured. His grip on Roses fingers tightened. *"El Mono..."* he breathed and crossed himself.

Hana took a very great, deep breath and made a visible effort at calming herself. The thunder cloud faded. She looked at her feet, then sank to her knees in front of a clearly astonished Franco. Hana placed her hands on the grassy plain and pressed her pretty nose into the dirt.

"Please, Veda Franco," she said. "Allow me to offer the deepest and most sincere apologies on my partner's behalf. Though his transgressions are unforgivable, I beg your forgiveness. There is no excuse..."

Rose and Franco just stared at her, unsure of how to respond, but Hana did not budge from her apologetic posture. Finally, Rose gave the brown boy's ribs a poke with her elbow.

"Y-Yeah," he stuttered, making an attempt at a nonchalant head toss. "Whatever... Don't worry 'bout it..." He cast another nervous glance back at Mikoto's forbidding structure. "H-Hey... How 'bout we bounce, yeah?"

"Of course," Princess Hana looked up from her prone posture on the ground. "Indeed... You have been greatly wronged," she lamented sadly, "but let us dwell no more upon it!"

She brightened as she stood up. Hana smoothed her features and made a respectable effort at a friendly smile.

"Come Rose," she said. "Let us take him to make a place for himself! Take his hand."

Rose did not need to comply. Franco was still crushing her tiny, white digits in his large, dark paw. Hana leapt into the sky and without really thinking much about it, Rose followed.

"Whoa! WHOA!" cried Franco in alarm as they abruptly soared thousands of feet above the plain. Then he yelled out something in Spanish that Rose did not understand and crossed himself again.

Rose caught sight of his terrified face and laughed. Franco shot her a glare that was as furious as it was incredulous. It was an expression that broadcast vividly he thought she was quite mad.

"I'm sorry, Franco," she apologized, with a helpless laugh. "I should have warned you, but you don't have to worry. Nothing can hurt us here. You can do it too! Come on! Enjoy it!"

His machismo was obviously bruised by the little white girl laughing at his fear. Franco jerked his hand away, determined to prove that he was certainly *not* afraid. He plummeted.

Franco's arms flailing wildly, both Hana and Rose dove after him.

"Don't try so hard, Franco!" encouraged Rose. "Just see yourself flying in your own head!"

"There is nothing to fear here, my partner's Veda," lilted Hana falling right alongside Franco, but in an unperturbed upright position as if she stood upon solid ground. "Fear is a thing of Before. Let go of it. Embrace joy!"

At just the same time, Rose and Hana reached out their hands and touched Franco. As soon as their fingertips brushed his skin their meteoric descent abruptly halted inches from the ground.

Franco's eyes were wide. His hair was drenched in a sweat, and he panted in obvious terror.

"Calm your mind," Hana encouraged. "You cling to your old ways of being. Those have all passed away. The limitations of your old life no longer hold true. See yourself as you would like to be, Franco. Nothing is impossible here. The only thing that prevents you from doing... from *being* whatever you want is your lingering doubt."

Franco looked away, brown cheeks flushing furiously red.

"Relax, Franco," added Rose sympathetically. "I had trouble in the beginning too. You shouldn't feel embarrassed. You just have to try. You'll pick it up. It's easy! Just think 'up' and up you'll go! Try it!"

"Not embarrassed..." Franco growled sulkily, his face still flushed furiously red.

"Well, let's try then!" rejoined Rose with a wide smile. She took his hand again and squeezed it. "Come on! It's fun once you get used to it!"

The three hovered above the ground for a few additional seconds as Franco composed himself and adjusted his posture from wrong-side-up to upright once more. He swallowed heavily and gave his head a toss. The expression on his face was clearly an attempt to appear nonchalant again, but the embarrassment was not completely assuaged either.

"Think up, eh?" he said at last. "Just up."

"Just up," Rose repeated, giving his hand another firm squeeze.

"Okay then," Franco replied, a little confidence returning to his voice. He gently extracted his hand from Rose's and ran his fingers through his hair which snapped abruptly from hanging limp against his head to being spiked up as if he had just applied a healthy dollop of hair gel. "Up…"

Hana smiled and nodded supportively, and Franco's face hardened. He took a deep, steadying breath.

"Well then," he stated determinedly. "*UP!*"

He shouted the last and shot skyward like a rocket. Rose and Hana raced to catch him. Franco swooped and swirled. He dove then climbed again and made wide loops in the air. He screamed - this time not in terror, but elation.

Flames burst from his lower extremities and he left a billowing vapor trail across the sky. He wrote his name "F-R-A-N-C-O" in huge, 100-foot tall letters among the clouds. Then he plummeted to Earth like a comet. It was all Rose could do to keep up. He struck the ground with a great and powerful concussion, leaving a wide, smoking crater on the otherwise pristine grasslands, and Rose rushed toward the smoldering hole in concern.

"Franco?" she called uncertainly.

The gentle breeze soon dispersed the smoke and dust to reveal Franco standing unperturbed in the wide pit he had made. His hands were on his hips and his head thrown back. He laughed heartily. No longer was he dressed in his torn and bloodied T-shirt and blue jeans, but rather was attired in something akin to a superhero costume – red cape billowing in the wind.

"Franco?" Rose ventured again.

He turned toward her voice, and the superhero tights were replaced by a half-open, button-down, white shirt and painted-on black slacks. His neck was hung with a heavy gold chain. He pumped his fist and said something very fast and intense in Spanish.

"That's *alright*, Rose!" he exclaimed looking up at her with a wide smile. "Let's do it again!"

He leapt back into the air. Rose watched him go with a grin as Hana landed next to her. She pursed her lips, as if she had considered frowning, but then thought better of it. Instead she sighed, held out her hand, and smoothed over the huge hole that Franco had made in the ground. She shook her head.

"Boys being boys, I suppose…" she lamented mildly as she repaired the scorched Earth. She brought up a fresh layer of tall grass with a raise of her hand "At least he's in a better mood now…"

Rose watched Franco swoop and soar high above her. Even thousands of feet below, she could still hear his exuberant cries as he played among the clouds. She suddenly wanted very much to join him. She gave Hana a gentle poke.

"Race you back to the mansion!" She challenged with a mischievous grin.

Hana raised an eyebrow even as she continued to worry with the damaged grass.

Rose laughed at her expression. Then she leapt into the air herself.

"You're already behind, Princess!" she called as she shot upwards. "You had better get moving! Last one makes the tea!"

Hana stood below her a moment longer, but then smiled broadly. She zoomed up into the sky, in hot pursuit of the two new Vedas of Aaru.

Chapter 7

Pandadora

Koren was wearing a silky pink nightgown, but she was not sleepy yet. Again, she sat alone in her room in the dark, but her mood was not at all the same as it had been the last time. Before, she had been wallowing in self-pity and despair. Now she was bubbling over with anticipation.

The techs from Elysian Industries had just left after setting up a huge, ninety-inch monitor. It took up nearly the entire wall where her mirror used to be. Koren faced it as she sat on the edge of her bed, staring raptly at the massive display, even though at the moment it only featured a single flashing word.

Loading...

Koren was giddy with excitement, but also, and quite strangely she mused, nearly paralyzed by nervousness. She could barely wait to see Rose again. Ever since the limo pulled away from Elysian Industries to take her and her parents home, she had earnestly begun drafting a mental list of the *millions* of positively vital things she just simply *had* to tell Rose.

At the same time, she could not completely banish the feelings of apprehension that were tying her stomach into uncomfortable knots. She was not sure exactly why she should be so trepidatious, but neither could she deny it. It felt very much the same way she remembered back when she was eleven or twelve and had gone over to a friend's house for a slumber party one night.

The neighbor girl had turned all the lights off, lit about a dozen candles and pulled out an Ouija Board. The questions and answers had been silly, but the idea that they were doing something supernatural had both unsettled and excited her. She knew the glowing monitor was just a piece of hardware that could have been bought at any big-box electronics store, but the feeling that she was about to communicate with her sister beyond the grave would not completely leave her.

The screen flashed, and the Elysian Industries trademark appeared. Koren stood from her bed and stretched her fingers out toward the gently glowing button marked 'login', but she hesitated.

Her breathing accelerated, and her heart was doing flip flops in her chest. She wasn't sure whether it was from anticipation or fear. When she had called Rose the first time, she had absolutely expected the whole thing to be proven a sham. Now she knew that it wasn't. Now she knew when she called, Rose would answer. She swallowed.

Then she scowled.

I'm being silly, Koren thought. *What exactly am I worried about?*

Even if it *was* a ghost she was about to talk to (and she had been told in no uncertain terms by Mr. Adams that it most definitely was not) it was still Rose. Rose would never hurt her. Rose loved Koren, and Koren loved her! More than that, Koren *missed* her sister. She missed her so badly that it made her ache. What on Earth was she waiting for?

She pushed the login button.

"Enter login information," stated the musical female voice she remembered from the demonstration earlier in the day.

"Koren1," she whispered, her voice cracking.

"I'm sorry," apologized the disembodied voice. "I didn't quite understand that. Please repeat your login information."

"Koren1!" Koren stated more forcefully after clearing her suddenly husky throat.

"Password please," requested the voice.

Even though she was unquestionably all alone, she still looked sheepishly left and right before uttering the password she had chosen.

"Pretty Pandadora" Koren said at last, using the name she had decided to give Rose's panda bear doll. It sat at the head of her bed on a pillow behind her, beneath her shirtless Jonas Perry poster.

The silhouette of the great tree and lightning bolt appeared along with the words 'Elysian Industries'. Then came the dazzling blue sky and fluffy white clouds followed by the same effulgent fanfare. The three buttons appeared with a whoosh and the gentle sound of wind and birds filled her bedroom from top-of-the-line, surround-sound speakers.

"Good evening, Koren," the female voice intoned pleasantly.

Koren pressed the red 'connect' button. The sky scene darkened to twilight, and the female voice called out.

"Connection ready. Input user please."

Koren swallowed. "Rose Johnson," she said.

"Establishing connection. Please wait," answered the computer. "Access granted."

The rainbow tunnel swirled. This time it felt like it took *forever* before the speakers pinged, and the voice finally stated, "Rose Johnson connection established. Configuring video feed."

Koren waited.

Even though she had been expecting it, she still gasped as the hand appeared on the screen. Koren gently pressed her own fingers against it, and her sister materialized in the window. Rose's face broke into a happy smile.

"There you are!" Rose exclaimed happily. "I wondered when you would come back."

Koren could momentarily think of absolutely nothing to say. Seeing her sister again like this was still confusing, and the emotional dagger she had felt buried in her heart at their initial reunion had lost none of its potency. All Koren could think about was how beautiful Rose looked and how bewildering it was to see her again.

Rose was still wearing the elaborate Japanese costume from before, but her kinky, chestnut hair was down. Behind her, instead of the wide azure sky, it appeared Rose was standing on a vast grassy plain. There was a tall rocky hill with a castle on top in the distance to the left and a long winding river, clear blue water sparkling brilliantly in the sun on the right. She giggled.

"Are you just going to stare at me with your mouth open?" Rose asked with a grin. "Or are you actually going to talk with me?"

Rose's laughter sounded like euphonious music to her sister. Koren felt the tears coming and wiped at her eyes fiercely.

"I missed you!" she managed at last though her voice broke. "It's been so hard... Yes! Yes! I want to talk to you! I *need* to talk with you! Things have been so horrible since... since..." she trailed off and pressed her cheek against the screen.

"I missed you..." Koren murmured at last, still at a loss for anything more to say.

Rose brushed the back of her hand against her side of the glass where her sister's face touched.

"I've missed you too, Koren," she said. "And I've got *so* much to tell you. It's wonderful here, and I've been dying to tell you all about it!"

Koren let go a single bark of teary laughter at Rose's ironic choice of words. She sniffed loudly and then wiped her eyes again.

"Me too, Rose," she said regaining a little of her composure. "I've got *tons* to tell you too. A lot has been going on. It's been a *crazy* day."

"I can't wait!" exclaimed Rose clapping her hands together with another pleasant giggle. "Hey! Is that my panda bear doll that Mom gave me back in the hospital behind you over there? She indicated the stuffed animal on the bed behind Koren with a pointed finger.

"Yeah," replied Koren shyly. "I named her Pandadora. I hope you don't mind. I keep her with me when I... when I miss you..."

"No, that's a great name!" Rose exclaimed with another smile. "I'm just glad she's got a good home!" Then she smoothed her features and looked deeply into her sister's eyes.

"It's good to see you." Rose murmured sincerely. "Although..."

She straightened, putting her hands on her hips and knitting her eyebrows together.

"What on *Earth* are you wearing?" she asked critically. "You look like the girl from *Beetlejuice*! I hope you're not sitting around writing bad poetry about how sad and miserable you are all the time."

Koren chuckled.

"No, "she replied. "No poetry."

"You looked pretty as a blonde, you know," Rose continued wryly. "And you should think about dressing like you're *not* going to a funeral too! You know, we used to make *fun* of emo kids who dressed like that..."

"Yeah, we did," acknowledged Koren. Her smile faded.

Rose's eyes widened. Thinking perhaps she had gone too far, she hastily added, "You still look really pretty though! Don't let me hurt your feelings. I was just teasing. You'd look hot wearing a potato sack!"

Koren giggled, and a contemplative smile came to her face.

"You didn't hurt my feelings, Rose," she murmured. "You're right. I guess, I... I guess I just kinda fell to pieces without you. You know, two days ago I would have sold my *soul* for just a minute of your teasing..." She felt herself tearing up once more. "You have no idea how good it feels to have you back!"

They were silent for a long moment, just looking at each other.

"So," Koren ventured at last. "How is it in there? You said you like it. What's it like?

Rose's face lit up.

"Oh, Koren," she breathed. "It's *so* beautiful here... I wish I could show you! The weather is whatever you want it to be. You can build or change or create anything you want and you can *be* anything!"

"Is that why you're dressed like an *anime* princess?" asked Koren with a laugh. "I like it though. I'd probably dress that way every day if I could!"

"I guess," Rose demurred. "When I'm not really thinking about what to wear, this seems to be what pops up..."

The kimono shifted and blurred until Rose was wearing a light yellow sun dress. Her hair was suddenly clipped back with silver burettes that had tiny pink flowers on them.

"How's that?" She asked. "It takes a little concentration, but it's still easier than having to shop. You know I always *hated* shopping for clothes. Everything good at the store is made for size zero stick people..."

"I remember," murmured Koren.

Rose grinned.

"Of course you do!" she exclaimed. "You *are* size zero stick people!"

They both laughed. Then Rose seemed to remember something. Her eyes brightened, and she changed the subject excitedly.

"Oh! Oh! Oh!" She exclaimed. "There's big news here! I told you about Hana before, right? Well, a new boy just came too! He said he's from somewhere in California. His name's Franco."

"*Reeeally?*" Koren drew out the word with a sly smile. "*Franco*, huh? Not Frank? Sounds like a Latin man then. Is he cute? Does he look like Ronaldo Casillas? I know you are *so* into Hispanic guys!"

Rose smiled, and her cheeks flushed.

"I guess he's pretty cute," she bashfully conceded. "He can get a little prickly and grumpy when he can't do things though... Especially, if I can... Mostly he's just a pretty fun guy to hang out with. I taught him how to fly today..."

"Wait…" Koren held up both of her hands. "You taught him *what* today?"

"Flying," Rose repeated. "Oh yeah… We can do that too."

"That's so *cool!*"

Rose smiled again, clearly pleased by Koren's approval. Then she launched into a detailed retelling of all of the simply amazing things she had been doing since coming to Aaru. Building her castle, creating her flowers, trees, and gardens, filling them with fanciful animals, and then bringing them all to life – she told Koren everything. As she spoke Koren's eyes grew wider and wider. She sat cross-legged on her bed and listened to her sister with rapt attention. Aaru did indeed sound wonderful.

…And Mr. Ashe has asked me to help him bring it to the whole world…

The enormity of what she was about to be a part of struck her abruptly. She was suddenly *very* proud. Koren tried hard to keep her attention fixed on Rose, but it was more difficult as her own flurry of thoughts kept intruding.

When Rose had finished her telling, Koren's head was spinning. It was hard to accept that such fantasy could be even remotely similar to anything real.

"I wish I could come visit you there, Rose." She sighed. "Aaru sounds great… Like a dream…"

"I wish you could too… Who knows?" she ventured hopefully. "Maybe you can someday, but you know what? I've been doing all the talking. Tell me about you! What's your big news?"

Koren made a small smile and looked down at her lap shyly. "Nothing as amazing as you, but…"

"But what?!" exclaimed Rose impatiently. "Come on! Give! What's up?"

"Mr. Ashe… You know, that's Mr. Adams' boss… He asked me to be their 'spokesperson'. He wants me to go around and tell everybody how great Aaru is and how they saved you. He even wants to put me on TV!"

"That's great, Koren!" exclaimed Rose. "You said yes, right? It's *so* wonderful here… You have to tell everyone. You have to get *everyone* to come!"

"I said yes," she replied softly.

Koren had agreed to Askr Ashe's offer on an impulse, but still felt nervous about it. However, seeing Rose again like this, seeing her so happy and healthy, listening to all of the amazing things she could do in Aaru – that finally convinced her. With those three words, Koren decided, she wasn't just going to do it either. She was going to *crusade* for it. She was a true believer. Aaru was everything Askr Ashe claimed and much, much more.

"Well, I'm proud of you, Koren." Rose said making the other girl blush with pleasure.

They chatted a little more of this and that. It was mostly just about little, mundane things - the family, friends, what was going on at church and school - but it felt good. Her room finally felt right again, Koren realized. *She* finally felt right again.

Immediately after the two sisters signed off and parted ways for the evening, Koren could not help releasing an ecstatic and exceptionally shrill squeal of pure joy. She jumped on her bed for a few minutes in elation. Then she indulged in a long, celebratory kiss with Jonas Perry on her poster. Rose had *really* come back to her!

As she laid her head on her pillow that night, Koren could not seem to wipe the silly grin off of her face and fall asleep. She just lay in the darkness, staring up at the ceiling thinking about Rose – how happy and beautiful she looked. She clutched Pandadora tightly against her chest and thought about how wonderful it would be when everyone understood about Aaru the way she did now. It really *was* going to change the world.

When Koren finally fell asleep, she dreamt magnificent dreams. They were filled with fanciful flying creatures, cute Latin boys, castles in the sky, and most importantly, Rose. In her own way that night, Koren *was* in Aaru, and it was a wonderful place to be.

Chapter 8

Back on the Pitch

Rose had told Koren that a lot had been going on, and that certainly did not change. Soon, other new Vedas began to arrive – one for each Lord and Lady of Aaru – nineteen in all. Rose met them in due course, but there were really five that she began to get close to. This was good, because as they prepared to, as Mikoto had said, "go live" Hana had less and less time to spend with her, and when she did, she was almost always complaining about Mikoto's side of Tenkoku.

Today, Hana had told her, she needed to meet with Lord Draugr about something. Lord Draugr was apparently the chief among all of the Aaru Lords and Ladies. Rose had never met him herself, but Hana conferred with him often. She described him as a huge, red haired, heavily bearded man with a booming voice.

"He can be a little intense," Hana had confided with a giggle, "but he's mostly just loud – all bark and no bite. I can usually get my way with him if I smile sweetly and say, 'please'."

In any case, since she was otherwise unengaged, Rose had decided to depart her mansion and go in search of her new friends. Now, the six Vedas zipped over the wide and empty Aaru plains.

They were not going anywhere particularly. Rather they simply exulted in the thrill of speed and flight for its own sake. Astride winged, purple horses, they galloped madly across the sky upon a thin layer of fluffy cloud that moved right along with them. Auset had cooked them up.

Auset was a small, quiet, dark-skinned girl. She was dressed like an Egyptian princess draped in gold and jewels with carefully painted, sable eye makeup. She was clad in a simple white, linen dress, her arms bare from the shoulders. She had arrived shortly after Franco and was sweet, but Rose found her to be very, very shy. She was the Veda of Lady Nu, who was a close friend of Princess Hana. Hana had been quite insistent that Rose try to make friends.

That had not particularly bothered Rose of course. She did not mind making more friends, and Auset was nice enough. She was extremely creative, Rose thought – her own mansion a testament to the fact. It was a massive stone affair of Greek-style columns colored all over in a rainbow of Egyptian hieroglyphics and set right on the edge of the great river. Auset also had a large Ibis-headed boat that they would sail around on lazy days observing the hundreds of fanciful creatures the girl created to inhabit the waters and banks around her estate.

Beside her was a boy that must have been equivalent in size to three or four Ausets. His name was Kurt and he was the Veda of Lady Embla. He was loud and jolly and wore a shirt that looked like something out of a fantasy movie – a sleeveless cross between armor and a leather doublet – along with fur-lined leather pants and boots.

Runa, Lord Epimetheus' Veda, rode an enormous winged polar bear behind him. Her pale, pretty face was framed with platinum hair and a white, fur-lined hood while Lord Wurugag's Veda, Derain, a black-skinned Australian boy, rode beside her. Franco soared next to Rose, as always taking the lead.

"There!" Franco pointed excitedly down at the ground, but Rose could tell no difference between that particular bare patch of grassy plain and any other. "It's perfect!"

"Perfect for what?" Rose asked with a raised eyebrow.

"You'll see!" Franco replied with a wink. "Come on!"

He jerked the reins of his periwinkle mount and plummeted. Rose was quick to follow. He pulled up hard and leapt from the back of his steed to hit the turf at a run. Rose pulled up beside his pegasus and simply watched him. Runa and Auset landed next to her.

"What ever is it that Franco is endeavoring?" asked Runa in a very precise voice that had initially struck Rose as haughty, but she soon decided was simply academic – as if Runa's strongly stilted English was a trick that she had mastered, but seldom used in actual conversation. "He seems quite excited about whatever it is he thinks that he has come upon."

"Yeah!" cried Kurt, cupping his hands up to his mouth, even though his loud, deep voice hardly needed the help. "What are you doing, Franco?!"

Franco turned in a circle and drew a large, white rectangle on the ground with an extended hand.

"Come on, mate!" laughed Derain, his flying horse kicking up dust as it touched down. "What are you on about?!"

"You guys couldn't figure out what to do today, right?" He answered. His white rectangle was bisected by a white line, and he quickly drew a large circle in the middle of it. "Well, I just thought of something! It's something Rose told me she wanted to do actually, but we only just got enough people!"

"Is that...?" began Rose just as two white, metal cages all covered in netting appeared at either end of Franco's big, white box.

Franco's skinny jeans and half-undone white shirt were suddenly replaced by a jersey with vertical red and gold stripes. The number ten was emblazoned boldly in navy blue on the back. A white sphere appeared under his arm.

"Huh?" started Kurt, but Rose squealed.

The kimono she was wearing was quickly replaced by a jersey of her own, but this one was white, with a blue number 7. Franco made a face.

"Ugh," he groaned in disgust as he caught sight of her wardrobe choice. "Seriously?"

Rose flashed him a coy smile. "You're just mad that my side always beats your side."

"Well, I *was* going to invite you to be on the *winning* team, but..." began Franco.

"Don't do me any favors!" laughed Rose. She turned back to their four companions who were still watching the pair curiously. "You guys know how to play, right?"

"What?" asked Kurt, rubbing the back of his head. "Soccer?"

"Football," Franco and Runa corrected simultaneously.

Runa's fur ensemble was quickly replaced with a deeply orange jersey, black number 19 on it. She smiled and leapt from the back of her polar bear. "Yes, I am in fact quite familiar actually."

"Well," interrupted Kurt with a grimace. "It is certainly *not* football, but yeah, I can play soccer."

"Why not?" added Derain, also jumping down with a laugh. "It's som'thin' to do, right?"

"I'll take Auset and Runa then!" announced Rose, with a wide grin, "girls against boys!"

"Whatever, Rose," scoffed Franco. "It's your funeral. We'll beat you a hundred to nothin'!"

"I'm not really very good at sports, Rose," whispered Auset, kicking her mount forward so she could lean down to urgently tug on Rose's sleeve. She seemed to shrink where she sat on her purple pegasus and gripped the reins more tightly.

Rose smiled. She took Auset's hands to help her down. Then she leaned in to give the smaller girl a tight hug.

"This is Aaru, Auset," she whispered conspiratorially. "Everyone is good at *everything*!"

"But some people are better at everything than others!" exclaimed Franco, as he launched the white ball into the air and executed a perfect bicycle kick. The soccer ball gave off flames like a comet's tail as it left his foot to streak into the net on the other side of the field. Franco did a running slide on the pitch with his head thrown back, both hands raised exultantly toward the sky.

"That doesn't count and you know it," complained Rose in irritation, scowling with her hands planted on her hips. "We weren't ready! We haven't even lined up for kickoff yet! Why do you have to be such a show off?"

"Don't be such a spoiled sport, Rose!" Franco retorted with a mischievous grin. "We'll spot you girls one."

"Spot us…?" Rose began. Then her mouth fell open. "It won't matter anyway!" she exclaimed. "We'll beat you guys by at *least* two!"

She and Runa stuck their noses in the air and stormed over to midfield. Auset followed them reluctantly. The white soccer ball suddenly appeared in Rose's hands. She dropped it on the center line and rested her right foot on top of it.

"Well?" she demanded glaring fiercely at Franco and the other two boys. "Are you going to get in position? Unlike you *we're* waiting. *We're* not big cheaters. We'll even let you kickoff first!"

She kicked the ball to Franco, who trapped it against his chest then juggled it a few times off his feet and knees.

"You heard her guys," he replied with a chuckle. "Let's do this!"

Auset and Kurt dropped back to their respective goals while Rose and Runa faced off against Franco and Derain. A whistle blew, although it was anyone's guess from whence the sound emanated. Franco rolled the ball across the center line with his toe then fired off a backward pass to Derain.

The aboriginal boy trapped the white sphere deftly and fired it downfield as Runa rushed to engage him. Franco got to the rolling orb an instant before Rose. He faked to his left then surged to his right. Rose was forced to spin and chase after him, no one between Franco, a visibly trembling Auset, and a wide-open goal.

Franco fired another bullet, and the ball again ignited as it streaked toward the quivering girl. She squeaked in dismay, and a stone wall suddenly sprung into existence between herself and the hurtling comet. It made a hollow *thunk* as it ricocheted against the barrier.

"Hey!" cried Franco. "What gives? You can't just throw a *wall* up in the way! That's cheating!"

"Takes a cheater to know a cheater!" laughed Rose, sticking her tongue out as she dashed away with the idle ball. A tiny rain cloud appeared just before her foot made contact, to extinguish the smoldering projectile with a hiss. "Are you gonna play, or just stand there and *whine*!?"

She faked toward him, then drove hard toward the goal, and Derain rushed to meet her. Rose faked again to the left then kicked the ball ahead of her to the right. She beat the Australian boy, but he raised his hand and a great stone pillar erupted from the ground directly beneath the soccer ball, carrying it high into the blue sky.

Derain leapt after the rising orb, climbing hundreds of feet in the air. Just as it reached apogee he spun his body in a dramatic bicycle kick. The ball hurtled back toward the pitch like a meteor. Runa streaked up to meet it - a pale defensive missile. She deflected it away from the goal with a sideways toss of her blonde head. The ball struck the pitch at midfield with deafening crash that left a ten foot crater.

The players fell back to Earth and looked at each other, then over to their captains.

"Penalty kick?" Rose and Franco ventured at the same time. Then they laughed.

Franco lifted his hand, and the Earth rumbled. Soil rose up beneath the soccer ball, lifting it up out of the hole. He rushed over to fire it sideways to Derain.

Runa was swift, however. She darted past Derain little more than an orange blur, even as the aboriginal boy fell flat on his back trying to fire off a shot with a ball that was no longer there. Franco flew across the field to meet her, and the two collided just as Runa zipped a pass to Rose. They flew backwards in opposite directions, digging long furrows across the ground.

Rose charged on goal, Kurt now the only thing between herself and the net. She pulled up short and fired, but not with the ball. Instead she launched a large muddy divot toward the upper right corner of the goal. Kurt made a spectacular dive towards it before he realized what Rose had done. She fired the ball to the left, and it nearly pulled the net off of the posts as it streaked into the corner.

Rose threw her hands over her head and sprinted back toward her side in celebration just as Runa rushed to meet her. Auset waved her hand over her head, causing another explosion of dirt on the sideline. A wide section of bleachers erupted from the ground filled with a rainbow array of fanciful creatures all cheering and screaming in celebration at the girls' fine play. Auset and Rose embraced and Runa gave her teammates enthusiastic high fives, apparently none the worse for wear for being driven into the turf by her impact with Franco.

Franco applauded slowly and deliberately, an expression on his face somewhere between bemusement and irritation.

"Very nice, Rose," he growled in grudging congratulations. "Is it legal where you're from to kick dirt clods at people?"

"Is it legal for you to light the ball on fire?" she countered. "I think we can all agree that we're not exactly playing by FIFA rules…"

"What troubles you, Franco," Runa slyly asked in her just-a-little-too-correct English, giving her platinum head a toss. "Does the fact of three girls tallying a point more than you cause you to become worried?"

"A point more?" countered Kurt leaping from the goal to the center line in a single step. He shook the remains of Rose's dirt clod from his short brown hair.

"Yeah," agreed Derain. "We're all tied up, yeah? Rose said Franco's first shot counted," he argued.

"I did not!" protested Rose. "I called him a cheater!"

"Yeah, well," countered Kurt. "You also said you girls could beat us by two, so the way I see it, you're still down by one!"

"That's right!" Exclaimed Franco, throwing his head back with a hearty laugh. "And now it's our kickoff again, so you'd better get set!"

The multitude of elves, fairies, pixies, and other less readily identifiable creatures in the bleacher box booed loudly.

"Fair warning!" Franco cried.

A whistle materialized in his hand and he blew it loudly.

Auset's eyes grew wide and she launched herself backwards toward the goal just as the soccer ball rocketed from his foot. It left a vapor trail in its wake. She managed to get a hand on hurtling orb, deflecting it upwards, but it was not quite enough. Both she and the screaming missile sailed into the net. The crowd in the bleachers roared in dismay.

Franco ran across the field and slid on his knees, once again digging two deep furrows across the pitch at the same time he ripped off his shirt and swung it triumphantly over his head. Derain and Kurt quickly rushed their teammate and tackled him in a crushing embrace while at the same time screaming "Gooooal!!!" at the top of their lungs.

"Come on Franco," Rose complained. "That was another cheap one and you know it!"

Franco shrugged helplessly.

"Hey," he said. "I told you to get set. It still counts! We're up two one!"

Rose scowled at him a moment. Then she angrily spun on her heel to march back over to her team's side of the field.

"All right girls," she spat, fixing Auset and Runa with a serious gaze. "Play time's over! Let's do this!" She rounded on Franco. "Next point wins!" she cried.

"Whatever, Rose," Franco shot back, a maddeningly contemptuous smirk on his face. "We could spot you a couple more if you want, you know. Are you sure?"

"You are needing the teaching of a serious lesson!" retorted Runa, jabbing her finger at Franco. "And it shall be we who does the teaching of it to you!"

"Teaching what!?" scoffed Derain, "How to watch a ball go into your own net?"

"Oh, it's *so* on!" shouted Rose. Her eyes flashed and flames leapt from her head and shoulders.

A whistle sounded somewhere, but again there was no visible source. Rose leapt from the half line, dribbling the ball determinedly before her and leaving charred grass in her wake. Derain charged to meet her, encasing himself in a giant ball of water. The two collided with a hiss as Rose launched a pass over to Runa. Franco moved to defend, but the blond girl exhaled a deep, deliberate breath and the ground beneath the Latino boy's feet froze solid in a wide sheet of ice. As soon as he hit it, he crashed to the ground and slid across the field in a heap. Runa charged the goal, and Kurt rushed out to meet her.

Runa darted to the right of the goal, but let her shot fly to the left. Kurt crashed to the ground, but stretched out with his right arm until it was impossibly long. At the last moment he swatted Runa's shot away.

By this time Rose and Franco had both picked themselves up and charged toward the ball. Rose slid towards it, but Franco got there first. He pincered the ball between his feet and flipped it up into the air just as Rose arrived. Derain picked up the pass and dashed toward the girls' goal. He let a devastating shot of his own fly toward the upper left corner. Auset stood as if frozen, eyes wide mouth gaping. Then she leapt up, grasped the crossbar and pulled it down to the pitch. The shot flew high.

"Now wait a minute!" protested Derain. "You can't move the goal!"

"Auset did not touch the ball and you missed!" cried Runa with a wide grin. "Goal kick!"

The Netherlander put her words into action and launched the ball downfield to a waiting Rose. She trapped it against her chest and charged towards the boys' goal again. Franco picked her up, matching her stride for stride.

Rose flipped the ball sideways, but Franco was ready. He stuck out his foot and managed to deflect it back the other way. Rose recovered it and pulled up hard. She and Franco faced off, and Rose feinted again – first left, then right, then straight up the middle. Franco again got his foot on the ball knocking it away from her, but Runa was nearby. She flipped it over Franco's head as Rose darted past him.

Rose leapt high, apparently ready to unleash a devastating bicycle shot on Kurt. He leapt to meet her, but instead of kicking the ball, she twisted sideways. The ball glanced against her temple and went low. It smacked against the grass with a dull thud and slowly dribbled across the goal line.

The crowd of creatures in the bleachers erupted. Rose landed gently on the pitch as Kurt crashed down with his feet in the air. She caught Franco's disbelieving eye and winked at him. Then she ripped off her Jersey and slid across the pitch on her knees in imitation of Franco's earlier celebration.

At first he looked incensed, but as Franco gazed down at her, her slim figure glazed in sweat, smeared with dirt, chiseled stomach bare, his face softened. Runa and Auset tackled Rose, laughing and screaming, shamelessly wallowing on the ground in celebration.

Derain swore. Kurt groaned, but Franco just smiled. He walked over and offered Rose a hand up. Rose quieted her laughter and smiled back up at him shyly. Then she wrapped her fingers around his. He pulled her to her feet so that she was standing almost nose to nose with him.

"Good game," he whispered in a husky voice.

"You too..." Rose murmured.

They stared at each other a moment more, acutely aware of the eyes of their friends resting expectantly upon them. Rose craned her neck up and kissed Franco, just under his chin where his jawbone met his neck. It was a swift peck, warm and soft and very, very brief, but it made him gasp anyway.

"Thanks," she said. "That was fun."

Rose turned back to the girls and raised her hands over her head as Franco conspicuously admired her lean, well-muscled back.

"We win!" She cried with a gleeful giggle, and the other girls squealed.

"Whatever!" Retorted Derain. "You only went up by one and you said two! Sounds like a tie to me!"

"I am sorry, Derain," shot back Runa officiously. "But Rose most clearly stated that the next point would determine the victor, and Franco agreed!"

"Don't be a sore loser, Derain," added Auset in a tiny voice, but they all turned and stared at her anyway. She blushed furiously pink beneath her dark, skin. Rose hugged her around her narrow shoulders with a pleased laugh.

"Don't be embarrassed, Auset!" She reassured. "It's about time you spoke up! And you are quite right..." she fixed Derain with an imperious look. "Derain indeed does not need to be a sore loser. He needs to take his whoopin' like a man!"

Derain continued to grumble, but Rose could not hear what he said.

"You guys wanna eat something?" Asked Kurt plaintively, still shaking dirt from his hair.

"That sounds great..." sighed Rose.

They never really felt hungry in Aaru, but eating was still something fun to do. Besides, it just felt natural after a game.

"Perhaps we can go to my mansion?" Suggested Runa politely. "It is not far, and I have made many improvements and addendums since last you made a social call."

And so it was decided. After smoothing out the devastation caused by their soccer match, they hopped back onto their mounts and soared off into the sky.

Rose liked Runa's mansion. It was nestled down in a snow covered valley rather than on a tall mountain like hers, and Runa had constructed a great castle made completely out of ice, though it never felt cold. It was beautiful as the sunlight sparkled through its diamond facets, reflecting and refracting to gorgeous, rainbow effect.

They landed at the gates, and two enormous polar bear guards pushed the heavy, glistening portal open to admit them. Runa led them through a series of wide corridors, roof suspended by rows of thick shimmering columns, until they came to a large banquet hall. The six Vedas seated themselves around a long wooden table on blocks of ice covered with thick furs and fluffy pillows.

Runa rang a little bell. A series of doors opened along the walls, and a waddle of penguins tottered in, each carrying a covered tray. The first wave set the trays before each Veda. Then a second group brought out steaming mugs. Rose tasted hers to discover it was a wonderfully rich, hot cocoa. She purred in pleasure taking a moment to drape one of the many furs about her shoulders.

"I trust you find it pleasing?" Ventured Runa, and everyone agreed. She gave a small self-satisfied smile.

The food before them was even better. Whatever they wanted most appeared as they lifted the silver cloches covering their respective trays. A steaming platter of tamales appeared before Franco, while Kurt revealed a pizza nearly as big as a wagon wheel. Auset received a shallow dish of meatballs served in some sort of yellowish-brown sauce while Runa had a bowl of something that resembled a steaming porridge chocked full of large slices of summer sausage. Derain had a big plate of roasted meat, but Rose could not have ventured a guess as to what kind of animal the pieces might have come from. On her own broad platter materialized a juicy cheese burger and fries. She sighed contentedly, raised the sandwich to her lips, and took a big bite.

Just like they were never really hungry, they didn't exactly get full either. They simply ate until they got tired of the sensation.

Runa's penguin servants came to clear the dishes away, and they all lounged around contentedly chatting of this and that. As their conversations often did, they soon found themselves talking about Before.

Before – the time before Aaru that is - seemed to grow dimmer in their memories by the day. However, as hard as things had been in her own Before-life, and as beatific as her life certainly was now, Rose still did not feel quite ready to let it go.

She talked a little about her cancer, but it seemed distant, almost like it had happened to a different person. Franco followed her and briefly mentioned his traffic accident, but left out most of the details he had shared with Rose previously. Kurt had a heart valve problem. Runa had been caught in a fire, which explained to Rose her affinity for ice, and Derain had been bitten by a poisonous snake in his back yard.

Rose had heard all of their stories before, of course. It was almost a formalized part of meeting someone for the first time in Aaru – What's your name? Where are you from? How did you die?

"So…" Kurt ventured at last. "What does everyone want to do now?"

"Wait a minute!" Interrupted Derain. "What about Auset?"

"Indeed," agreed Runa. "Though she may be unassertive, she should also have a turn at telling as well."

"Yeah, Auset," noted Franco thoughtfully. "I don't think I've *ever* heard yours before."

Auset stiffened and looked down at her hands.

"No," she murmured. "I don't suppose that you have…"

"Well?" Prompted Kurt with a broad, easy grin. "What was it? Train wreck? Bubonic Plague? Parachute didn't open?"

"No," whispered Auset, shrinking even deeper into the heavy furs on her chair. "Nothing like that…"

"Well, what then?" Franco asked insistently. "You know all of ours…"

"Franco!" Rose exclaimed, noting Auset's obvious discomfort. "Leave her alone! If she doesn't want to talk about it then we shouldn't force…"

"No, Rose," Auset spoke up quickly, though her voice was still barely audible. "He's right. We're friends after all. I should tell you…"

"Are you sure?" Rose asked uncertainly.

Auset seemed to want to melt straight through the floor. Despite what she said, she did not look at all to Rose like someone who was burning to share a secret.

"It is not that I want to keep it secret, really," Auset said. "It's mostly just because I haven't quite decided what I feel about it myself. I am still… confused by it all…"

Auset took a deep breath and met their inquisitive gazes. Her eyes were grim.

"I was killed," she stated matter-of-factly.

Everyone sat up. They stared in surprise.

"What do you mean 'killed'?" asked Kurt.

"By who? How?" Derain quickly followed.

Auset's voice was cold. "I was murdered."

She stated the fact neutrally enough, but her brows knitted together and her expression hardened.

"It was by my father and my brothers and my uncles and cousins…" she continued. "All the men in my family."

"What?!" exclaimed Runa in disbelief. "Why?!"

"My mother moved to the US – Chicago - with me when I was a baby and divorced my father," She replied in the same neutral voice. "But we had to go back to Pakistan because my grandmother got sick. She was dying, and my mother felt that she just had to see her before the end. My father found out. He came to my grandmother's house where we were staying. He said we had dishonored him and the family – her for leaving, me for being too 'Western'. He said I sinned against them and against God… Then…" she paused.

"It hurt, and I was afraid, but I don't remember much after…" her voice broke a little. "After they drug us through the village, everyone screaming and calling curses at us… spitting on us… all the way to the town square. They began throwing stones…"

She trailed off and the room was silent. Everyone stared in horror.

"I think I woke up in the hospital a couple of times," Auset continued at last. "I don't know how I got there. I expected to wake up in Hell, really, but instead I eventually awoke here. I couldn't understand why my mother wasn't with me… I feel… I feel… I… I guess I don't know what I feel…" She trailed off. Then her face slackened, and she sighed in apparent defeat.

"It still confuses me…" She trailed off again.

Everyone continued to stare, unsure how to respond.

"It's funny, actually," Auset went on after a moment of uneasy silence. "I try to think about it now, and I remember that it happened, but I can't really *think* about it, and by that I don't mean I don't *want* to think about it. I just literally can't! I try, and I can tell you what happened, but it's almost like I am telling a story I heard from someone else... All words, but no substance... It's strange."

"Isn't that a good thing?" asked Kurt with a shudder. "Why would you *want* to remember something like *that*? It's... That's... That's just awful."

Auset furrowed her brow as if concentrating very hard, then shook her head in apparent defeat.

"I suppose you're right," she answered at last. "It's just... I feel like I need to... I don't know... sort things out in my head, maybe. Why did it happen? What happened to my mother? I feel like I should be angry at my father, like I should *hate* him, but can't... can't quite... manage it, I suppose. I'm certainly happy now. It's beautiful here, and I can do or be anything I want! But I keep thinking, should I be? I... I don't know... Maybe I'm being silly. I should just be happy that I'm not dead, I guess... Or maybe that I *am*... I... I don't know..." She trailed off into silence.

Rose got up from her seat and walked around to where the other girl sat with her head on one hand. Auset was mushing what looked to be chocolate cake through the prongs of her fork with the other. Rose crushed the smaller girl's head against her breast in a tight embrace.

"I understand," Rose said softly. "I've tried to think back about being sick a few times myself, and it's just the same for me. I remember it happened, but can't summon any of the details of what I felt. It's more like remembering a movie I watched. We could go talk to Lady Hana about it if it's really bothering you, or maybe your own Lady... Lady Nu? I'm sure they could help you..."

"I might talk to Lady Nu about it..." conceded Auset with a sigh, pushing gently away from Rose. She noted everyone's somber faces and looked down sheepishly before giving a nervous laugh.

"Now look!" she cried. "I've gone and depressed everyone! This is supposed to be a party!" Auset made a great show of brightening. "Would you like to go back to my mansion and take my boat down the river? I've put some new animals in the water that I want to show you…They're called *amermaits*… They're part lion, part crocodile and part hippo…"

"That sounds really *weird*!" exclaimed Kurt, with perhaps slightly overwrought enthusiasm. "Let's go see 'em!"

"Sounds pretty cool, Auset," Derain agreed. "Let's go!" He leapt from his seat.

The others quickly agreed. They all made similar approving comments as they filed back out to where they had left their mounts, clearly happy to be talking about something else. The penguins came in once more to clear the last of the dirty dishes away.

Rose followed her friends, but remained quiet, suddenly unsettled. She tried again to recall her illness. She tried to imagine the way she felt back then, the miserable weakness, the cold steel of her hospital bed rail, the pinch of the needles piercing her arms, the hopeless despair, but could not. Just as Auset said, she recalled it happened. She *knew* that it happened to her, but at the same time it didn't really feel like it was *hers* anymore – like it was a story someone had told her rather than the single most devastating experience of her life.

She wasn't exactly sure why it should bother her so much. Rose certainly had no desire to go through anything like her cancer treatments ever again, but the apparent loss of those trials upset her. Where had those memories gone?

"Everything okay, Rose?" Franco asked solicitously as he walked up to her and gave her hand a shy squeeze. "You alright?

Rose gave a weak smile.

"Yeah, Franco," she answered.

Then Rose took a deep breath and made a much better effort at a grin. She tried to put her discombobulation out of her mind, and squeezed Franco's hand back gratefully.

"I'm great! It's a beautiful day, and the river will be *awesome*. Let's go! Race you there?"

Franco took a deep thoughtful breath, apparently considering. He opened his mouth as if to answer, but then spun on his heel and darted away toward his winged pegasus instead.

"Franco!" Rose called after him with a deep scowl. "You're a big, fat cheater! You know that, right?"

Franco hopped on the beast's back and flashed a mischievous smile. "You gonna stand there and whine, or are you gonna race?"

He laughed. Then he snapped the reins and took off into the sky.

Rose opened her mouth to shout out a retort, but instead just rolled her eyes. Then she giggled and raced toward her own purple pegasus. Soon, she was zooming across the blue sky after Franco and another blissful afternoon in Aaru.

Chapter 9

That's Just Showbiz

Koren stood in front of a three-way mirror with her arms extended. All around her three smartly dressed young women touched up her make-up and adjusted her clothes. Miss Hanasaka had dispensed with her conservative business suit and instead wore a short, hip-hugging black miniskirt with dangerously tall, strappy high heels. Koren thought she looked devastatingly beautiful. Miss Hanasaka stood behind her gazing approvingly into the mirror over her shoulders, which were beginning to ache. They must have been at this for two hours or better.

"You look beautiful, Koren," the Japanese whispered in her ear. "Are you ready for your big moment?"

Koren nodded, but was not sure her answer was the truth.

When she had agreed to be the Elysian Industries' spokesperson Koren had been highly emotional about seeing her sister again. She had also been admittedly flattered. Her later conversation with Rose had then reaffirmed her decision, but now she was starting to rethink it. She had already shot a half-dozen commercials for Aaru and was just beginning a tightly packed talk show and public appearance tour. The first commercial had aired in prime-time just last week, and Koren still remembered the surreal experience vividly.

She had been alone in her room having just talked with Rose again via the Aaru console in her bedroom. Her sister seemed happy enough, but distant and distracted somehow. Koren's feelings were a little bruised, but she hadn't had long to dwell on it. As soon as she broke the connection, and the large HD monitor faded to the now-familiar, cloudy sky start screen, her mother had burst in and demanded she switch the monitor over to its TV setting.

There she was on the screen, her sorrowful face filling the full 90 inches - Sable hair limp against her scalp, the tracks of her tears drawn starkly upon her ashen cheeks in running, black mascara. A fat teardrop rolled down her face in slow motion and the picture faded into a wide shot of Rose in her hospital bed – pale, hairless, skeletal, eyes closed.

Ominous music played, and the steady rhythm of a respirator was amplified to near deafening volume. Then the screen faded to black and stark white letters appeared: "Name: Rose Johnson, Age: 16, Diagnosis: Leukemia" the words disappeared to be replaced by a single line: "Prognosis: Terminal."

The words faded.

"Maybe you can forget all about Rose like she never existed," Koren heard her voice scream. It quivered with unsuppressed anguish. "But I can't! I won't! I'm not going to be all nice and good like there's nothing wrong!"

That had shocked her. She remembered the argument, of course. It had been with her mother in her own bedroom. Koren had no idea how anyone could have gotten a recording of it, but that was undeniably her own heartbroken voice coming out of the surround sound speakers, profanity skillfully censored.

The black screen quickly brightened to radiant white. A vague outline of a slender person solidified to reveal a smiling blond girl with perfectly applied make-up. She wore a short, white sun dress that was girlish and vestal yet subtly erogenous at the same time. Eyes that looked far too large welled with barely contained joy. Koren hardly recognized herself.

"Rose?" she breathed affectedly. "Is it really you?"

The black screen returned, and more white words appeared: "Tragedy need no longer separate us." It said. "Oh Death, where is thy sting?"

"Thank you," Koren heard herself gasp. "Thank you for saving my sister!"

The commercial closed with a cloudy blue sky and the word, "Aaru" filling the azure firmament.

Koren had not been at all sure how to react. On the one hand Elysian Industries had apparently invaded her privacy to record her voice and take unflattering pictures of her in her grief-stricken Goth getup. Then they had also clearly gone crazy with the Photoshop. Who *was* that girl anyway? It sort of looked like her...

Her mother had been dismissive of her reticence. That was just the way big business types did things. This was 'showbiz', and all that was just a part of it. One had to expect little changes like this if they were going to be a celebrity. Koren really did look very pretty after all, and Mr. Ashe had paid them a great deal of money for just that one commercial appearance with the promise of many more to come. Jesus had bestowed this incredible blessing upon them, and it was ungrateful not to embrace and accept it! Koren had reluctantly allowed herself to be mollified.

Now, she felt like she practically lived in a makeup chair.

That very day another limo had rolled up in front of her house to whisk her away to a dizzying succession of briefings, commercial and photo shoots, as well as an array of other harried engagements. The three women fussing over her now were almost constantly with her – painting this, pinning that, sewing up this other thing. Then of course, Miss Hanasaka was always following close behind to tell her how beautiful she looked and how wonderfully she had done at each new appearance.

Koren felt like she had been hijacked by her childhood pastimes and made into a living Barbie doll. Her time was never her own any longer. It seemed like there was always someone around to tell her where to be, what to wear, what and when to eat, when to sleep, and when to wake up and do it all over again.

"Dear," protested one of the women in a sweet, but clearly exasperated voice. "You really do need to keep your arms up."

Koren was about to apologize, but the half-formed response stuck in her throat as the woman unceremoniously jerked her top down, mashed her small breasts together and affixed a six-inch strip of silver tape beneath.

"There we go!" she exclaimed approvingly as she replaced Koren's bodice to its appropriate concealing position. She tugged on it sharply to reveal just the right hint of developing cleavage.

"You know," the woman added considering. "You really might think about getting a boob job. That would make this a lot easier..."

"I... I'm thirteen..." Koren stammered.

"Alright," cut in another woman, who pressed Koren downward into the make-up chair by her shoulders. She was slightly built and in her mid-twenties. Her hair was closely cropped and dyed brilliantly pink. She clutched a broad hairbrush in one hand and a can of hairspray in the other.

"Go ahead and put your arms down." She instructed shortly. "I want to touch you up just a little. You go on in three minutes!"

There were a few seconds of tugging and pulling at Koren's once again blonde hair, then a few more of spraying that made her choke. Just as she was getting her coughing under control, the third woman – also very thin, but dark haired and severe – wordlessly forced her chin up and stuck a thin mascara brush in her eye. Koren started, but the woman forcibly turned her chin back toward her.

"You look quite fetching, Koren," Miss Hanasaka gushed over her shoulder. "All of America is sure to love you!"

"Thank y…" Koren began, but the make-up artist interrupted her unapologetically.

"Don't move," she commanded shortly with a pronounced French accent.

After a moment longer of painting, she took a step back and regarded her work critically.

"Well," she sniffed. "I suppose it will do."

When the French woman stepped out of the way Koren caught sight of Askr Ashe sitting in a large, plush chair across from her. His usually wild and unkempt hair was tamed with what must have been nearly a whole bottle of gel. He was chewing something and held a glass tumbler full of a dark, amber liquid in his right hand. His suit was grey with a white button down shirt and no tie. His sport coat gaped open casually. Askr smiled at her and brushed the crumbs from his chest.

"So, Koren," he ventured. "Are you ready? Are you ready for your big debut?"

"I guess so…" replied Koren uncertainly as she shifted in her chair. The tape under her breasts was starting to pinch. "It all seems like so much… Maybe it's *too…*"

"I understand," Askr cut her off with a dramatically sympathetic expression. "I know you've been very busy lately, but it will all be worth it in da end. I promise!" He took a swig of his drink and wiped his mouth with the back of his hand. "People love you already! You should see da social media posts! Across da board everyone is going *crazy* for our poor, pretty, melancholy girl. Our first three commercials have already been viewed on-line over eighty *million* times all together. Dat's just in da first ten days alone and doesn't even *begin* to count all da viewers of regular TV spots! After tonight, yours will be da most recognizable face in da *country!*"

"Do not be nervous, Koren," instructed Miss Hanasaka behind her, again resting both of her warm hands on Koren's bare shoulders. "You will be charming and wonderful! You will steal everyone's heart!"

Koren nodded, but did not reply. The idea of being a celebrity sounded a whole lot scarier all of a sudden, but Askr Ashe and Miss Hanasaka were far too caught up in their own euphoria and excitement at how splendidly everything was going to notice her unease.

"'David O'Brian Live' is da most widely viewed late-night show on TV!" Askr went on. "After tonight, interest in Aaru is going to *explode!*"

"On in thirty, Mr. Ashe," said a middle-aged man from around the corner of a large curtain to their right. He wore a big pair of black headphones.

"All right, Koren," Askr said as he leapt to his feet and straightened his clothing. "Showtime!"

"Good luck!" cried Miss Hanasaka giving Koren a quick hug around her shoulders.

Koren swallowed the lump in her throat and bit her lip nervously as she nodded and stood.

The drummer out on stage struck an upbeat cadence, and the studio band quickly joined in marking the end of the commercial break. The man in the head phones vigorously gestured Askr and Koren over and indicated they should stand behind a strip of red tape on the floor just off stage. Koren could see out into the studio for the first time.

The stage lights were blinding, which washed out most of the audience from her view and actually made her feel a little more confident. She could see David O'Brian himself sitting at his desk, silver hair perfectly coifed, smiling broadly into the camera. Koren's parents watched this man's show religiously, so Koren had to admit, seeing him right in front of her in person, she was a little star-struck.

"Welcome back everyone!" he called out genially. "Now, I'm sure all of us have our opinions about life everlasting and what happens in the hereafter. Like hereafter I'm pretty sure I'll be drinking a fifth of scotch!"

The crowd roared with laughter. When it died down he went on.

"But seriously folks, our next guest not only says he knows what it will be like, but he is willing to sell it to you for a nominal fee. I'm sure you've all seen his commercials blowing up the social media universe this past week, and just like me are all wondering what the hubbub is about, so let's get the real inside scoop from the man himself. I'd like you all to welcome Askr Ashe and the haunting young lady from Aaru, Koren Johnson everybody!"

The audience applauded and the man in the headphones jabbed a commanding finger in their direction.

"Remember to smile," whispered Miss Hanasaka pointing vigorously at the corners of her own mouth as Askr led the way out onto the stage.

They must have rehearsed this three dozen times at least, Koren mused, but it had taken every bit of the practice to get to where she was unlikely to humiliate herself. She did her best to balance on the ridiculously high stiletto heels her wardrobe team insisted she wear while smiling pleasantly and waving to the crowd. She swung her hips slightly just as she had been instructed and said a fervent but silent prayer that she would not trip and fall flat on her face. They quickly traversed the stage and seated themselves in two overstuffed chairs to David O'Brian's right.

"So, Mr. Ashe," O'Brian began with a sudden mock serious demeanor. "I understand you have condos in Heaven for sale?" The audience laughed, and the talk show host waited for the noise to die down before continuing. "Does it like... cost extra for a pool, maybe a membership at the golf club? And when they say Saint Andrew's they *mean* Saint Andrew! Can you like get him to caddy for you and stuff?"

Askr Ashe laughed good-naturedly and slapped at his knee in apparent appreciation of the joke.

"Not quite, Dave. Dey're actually *'mansions'*," he corrected maintaining a broad and toothy smile. "Da pool membership is included and we play croquette rather dan golf!" He grinned full into the camera as he delivered the rejoinder and the crowd crowed its approving mirth.

"Right," chuckled O'Brian. "Seriously though, what exactly *is* all the excitement about? I must admit that when I saw the first commercial last week, I wasn't at all sure what it was for. I guess my first thought was that it looked like a movie trailer, and I was like all 'Oh yeah! I am so camping out at the theater for this one!'"

"So I guess you were disappointed then?" Quipped Mr. Ashe earnestly.

"Yeah, I kinda was actually," replied David O'Brian. "Stupid eternal life! I wanted another big-budget, mid-summer blockbuster, damn-it! I was hoping for like *Transformers 11* or *Son of Birdman* or something like that!"

The crowd roared again and David O'Brian acknowledged them with a casually waved hand and appreciative nod. When they quieted once more, he looked at Mr. Ashe seriously, hands folded before him on his big desk.

"So," he said. "Tell us all about it then. What exactly is this thing you're calling 'Aaru'?"

"Well," Askr began. "Da best way to describe it is an enormous bioelectrical data storage system."

"So it's like the world's biggest flash drive," interjected the host, and the crowd crowed. "Hmm... Flash drive Heaven... Talk about saving things to your Cloud now!"

"I suppose it's something like dat," agreed Askr, once the roar of the audience died down. "Although, instead of just saving your Excel worksheets and Word documents and MP4s..."

"And porn," interrupted Dave. "Can't forget the porn - Gigs and gigs of porn!" He raised his hands high above head gazing aloft with a comically ecstatic expression on his face and the crowd howled with laughter. Then he cleared his throat and made a great show of straightening his tie.

"Sorry about that," he apologized in mock chagrin. "As you were saying..."

Askr chuckled, "Right..."

"It's just, that's the first thing I think of when I think of flash drives." Dave cut in again in a theatrically murmured aside.

"Of course," nodded Askr. "Da ever ubiquitous porn..."

"I don't actually know what that word means, but sure, whatever," said O'Brian again to even more raucous guffawing from the audience. Koren's face turned bright red, and she was starting to feel more than a little bit uncomfortable.

"Anyway!" stated Askr a great deal more forcefully, though still smiling. "Just so you all know. Aaru has nothing to do with porn!" He made a wide gesture in an X pattern to punctuate his exclamation.

"Disappointing..." muttered Dave.

"Aaru is a system by which we can save whole people," Askr went on. "Save whole minds. Every thought and feeling, every memory and emotion dat you have ever had or ever might have can be stored forever in Aaru. All joking aside, what we've done is essentially figure out how to save da essence of a human being – dat little spark inside all of us dat makes us who we are. Our bodies might fail us, but now our consciousness can live on forever!"

"If it's true, what you are claiming is amazing certainly," David O'Brian commented. "But how can all the viewers out there be confident that what you're saying isn't well... you know... an enormous load of crap!"

Askr laughed again, but Koren thought she detected the slightest bit of irritation creeping into his expression – maybe it was a subtle tightening at the corners of his eyes or his mouth, but if Askr was annoyed, he did an admirable job of disguising it.

"It kinda sounds like you might be trying to sell me a star or something..." O'Brian finished to more laughter.

"Well Dave," responded Askr evenly. "We completely understand dat people might be skeptical. Dis breakthrough is Earth shattering to say da least. It will change da way humanity looks at life and mortality forever. Death as we know it is *over*. Dat is a very difficult concept for people to grasp, and I completely understand dat dere will be doubters. If I might mention my companion here..." he turned to Koren. "She was a doubter herself in da beginning."

"Now, I need to apologize for being rude," said Dave. "I certainly was not trying to ignore Miss Johnson over there, the radiant if *seriously* depressed beauty that has so captivated the cyber-universe. You know sweetheart, you make miserable look so darn *sexy!*"

Koren laughed nervously, not at all sure how to respond.

"How old are you, again?" he asked.

"I'm thirteen and a half..." Koren answered.

"Whoa!" exclaimed the host with a highly orchestrated grimace on his face. He rubbed his hands over the lapels of his suit coat as if scrubbing himself. "Wow! I'm gonna need a cold shower after this one folks... Seriously?! *Thirteen?!*"

More laughter.

"And a half!" added the band leader - A bald, heavy-set black man in dark sunglasses holding a trombone at the front of the orchestra.

"Well, yes," conceded Dave. "There is the half... Man! *Thirteen?!*" he repeated in mock surprise. "Thanks a lot Miss Johnson. Now I feel like a dirty old man... Seriously though, you do look quite ravishing tonight." He cleared his throat and straightened his tie again. "Can you back up what Mr. Ashe here is claiming? Tell us about your experience with Aaru."

Koren swallowed. She folded her hands demurely in her lap. When she spoke it was in a tiny, shy voice that was at least an octave higher than the way she usually talked.

"Mr. Ashe is right, Mr. O'Brian," she began and there was a collective 'Ahhh...' from the audience. "I didn't believe any of this either. I thought he was trying to trick me."

Mr. O'Brian's voice took on a decidedly gentler, more sympathetic tone, and he looked deeply into Koren's eyes from across the desk. She thought it was a little creepy.

"So what changed your mind?" he asked consolingly.

"My sister," she replied sadly. "My sister Rose had leukemia. She died."

The audience gasped.

"Before she died, though," Koren went on. "Mr. Ashe sent someone to make a scan of her brain. I didn't know anything about it at the time... Or at least I didn't really understand what it was all about. It was after Rose's fu... funeral..." her voice cracked and a tear trickled down her cheek. She saw the camera zoom in close on the monitor just off-stage. Koren wiped her eye and continued. "Anyway, they brought me and my parents to their facility and had me call out to Rose on the Aaru system. I thought it was all b..." she caught herself, "...not true, but I saw my sister! I mean really *saw* her! And when she talked to me, she knew things... things that only Rose could know.

"In the hospital," Koren continued. "She had been so sick and weak. She had lost all of her hair and could barely move, but in Aaru, she was healthy and happy again!"

Koren's voice began to quaver and she could feel those same powerful emotions boiling up surface once more.

"That was when I *believed*," she finished intensely. "That was when I knew it was all true..."

"I believe we have a clip of that," added David O'Brian. "Roll film!"

It was another piece of video that Koren never knew existed. It was obviously cut up and spliced together so that it was shorter than actual events, but it still showed her in all of her sable, Goth glory, standing before the huge Aaru console in the conference room. It showed her initial anger, then her shock, and finally her

---

tearful reaction when Rose apologized for leaving her. There was not a dry eye in the house.

When the video clip ended, David O'Brian turned back to Koren. "So I guess this has been quite a life changing experience for you." He noted somberly. "It's changed out your wardrobe at least!"

The mood immediately lightened and the audience laughed again. Koren ventured a tiny smile.

"Yes, it has," she whispered affectedly. "I'm happy again and so is Rose. I just feel so grateful and... and... the feeling is just too big to keep it inside. I want to share it with everyone... With the whole world!"

That last bit had been scripted by Mr. Ashe, but Koren did not entirely disagree with it. She could still scarcely believe what had happened to Rose - how they had managed to save her. It was amazing.

"Well folks that's just about all the time we have," David O'Brian cut in. "Just remember that the full version of the clip we just watched can be found at..."

He went on to give the web address of the complete video and introduce the musical guest who would close the show. He shook Askr Ashe's hand and gave Koren a tight hug. Then he smiled and waved at the camera as the closing credits scrolled down the screen in front of the raucous audience on the monitors just off stage.

Once they got backstage again, Askr beamed into Koren's face, and Miss Hanasaka gave her a tight hug.

"You were brilliant, Koren!" Mr. Ashe gushed. "Just *brilliant!*"

"You were perfect!" agreed the pretty Japanese woman clapping her hands together in obvious delight. A wide smile split her face. "Just like we practiced!"

"And da tears?" added Askr. "Excellent touch! You melted every heart in America!"

Koren smiled, quite pleased at the effusive praise, but that grin turned into a grimace as she noticed her fashion team saunter up behind the two Aaru board members.

"Now," Mr. Ashe stated matter-of-factly. "We'll have to hurry to finish up and get you to our next interview. You can eat dinner in the limo on the way. Once that's done, it'll be back to the hotel and bed. We've got to be at *America's Wake-up Call* bright and early - 5:00 am tomorrow morning. Ladies..." He addressed the three women whose names Koren still did not know. "Please, hurry and get Miss Johnson changed and freshened up. We have a photo op to knock out downstairs in about fifteen minutes."

Koren groaned, as she allowed herself to be bullied back over to the make-up chair, stripped down, and dressed up again in typical Barbie Doll fashion.

*

When Koren finally got back to her hotel room late that night, she was exhausted. Her parents were staying in the adjoining room, so she cracked the door to check on them, but they were already asleep. She quietly shut the door again.

Her face was still heavily caked with make-up, and she was wearing the designer outfit that she had been dressed in for her last interview that day. Briefly, she thought of talking to Rose, but of course the Aaru access port was back in her bedroom at home, so that was impossible.

Instead, Koren walked over to the mini-fridge and pulled out an Evian. That was the only thing it contained. She popped the lid, kicked off her shoes, sat cross-legged on her king-sized bed, and rubbed her aching feet and ankles. She flipped on the TV, and as luck would have it, Koren was greeted by her own sad face. They had washed all the color out of the shot so she looked especially forlorn, but hauntingly pretty also. She was dressed in the short and low-cut, white sundress.

"Never say goodbye again," her voice came from the TV in a sultry murmur. The camera zoomed in on her perfectly painted, pouty lips. She whispered the word 'Aaru' just before it flashed across the screen along with a web address. It was only the tail end of the spot, but Koren still found it surreal.

She remembered shooting that commercial. She remembered the marathon hair and make-up session that preceded it too, but it still all felt disconnected from her somehow. It was like that girl on the screen was a totally different person.

She watched the last twenty minutes of a Jonas Perry documentary and thought about her poster at home. Koren wondered if *he* ever felt the way she did now – like they were trying to turn her into something she wasn't.

I bet he would understand, she thought with a sigh. *He's so cute and seems so sweet!*

An old sitcom came on after that. It was not one she was familiar with. It wasn't even really that funny, but she watched it anyway as she continued sipping on her bottled water in the dark by herself.

So this is what it's like to be famous, she thought ruefully.

She took another sip and sighed. Koren knew she really should go to bed. It was well after midnight, and her handlers would be back, banging on her door again in just a very few hours from now.

Maybe she just wasn't giving it a chance. She couldn't possibly stay this busy forever. Perhaps after she had some time to stop and catch her breath, after this initial media blitz was done, then she could enjoy the experience a little more. Maybe she would feel better after talking to her sister.

Koren set the half-finished bottle of water on the night stand and flipped the TV off. She laid back and closed her eyes, but could not sleep. The image of her sad, sexy self on the TV kept passing before her eyes – visions of a girl who did not really exist.

That's not me... she could not help from thinking, but if not her then who was it? Who was this girl that everyone suddenly wanted to see and talk to?

"All part of da game," Askr had reassured her.

"That's just the way it's done," her mother had insisted "That's just the way they do it in showbiz, honey," and her father had silently nodded his agreement.

Koren sighed again. Maybe they were right. This was all very new to her. Maybe she just needed time to adjust.

Her stomach grumbled plaintively, but there was nothing to be done about it. The hotel kitchen was closed at this hour, and there was nothing edible in her room but for cases and cases of Evian. The small dressing-free salad topped with a tiny spoonful a shredded salmon that she had been fed in the limo was well gone.

Koren growled grumpily. She wanted a cheeseburger.

She made a conscious effort to slow her breathing, but the unsettled feeling would not pass. Koren did not think it was just her hunger either. The sexy girl who was and was not her shot her a seductive glance in her mind's eye. Her huge eyes welled with barely suppressed tears. She blew Koren a sad, sultry kiss. Who was that person? Who were these people trying to turn her into?

About the time Koren finally managed to doze off there was a cursory knock at her door, but the three members of her fashion team followed closely by Miss Hanasaka did not wait for her to answer. They barged right in, with a loud "Good morning sleepy head!" from the Japanese woman. Then they dragged her out of bed, fed her half a plain, wholegrain bagel, and whisked her away to her next interview location where she soon found herself tossed into yet another make-up chair to be transformed into the sad, sexy girl Askr insisted the whole country was falling in love with.

Chapter 10

Flowers and Fountains

The days were hard to measure in Aaru. Rose never felt any need to sleep, and she only ate when she felt like tasting something. It threw off her whole appreciation of time's passage. Additionally, although there was a brilliant sun in the sky whenever she wanted it, the deeply orange harvest moon and all the stars of creation were hers to command as well. Day and night were only what she made of them. However much time there was though, she began spending a very great amount of it with Franco.

She helped him build his mansion, of course. It was a sprawling, walled structure with a reddish-brown, clay-tiled roof and looked like it might have been inspired by a combination of the villa of some ancient conquistador and the Spanish fortress at St. Augustine that Rose remembered visiting on a vacation to Florida once as a child. When they finished it, they stood staring up at the magnificent structure in silence. Franco's face bore a deeply affected expression.

"Feel glad it's done?" Rose ventured. "You took long enough to do it. Of all the Vedas, yours is the last one to go up…"

"I never thought I'd ever get to have anything like this," he murmured. "My family… well… there was seven of us all living in a two bed-room apartment. My mom and dad had one room. My sisters shared the other. Me and my brother slept in the living room on the couch… It still doesn't seem real…" He trailed off. "Is this thing really all mine?"

"That and anything else you want, Franco," Rose replied softly. "It's perfect here. You can do anything, be anything, *have* anything …"

Franco turned his face toward her with a curious half smile. Something in the way he looked at her made Rose catch her breath. Maybe it was the intensity that seemed to ever burn in his large, dark eyes or perhaps it was his strong angular features and high cheek bones, but when he looked at her like that, right at her, like he couldn't see anything else, it stole the thoughts from her head and words from her lips. All she could contemplate was how utterly handsome he was.

"Can I?" he asked coyly. "I'll have to think about it… What about you though, Rose? What do you want? What do you want to *be*?"

The question took her off guard. She hadn't thought about it in quite a while. There had been a time when she wanted to be a doctor or a professional soccer player – the first woman to play for Real Madrid! Maybe president. Why not?

Her illness had stolen all of those dreams away a long time ago, however. Could she have them back now, here in Aaru? Was not anything possible here?

As she thought about it some more though, they seemed less and less relevant. Why be a doctor in a world with no disease? What use was a president where everyone was a princess or king? What *would* she be?

Hana had told her that she was a Veda, but that was still just a word. It didn't really hold any meaning for her. She thought back on the previous four long years – the constant sickness, the weakness, the fear, the pain.

Rose met Franco's gaze earnestly. "I want to be happy."

Franco chuckled and turned away. He stuck his hands deeply into the pockets of his skin-tight slacks. The heavy gold chain around his neck clinked softly as he looked down. Then he turned back to at her with a smile. He took Rose's hand and squeezed it.

"Me too, Rose," he agreed. "I think that's a great thing to be."

They stood there for a long time simply looking at each other, both unwilling to bring the moment to an end, but equally unsure of how they should proceed.

"Walk with me?" Rose ventured shyly at last.

Franco nodded.

Rose turned, but did not release Franco's hand. She swept her free hand in a wide arc, and the sun slid across the sky to disappear below the horizon. It was replaced with an impossibly large full moon and a billion, billion stars, twinkling brilliantly in sable firmament.

"Wow," Franco breathed, awestruck by the sudden celestial display.

Rose gave his hand a tug, and he wordlessly followed. They wended their way down the hill upon which they had built Franco's mansion. Every so often Rose would pause and raise up a glowing flower. They were not a variety she had ever seen before except perhaps in a dream.

The vividly green leaves shone faintly in the darkness with an emerald luminescence. The tiny glowing flowers drooped like bluebells and gave off a gentle turquoise light. Rose's quotidian kimono shimmered and changed into a translucent, blue gown to match them. It twinkled all over as if covered with diamonds. She met Franco's wondering gaze with a coy grin of her own.

His expression suddenly struck Rose as hilariously funny. She threw back her head and laughed, and as she did so she spun in wide circles, dancing across the grass in unabashed joy. Everywhere her feet touched more of the shimmering flowers sprang to life. Soon the hilltop sparkled as if someone had spilled a million sapphires all over the grass.

Yes! She thought euphorically. *Happy is what I'll be! Happy forever!*

Again she laughed, and as she did, tiny spheres of light issued from between her lips to camber and warp into minikin, winged people of every color of the rainbow. The faeries born of her laughter quickly flew away to gather dew from the softly chiming glowbells - at least that was what Rose decided in that moment her flowers should be called. The tiny people soon took up a wordless, haunting tune.

She continued her rapturous dance, the outline of her slender silhouette faintly visible as the brilliant moonlight shone down through her diaphanous gown. She spun in a dizzying pirouette, and beneath her feet, a tall marble structure erupted from the loamy earth. Fourteen feet tall it rose, layered like a wedding cake, and when it was fully exposed, the beauty of everything that had been wrought of her joy struck straight to Rose's heart.

A single tear rolled down her cheek and dripped off her chin. Where it struck the top of the alabaster monument, it burgeoned and grew until cascades of cool, shimmering water flowed down the moonlit fountain in murmuring effusion. Franco said nothing, but simply stared up at her in amazement.

Rose blushed furiously pink, chagrined at how thoroughly she had allowed herself to be carried away. She nervously giggled.

"Something to remember me when I go home," she ventured sheepishly. "I hope you don't mind…"

"It's beautiful," Franco replied, eyes never straying from the vivid outline of Rose's slim silhouette, illuminated starkly through the gossamer dress by the battened moon behind her. "You're beautiful…"

Her cheeks flushed from roseate pink to beet crimson, but Rose was not at all displeased. However, her dress did darken a bit so that it was not quite so see-through. She hopped down off of the enormous fountain she had created to stand in the pooling water at the bottom. She lifted the hem of her sparkling gown, which shifted from a pale blue to milky white. She waded over to seat herself on the side, feet dangling in the cool water. Franco moved to shyly sit beside her.

He stared at his hands, folded in his lap and chuckled.

"What?" asked Rose warily, terrified that she had just made a total fool of herself and that her new friend now thought her quite insane.

He looked up at her with a wide grin. "Nothing, Rose. I just hope I can be as happy as you someday."

She blushed even more fiercely. Franco pivoted and stuck his own feet down into the water beside her. The dark alligator shoes he was wearing disappeared to expose bare, brown feet as they broke the surface. He scooted just a little closer and gazed thoughtfully up at the gorgeous night sky.

"You made all that, huh?" he asked at last, scooting another inch nearer. "It's real pretty. I wish I could do something like that…"

"Oh! But you can!" exclaimed Rose. "You just have to imagine it. You just have to get used to it, and then it's easy!" She put a small white hand on his shoulder. "I'll… I'll show you how if you want me to…"

"Oh, I don't know," Franco stood up in the fountain and stretched. His pants were suddenly rolled up baggy jeans and he was shirtless. He reached down and splashed himself with the water from Rose's fountain then ran his dripping fingers through his inky black hair. "Maybe I'll just call you up whenever I need something, and let you do it." He crossed his arms and nodded in approval. "Quality work here…"

Rose gasped and kicked her legs out, splattering Franco with a great wave of water.

"Lazy!" she cried offendedly. "I don't mind showing you how, but I'm not here to be your servant!"

"You sound like my Mom!" retorted Franco dripping.

He shook the droplets from his head and fingers. Then he gave her a wicked little grin and bent over. He stuck both arms into the water and then unleashed a splashing barrage of his own that had Rose soaked to the bone in seconds.

She squealed in surprise, but quickly responded with a counter attacking deluge. Soon they were both dripping wet and laughing quite madly. They splashed and kicked and threw water on each other until Franco grabbed Rose's wrist and pulled her so her head was squarely under where the water cascaded down from the top of the fountain. This was clearly cheating, so Rose had no compunction at all about hooking her foot behind Franco's ankle and toppling him over backwards with a great splash. Then she mercilessly baled water over his spluttering head.

"Okay! Okay!" he protested with his hands up protectively. "I give! Truce! Truce!"

Rose stopped splashing and reached down to help him up. Franco took her hand, but instead of letting her pull him to his feet, he gave her arm a tug and sent her sprawling in the fountain. Rose leapt to her feet and stood still, staring at Franco with her mouth opened. Her gossamer dress clung to her slender frame and her hair was sopping wet. Her eyes narrowed, and she pounced on the treacherous boy dunking his head under water over and over again.

"I'm sorry! I'm sorry!" Franco helplessly spluttered, laughing. "No more! No more! I mean it this time! You win!" He pushed himself backwards until his back rested against the side of the fountain. Rose quickly moved to kneel beside him in the water.

"You're a big cheater!" she exclaimed, poking an accusing finger into his broad, brown chest. "You know that, right?"

"Yeah," he chuckled. "But you won anyway. You were savage! What was up with that?"

Rose gave a pert smile and sat beside him.

"I don't like to lose." She said simply.

Franco chuckled again. He stretched his arms out along the sides of the fountain. His left arm came to rest around Rose's narrow shoulders. They looked up at the stars together, half submerged in the sparkling water.

"Is all of this really ours?" asked Franco at last. "What's the catch?"

"It looks like it is," replied Rose, timidly leaning her head against Franco's chest. He smiled and squeezed her more tightly.

"I'm glad you're happy, Rose," Franco murmured. "It's just..." he trailed off.

"Just what?" she asked.

Franco sighed. "It's just that nobody ain't never given me *nothin'* before... Why all this? Why me? Why now?"

Rose wrapped her arms around his torso. She liked the feel of his warm skin against her cheek and bare arms. She squeezed him and sighed contentedly.

"Maybe we're just lucky," Rose ventured. "Maybe it's just our turn. I don't know about you, but this is the first time anything has gone right for me in *years*. I feel like maybe karma has caught up with me finally. Maybe God just decided I deserved a break; that it's just time for something good to happen."

"Maybe..." replied Franco dubiously.

Rose pressed her index finger against his lips.

"Hush," she breathed. "Don't think so much. Tonight is a good night. We're here together, and that's all I want to think about... You do like it here with me, don't you?"

"That's not what I meant!" exclaimed Franco. "I mean... of course I like being with you... it's just that... well... I look back at my life Before, and as soon as something good happened, it was taken away, or just something really bad came after... Every time! Ya know, the day before I got hurt, my Ma found out that we'd won the lottery!"

"So you were rich?" asked Rose puzzled.

Franco laughed. "No, no, not *that* lottery – the lottery to get into the Pamona Cambridge Prep Academy. It's like this new super-school or somethin' that opened up a few years ago. My Ma was all into it. There's so many people who want to get in that you gotta enter a lottery for it. If they don't pick your name then you just gotta go to like, the regular dummy school I guess, but my Ma was like at the church every day with her rosary just prayin' and prayin' that we'd get in. She said it was our ticket out of the poor house and to go to college and stuff. Then both me *and* my brother got in! Ma was all cryin' and happy, and we went out for this big dinner at a restaurant and everything!" He got more and more animated as he talked. Then his face darkened. "The next day I went out with my homies, ya know? Riding bikes just like we were little kids and stuff, yeah? Everybody was super happy and laughin', then *BAM!* Lights out. It's all over…"

He fell silent and Rose snuggled closer against his chest. She looked up into his face sympathetically even as Franco continued to stare straight ahead.

"I… I don't know, Rose," he murmured. "It's just… Whenever somethin' good happens to me, I can't help thinking it's not gonna last. I just keep waitin' for someone to come along and jerk it away…"

Rose kissed his cheek, and Franco started. She gave him a sympathetic smile.

"I know how you feel, Franco," she murmured. "I really do… But no one's gonna jerk anything away tonight, are they? Tonight it's just us, here together with the stars. For tonight anyway, isn't that enough? Do you think you could be happy just for tonight at least?"

He looked down at her a moment. Then he chuckled and squeezed her.

"Yeah," he replied huskily. "Yeah, I guess so."

They stayed together that way, holding each other and staring up at the countless stars. Hours, days, years, eons – it could have been any of those. They didn't know how long they stayed there, and it didn't matter either. They just knew they were together, and here in this place, right now, they were really and truly happy. For tonight at least, it was more than enough.

*

The two spent a lot of time together after that. Rose did her best to teach Franco what she had learned about manipulating Aaru to her will, but Franco was resistant. For whatever reason, it seemed like Rose was much more natural at it, and it irritated his last nerve a girl could be so much better at something than him.

Despite his occasionally overblown machismo however, that did not appear to weaken his desire to be near her. For her own part, Rose wanted to be near him too. Often it was all together with Runa, Kurt, Auset, and Derain, but more and more often it was just the two of them alone.

There was a strength about Franco as well as a vulnerability that Rose found charming. Oh, he tried his best to hide it of course, but she could always tell when he was feeling his most insecure about the strange, new world in which they found themselves. That was almost always when he put on his most elaborate displays of bravado and went to the greatest lengths to impress her. These usually did a great deal more to amuse rather than entice however.

Whether it was rolling up to her mansion one day in the most preposterous purple vehicle she had ever seen - (It had been something akin to a low-riding, purple monster truck on hydraulics - exposed engine so massive that it surely must have been impossible to see out of the windshield. It belched fire from a dozen exhaust pipes, and was plated all over in gold rather than chrome) - or appearing shirtless at her door in a musclebound body so huge that he could barely move, it pleased Rose that he tried so hard. Though his most ardent attempts were just plain silly, Rose still appreciated the effort.

In the beginning, they felt compelled to converse, whether they really had anything to say or not. Mostly the talk was inconsequential - telling each other innocuous anecdotes about their families or mundane events they recalled of their time Before. They had both made great efforts to awkwardly fill the silence.

As the time passed however, they were more and more often quiet – content simply to be in each other's company. Whether walking hand in hand through one of the many fragrant gardens Rose created, or laying side-by-side on the grassy plain together looking up at the flawless, cerulean sky, being together started to feel easy. It was these moments of tranquil serenity that Rose liked best – the times when Franco let his guard down and allowed her to get a glimpse of what was inside. She was beginning to very easily see herself content to go on this way forever – an eternity of long strolls, restful afternoons, tender touches, and sweet stolen kisses.

Chapter 11

A Million Dollar Video Game

Koren was sitting in her hotel room after another whirlwind of interviews and public appearances. The TV was on, and a new Elysian Industries ad had just played, but that was not what held her attention now. She had become somewhat accustomed to seeing her own, heavily made-up face all over TV, the internet, and billboards.

Rather, the ad had played on "The Dave O'Brian Show" as an introduction to the show's next guest. Koren did not recognize him, but was intrigued none-the-less. She assumed it must be another spokesperson or board member, but was a little surprised because she thought she knew everyone of significance from Elysian Industries, and this man was no one she had ever met.

"I'd like to introduce our next guest, Alabama Senator James Rook!" Dave called out.

The band played a spirited fanfare and a dapper, middle-aged man strode out across the stage with a well-practiced grin and a wave to the audience. He was a handsome man, Koren thought. His mostly brown hair (there was just a spattering of grey around his sideburns) was carefully coifed, and his stylish, charcoal suit freshly pressed and conservatively correct. He shook Dave's hand across the desk before seating himself in the very same chair that Koren had occupied just a few short weeks ago.

Dave made a wide cutting gesture with both hands and the band stopped. The audience clapped politely. Dave sat back in a casual manner and fixed the Senator with a good natured smile.

"So," began Dave. "I take it you recognize that commercial we just showed. Aaru from Elysian Industries seems to be all anyone is talking about these days. They claim to have finally beaten death! You can have your brain saved onto a hard drive and live forever. We had the young lady from the commercial, Koren Johnson, on just a couple of weeks ago in fact... But I understand that you are not a big fan."

"I'm afraid not, Dave," Senator Rook shook his head with a grimace. His southern drawl was pronounced, but carefully precise, in a register that was deep and velvety. Completely independent of anything he had to say, Koren found it pleasant to listen to. "I must admit that I am far from as enamored as everyone else seems to be..."

"Well," Dave laughed in an ironic sort of way. "You certainly made *that* clear last week on the floor of the Senate. Roll that tape!"

The camera cut away from Dave and Senator Rook to a shot of only the senator standing behind a podium.

"It is absolutely unconscionable that this body allow the wholesale fleecing of the American People!" He proclaimed in a loud clear voice, his thick eyebrows knitted together in clearly affronted outrage as he pounded his palm with his other hand. "I'm from the South, and let me tell you friends, down there we know snake oil salesmen when we see them, but this so called Elysian Industries takes the cake!

"They abuse families when they are emotionally vulnerable. They sell lies and deception to the gullible and the hopeless. Then they promote it all with a massive corporate marketing campaign that includes testimonials, merchandising, and even a reality show yet to come! Much more than phony weight loss pills, hair regrowing ointments, or masculine enhancement scams, these people prey on the insecurities and fears of others. They essentially trick them into buying a million dollar video game!

"In the past, this body has moved to regulate professional football and baseball. It has even stepped into the fray when television game shows were accused of cheating. How much more are we obligated to prevent unscrupulous persons from taking advantage of the grieving with slick marketing, a pretty actress, and an impossible promise?"

Koren gasped. Was that man suggesting she was faking?

The clip ended, and the camera turned back to Senator Rook and Dave O'Brian. Both men bore expressions that were exceedingly grave.

"Wow," commented Dave seriously. "A million dollar video game... That's a pretty strong statement, and it's certainly the one the various media outlets have grabbed a hold of. So you don't buy into this idea of scanning someone's brain and saving it to a computer at all then? You're not convinced by Koren Johnson's story?"

"Not in the least," Senator Rook stated decisively. "I think Elysian Industries has hired a very pretty, very talented young actress who is making a whole lot of money off of other people's grief."

"So you're saying she's lying," Dave pressed.

The senator shook his head and exhaled heavily, "I'm saying that what she's telling everyone can't possibly be true. I have no idea how much of the inner-workings of the company she's involved with. What I think a lot of people forget is that as beautiful as she is, and as much as they dress her up like a high priced prostitute, she's still a very young girl…"

"Yes, she's twelve I think…" added Dave.

"Try thirteen and a half…" Koren muttered at the screen.

"See?" agreed the senator. "There you go. That's a completely separate issue right there… I think it's totally disgusting the way they have 'sexed up' this little girl to sell their nonsense. The commercials, the reality show… You know, I even saw a Koren Johnson doll the other day, complete with stiletto heels and a skirt that any normal person would wear as a shirt! I can't understand any parent putting up with it no matter how much they're being paid. God only knows what this kid is exposed to being pressed into an adult celebrity lifestyle so young… but in any case, I think it likely that she's a victim of all this too – taken advantage of by greedy businessmen and her own parents even! But here's the thing, Dave…" He leaned in closer, extending both of his palms toward the talk show host with his elbows at his side.

"The worst part of this… The part that scares to bejesus out of me frankly is in the possibility, however remote I think it probably is, that they're *not* lying. It's infinitely more problematic if they *are* telling the truth."

"So then you're not *completely* discounting the possibility that Aaru is in fact *not* a 'million dollar video game' like you stated on the senate floor…" Dave O'Brian cut in.

James Rook chuckled and raised his hands in a prohibitive gesture.

"Let me be clear. I'm *almost* completely discounting it, but let's let our imaginations run wild for a moment. What if Elysian Industries *could* save a person's brain after their death? What if they could in fact make the people *they* choose live forever? Would you be comfortable allowing some corporate executive in Manhattan or Los Angeles usurp the judgment of Almighty God and determine who does and does not get saved? What would *you* give to live forever? More importantly; what would you be willing to *do* for them? If that's not playing God, then I don't know what is…"

"Wow," commented Dave gravely. The audience murmured in uneasy disquiet. "That's an interesting point."

"And how about this?" continued the senator, grey eyes intense as they gazed into the camera, which zoomed in closer. "I like Miss Johnson's story about saving her poor dying sister too. It's a real tear jerker to watch a little girl, however tarted up, boohoo about her dead sissy. I think it resonates with a lot of people. I mean, and I think this is true of almost everyone, who *doesn't* want to save poor, suffering little girls with cancer?"

Dave nodded conceding the point as Senator Rook continued.

Koren was mortified. She did not care for his tone at all. She thought it totally disrespectful of Rose. That was even worse than the horrible things this man was saying to the whole world about her and her parents. …And "*tarted up*"?! She felt her face grow hot.

"What is our guarantee that these people, who clearly have no morals or values apart from making money, what is to guarantee that they continue to just save poor little girls with cancer?

"If I was a neo-Nazi," Senator Rook went on. "Who would I want saved on my computer, hmm? What if I was a card carrying member of Al Qaeda or ISIS? Don't you think the North Korean government would like to have Kim Il Sung back?" He grew intense as he spoke. He lifted his hand and began to raise one finger at a time.

"Adolf Hitler, Al Capone, Osama Bin Ladin, Joseph Stalin, Pol Pot, Mao Zedong, Caligula… Are these people who you'd like to see live forever? The blight of humanity? Continuing to run their oppressive, violent, and criminal endeavors from beyond the grave? Elysian Industries might *claim* that they would never allow people like this into their system, but once the genie's out of the bottle, he's out! If by some miracle, this technology is real, it's just a matter of time before someone with less than pure intentions can make use of it."

The grumbling of the audience grew louder. Here and there a few people called out words of agreement.

"I can't think of anything that could possibly be more dangerous for the whole world," he finished in a low, grave voice.

"The way I see it Dave, there are two possibilities," Senator Rook continued after a long dramatic pause. "The first is that these people are playing God by usurping *His* Holy judgment and putting the whole world in terrible danger. If this technology can be used by good people for what they think are good reasons, then it can certainly also be used by the most evil people on the planet to extend their wickedness forever..." He paused again.

"The other..." he began then made an obvious show of brightening. "The other is that the whole thing is total bunk and these people are just using and abusing a cute little girl to rip people off!"

The audience roared with laughter, clearly pleased by the suddenly lightened mood. Senator Rook sat back in his chair, folded his hands in his lap, and fixed Dave with a self-satisfied gaze.

"Either way," he concluded, spreading his hands. "These people need to be shut down, jailed, and if it is even *hinted* that anything they've developed comes anywhere close to doing what they say it can do, then it needs to be confiscated by the US government in the interest of national security. It's dangerous. It's blasphemy. It's just flat out wrong!"

"Wow," Dave commented seriously again. "That's certainly an interesting perspective. You've given us a lot to think about... Senator James Rook everybody!" He thrust his hand in the direction of the senator who smiled and waved appreciatively. The band played and The David O'Brian Show cut to commercial.

Koren glared at the screen fuming. She was explosively furious. What right did this guy have to come on TV and talk about her that way? 'Sexed up?!' A *'tart'*?! *A high-priced prostitute?!* Who the *Hell* did he think he was?!

Her stomach lurched suddenly and her eyes widened. Could he really do what he said? Could the government really come in and turn Aaru *off*? What would happen to Rose? Koren put both hands over her mouth. She ran to the hotel bathroom and threw up in the toilet.

When she was finished, she wiped her mouth with a towel and drank some water directly from the faucet. Then she hugged herself and bit her lower lip.

What am I going to do?

The TV continued to blare – some insipid commercial for shampoo or something, but she did not really hear it. If they turned the machines off wouldn't that mean that Rose would...? She began to feel sick again.

127

The phone rang.

It startled her, but she did not react. She just stood in the bathroom staring, but the bedside phone did not stop ringing. Slowly she made her way across the hotel room.

Who could that possibly be? Was it maybe Mr. Ashe?

She quickened her pace, suddenly wanting very much to speak with the Elysian Industries CEO. She lifted the receiver.

"Hello?" she answered nervously.

"Miss Johnson," blared the voice on the other end. "This is Steve Parsons from News Corp. I was just wondering if I could get your reaction to the accusations made against Elysian Industries today by Senator Rook? Do you personally have any knowledge of wrongdoing?"

"I..." Koren began.

The door to her room flew open with no knock or announcement. Askr Ashe stood in the doorway disheveled and wild-eyed. His shirt was untucked, he wore no tie, and he appeared to be wearing two different shoes and no socks. He bounded across the room and ripped the phone from Koren's flabbergasted fist.

"Miss Johnson has no comment at dis time!" he shouted into the phone before slamming it down on the table. He rounded on her.

"Did you say *anything*?!" He demanded. "I must know what you said and who you've said it to!"

Koren was taken aback. All she could do was blink stupidly with her mouth open. Askr laid his hands on her bare shoulders.

"What did you say?!"

"N... nothing..." She stuttered. "All I did was say 'hello'!"

Askr Ashe took a deep breath and collapsed onto her bed. He was immediately calmer.

"Good... dat's good..." he murmured. Then he took another deep breath before looking up into Koren's stricken face. "Dey told me da show wouldn't air until tomorrow night. I was going to talk to you about it in da morning... I must tell you dis was not completely unexpected, but I hoped..." He shook his head. "No, I should have known. I should have prepared you for it sooner... We need to get you back to headquarters. We have to decide on a response."

"Now?" Koren gasped. Then she looked down at herself. She was wearing nothing but a thin, translucent slip and her underwear. She felt suddenly very exposed and crossed her arms over her chest self-consciously. "It's nearly midnight, Askr! I'm not even dressed!"

"I'm sorry, Koren," apologized Mr. Ashe, failing to notice her distress in his own agitation. We have to go *now*. In a few minutes dis place will be swarming with reporters and paparazzi. Leave your stuff. I'll have someone send it on later."

He rushed over to the closet threw open the doors and began riffling about within. After just a few seconds of searching, he grasped a dark colored garment and threw it at Koren's head. It was a brown, knee-length leather coat belted at the waist.

"Put dat on!" He directed sternly.

Koren was still in shock, but she nodded numbly and complied. She soon found herself surrounded by a half dozen burly men in sunglasses being whisked away through the lobby and out to a waiting limo. Outside the hotel there were already a good dozen or so people gathered. Two held TV cameras. The numerous flashes nearly blinded her as she rushed by, and people shouted questions.

"Miss Johnson, what do you think about James Rook?"

"Have you been lying to everyone the whole time!"

"He claims that you could be putting the whole country in danger. What do you say to that?!"

Koren just shook her head with her eyes clenched tightly shut. She was bundled into the limousine where her parents were already waiting, looking just as out of sorts and unkempt as she did. The vehicle screeched away from the curb before the door was even completely closed. She put her face in her hands wearily.

It was then that she noticed her feet. She hadn't put any shoes on. It didn't really make sense she knew, but for some reason that seemed like the most upsetting thing of all.

She wept all the way to the airport.

*

Of course, her barefoot retreat was the only thing people were talking about on TV and *every* social media site the next day. Koren felt completely humiliated and didn't even really understand why. Was there any truth to what the senator said? Was she involved in something dangerous? Clearly he was wrong about Rose. That was true, she was sure. Nobody was tricking her! ... Were they?

High-Priced Prostitute...

"Koren?" said Miss. Hanasaka quietly. She laid a warm hand on Koren's shoulder.

Koren started and looked up. Miss Hanasaka smiled gently. Sympathy shone in her eyes.

"Mr. Ashe will see you now," she told Koren softly.

Koren was sitting in a plush chair outside the conference room where she had first met with the Elysian Industries Board. She had brought Pandadora with her for silent support and squeezed her to her chest. Maybe it was a little childish to bring a doll, she thought, but the smiling panda princess made her feel better. It made Rose feel closer, and *boy* would she like to talk to her now!

She had been waiting here all morning after flying all night on the company's private plane. Another limo had picked her up on the tarmac and deposited her directly at the huge warehouse that contained the Aaru super-server. She had arrived well before dawn, and since then had sat in exactly this same spot while some sort of meeting was going on within. It was nearly noon now. She felt like she was in trouble – like waiting at the door of the principal's office at school - but could not conceive of anything she might have done wrong.

As she rose, Miss. Hanasaka leaned over and whispered in her ear. "Don't worry, Koren. Mr. Ashe will fix all of this. You don't need to be concerned."

Koren ghosted a tiny smile, but truth be told did not feel a great deal better.

She gave Pandadora another squeeze as Miss Hanasaka pulled the door open for her. The Japanese woman put a supportive hand on her shoulder, and they entered together. Inside the room, she could clearly hear her father's loud, angry voice.

"...I mean goin' on TV and callin' a *thirteen* year-old little girl a *whore*?! Doesn't the man have any decency at all?! What're you gonna do about this, Mr. Ashe? I won't stand for it! This was never part of the deal! I thought she was just supposed to be in some commercials and take some pictures and stuff. If Koren is gonna be slimed on every TV show in the country then you can just..."

"Mr. Johnson," interrupted Mr. Adams in his customarily neutral way. He stood ramrod straight behind Askr Ashe's chair, as always dressed in his spotless lab coat. "Trust me when I say that we are every bit as outraged as you are. There was no shortage of things wrong with what Senator Rook said last night, and be assured that we shall certainly respond in an appropriate fashion."

"I totally understand why you're upset, Bill," added Askr companionably.

His demeanor was the polar opposite of the way he had reacted last night. His voice and posture seemed once again relaxed and unconcerned.

"I'm upset too. It's absolutely ridiculous da things dat man said about Koren yesterday, and please believe dat we are going to continue to do everything we can to protect her. Dat's absolutely why we cut da trip short and got her back here before she could be ambushed by da paparazzi. We're on your side, Bill, and we've spent da morning deciding how to respond..."

"Zat doesn't even begin to touch on how much he lied about za technology," muttered the fat German scientist. "He can't possibly be zat ignorant! Calling Aaru 'dangerous' ... Self-aggrandizing..."

"That is of lesser importance right now, Dr. Heidler," interrupted Miss. Hanasaka smoothly. She regarded Koren's father contritely. "We are of course here to talk about protecting Koren. That is our greatest concern. That is why we've called her and Mr. Johnson here this morning..."

"Of course, Miss Hanasaka..." he replied apologetically.

Mr. Ashe appeared to notice for the first time that Koren had entered the room.

"Ah, Koren!" he exclaimed with a wide smile. "I didn't see you there. Come in! Please have a seat here in front of me."

Koren moved toward the chair on the other side of the room, but her father intercepted her. He crushed her against his chest in a fierce embrace.

"Don't worry, sweetie," he whispered into her ear. "I'm gonna take care of all this. Don't you worry about nothin'..."

Koren appreciated his outrage certainly, so she let him hug her for a few additional seconds before pushing away. She might have reacted more strongly under normal circumstances. She was absolutely upset by the unexpected ordeal, but right now her overriding feeling was one of exhaustion. She had already endured a whole, long plane ride of her father's outrage and it was starting to grate.

"I'll be fine, Dad," she sighed.

Askr stood up and reached across the table to take both of her hands in his own. She had to tuck Pandadora up under her arm. Askr's expression was profoundly apologetic.

"I just want to reiterate how extremely sorry I am about everything dat has happened. Dis really has been unpleasant for you, and we should have been better prepared. I…"

"Yeah!" interrupted Koren's father angrily. "Why *weren't* you better prepared?!"

"Dad…" Koren's protesting tone begged her father to calm down.

Askr Ashe sighed and released her hands.

"Please have a seat," he repeated before sitting himself.

Koren complied.

"Your father is quite right to be upset, Koren," admitted Askr. "We were careless. Senator Rook made his senate speech three days ago, and we knew about it, but we weren't particularly concerned. He's a freshman senator, and he gave the speech at five in the morning to a completely empty chamber. It was only carried by CSPAN2 so da audience was minuscule."

"Well that's fine!" shouted Bill Johnson. "But what about David O'Brian!? That was the big problem!"

"I was just getting to dat…" replied Askr, a hint of irritation showing through.

"Come on, Dad," Koren wearily entreated. "Let the man talk."

Her father quieted, but looked no less outraged. Mr. Ashe took a deep breath.

"What we didn't know was after his speech he was scheduled as a last minute replacement guest on da Sean Savage Show. It's a political talk show and has a very conservative viewership. Once he went on da story exploded on right-wing social media. Da speech got over three million views on YouTube in mere hours. Suddenly, it was a big story. Dave O'Brian's people called me and told me dey were going to have Mr. Rook on today, but den something happened – a cancellation or something – and dey moved him up to last night. We were completely caught by surprise, and we shouldn't have been. I'm sorry."

"It's okay," Koren said.

"Well, dat's very kind of you, Koren," replied Askr Ashe gratefully.

"Koren," Miss Hanasaka gently added. There was real concern in her voice. "I'm sure yesterday must have been very confusing for you. I would really like you to tell us how you are feeling. Are you alright? Truly?

Koren wiped a stray strand of hair out of her face with the back of her hand and shrugged.

"I am sure you will have some questions for us," the pretty Japanese woman pressed then waited for Koren to reply, but Koren did not respond.

She was feeling uncertain about this whole Aaru thing again but didn't feel comfortable talking about it in front of all these people. Maybe if it was only Miss Hanasaka... Koren thought she was nice, so...

"Surely, Koren," said Miss Hanasaka insistently. She seemed to sense the doubt in Koren's downcast eyes. "Surely you must have at least one question. Please try to ask at least one..."

"If she doesn't have any questions, then she doesn't have any questions!" cut in the young Indian scientist seated to her left. "Don't badger her, Kiku!"

Miss Hanasaka ignored Dr. Kapoor. She just kept looking at Koren expectantly.

"Could..." Koren shyly spoke up at last. "Could..." she hesitated.

"What, Koren?" prompted Miss Hanasaka flashing the scientist a quick triumphant glance. "Please don't be nervous. Ask us anything at all. We want to reassure you."

"What will happen to Rose if Senator Rook shuts down Aaru?" Koren blurted. "Will she die?"

"No, Koren" Askr spoke up quickly. He sounded uncharacteristically sincere. "Dat will *never* happen. Dis Senator Rook person has no authority to do anything like dat, and we are doing absolutely *nothing* illegal. Our lawyers are already prepared, if he decides to pull any shenanigans. He's a little man with a big mouth looking to gain notoriety by attacking something popular."

"Even if he *could* turn za system off," the German scientist added. "Sink of Aaru like a much, much bigger version of your computer at home. Za data is saved on hard disks, and we update zose every four hours. Even if za system was shut down, zat would not affect za data. Perhaps it would be like everyone go to sleep, you know? Until za power turns back on. Zen it's all fine again."

"We promised you that we would save Rose, Koren," added Mr. Adams. "We did that, and we will continue to. You need *never* worry about Rose dying again. No one will. That's why we built all of this."

"The only way that could happen," said Dr. Kapoor, "would be if the hard drives were erased, and that could never occur. We have too many fail safes – We have multiple proxies in a number of other nations. We employ regular back-ups, RAID 10 storage virtualization for redundancy, emergency power…"

"You do not need to worry for your sister, Koren," soothed Miss Hanasaka. "Be at ease regarding that, but tell me about you. You are the one I am most concerned for."

"Well… Also, I was worried…" Koren trailed off.

"What about, Koren?" prompted Mr. Ashe.

"Could a bad person get into Aaru? Like… like Hitler or… or those other guys Senator Rook talked about?"

"We are *very* careful about who we let into Aaru," Askr Ashe said rigidly. Despite what Jim Rook might think or says he thinks, we are not in dis for da money. We are in dis to change da world! No amount of money could get someone in who we deemed unsuitable and if someone is a perfect fit dey would be in regardless of deir ability to pay."

"Like Rose," said Mr. Adams evenly.

"Right," agreed Askr. "Just like Rose. It won't happen"

"And even if it did," spoke up Dr. Kapoor, "they couldn't do anything because of the Harm Failsafe."

"Yes," said Miss Hanasaka. "No Resident of Aaru can hurt any other Resident. The coding won't allow it."

"And even if zat *wasn't* so," said the big German. "Because each individual's data is allocated to a unique storage unit, if by chance someone *did* get in who wasn't supposed to, it would be fairly easy to remedy. We would just have to locate zem on za system and delete or quarantine za file."

"So no," stated Askr Ashe forcefully. "In answer to your question, what Mr. Rook suggests just simply is not possible."

"Is there anything else, Koren?" Miss Hanasaka asked solicitously. "Any other questions at all? Do you feel better?"

Koren was silent for a long moment. She did have one more question. It was actually the thing that was bothering her the most, but she was reluctant to ask it.

"Koren?" the slim Asian woman prompted. "What is it? What else is bothering you?"

Koren swallowed. "Does everyone…" her face blushed brilliantly pink and she stumbled to a halt.

"What, Koren?" Askr asked kindly.

She squeezed Pandadora tightly for strength.

"Does everyone really think I… I'm a '*tarted-up, high priced prostitute*'?" She forced the words out and was immediately embarrassed by them.

The room fell silent. Mr. Ashe clearly looked aghast by the question, but he took a deep breath, looked down, and then met her clear, blue eyes steadfastly.

"No one in dis room thinks anything at all like dat," he stated gravely. "*No one.* Also, dere are a lot of people who were *thoroughly* offended by what Senator Rook said about you. It was mean spirited and untrue. It clearly crossed a line, and I really hope you will not take it to heart. When you are in da public eye, dere will be many who are jealous of what you have or want to use you to somehow further whatever deir own personal goals and agendas are. You mustn't let dem define who you are, Koren."

"You are a beautiful and sweet young girl," Miss Hanasaka added, "and I like you very much… We all do."

"Indeed we do," said Mr. Adams. "That is why we chose you, but I know what the Senator said was hurtful. It would have upset anyone, and you certainly have a right say so. We have been discussing an appropriate response all morning."

"Response?' asked Koren unenthusiastically.

"Yes," answered Kiku. "We definitely must respond and soon. The longer we are silent, the more time and space Senator Rook has to spread his nonsense and lies. If he's the only one talking, he'll also be the only one people listen to as well. If we don't counter what he says, people might start to believe that we *did* do something wrong."

"Do *I* have to do it?" Koren asked with a decided sinking feeling in the pit of her stomach.

"You absolutely do not!" shouted her father, unable to contain himself any longer. "You folks've got no business putting a little kid out in front of a bunch of cameras and reporters to take on some slick, rich politician!"

Askr sighed wearily. "You do not *have* to, Koren."

She relaxed slightly.

"But," Mr. Adams added. "It would be better coming from you."

"What I propose," said Askr wearily, but still too quickly for Mr. Johnson to interject, "is we make a joint public statement together. We can prerecord it so you don't have to deal with da media, but *you* really should speak out."

"You are a celebrity, Koren," stated Miss Hanasaka. "It is you who Senator Rook most wronged, but you are also the one people *love*. You might not fully realize it yet, but you have *millions* of fans who will support you. If you come out and say the system is safe, they will believe you. If you tell them how much this man hurt you, they will have sympathy for you and defend you in social media."

"We will help you to prepare a statement," added Mr. Adams. "We can record it this afternoon. Then we will release it to the major news outlets and on the Elysian Industries' web site this evening."

"Also," added Askr sympathetically. "I understand you have been struggling a little with da tight schedule lately. It was inevitable as part of our initial media blitz, but I think I can cut down on da public appearances a little bit, at least until da reality show comes out."

"Thanks," Koren murmured gratefully.

"After we finish recording," he continued folding his hands together. "Dere are some people I'd like you to meet. I think dey are people you will have a lot in common with… who are in da same situation as you."

Koren looked up, her brow creased quizzically. "What do you mean?" She asked.

"Koren," answered Mr. Adams. "You are our spokesperson for all of North America's English speaking outlets."

"But," added Dr. Kapoor, "you are not the only spokesperson."

"The US is our biggest market," said Miss Hanasaka, "but we executed a *worldwide* release."

"Right," added Askr. "We also have spokespeople for eastern and western Europe, Australia, Russia, Latin America, and Spain, southeast Asia, another for the US Spanish outlets… They are promoting Aaru through Univision and Telemundo in addition to Latin radio and Spanish online venues…"

"Among many others," interrupted Miss Hanasaka, apparently sensing that the men were starting to ramble. "The point is, Koren, you are not going through this alone. I think it really might help you to meet some people dealing with very much the same thing."

"Yes," said Askr. "The families we selected were picked using similar criteria for each region, so I think you'll have a lot in common. There are nineteen Beta families spread over many nations, all chosen very carefully. You and Rose were our choice here. We have found dat people react better to people more like demselves – same racial background, same language, same religion, etc. We have further found dat children are regarded more sympathetically."

"Zey have za most to gain when zey are added to za Aaru mainframe," added Heidler. "Zere is nothing sadder zan a young life cut short."

"Wait… When you say you *'chose'* me for this *'market'*… You mean this… this is all just *marketing?*" Koren asked sharply. The idea offended her. "You picked me and Rose just so you can make more *money?!*"

"Now, now, now," protested Askr, making a calming gesture. "It really isn't like dat! Rose was chosen because, first and foremost, without our intervention, we would have lost her."

"However," added Miss Hanasaka. "She was also chosen because we knew people could relate to her… and to you. *You* were also a big reason we chose Rose."

Koren bit her lower lip in distress.

"That doesn't seem… I don't know… fair, I guess." She looked away and hugged Pandadora.

Was the senator right? Was she being used?

"So," she went on, "were there other sick girls you passed over because you liked *me?* Is there someone out there who *died,* because you thought I could sell Aaru better for you?"

"Everyone we scanned either has been or will be added to the system," stated Mr. Adams firmly. "*Not* everyone was included in the Beta Test. No one died because we chose you, but think of it this way, Koren. You understand how people are reacting to the things Senator Rook said, don't you? Like Kiku said, you have millions of fans, and they are furious with the senator *for* you. They have come to *love* you, just as we knew they would."

"We would have been very naïve indeed to assume every human being on the planet would welcome a system like Aaru with open arms," he continued. "There are lots of people who will be opposed to it for many, many different reasons. Some will find it flies in the face of their ideas about religion. Some will oppose it on economic grounds because it is very expensive, just as any new technology is in the beginning. Others will simply fear it, because it's too new and different for them to fully comprehend, and people often fear that which they do not understand..."

"Da point, Koren," interrupted Askr. "Is we knew a certain level of protest from people like Mr. Rook was inevitable. We knew we would need someone to defend Aaru once it was revealed. We needed someone who da public would like and trust... Someone dey would feel real sympathy for..."

"And someone who we knew was strong enough to stand up to the criticism," finished Miss Hanasaka gravely. "That someone was you, Koren, but I know it is not easy. There is no need for you to do this alone. We are here for you, and the other spokespeople have expressed similar concerns as you. I think meeting the other families will help you... Give you someone to talk to who really understands what you are going through, but please don't let hurtful words sour your experience with Aaru. This has *never* been about money for us."

Koren swallowed. She did not feel very strong at the moment. She felt overwhelmed. What the Elysian Industries Board was saying made sense she supposed, and she had to admit being more than a little flattered, but something was still not hitting her quite right. She held Pandadora a little closer.

"Do you doubt da impact of dis technology," Askr asked quietly, detecting her reticence. "Do you doubt da good it can do... dat it has done already?"

Koren had sudden flashes of memory at his words. She saw Rose happy, healthy, and smiling in Aaru. She saw her lying dead and still in a narrow, pillowed box. She saw her flying joyously across an azure sky. She saw her sick, hairless, and pale in a hospital bed.

"No, Askr," she shook her head firmly. "No, I don't."

Whatever her misgivings at everything that had happened over the past twenty four hours, she would not have traded Rose's return for anything. This senator was either being dishonest like Askr and the other board members said or simply foolish. He flat out didn't understand what he was talking about.

Askr nodded slowly.

"Dat's good Koren. I'm glad to hear it. We're da good guys here. We're da ones out to save da world, you know? I really believe dat. So…"

He stood and his tone became more business-like.

"I have taken da liberty of ordering some lunch. While we eat we shall work up a draft of our response. After dat, Koren, I think it would be nice for you to make some new friends. Dey are truly good people, and I believe knowing dem will do you a lot of good as well."

"Why don't you sit with me?" Invited Miss Hanasaka with a friendly smile. She patted an empty chair beside her. "We can talk about more pleasant things while we eat… Did you happen to see the Jonas Perry documentary last night by any chance? I know you're a big fan…"

Koren nodded. "I guess it was a rerun. I saw it a week or two ago…"

"Well then," the pretty Japanese woman continued airily. "Let us talk about it. After you have eaten and feel a little more settled, we can think about what to do in addressing all of this unpleasantness. Then let us help you make some new friends."

Koren took a deep swallow and set her face determinedly. She nodded.

She did not mind making new friends. Miss Hanasaka was right. It *would* help to have someone to talk to besides her parents. After all, it made her feel better just to know she was not in this fight alone, and she could not deny it; whatever her lingering doubts, Koren truly believed in Aaru. It was something worth fighting for.

What the senator said about her upset Koren certainly, but the fact that he was threatening Rose? That was unforgivable. She *was* ready to fight back, she realized. She couldn't let this hateful person get to her. She would fight for Rose. Koren was ready, like Mr. Ashe had said, to start saving the world whether Senator James Rook liked it or not.

Chapter 12

The Mega Bite

The scruffy, unkempt man who entered the café wore large, dark sunglasses, a camouflage ball cap pulled low, and a long leather trench coat with broad collar pulled high. His face was covered with a few days growth of salt and pepper whiskers. He stood in the entranceway and urgently surveyed the dingy, outmoded restaurant.

The decor had a very late-nineties, early two thousands vibe, and the furniture showed a lot of obvious wear. There were only one or two other patrons at this late hour, but he still moved to seat himself in the rear-most cubicle of the twenty four hour Mega Bite Internet Café. He did not like doing this someplace so public, but he was in a hurry.

The lone waitress came over and took his order, which he gave shortly.

"Large black coffee," he growled, but wasted no time with other niceties.

The girl wasn't bad to look at really. She was thin, and her curly brown hair was tied back in a neat pony tail. Her face was pretty enough if a bit sleepy looking, but he was not interested in her. He was only interested in the alert that had just buzzed into his phone. Now the infuriating device was flashing its battery warning, and he was positively desperate to get somewhere with Wi-Fi.

The waitress scowled at his abrasiveness, but went behind the counter to pour his coffee. He couldn't seem to get his pre-paid debit card out fast enough to log into the obsolete desktop computer terminal. It was honestly rather appalling that any of these sorts of places still existed, he thought.

The connection is bound to be slow, he lamented to himself with a grimace.

Still, it was better than nothing, and he did not think he could contain himself long enough to get to his own, far superior equipment. The waitress came back with his coffee in a paper to-go cup.

Freaking dive, he thought to himself in disgust. *Can't I even get a real mug?*

She stood there another minute, but when he said nothing she cleared her throat and asked in an annoyed voice, "Can I get you something to eat?"

"No," he answered without looking up.

"Do you need anything e…"

"*No!*" he stated more forcefully and sipped slowly from the paper cup. He made a face. The coffee was lukewarm.

The glow of the monitor reflected off his sun glasses to unsettling effect as he stared intently at the screen. The waitress gave him a funny look, shrugged, then stormed off in a huff. She quickly retreated to the kitchen grumbling under her breath.

Fuck her, he thought uncharitably.

She was bothering him – wasting his valuable time. She wasn't *why* he was here. She didn't matter.

He opened the web browser and typed an address into the navigation bar. The homepage of Elysian Industries popped up, but painfully slow. At the top of the page was an alert message flashing yellow and urgent. It was just like the one that had come into his phone minutes before:

Koren Johnson Releases James Rook Response, it said.

He clicked the link but groaned internally at the snail's pace of the outdated hardware. He had been nearly frantic since that lying southern hick of a greasy politician said all of that insidious filth about Koren on the David O'Brian show, not to mention on all of the equally intolerable appearances elsewhere. It was about damned time she had a response!

The man forced himself to calm. He really ought to be more charitable. As angry as it made him, it must have been *devastating* for her. He could see those huge blue eyes filling with tears right now, and felt a stab of remorse at his impatience, but the waiting had been *killing* him.

After the 'loading' icon spun for what felt like forever, the video finally started. He stared at the Elysian Industries webpage intently as the audio clicked in. Then he gasped. There she was.

Koren Johnson stood behind a wooden podium. She was dressed more conservatively than he was used to in a simple but feminine, white suit with long sleeves and the same colored skirt of medium length. It was bound at the waist with a thin black belt.

He frowned.

He liked her better in her sun dresses, but decided she could be forgiven under the circumstances. It was important to look professional for this, he supposed. Still, Koren's make-up was perfect as always and her large azure eyes flashed with determination, angelic face perfectly framed by lusterous blonde hair. The lapels of the white suit cut *almost* low enough to reveal cleavage.

Women's modesty generally increases with their beauty, he mused philosophically. *It does invite one to imagine.*

He flashed a leering grin and clicked into full-screen mode. *Wow, is she stunning!*

The man released a deep sigh, as Koren suddenly filled the monitor. He adjusted slightly in his seat before taking another long sip of lousy coffee.

Then he scowled in distaste. Koren's parents, Bill the mechanic, thirty-nine and Gypsie the waitress, thirty-seven, (though she always claimed she was only thirty five), stood behind their daughter along with the CEO of Elysian Industries, Askr Ashe. The Norwegian CEO was standing far too close to Koren for the man's liking, but he quickly forgot his irritation as the camera zoomed in on the girl's porcelain face. She looked straight into the camera.

So beautiful...

"It pains me to have to make this statement," Koren began, crystalline eyes and musical voice both hard and clear. "But recently an individual has been making absolutely irresponsible and slanderous statements about me in the public media to the extent that I feel I must respond. Senator James Rook is an elected member of the US Senate, and a fully grown adult.

"He is also a bully," she stated coldly, "who has decided to use his power, influence, and speaking platform to call a thirteen year old girl a 'high-dollar prostitute' and a 'tarted-up whore' in front of millions of people on national television."

Her eyes flashed and she jutted her pretty chin defiantly.

"Well, I would like to take this opportunity to emphasize that I am most certainly *neither* of those things. I find it quite disgusting, Mr. Rook, that a man of your age and position could be so comfortable flinging these kinds of totally unsubstantiated and demeaning sexual innuendos at someone so much younger than you..."

"You tell 'em, Honey," murmured the man. She was *so* cute when she was angry. He felt a little flushed and had to adjust again.

"Furthermore," Koren went on, "apart from my belief that making such sexually charged comments about a girl young enough to be his granddaughter is totally inappropriate, what I find most reprehensible is his suggestion that I am either too stupid to realize I am being taken advantage of or so shallow I would lie to millions of people about the single most emotional, devastating, and powerful experience of my whole life! This is then not to mention the terrible things he has suggested about my parents who have done nothing but their absolute best to support me in emotionally difficult times.

"Why is it…" she went on, "whenever a young woman is successful and in the public eye, there are always cynical men waiting in the wings to dismiss that girl as some sort of brainless doll? I assure you sure, sir, I am more than the television eye-candy you would reduce me to."

The man in the sunglasses nodded vigorously even as the hand not holding the coffee strayed to his lap.

No Koren, he thought. *Not* just *eye-candy… You are that and* so *much more!*

"I want to state definitively. What I witnessed of Aaru is real! Everything I've said is true!" Koren laid a hand on the podium and leaned in to the camera. "I do not believe for a *second* that anything I have seen could have possibly been faked. My sister, Rose, *is* alive today because of Aaru.

"Without it," Koren continued lower lip trembling and eyes welling with emotion. "She would be dead. I reject outright the assertion that Aaru is anything at all menacing or dangerous. Rather, it represents an enormous step forward for all of humanity. It represents hope for people who in previous generations would have had none. It represents relief to those who have been forced to know nothing but pain. Aaru is a blessing and a marvel that we should welcome and embrace instead of fear. Aaru is safe. It is secure, and it represents salvation to millions of people who have exhausted every other option for treatment and care.

"I will now let my friend, Askr Ashe, CEO and Chairman of Elysian Industries speak to those particulars in greater detail…"

"That's right, Little Koren," the shaded watcher murmured to the screen, squirming in his chair. "You're smart enough to know what's *real* when you find it… Or when it finds you…"

Mr. Ashe pushed his way to the podium. He patted Koren's back and hugged her briefly as he passed. That made the man in the trench coat instantly jealous. He took another long pull of cold coffee and growled as Askr Ashe settled himself. The young CEO cleared his throat. Koren stood beside him, looking up into his face doe-eyed and expectant.

Wouldn't it be excellent if she would look at me *that way?* The man in the trench coat mused with a sigh. *Who knows? Maybe she will yet...*

"First of all," Askr started with none of his usual laid-back swagger. "I would like to reiterate my utmost contempt for da totally sexist and misogynistic comments made by Senator James Rook about Koren Johnson - a fine young woman who has done nothing at all deserving of ire but tell about her own personal, life changing experience dat has forever impacted her family and will in due time change all da world as well. I would like to request of Mr. Rook in da future, if he feels da need to call somebody names he pick on *me* and not young, teenage girls.

"I am a grown man, Mr. Rook," Askr stated sternly, "and am completely capable of enduring such nonsense. A child is not, nor should she be expected to do so. Also, you have no basis by which to question Miss Johnson's truthfulness, especially in da very crude and public way you chose. It is a vile insult."

It still bothered the man how close Askr was to Koren, not to mention how intently she was staring at him. It made him squirm in his chair, a roiling emotional mess of anger, envy, and dismay, but he couldn't disagree. James Rook was clearly a villain!

"Having said dat," Askr continued. "I feel I must also address Senator Rook's patently false accusations regarding da nature of Aaru itself. All of his objections are based on fear, ignorance, and innuendo, not fact.

"First..." He held up his index finger. "In regards to da assertion Aaru is 'a scam' or a 'million dollar video game'. I would like to point out we hold multiple patents from da US government as well as other world governments for much of da technology involved. Da White Papers are available online. I invite anyone with a background in neuroscience, computer engineering, or bioelectric engineering to examine our work..."

The man in the sun glasses smiled smugly to himself.

"Oh, I will, Mr. Ashe," he replied under his breath. "I will..."

"If lawmakers are concerned," Askr Ashe continued. "I invite dem to tour our facility. What we have achieved is indeed very real. Assertions about our capabilities are not da least bit exaggerated or overblown. We have nothing at all to hide from *anyone.*

"Now…" The CEO leaned forward on the podium and pointed straight at the camera. "In regards to Mr. Rook's claims dat what we are doing is somehow dangerous… Elysian Industries has multi-layered and highly redundant fail safes in place to not only insure da integrity of da system itself, but also da safety of our Residents. No Resident of Aaru can hurt any other. Da system will simply not allow it.

"I would also like to take dis opportunity," he said with a deep scowl. "To emphasize his concerns about someone 'saving Hitler's brain on a flash-drive', are completely unfounded - utter unadulterated fantasy.

"In da simplest terms possible, what our technology does is scan da structure of da brain along with all of da bioelectric impulses and chemical reactions dereof which den allows us to recreate dat structure *exactly* in virtual form. In order to do dis, we must have a *living* brain to scan. Non-living brains don't have electrical impulses! Like any other technology effecting medical outcomes, ours is only effective while da patient is *alive*. Furthermore, da selection process for Aaru is rigorous specifically to prevent da nefarious and da criminal from taking advantage of da system.

"Finally, da charge to which I take da most exception," said Askr standing straighter, "is da suggestion we are somehow acting immorally. Dis deeply offends me. I would submit it is in fact da Senator himself who lacks compassion for da families of individuals we help. If he was allowed to have his way, all of dese people would be dead - lost to deir loved ones forever. Aaru offers families a chance at *life*, albeit in a different way dan it was lived before, but is it really any different from a wounded soldier who receives an artificial leg or a baby with a defective heart who gets a transplant? When da body or parts of da body fail, dey must be repaired or replaced. Dis is what Aaru does. Aaru *saves* lives, and how can any reasonable person possibly find fault with dat?"

"In conclusion, Mr. Rook," stated Askr forcefully. "No one is going to force you to like dis technology. In every chapter of human history have been dose who simply refused to accept a world different from da one dey grew up in. Da people who persecuted

Socrates and Galileo... Individuals who insisted da world was flat, and Earth da center of da universe, or even today with people who refuse all modern medicine based upon some vague idea God disapproves somehow - you sir are no different from any of dem. You have every right to your opinion, but please do not try to steal hope from others, and do not seek to dehumanize and objectify a brave young woman who is only guilty of finding joy again in a life she once thought had none left. Aaru represents good in dis world, and hopefully in coming months and years, we will be able to convince you and everyone else who doubts dis groundbreaking new technology. Thank you."

The video window flashed the Elysian Industries trademark logo faded to black. The man in the sunglasses settled back in his chair thoughtfully. He really wished there had been more of Koren and less of Askr Ashe, but the executive had a point. The shrouded figure found himself simultaneously wanting both to strangle and cheer the man. He watched the whole video again from the beginning, then stared at the screen.

"Right," he breathed and drained off the last of the coffee. "Who *could* object to that? Saving lives, Mr. Ashe... That's what we're doing here... That's what we're *both* doing here..."

He clicked the 'back' button, then selected the link to the Elysian Industries photo gallery. He located his favorite image file and clicked it. It opened to reveal a promotional photograph of Koren Johnson at the beach on a cloudless sunny day,

Maybe a day like Rose might have in Aaru, he mused with a wistful smile.

Koren's innocent blue eyes were turned upward. Her sleeveless sundress was cut exceedingly low and was a length to reveal a dangerous portion of porcelain thigh as she ran bare-foot across bleached, white sand. He stared at the image and smiled again, both hands now under the computer table.

He noticed the waitress staring at him. Her expression was vividly repulsed. The man hit the 'close' button and stood. Then he threw a few crumpled dollars on the table and stormed from the café.

Horrible place!

He was not embarrassed really. He simply disliked the scrutiny of others. Who cared what the girl thought anyway? She was nobody.

In any case, now that his initial urge was satisfied he could think a little. He had a great deal to do, but not here... someplace more secure. Then it would *really* be time to start "saving lives" as Askr Ashe had put it – Koren Johnson's not least of all.

It was late, so the street was deserted, but he looked left and right just to make sure. The street light above him flashed and flickered but would not come completely on. It cast only dim illumination on the corner where he was standing. The man in the trench coat unbuttoned the garment briefly to reveal a pink T-shirt beneath. It was emblazoned with the cartoon image of a panda bear in a kimono holding a paper fan.

He pulled a brand new iPhone from his pocket and closed his coat. Then he tapped the device to turn the screen curtain off. When his custom wallpaper flashed into view, he caught his breath like he did every time he beheld his creation.

Beautiful...

It was a gorgeous picture, and he was quite proud of it. It had taken a great deal of time to find just the right images and piece them together – just the right body, just the right pose, just the right head shot, just the right longing, sorrowful expression – everything lovingly tweaked and manipulated just so in Photoshop...

So sad... he thought, *So, so sad, but God! Koren Johnson is so gorgeous... so pure!*

And this image was almost exactly the way he wanted her – the way she *should* be... Almost... He sat up nights wondering about what made her look so tragic. What weight still lay upon her delicate heart even after the miraculous return of her sister, Rose?

He knew so *much* about her! More than anybody! But then again so little – not enough, not the most important things... not yet anyway. He had to discover *everything*!

But there was one thing in particular...

If he could know that thing; *that one thing* that cast the shadow over her pure and radiant soul... If he could find *that* out, surely, she would be grateful. *So grateful!* Then she would look at him the way she looked at Askr Ashe.

She would smile up at him, blue eyes sparkling with amenable joy and, he was sure, be quick to demonstrate her gratitude. He was convinced that she *needed* someone to find the one thing out for her and make her complete... Make her into the perfection he knew she could be. He intended to be the one to do it, too. He would just have to keep digging.

A car drove by, and the heavily obscured man stuffed the phone back into his pants pocket. That was *their* special picture – his and Koren's. It was for *his* eyes only. He glanced around nervously; suddenly suspicious he was being watched. One could not be too careful after all.

He huddled more deeply into his long, heavy coat, and pulled his baseball cap lower over his eyes. He shoved his hands deeply into his coat pockets. Then he spun on his heel and disappeared into the night.

Magic Man had things to do.

Chapter 13

Those Who Come After

Rose watched her sister's face fade from the black window. Then the window itself disappeared. She was sitting in one of her many fanciful gardens, perched daintily on a flowering vine she had manipulated to grow into the shape of a wrought-iron chair. As always, it was a beautiful day, but she was troubled.

Koren had looked *really* tired. She said as much in fact, but provided frustratingly scant details. She had insisted she didn't want to talk about it right now but would explain everything tomorrow after she got some sleep. Koren just really needed to hear Rose's voice for a few minutes before going to bed, she said.

Koren had sat all wilted and slumped forward on the end of her bed in a thin, pink nightgown. Pandadora was clutched fiercely to her chest, and she swayed as if she could barely remain upright, so Rose had not pressed her. Her strongest impulse had honestly been to hug her sister, but of course that was not possible. They could see each other. They could talk to each other, but the black rectangular window pane stood ever a barrier in between.

Rose tried to put it out of her mind. Surely Koren would feel better after some rest. As soon as she was ready, Rose would do her best to help, but at the moment she had other things to think about. She had become quite busy lately.

Newcomers had begun arriving to Aaru in droves. They were not Vedas, Hana explained, rather most of them were classified simply as 'Residents'. Rose was starting to get a better idea of just what it meant to be a Veda, and honestly, she thought with a tiny frown, had she known what it entailed, she might have reconsidered accepting the position.

Apparently there were different levels of users in Aaru. Those with the most privileges were of course the Lords and Ladies, like Princess Hana and Lord Mikoto who could manipulate any part of Aaru and anyone in it at any time as they saw fit. Then there were the Vedas like Rose and her friends. They had unlimited power to modify any of the physical structures in Aaru and, like the Lords and Ladies, were of a select, set number.

Everyone else was a 'Resident'. Each Resident could travel anywhere in Aaru and conjure up any object that was not a permanent component of the landscape, but were each assigned a small, set plot of space that was theirs to manipulate however they pleased and build their own castles and mansions any way they wished. Additionally, if two or more Residents got together they could set up public spaces in other specially demarcated areas. These were steadily becoming more numerous as well.

Hana had mentioned there was also a way in which Residents might be promoted to 'Overseers', who evidently had a few more powers and privileges, but she had not yet explained to Rose how exactly that worked. She hoped Hana would find the time to elucidate her soon however, because she could really use some help.

Hana had asked Rose to act as a 'cicerone', a kind of guide and mentor, she explained, for the new Residents as they arrived. This was proving no easy task if for no other reason than the sheer volume of new arrivals. As always the passage of time was difficult to gauge in Aaru, but since Hana had asked for her help, Rose had imparted a working understand of the infinite plains to dozens of people.

Even as she contemplated her recent efforts, she perked up, suddenly alert. It was as if chiming music was ringing inside her head, and her attention was immediately focused on a blank square of ground far away on the verdant Aaru plain. She felt strangely compelled, as she had every time this had happened so far, to leap into the sky and hurtle towards it.

"New Resident arrived," a feminine voice lilted in her head. "Resident arrived…"

"I know it's a Resident," Rose muttered back to the unresponsive voice. "You don't have to tell me every time!"

As Rose drew closer, she noted a solitary figure standing in the middle of the plot. Rose could not really say by what means she could delineate its borders, but she had no trouble recognizing them. What ensued was highly typical of her cicerone experience thus far.

Some of the new arrivals had been older than her, some younger. This particular Resident was easily the oldest she had encountered. She was a woman in her seventies at least if Rose had to guess. She stood blinking in confusion, dressed in a blue hospital gown.

Rose alighted before the astonished older woman, her brown hair and beautiful kimono billowing as if tossed by a strong wind.

She had actually been making a conscious effort to refine her welcoming performance.

If I have to do it, I might as well make it fun, Rose decided. She smiled warmly.

"Welcome to Aaru, Dear Chloe," Rose called in a voice that rivaled Hana's for saccharine sweetness. Though she had never seen this person before in her life, Rose knew her name as easily as if it was tattooed on the old lady's forehead. "Let me be the first to welcome you to a new life everlasting. It will be filled with joy, free of pain and suffering. Here you can do and be whatever you like, freed from the limitations of your Beforelife."

A flock of lily white doves took wing behind her as she spread her hands dramatically.

"But first," Rose went on with a pleasant giggle. "How about we clothe you in something more festive and befitting of the occasion?"

She was not exactly sure by what means she knew, but as a Veda, one of Rose's privileges was to read the information of anyone who was equal to or lower than her in rank. She immediately knew exactly what the new Resident would find most pleasing.

Rose put her hand to her mouth and blew. As she did so a sparkling, opaline powder cascaded around the old woman in a shimmering shower. Suddenly, Chloe was no longer wearing the hospital gown. She was instead clothed in a beautiful glittering ball gown like Cinderella might have worn. The woman laughed in delight as her wrinkled face smoothed, and her grey hair changed to yellowy gold.

After Chloe's protracted paroxysm of joy - which was again typical of everyone Rose had greeted so far - and profusion of thank yous and questions, Rose proceeded to demonstrate just how the woman could manipulate her plot to her liking. Then Rose invited her to explore the new and beautiful world in which she found herself.

As Rose bid the ecstatic Chloe goodbye, she rose into the air feeling quite pleased with herself. It really *did* feel good to be a part of that initial euphoria, that first moment of elation when someone realized that they were not in fact dead, that life would go on and be even better than before. However, Rose did not have long to ponder the gratifying sensation. Almost as soon as her feet left the ground, the chiming music came again.

"New Resident arrived," the voice announced. "Resident arrived…"

"All right, all right…" Rose muttered and rocketed off to the next, new plot.

This space was not far from the one where she had just left Chloe. It was near the great river, on Hana's side. Rose wrinkled her brow as she drew nearer. Something felt different… *off* somehow.

Rose noted the silhouette of a single individual below and descended towards it, just like before. Kimono and chestnut hair once again billowing, she began.

"Welcome to Aaru, Dear…" Rose stopped.

No name was coming to mind. It had always been automatic before. Moreover, now that she saw the person, she could tell that something was *seriously* wrong.

She thought it looked like it was a man, but horridly misshapen. The form flickered and warped, remaining indistinct. The person had all the right parts; arms, legs, eyes, mouth, nose, etc., but they were amorphous and shifting. The misshapen face looked up. Then it threw back its head and screamed.

It was a terrible, wordless shriek - An incomprehensible howl of misery. It stole Rose's breath, and she fell heavily to the suddenly grey and barren turf.

As she found her feet, an alarm blared, shrill and deafening. The female voice from before was replaced by urgent male shouting. "Error! Error! Resident upload failed! Data corrupt - lines 10, 67, 102, 406…" It continued rattling off a long list of numbers that were utterly meaningless to Rose.

The humanoid creature turned its malformed visage towards her, features shifting and drooping like melting wax beneath a sweltering sun. For the first time since Rose had come to Aaru, she was afraid.

The ground beneath her feet warped and bulged. She lost her balance and tumbled to the colorless turf once more. The creature lunged at her, and Rose screamed, throwing her hands up to ward off the attack.

A higher pitched siren wailed and there was a flash. The malformed apparition vanished, only to reappear about ten feet away. The female voice returned.

"Harm Failsafe engaged. Harm Failsafe engaged…" it repeated over and over.

Rose screamed again as the roiling monstrosity lurched towards her. It reached for her with scabrous, twisted hands.

"Hana!" she cried and her piercing wail echoed across the plains like thunder. "Princess Hana, help me!"

A shadow passed before the sun. Then with a cry like an eagle, a winged shape plummeted towards her. The Earth shook as it struck in the center of the distorted plot and dirt erupted into the air.

What appeared to be a giant man, dressed in the baggy *hakama* pants, *haori* shirt and the patterned vest of an ancient Japanese warrior, raised himself from the smoking crater. His face was crimson and his nose comically long. He bore a thick white mustache and his expression was fierce. He positioned himself between Rose and the twisted apparition. Then he raised a hand and pointed at the monstrosity clawing toward Rose.

"Delete!" the voice rumbled.

The misshapen creature turned away from her. It raised its arms high above its head with a deformed and contorted posture and wailed out another deafening shriek of despair. Then it disappeared in a flash of light and a cloud of tiny green squares that quickly dissipated into the ether. It was silent again, and the abrupt quietude rang in Rose's throbbing ears.

The *tengu* lowered its arm.

"Are you alright, Rose?" It rumbled.

Rose could not manage speech yet. She just laid there, a huddled mass on the ground. The giant waved a hand over its head and shrank. It moved towards her and held out a hand.

Rose recoiled.

"It's okay, Rose," it said in a much more normal sounding voice.

Rose ventured a peek. A young man with thick, black-rimmed glasses and dressed in disheveled blue shirt and orange pants was holding his hand out to her.

"Mikoto!" she exclaimed as she recognized the Aaru Lord.

She quickly took his proffered hand, and he hauled her to her feet. Rose looked into his face in bewilderment for a moment then wrapped Mikoto in a fierce embrace. She cried hard wracking sobs into his shoulder.

Mikoto patted her shoulder clumsily.

"It's, uh... It's okay, Rose..." he mumbled. "Really..."

"Rose!" screamed another urgent voice behind her.

She was practically tackled from behind as Hana wrapped her in a crushing hug. The Flower Princess extracted Rose hastily from Mikoto's uncomfortable grasp with a poisonous glare at her partner. She squeezed Rose against her chest and stroked the younger girl's hair as Rose cried.

"It's alright Rose," Princess Hana soothed, rubbing her back with the other hand. "It's all over now... Shhh... Hush, now, hush... You are safe. You will always be safe here. No need to cry... There are no tears in Aaru, remember?"

Rose looked up at her, and Hana brushed the tears from her cheeks with her index finger.

"Remember?" she whispered again.

Rose swallowed, sniffed, then nodded. Hana answered with a gentle smile, and a soft peck to Rose's cheek, before rounding on Mikoto in a blazing fury. It was so intense that lightning crackled from her whole body and thick black storm clouds formed to roil and rumble around her perfectly styled head. Her face was vividly flushed as she stalked towards him.

"How could you allow such a thing to happen!!!" she roared at her compatriot jabbing an accusatory finger squarely into the middle of his narrow chest. "How *dare* you allow a Veda to be endangered within the very sanctity of Aaru!!! Lord Draugr shall hear of this!!! I swear that...

"Calm down, Hana," interrupted Mikoto with a profoundly annoyed voice, rubbing the spot where he had been poked by Hana's thrusting digit. "I didn't *endanger* anyone. All the warning messages went off. The Harm Failsafe engaged. Everything worked the way it was supposed to work! Everything was *perfect*!"

Hana gestured to the devastated plot around them. The earth was twisted into unnatural shapes. It remained a maudlin shade of grey. Then she gestured toward Rose's tear stained face.

"This is your idea of 'working perfectly'?" she screamed incredulously. "This is *Aaru*. No Resident should *ever* have to witness something like that! Especially not a *Veda*!"

"So, there might be a few style bugs to work out..." Mikoto conceded with an unconcerned shrug. "But the fact remains that all of my systems did what they were supposed to do and removed the threat!"

"What *was* that?" Asked Rose shakily. "What happened?!"

"Corrupt data," answered Mikoto nonchalantly. "Bad upload. It happens sometimes."

"So," began Rose. Dread crept into her voice. "Was that a *person*? You said 'delete'... Does that mean they're..."

"Most likely not," interrupted Mikoto quickly, before Rose could finish the dire thought. "What usually happens is that there is some kind of interruption during upload – like a power surge, or disconnected cable for instance – that interrupts the transfer." He tossed his head in the direction of where the creature had stood. "That was *obviously* an incomplete file. Whoever it is, they'll most likely be fine. All you have to do is delete the corrupted file and then reload the data. They won't even remember it happened."

"*Most likely?*" Rose repeated Mikoto's words uneasily.

"I am sure there is nothing to worry about, Rose," cut in Hana with another offended scowl at Mikoto. "The Makers have been notified and the situation will be resolved. Would it make you feel better if I check to make sure all is well with that young man after everything is sorted out?"

Rose sniffled and nodded. Hana hugged her. Then she took a step back.

"I'm sorry that happened, Rose," Hana apologized with a deep bow. Then she shot Mikoto another poisonous glare. Mikoto rolled his eyes.

"Just remember, Rose," he said before giving her an awkward shoulder pat. "This is Aaru. Nothing can hurt you here. It just can't happen."

Rose nodded. Then she straightened. She heard the chiming music again.

"New Resident arrived... Resident arrived..." the bland female voice called.

Rose turned to Hana plaintively.

"You know," ventured Mikoto over his shoulder as he turned away. "If you want a break, you can turn that off for a while. I'm surprised Hana hasn't shown you how yet."

He sniffed once, leapt into the air, and was gone.

Hana fumed at Mikoto's parting shot, but took a deep breath. She looked Rose straight in the eye and made a cutting motion with her hand. The blaring newcomer alarm went silent.

"There," said Hana. "Better?"

Rose nodded. Then Hana put both of her hands on Rose's shoulders. Her face bore a profoundly apologetic expression. The Flower Princess squeezed Rose tightly and whispered in her ear.

"Why don't you go find your friends?" she suggested. "Mikoto is right in at least one thing; It would be good for you to take a rest. Perhaps some time with them would relax you. I can stay here and finish cleaning up this mess. How does that sound?"

Rose nodded, and Hana gave her a gentle push. She wiped her eyes and nose on her sleeve. Then Rose flew off into the brilliant azure sky glancing back once to see Hana straightening out the scorched rectangle of the ruined plot. The Flower Princess filled in the craters, smoothed out the twisted Earth, and raised up the tall plains grass once more. Rose exhaled deeply.

Everything was okay again. Everything was fine. Both Hana and Mikoto said so. She was just a little bit unsettled. That was all. Still, Rose could not completely dismiss her disquiet, so she decided that she would take Princess Hana's advice and go find someone to talk to.

Her first thought was of her sister, but Koren was most likely still sleeping, and there was no telling when she would call for Rose again. Furthermore, as much as Rose hated to admit it, she doubted Koren would be quite able to understand what had just occurred or fully grasp how she felt about it.

She briefly considered looking for Franco. If she told him what had transpired, he would certainly have lots of hugs and kisses to make her feel better. He might even take off his shirt again…

That was always nice she supposed, but her mind was still uneasy. Rose realized that she didn't feel quite up to it. There would be plenty of time for kissing and snuggling after she calmed down and sorted some things out. Still, Rose felt she really needed to talk to *someone*. Who would *really* understand?

Rose did not ponder long. She soon found herself following the sparkling blue ribbon of water towards the riverside mansion with the Egyptian hieroglyphics and Greek columns. She wondered as she skimmed over the silvery surface if she might find Auset at home.

*

When Rose alighted on the docks in front of Auset's mansion, she was not at all sure what she wanted to say to the other girl. As luck would have it however, Auset was nowhere to be seen. The Pakistani-American girl did not appear to be at home.

Still, there were ways to find people you wanted to see in Aaru, especially if one was a Veda. Rose walked to the end of the dock where Auset's Egyptian pleasure barge gently bobbed up and down in the water. She placed a hand on the bow, looked up into the clouds above, and said, "Auset," in a clear, quiet voice. Then she knew. She leapt once more into the sky.

As with many things in Aaru Rose did not know exactly how or why she knew them. They just sort of appeared in her brain. Though she could never have explained where she was going had someone asked her, she still streaked unerringly towards the place she was sure she would find her friend.

Rose came down on the edge of a dark forest. This was something she was sure had not been here before. Perhaps it was some creation of Auset's – another whimsical menagerie for the fanciful creatures she was so fond of making. In spite of Mikoto's assurances that nothing in Aaru could harm her, Rose could not help but experience tremblings of foreboding and dread as she stepped beneath the thick and shadowy boughs.

It was cool here, but not unpleasantly so. And although it was dark, here and there at the roots of the great trees were clumps of softly glowing mushrooms to light her path. Rose could hear the singing of birds high above in the towering branches, and the wind rustled the thick leaves as it gusted among the treetops. Unconsciously, her clothing changed from her ubiquitous kimono to a sleeveless shirt, tight shorts, and thick pair of hiking boots like she wore sometimes when she and Koren used to go camping with their dad.

Rose heard a low growl to her right and spun in alarm. Staring back at her was what looked like a family of large bears, but with the bushy manes of lions and thick wooly fur that was vividly pink. One of them sniffed in her direction, but quickly lost interest. They lumbered away deeper into the forest. Rose released a breath she had not known she was holding and continued on her way.

She was not at all sure how far she walked, but after quite some time of climbing over roots and weaving among massive trees, she thought she heard a faint sound coming from further ahead. It sounded like singing.

Rose redoubled her pace and turned toward the haunting melody. She burst out into a broad clearing before she noticed it was upon her and caught her breath. It was beautiful.

An emerald pond surrounded by lilies and cattails that glowed and shimmered like gems met her eyes. Faeries and sprites flitted over the surface, and the banks were covered with what must have been a thousand different kinds of flowers, each winking and glowing with their own subdued inner light every shade of the rainbow. Bioluminescent fish and frogs of blue and green swam and leapt in the still water and everywhere were more glowing mushrooms. It was breathtaking.

Then she saw her – a huddled little shape on the far bank. Auset sat with her knees pulled up under her chin staring straight ahead. She was singing a song, but Rose could not understand the words. It was beautiful, but also very sad.

Rose hurried around the edge of the lake to hail her friend, but when she drew near she slowed. Auset's pretty brown face was serious and unpainted, and she was not clad in her customary Cleopatra-themed clothing. Instead, she wore an unadorned grey dress that looked as if it might have been a sack at one time. Her head was covered with a colorless *hijab*.

"Hello, Rose," she said quietly as Rose walked up to her, but she did not turn. "I don't think I'm in the mood to play today."

As she said the words a soft drizzle began to fall, and thunder rumbled softly in the distance.

"That's not why I came looking for you, Auset," Rose answered uncertainly. "I... Are you okay?"

Auset sighed.

"I don't know Rose," she said and leaned her head against her knees. "This is my thinking place. I'm just... thoughtful today, I suppose... Yeah, I guess I'm okay... No... Well, I... I just don't know..."

Rose took a step closer.

"May I sit?" she asked hesitantly.

"Sure," answered Auset with a shrug. "I don't mind. I just don't know if I'll be very good company..."

Rose sat beside her. She thought Auset looked terribly sad. That wasn't supposed to happen – not in Aaru. It seemed that lots of things that were not supposed to happen in Aaru were occurring today.

Rose wasn't sure what to say, so she just sat cross-legged in the sparkling sand, following Auset's gaze across the enchanted glade while fairies danced above the water, and the shimmering flowers played chiming music as they blew in the wind.

"'Allah hath promised,'" Auset stated suddenly, "'to Believers, men and women, gardens under which rivers flow, to dwell therein, and beautiful mansions in gardens of everlasting bliss... *Sadaqa Allahu Al-Azhim...*'" She sighed deeply and looked over at Rose at last. "That's what the Holy Koran says anyway... about *Jannah...*"

"Does it?" asked Rose uncertainly, not at all sure what the other girl was getting at. "I guess that kinda sounds like..."

"It also says," interrupted Auset insistently, her voice quavering, upon the verge of tears. "It also says, 'They shall enter there, as well as the righteous among their fathers, their spouses, and their offspring. Angels shall enter to them from every gate with the salutation: 'Peace be with you because you persevered in patience! Now how excellent is the final home!'"

Her voice grew louder as she recited the quote and a tear leaked from the corner of her eye.

"Auset?" Rose asked in concern. "What's wrong?"

"The *righteous* among their families, it says, Rose," her voice cracked. "*Only* the righteous..."

"Auset," Rose laid a gentle hand on the other girl's shoulder. "Really... What's the matter?"

Auset could only sob. Rose gathered her to her and held the smaller girl close. She pulled Auset's head tightly against her shoulder.

After a few minutes Auset looked at her miserably.

"Where's my mom, Rose?" Her words were barely intelligible. "Why isn't she here?"

Rose had no answer for that, so she just held her. Auset was so slight and small... She felt tiny. It was just like the way it felt when she used to hold Koren as a little girl. The realization made Rose feel a little teary herself.

"And if..." Auset went on, choking on her sobs. "And if... She's... not... here... then... she... must... be... in..."

"Hush now, Auset," soothed Rose, suddenly comprehending her friend's fear. "You don't know that. We don't know this is even... well... That this is... *Jannah*..." Rose stumbled over the unfamiliar word. "If what you just said is true, then how am *I* here? I'm Methodist."

Auset sniffed and wiped her eyes.

"Who knows," Rose went on. "There's tons of people arriving every day. She might just not have shown up yet! You never know..."

Auset took a deep calming breath. She nodded.

"Maybe you're right, Rose," the smaller girl conceded, but then timorously met her friend's gaze.

"Where are we, Rose?" She asked. "It's not *Jannah*, is it? ...But we're *dead*, right? So... What is this place, Rose? What is it *really*? Where are we? *What* are we?"

Rose thought for a moment and took a great swallow. She wanted to make her friend feel better, but her uneasy feelings were returning. This couldn't be Heaven... At least not the Heaven she had been taught about her entire life – all full of clouds, and angels with harps, and pearly gates. At last she placed her hand against Auset's cheek.

"This place..." she began, but then stopped to think.

"This place is Aaru," Rose stated finally with much increased confidence. "This place is *ours*. And where we are? We are together... Two friends together, Auset... That is what we are."

Auset nodded and wiped at her eyes again.

"I'm sorry, Rose," she apologized as she struggled to regain her composure. "Look at me. I'm such a mess!"

"Don't apologize," Rose replied. "I'm a mess too. That's honestly why I came looking for you... I hope I made you feel better..."

"You did, Rose," answered Auset, snuggling closer against Rose's side. "Thank you..."

She trailed off, and they were silent for quite some time, just watching the creatures of Auset's menagerie frolic around the peaceful, jade pool. It felt good to hold another warm body so close. Rose missed this with Koren, she realized and the thought made her suddenly and poignantly miss her little sister.

Then Auset had a sudden thought. She sat up straight.

"Wait..." she said turning to face Rose. "You said you came looking for me because *you* felt a mess? I'm being so terribly selfish! You are being so sweet to listen to me weep like a little child, and I have totally ignored you! What is troubling *you*, Rose?"

"Don't worry about it," demurred Rose. "The hugging made me feel better too..."

She briefly considered letting it go. She was probably just being silly anyway, but... Rose really wanted to talk to someone.

"Something happened today," Rose began in a low, hushed voice. "Something... disturbing... Something scary... It really bothered me, and I don't really know why. It's probably nothing... After all, both Lord Mikoto and Princess Hana said it was no big deal, so..."

"What was it, Rose?" Auset asked.

Rose told her about all of it – her shock at the abortive new Resident greeting, how Mikoto had flown to the rescue, and the horrible screaming the man-thing had made.

"It really sounded like it was... like it was in *pain*," Rose concluded with a shudder. "Mikoto dismissed it. He said it was no big deal, but Hana was *furious*! I've never seen her so mad, even at him!"

"That does sound pretty scary," Auset conceded, "but you said Hana would tell you when it was all fixed, right?"

Rose nodded.

"Well then maybe we should make a special effort to find that boy again when he is uploaded properly and make friends with him," Auset suggested with a smile that actually looked legitimate. "I bet it would make you feel better... Probably him too."

Rose giggled.

"You're probably right, Auset." Rose sighed. "I'm most likely getting all worried and upset over nothing."

"It wasn't *nothing*, Rose," Auset contradicted gently. "It was something that upset you. You needed to talk it out with someone... With a friend... That's what friends do... Thank you for thinking of me."

She took Rose's hand shyly and gave it a squeeze, and Rose leaned in for another firm hug.

"Yes they do," she agreed. "And no problem! Thanks, Auset."

"Thank *you*, Rose."

Rose stretched. Then she stood and reached out a hand to help Auset up as well.

"How about we find the others and go do something *fun*!" Rose suggested with a laugh. It seemed to dismiss the residual darkness she felt inside. "Today has been *way* too serious!"

Auset allowed herself to be hauled to her feet. She shook herself, grinned, and the drizzling rain ceased. Her grey, sack dress and tear stains were replaced with her Egyptian clothing, straight dark hair, and black eye make-up once more.

"I think that's a great idea, Rose," she said adjusting her grip on the other girl's hand. "Let's go."

And with that, they headed off through the forest together in search of their friends.

Chapter 14

A Troll in the Dark

The room was windowless. The only light came from dozens of digital photo frames set all about the cramped apartment and large, glowing computer monitors arranged precariously on a broad metal desk. The heavy piece of furniture was overflowing with electronic equipment, the purpose of which most laypeople would be hard-pressed to identify. An old rock song played quietly in the background from an even older eight-track tape player that looked strangely out of place among all the brand new, top-of-the-line technology. The muted song and the incessant clicking of the computer keyboard were the only sounds.

The cursor sailed across the screen. It stopped on a button marked 'post'. There was a click and the video quickly uploaded to a message board with the title "Unedited Koren Johnson Footage – Exclusive!!! – Another One From Magic Man". He smiled.

The skags in the 5Kun community were going to *love* this one! He couldn't resist hitting play again. The loading icon swirled for less than a second before the video clip started.

Koren Johnson was standing in front of the Aaru access portal in her bedroom. She logged in, and the camera angle changed to show the Aaru screen. Her sister Rose soon appeared, and they started talking. Their conversation was mostly about school, family, other mundane people and things no one important had ever heard of or cared about. It would probably not be of much interest to the creepers who generally posted on this message board.

The vast majority of the content in the Koren Johnson stream was simulated porn – both hardcore and soft-core images ripped off of other sites with Koren Johnson's face photoshopped into them. Magic Man had started out that way too. The day he saw her first Aaru commercial he had been inspired. Since then he had produced hundreds of "improved" Koren Johnson images, but that was old hat now.

In any case, the vast majority of the content was heavy handed garbage. The man who posted under the pseudonym 'Magic Man' browsed them often, although he rarely found anything he thought was even slightly interesting. Usually, his main purpose was to troll the lesser 'cyber socs' and 'newtinks' who dared think they were special enough to post content along with *his* pics and memes. *He* was the artist.

His was and would ever be the best original content. No one cared about Koren Johnson like *he* did. No one understood her the way he did, and he was always upping his game while every other wannabe on this board was still stuck on the same tired, old crap. Magic Man was the meme master, the creator of content, a single glimpse of which could break hearts and inspire souls!

Even so, every once in a while someone would surprise him. Occasionally he would find work he had to grudgingly admit was perhaps *marginally* good. His favorite pics, gifs, and video files he saved and loaded onto the digital picture frames – Koren Johnson on glowing display in all of her sweet, sensual glory. The *vast* majority of his collection was, of course, OC courtesy of Magic Man. He let out a quick, self-satisfied chuckle at how great he was then turned his attention back to his computer monitor.

At the end of Koren and Rose's conversation, Koren logged out. Now, *this* was where the *real* show would start for most of his loyal fans. As the Aaru screen went dark, Koren rose from her bed and laid Pandadora on her pillow. Then she walked over to a chest of drawers and pulled out a pink nightgown. She casually stripped down to white cotton panties, dropped her bra on the floor, and pulled the nightgown over her head. Then she got into bed and snuggled Pandadora against her chest. Koren rolled over to flip the bedside lamp switch off, and the screen went dark.

Money, he thought smugly.

His adoring skags would eat this stuff up. This was the most righteous post he'd ever made, and there was only going to be more where that came from. Unlike all of the excellence he had produced before, this was different. This was *real*. All his searching had finally paid off. He'd finally found the rabbit hole – the entrance to Wonderland.

Magic Man had to give the boys over at Elysian Industries credit. Theirs was a quality system – very well protected. It had taken him nearly two months to find the back door into their network. He had not yet met his goal of hacking the Aaru complex itself – that was a separate, closed system not connected to the internet or the other company computer systems, but what he *had* found turned out to be sublime.

An alarm buzzed, and he looked toward a second monitor. The screen was divided into nine separate boxes, each showing different parts of his apartment building. He saw movement at the main entrance and glimpsed the old lady who was always leaving notes on his windshield complaining he parked his car too closely to hers. She was just coming into the building with bags full of groceries.

He flipped on a speaker and waited until the security door closed behind her. She grumbled to herself as she struggled to balance her load and get to her apartment keys. Then Magic Man pressed a button and touched the screen. It went black.

There was an exclamation of dismay, a crash, and a stream of vivid cursing. He touched the screen again, and the lights came back on. The old lady was sprawled in the floor, groceries scattered. He chuckled as she picked herself up and gathered her spilled foodstuffs.

Serves the old hag right for being a bitch, he thought unsympathetically.

Magic Man had the whole building wired this way. Lights, elevators, fire alarms, sprinklers, security door locks – all he needed was a computer and a wireless connection… And not just in his building – given enough time everything was his to command… *Everything!* Trolling successfully completed, Magic Man turned his attention back to the main monitor.

He had heard long ago that a Koren Johnson reality show was in the works. It was going to be called "Love Beyond Death", which he thought was a cheesy title, but whatever. From what he had read about it, (and he had read *everything*), it was for all effects and purposes going to be a pretty typical program about Koren's life in the real world and Rose's adventures in Aaru – basically an hour-long commercial for the service.

The thing about reality shows, he knew, all of them had one common component – one particular need. In order to make a decent show where something actually happened every episode, one had to shoot *massive* amounts of footage.

About a week after he first breached the Elysian Industries firewall he had come across a folder labeled "Love Beyond Death Raw Footage". That was the happiest day of his life.

He had copied everything to his own hard drive. Then he carefully covered his tracks so no one would notice the content had been accessed. Since then, he had been spending almost every waking moment raking through hours and hours of footage for the especially jeweled morsels, those few exquisite, tasty bites like the one he just posted.

He didn't just mean seeing Koren naked either. Magic Man liked ogling his little, melancholy flower as much as anyone, but that was not what he was searching for. His endeavors were not so base as simple, carnal amusement. It was the '*one thing*' he wanted to find. *That* was always foremost in his thinking.

Somewhere in these hundreds of hours of footage he was sure it must be hiding. It was just going to take patience and determination. Once he found that…

Magic Man picked up the digital frame that was sitting on his desk. This particularly graphic picture was his favorite. That's why he kept it close. It was a larger version of his smart phone wallpaper.

"'An artist chooses his subjects,'" he whispered softly to the picture, "'that is the way he praises…'"

He brushed his fingers over the cool, smooth surface. Then he closed his eyes and kissed it.

"Soon, Little Koren," he murmured in his most seductive voice. "Soon my lithesome nymph, I'll find out all your secrets. I'll find the one thing to complete you… to complete *us*. Then…" He paused and set the image back on the desk. "Then '*the artist*' will paint upon your pristine canvas, and we shall realize your perfection *together*…"

***

Koren opened her eyes reluctantly. She had gone right to bed after talking to Rose, then slept a deep and dreamless slumber all night, but still she felt exhausted. The previous day, after her difficult meeting with the Board, they had spent the rest of the afternoon writing and recording her official response to Senator Rook. Then there had been retake after retake! They had not finished until after 1:00 AM, and then she had to wait around for them to edit and post it on the Elysian Industries website. The end result was she did not return home until well after three in the morning.

Askr and Miss Hanasaka had apologized profusely for keeping her so late, but the response really *did* have to be perfect. It was *vitally* important that it be released immediately, they insisted, and they needed her. She granted that was probably true.

Koren understood why it was so vital for it to be her who made the first part of the statement, but *ugh*! She hoped that she never had to do *that* again. It had been *so* tedious.

The night had stretched so late Askr Ashe had been forced to reschedule her meeting with the other Beta Families. Again, Askr had been full of apologies, but truth be told, Koren did not mind that so much. Honestly, she wasn't sure she felt up for it today either.

Almost as soon as she finished the thought, the alarm blared. She groaned, but forced herself to get up. It was already well after ten, and she had to be back over at Elysian Industries by noon.

Koren quickly stripped out of her nightgown. Then she wrapped herself in a fluffy, white towel and walked down the hallway to the bathroom for a shower. When she got back to her room, her wet hair tightly wrapped in a second, garishly pink towel, she let the white towel fall to the floor and began getting dressed.

As she pulled on tight, ripped blue-jeans she realized just how *good* it felt putting her own clothes on. This was the first time in *forever* she had not been dressed up by someone else. The idea tickled her.

It put her in a rather silly mood, so she grabbed up her hairbrush and jumped up and down on her bed singing along with the newly released Jonas Perry song she had just downloaded to her phone. She did this for a few minutes slinging water droplets everywhere as she tossed her soggy head to the beat. Then she gave her smiling poster a long, sweet kiss, jumped down, and walked across the room to get her hairdryer.

She sat on the end of her bed and dried her damp locks. When she was finished, she carefully brushed out all the tangles, fastened her bra and pulled a pink t-shirt over her head. Just as she was slipping into her shoes, the door opened, and her mother told her she needed to come down and eat breakfast.

"But I promised Rose that I would call her back this morning!" Koren protested.

Her mother shook her head.

"You're late getting up already," Gypsie stated sternly. "The limo is waiting outside, and you've got just enough time to choke down some cereal and go. We can't be late! The other families will be waiting, and Rose will still be here when we get back. I'm sure she'll understand."

Koren grumbled, but did as she was told. About fifteen minutes later, the black limousine roared away from the curb and back to corporate headquarters.

*

When she arrived, Koren and her parents were met at the door by the young blonde woman named Amy. She escorted them to a large conference room much like the one in which they had met the day before, but Koren did not think that it was the same place. There was a large table in the center, covered with food and drink, which frustrated her. Why on Earth had her mother practically force-fed her that nauseatingly sweet breakfast cereal before they came?

Time wasted that could have been spent talking to Rose... She thought grouchily.

A few caterers wandered about the room, putting the finishing touches on a table setting here or chipping a couple of last minute shards out of an ice sculpture there, but otherwise Koren, Bill, and Gypsie were the only other people in the room.

Amy smiled a toothpaste commercial smile and called out brightly. "The others will be here shortly. I hope you'll wait just a moment, please."

Koren's dad mumbled something like "Yeah, sure," but Koren couldn't be completely certain.

She felt another moment of annoyance. What was the use in being here early just to stand around? *More* wasted time she could have spent talking to Rose! Was it really that big a deal to be just a little bit late?

As it turned out they did not have long to wait. After about five minutes, the other families began to trickle in. There was a Hispanic couple with four children - one boy and three girls who ranged in age from about four up to around sixteen or seventeen. Next, was a family of four – Mom, Dad, Brother, and Sister – all of them with hair so blonde that it looked nearly white. Others followed, but the only other family that particularly stood out to her was a very dark-skinned couple accompanied by a girl with a huge halo of black hair that stood out from her head in every direction and who was about the same age as she herself. There was something unusual in their features that Koren couldn't quite put a name to.

After that, it seemed like everyone else was fairly nondescript. Some had kids, some didn't. Some looked quite a bit older than her parents, some looked about the same age. They all stood around nervously, shifting from foot to foot, and not looking at all sure what to do next. When Askr Ashe finally strode into the room, Koren counted eleven families.

"Welcome, everyone!" he announced bombastically. "I'm sorry we had to delay dis get together. Circumstances dictated we turn our attention to other matters, but still!" He exclaimed as he closed the doors behind him and glided across the floor. "We are so happy dat we can all gather today! Dis is not everyone exactly. Several families were unable to make it due to scheduling conflicts, but I'm so glad so many of you could take time out of your busy schedules to attend dis little meet and greet! I think it will be so nice for all of our Aaru families to get to know each other. So without further ado..."

Askr Ashe seized a champaign glass from a nearby table and rapped it smartly with the handle of a convenient butter knife. A clear, crystalline tone resonated across the room.

"Let us eat!" he proclaimed grandly. "And let us celebrate the return of your precious children!"

A line of servers walked in from the back of the room to pass out glasses. Champaign was poured for the adults, and Mr. Ashe proposed a toast to Aaru, which the families returned, if in a rather lukewarm and reserved fashion.

It was a nice party. The food was good. There were lots of items that Koren didn't recognize, so she assumed that meant they were expensive. She talked with a couple of the children in attendance, and they seemed pretty nice, although about half of the families did not speak English very well. In particular, she found the daughter of the two dark skinned people fascinating - she loved her unusual accent – but the conversations stayed peripheral. People seemed guarded for some reason, herself included.

Koren 's experience with Aaru had been so intimate and personal. It felt like a thing that was just hers and Rose's. Suddenly, there was this big crowd of people who were going through the same thing, and Koren was not certain how to feel about it.

After about an hour, Askr Ashe clanged on his champaign glass again to make the *big* announcement. Men dressed in light blue Elysian Industries jumpsuits wheeled in an enormous television monitor, and Askr introduced what Koren came to understand were a series of reality shows to be released in different countries and regions all around the world. Her portion was perhaps five minutes long and included mostly footage she had already seen – her screaming at her mother a few weeks after Rose's funeral, her near fainting spell when Rose's rebirth was first revealed – but then there were a few more scenes that she was not so sure about.

Much like the video clips she had seen for the first time on the David O'Brian show, these seemed just a little too intimate. They depicted time with her family she truly had no idea how they could have gotten. Some included footage of her conversations with Rose. Koren was not comfortable with that in the least.

She mentioned her unease to her mother, but Mom just muttered something about "contracts" and "blessings" and the "they just do things that way in show biz" quote that she had taken to repeating like a mantra whenever Koren voiced a concern. Then she told her daughter to be quiet and watch. Koren was not at all satisfied with the response, but did not feel like she had the energy for a conflict, particularly not in front of all these strangers. She decided to let the matter drop for the time being.

Each of the families in attendance had their time on screen. All of them went through a similar range of emotions, so after eleven straight portrayals of anger and suspicion followed by disbelieving joy, (particularly since many of them were in languages that Koren did not understand) she found herself getting a little bit bored.

The big surprise however, came at the end, and Koren had to admit the spectacle stole her breath. The finale was brilliant and beautiful - scenes from inside Aaru itself. They were breathtaking. Koren had never seen anything like them.

When she talked to Rose, it was always as though her sister spoke from inside a picture frame – something like a sentient portrait with a vague, painted background behind her. These shots however, were high definition, dynamic scenes that would put any multi-million dollar action movie to shame. Dramatic music played in the background.

The children shown in each scene swooped and soared through the bluest sky Koren had ever beheld - effulgent, bleached clouds sparkling in the radiant sun. With a wave of the Residents' hands trees, mountains, and castles erupted from the Earth and fanciful creatures, many of which Koren had no name for, were called into being. Every face bore an expression of unmitigated happiness.

Koren found herself with a palpable lump in her throat when an image of Rose flashed across the screen. Her sister's thick brown hair flew resplendent, her blue and white Ronaldo Casillas jersey flapping in the wind as she executed a perfect, slow motion bicycle kick. The scene then shifted to a wide shot of Rose, dressed in a beautiful gossamer gown, dancing before a towering fountain beneath a diamond-studded, sable night sky. The expression on her face was one of unabashed joy.

When it was over, everyone applauded enthusiastically. The conversation level picked up, and there was an air of excitement that had not been there before. Everyone was visibly emotional and could not wait for the debuts, which Askr Ashe informed them would be occurring all over the world the very next month.

While everyone was still gushing about how excellent it had all been, and Askr Ashe was indulgently reveling in the copious praise, the door to the hallway opened. A peculiar looking little man came in with obvious reluctance. He was Asian of some extraction, but was otherwise nondescript in his build and his features. What really stood out to Koren, however, were his clothes. They were garishly mismatched.

If the University of Florida had a collegiate math team their uniforms might have looked like the outfit the man was wearing. Thick, black-framed glasses made his eyes look tiny and his hair was unkempt and askew. However, what was especially noteworthy were his bright blue button-down shirt and vividly orange pants.

He scanned the crowd nervously. When his eyes fell on Askr Ashe, who was engaged in a laughing conversation with the Latin couple in Spanish, the man strode across the room with his head down. He pulled insistently on Askr's sleeve and then whispered something in his ear.

Askr's smile faded, and he nodded gravely. Then the man with the disheveled and mismatched clothes spun on his heel to stalk from the conference room as quickly as he possibly could without actually running. Mr. Ashe dinged on his champagne glass once more, and the low hum of conversation fell silent.

"I'm very sorry," he began with a dramatically disappointed expression on his face. "But something has come up dat I simply must deal with. However," he made a great show of brightening. "You all are welcomed to stay and eat and drink and converse as long as you'd like. We are doing something very marvelous here – something truly worthy of celebration, and I hope you will all take full advantage! I think Amy is actually going to fire up da karaoke machine in a few minutes, and I hope you all enjoy. Thank you for your strength and patience, and I bid you fondly adieu."

Then he set his glass down and stalked from the room almost as fast as the nameless messenger.

"I wonder what it could be?" Koren wondered aloud. "Is something wrong?"

However, the din of animated conversations around her was too loud for anyone to hear her. Her father, who had obviously been heavily indulging in the Champaign, was loudly proclaiming what an excellent singer his little girl was, so despite vociferous protest, a mortified Koren soon found herself frog-marched to the front of the room to perform a Jonas Perry song her dad always insisted she sing. After that harrowing humiliation, she could hardly wait to go home, but everyone was nice and complimented her on what a fine effort it had been.

A couple of other people took turns, which actually made her feel less embarrassed. Then the dark skinned girl (whose name was Bindi, it turned out) insisted they sing a pop song together that was popular in her home country of Australia. It was one that Koren did not know, so she struggled with the unfamiliar lyrics, but had to admit it was actually kind of fun. After it was over, she and Bindi exchanged texts with promises to stay in touch.

The party lasted about another hour after that, but then her mother insisted sternly to her increasingly inebriated father that it was *definitely* time to go home. Koren's dad protested half-heartedly, (more as if it was something he was expected to do than because he really wanted to stay) and fell asleep almost as soon as he plopped himself down on the plush leather seats of the long, black limousine. Koren's mother pulled a half-finished romance novel from her purse and began to read. The ride home was silent.

Koren was quiet too, but not because she was thinking about her embarrassing and infuriating parents. She stared out the window of the limo lost in thought about the coming reality show. Maybe it *was* all just typical showbiz stuff. What did she know about it anyway? But did she *really* want her private moments with Rose on display for the whole world to see?

She snorted to herself with a rueful laugh. Even if she did not, was there anything she could do about it? It was obvious that Mom and Dad were both sold on the idea. As long as the cash kept flowing so too would the video stream.

Koren turned her thoughts to the Elysian Industries CEO. She wondered what made Askr beat such a hasty retreat. It was probably nothing, she told herself.

Mr. Ashe was a busy man. It honestly could have been anything related to the running of his growing and expanding corporation. She doubted he had much spare time for partying with thirteen year old girls and their parents.

Koren tried to put her concerns out of her mind. She should just relax and enjoy this brief respite of relative inactivity. As soon as 'Love Beyond Death' came out, she was sure to be swamped again.

It was no use though. Koren just simply could not shake the nagging premonition that yet another disaster was about to befall her. Maybe she was being paranoid. Maybe she and Rose could sort it all out together after she got home.

The thought made her feel a little better, but the disquiet would not completely abate.

What on Earth have I gotten myself into? Koren thought with a deep sigh.

It was beginning to feel overwhelming again - like she had bitten off *way* more than she could comfortably chew.

Chapter 15

The Harm Failsafe

Magic Man did not like being out in public. He always felt there were far too many eyes upon him – spying eyes, judging eyes. There was little he required from the outside world anyway. He generally had most of the things he needed delivered - to a vacant apartment two floors up from his, of course – but there were times when he could not avoid venturing out into the world. Today was such a time.

He sat at the back table of a seedy diner drumming his fingers impatiently upon the scarred and scuffed table. He was agitated. He was nervous and more than a little angry at being kept waiting, but he was also excited.

Magic Man did not really have friends per se. One couldn't afford to trust people much past doing what they saw as being in their own self-interest. Most people mindlessly followed anyone whom they either hoped would benefit them in some small way or feared might damage them in some fashion - So quick to conform to the norms of society, so frightened of failing to 'fit in' and being culled from the ignorant herd.

Most people were fools, and Magic Man had no patience or regard for them.

'These poor creatures have no idea how blighted and ghostly this 'sanity' of theirs sounds'... He quoted mentally with a sneer.

The so-called *'normal'* people of the world were just sheep. Normal was nothing more than a synonym for mediocrity. How he hated them… and envied them, knowing he would never be one of them…

He shook his head and focused his thoughts, annoyed with himself for letting his mind wander. In any case, even though there was no one Magic Man would call 'friend', he did have his acquaintances and allies. They were mostly faceless drones from 5kun – unimportant, but occasionally useful people to be exploited and discarded. It was one of these he awaited now.

But every so often, he considered, *once in a lifetime perhaps, someone special comes along like a rare and precious gem - someone of greatness who seeks the immaculate vision rather than accept the grim realities of 'mortal existence.*

Magic Man saw himself as one of these – a dream seeker, an artist, a visionary!

Koren Johnson is another, he thought.

She was an excellent person - the perfect complement to his being. She was a kindred spirit, who had overcome the grey, cold world of conventional knowing and believing and proven them all lies. She had embraced the dream like the shining Dionysian revelers. Koren had rejected the most quotidian of human conditions, in fact. She had rejected death itself and become the first prophet of a new faith. She was a modern day sibyl preaching a new way of being!

Magic Man had no shortage of regard for his own unique superiority, but had to admit, Koren Johnson had well and thoroughly impressed him. By rejecting the old gods and religions, by embracing Aaru, Koren was very nearly liberated from this bleak mortal coil... almost... But soon Magic Man would see to it that the process was complete. He would free her from the corporate machine of Elysian Industries and with it the villainous, corrupting influence of plutocrat, Askr Ashe not to mention the plebian chains of Bill and Gypsie Johnson.

Together he and Koren would become something more, something unique - a new and revolutionary architype for languishing humanity to follow. Of this he was certain, for Magic Man was an individual of unique and profound artistic vision. Sweet, innocent Koren would be his ultimate canvass and muse.

"A man in this state transforms things," he murmured to himself, "until they mirror his power — until they are reflections of his perfection. This having to transform into perfection is *art*..." He smiled.

The little bell rang, and Magic Man turned his shaded eyes towards the front door. A lumpy young man in perhaps his mid to late twenties stood apprehensively in the entrance. He was dressed in a dirty black T-shirt with the name of some insipid rock band inscribed on the front. His face was pimply and uncertain as he scanned the nearly empty diner. When the young man's eyes at last fell on Magic Man huddled in the corner, he walked purposefully towards him.

"Hey," he said inanely as he came next to the table. Then he stood in silence.

Idiot, Magic Man thought in disgust and waited a moment longer.

Then he growled in irritation.

"Well?" he said expectantly.

The splotchy rocker looked confused for a minute, before his eyes widened, and he gasped in comprehension.

"Oh yeah!" he said, far too loudly for Magic Man's liking. The young man thought for a moment more, then recited. "Underneath this reality… in which we… in which we live and have our being, another and… altogether different reality lies concealed…" he finished with a slight grin.

Well, this is the one, it looks like.

"You have no idea what that means, do you?" growled Magic Man, tugging his trench coat around himself more tightly.

The young man stared at him blankly for a moment before opening his mouth, but Magic Man rolled his eyes and cut him off.

"Sit," he commanded coldly.

The other man complied.

"So," Magic Man breathed leaning forward in his chair. "Have you brought it?"

"Yeah," the young man said after a noticeable gulp. "It's out in my van… I'll show you where… Um… So, by the way… I guess, Uh… I should call you…" he began with his hand outstretched, but Magic Man cut him off again and remained motionless."

"*Don't* call me," he stated coldly. "And I don't care what you are called either. It's probably better for both of us if we don't know. Let's get this over with. Where are you parked?"

The young man swallowed and gave his head a toss.

"Out back," he stated trying to sound nonchalant, but he was still visibly uncomfortable. "There's a little alley between this place and the old, boarded up department store next door…"

"I'll leave first," said Magic Man. "Wait fifteen minutes and then come out. Order a Coke or something so it doesn't look suspicious…"

With that, he got up, plopped a couple of crumpled bills on the table, and stalked from the dingy restaurant.

As always when he ventured out, it was dark outside and very early in the morning. He preferred these aphotic times when the few prying eyes about could glimpse him only dimly. He walked in the opposite direction the young man had indicated and approached the tenebrous alley from the other side of the block.

He smirked to himself as he saw the outline of the nondescript, white van in the shadows. If this idiot had what he said he had, this would be a major next step. Not the last, certainly, but the puzzle pieces he needed for his ultimate vision would become many, *many* fewer.

He stood behind a rusty dumpster to obscure himself from any passerby who might glimpse him from the isolated back-street. Then he waited… but although he was peerlessly skilled at many things in his own estimation, waiting was not one of them.

Magic Man hated waiting. He preferred the virtual world to what the bumbling "sheeple" who crowded this planet like so many mindless cockroaches referred to as the "real" world. In the virtual world his needs and demands were met instantaneously. He would live there all the time if he could.

Perhaps that time is coming soon, he thought with another half-smile.

He briefly considered pulling out his phone, but decided against it. The glow of the screen might give him away. Still, he indulged in a brief erotic daydream about the gracile and seductive Koren Johnson of his doctored photograph to pass the time, so he was actually slightly annoyed when the cretin van driver appeared in the alley from the other end and hailed him.

"Hey, Dude!" he hissed out in a poor imitation of a whisper. It echoed off the brick walls of the narrow alley like thunder. "Over here!"

Magic Man rolled his eyes and stalked toward the young man. He grabbed the front of his black T-shirt and threateningly pulled his face close to his own.

"Shut… Up…" Magic Man spat in a low and threatening voice. "The whole point of meeting like this is to avoid notice. That goal is significantly compromised if you run screaming down the street!"

He released the pimply man who jerked away, smoothing his shirt offendedly where Magic Man had grasped it.

"Jesus, dude!" he protested. "What the *Hell*?!"

"Do you want to get paid or not?" Magic Man interjected. "Let's get this done. I want to see it."

The van driver looked not the least bit less offended, but he calmed down enough to stalk toward the rear of the van and throw open the back doors. Then he pulled a stained red blanket from where it was covering something on the floor.

Magic Man's eyes grew wide at what he glimpsed beneath the vermillion shroud. He reached towards it.

"Now, wait a minute, Dude," the chunky rocker exclaimed, stepping in between Magic Man and his prize. "Paws off 'til I get paid!"

Magic man regarded him stonily.

"If I can't look it over and prove to myself that this is what you say it is," he acidly rejoined, "I'm not paying you *shit*!"

The young man was reluctant, but moved out of the way.

"Fine, whatever" he said. Then he added defiantly, "you just... You just better have my money, is all!"

"You'll get your money," Magic Man muttered distractedly, his attention focused on the dark shape in the floor of the van. "As long as it's legit..."

He pulled a pin light from the folds of his trench coat to get a better look.

"And where did you say you got this?" He asked as he turned the object this way and that. Then he frowned. "It's broken..."

"Yeah, well... Friend of mine used to work for Elysian Industries as a delivery guy," the other man said with a nervous stutter, clearly having hoped that Magic Man would not notice the damage. "He got in a wreck, and this fell out. He didn't latch the door on the truck right or somethin'. They made him go back to the loading dock to give it back and file some paperwork saying he returned it, but then they fired his ass, so before he left he shoved this in a box and took it home. He owed me money, so I took this and called it even. I thought it looked pretty cool, but when I got it home I realized it was broken so... I just figured I'd try to get rid of it and make a few bucks..."

The more Magic Man looked over the object, the more he was sure it was real. Yes, the shape was right – kind of a white plastic box, helmet-shaped with part of one side cut out. All the ports seemed to line up with what he'd seen from the schematics he liberated from the Elysian Industries computer system. All the red, yellow and green lights seemed to be in their proper places.

He smiled, and his eyes lit up behind his sun glasses.

This thing is real.

"You done lookin' yet, or what?" The other man asked impatiently. "Make with the cash!"

"Give me your bank info," Magic Man instructed curtly. "I'll transfer it."

The man grumbled, but climbed into the van's front seat. Then he began rummaging around in the glove compartment. He soon returned with a battered and bent checkbook. The checks looked as if someone had spilled coffee all over them. Magic Man regarded the filthy paper distastefully.

"Just hold it up so I can see the routing number..." he said.

The other man complied then said, "So that's five thousand, right? That's what you said..."

Magic Man pulled his phone out of his coat pocket, but turned so that only he could see the screen.

"Yeah," he answered with an incredulous snort. "That was before I found out it was broken. I can fix it, but it'll be a real pain in the ass. I'll give you two."

"What the fuck!?" the young man exclaimed. "What kinda bullshit is this? How about you go and..."

"Do you want the money or not?" Magic Man interrupted curtly. "You can go try to sell it to someone else, I guess, but good luck. First, it's broken. Also, this isn't something you can just drag into any pawn shop. Almost nobody would even know what it is... Do you?"

The young man cursed a few more times, but finally agreed, "Fine, two thousand, you greedy bastard. Just hurry it up so I can get the Hell outta here. You're majorly starting to creep me out."

"The feeling is more than mutual, I assure you..." Magic Man replied wryly.

Just then, there was a buzz from the van driver's front jeans pocket.

"There you go."

Magic Man stuffed his phone back into his pocket. He picked up the helmet-shaped device, stuffed it up under his trench coat, and walked back up the alley toward the side street.

"Let me know if you come across anything else like this," he called over his departing shoulder. "You know how to find me..."

The young man was staring down at his phone.

"Yeah... yeah, Dude... Sure" he replied absently. Then he muttered under his breath. "Fucking weirdo..."

Magic Man heard him, but did not care.

The noble type of man, he thought with a sneer, *regards himself as a determiner of values. He does not require to be approved of. He passes the judgment.*

The van driver was a imbecilic plebe who was incapable of appreciating his greatness, and Magic Man was done with him. He had what he came for, and now he could barely wait to get it home.

So now I've got the key in, he thought to himself in satisfaction.

He walked down a few more twisting alleyways until he came upon a narrow vacant lot stuffed between two crumbling buildings. A late-model, black Ford Granada was parked there in the darkness. Magic Man quickly loaded his prize into the back and climbed into the driver's seat. He took a moment to once again appreciate his masterpiece there on his phone's wallpaper and ran a lascivious finger over the obscene image. He kissed it before firing up the engine. Magic Man drove off into the gloom determined and resolute.

It's time to open the door.

***

Rose sat by the side of the river dangling her bare feet in the cool, crystalline water. The effulgent sun sparkled and gleamed brilliantly off of the little waves and splashes she made with her toes. She gazed out at the frantic activity on the other side with a sigh.

What had once been nothing but empty, grassy plains were now teaming with activity. New mansions were popping up by the dozens, and excited new Residents bustled here and there. The sky was thick with them.

There was still plenty of space, of course. Aaru was so vast as to be virtually infinite, but Rose could not help experiencing a bit of a pang. It didn't feel like it was just hers anymore. She was a little ashamed of herself for the uncharitable thought, but the persistent sentiment was there nonetheless.

There were enough cicerones now that Rose only had to greet new arrivals if she felt like it, and she did so fairly often. It gave her no small sense of felicity to see the delight, even ecstasy, on the faces of the new Residents as they realized they were no longer ill, or old, or hurting – that they were alive like they had never dreamed possible before. It was wonderful to experience their joy vicariously, but... she did not really feel like it today.

Rose was troubled.

She could not help dwelling on her conversation with Auset. She was glad her words had made the other girl feel better. However as she turned her friend's concerns over in her head, the more those same fears and uncertainties kept intruding to needle her own troubled thoughts.

Adding to this unease, Rose still hadn't heard from Koren. Her sister was extremely busy these days, she knew, but Rose could not help feeling anxious about her continued absence. She wished Koren would call. It had been far too long.

There was a growing sensibility within her being - nagging and urgent, yet not fully developed. Some interminable cloud had cast a shadow over her heart, so that the shining immaculately of Aaru's inexhaustible days of perpetual summer felt muted and somber somehow. The sun did not feel as bright, nor did the sky appear as pristinely blue. The emerald splendor of the gently wind-rustled grasses seemed faded and wasting. Even when she was with her friends, her laughter felt forced, and their play seemed dull and trite.

She could not articulate any specific reason why. Everything she had been told about her recent traumas had been reassuring. By all accounts, everything was now just as it should be. Everything was *fine*, so why did her insides still feel such a roiling, disquieted mess? Rose could not even begin to iterate the emotions welling up inside of her, but neither could she deny them.

Rose had felt so agitated by everything recently that she had even prayed about it – something she hadn't done in years. The last time was just after she had received her terminal cancer diagnosis, in fact. She had prayed her hardest – begged even, down on her knees for hours. She had beseeched the Almighty to fix her and save her from what the doctors all grimly told her would be coming, all to no avail.

She still got sicker. The treatments did not work, and Rose lost hope. She grew to resent God, angrily certain that either He did not exist, or that He simply didn't care. Then she had died only to awaken in Aaru, not at all sure what she should feel about any of it.

Before her cancer, praying was what she had always been taught to do when she was distressed. Though never nearly so devout as her mother, it had been a source of some comfort to her. However, more so now than ever in her whole life before, it just felt like she was talking to herself – like standing in the middle of a very large room, screaming at the top of her lungs, but answered only by the deafening echoes of her own doubt and uncertainty.

"Hey, Pretty Princess," someone called out behind her. "Anybody sittin' here?"

Rose turned toward the voice. It was Franco. He had recently taken to calling her that, and it did not displease her. Unconsciously, her kimono changed into the short, yellow sun dress the Latin boy liked.

"Hey, Franco," she greeted mildly. "Nope, nobody here but me... Feel free. It's a big riverbank."

She smiled, but there must have been something sad in her eyes, because Franco noticed. His broad grin faded, and his handsome face took on a look of concern. He cocked his head to the side.

"What's wrong, Babe?" He asked as he seated himself next to her and put his arm around her bare, narrow shoulders. "What's up? You look upset."

"No," Rose demurred, but it didn't sound convincing even to herself. "Well... yes... I mean... maybe?"

"Oh!" She exclaimed in frustration.

Then she leaned her head heavily against Franco's chest. He seemed a little surprised, but pulled her close just the same. Rose let him hold her while she collected her scattered thoughts. She closed her eyes, indulging in the sensation. It felt good – warm and safe.

"I... I'm not sure what's wrong exactly," she murmured at last into his shirt. "I just feel..." She paused as she searched for an appropriate word. "*Unsettled*, I guess..."

Franco arched a quizzical eyebrow. "Why, Babe? What's up?"

Rose sighed. Then she told him all about what had happened with the corrupted new arrival and her subsequent troubling conversation with Auset. Even now, the more she talked about it, the more she *thought* about it, the more upsetting it all seemed.

"This... This... Isn't Heaven, Franco," she whispered affectedly as she concluded her retelling. Again, Rose was overcome by the amorphous realization that there was something inside her that needed to get out, something that needed to be purged, but for the life of her she could not figure out how to adequately express it.

"But... But we're dead, right?" She went on. "Why didn't we go to Heaven? It can't be because we were *bad*... I mean... This definitely isn't *Hell*... Or maybe we're stuck in between Heaven and Earth somewhere... It's just... Where are we Franco? Are we... are we like *ghosts* or something? *What* are we? I... I just don't know..."

She knew the confusion must be starkly painted across her face. Franco wrapped her in both of his arms. He had no immediate answer for her, but Rose was content to simply remain encircled in the comforting embrace. They stared out across the sparkling river in silence.

After quite some time, Franco looked down at her. He bit his lower lip – an apparent moment of indecision. Then he pulled her up to sit on his lap. Rose did not resist. He hugged her body against his, and Rose would have been happy to completely disappear in his arms.

Franco whispered in her ear.

"You know where we are, Rose," he breathed. "We're in Aaru... Just like I was in Cali before, you know? It's just another place... a different place, but still a place like any other, isn't it?"

"I... I..." stuttered Rose shaking her head in confusion. "I don't know...Not really? Maybe?"

Franco paused considering.

"Well," he conceded. "I guess it's a lot cooler than Pomona..." He chuckled. "I couldn't fly there..."

Rose returned his grin weakly and gave a very slight giggle, but it was a half-hearted effort.

"Yeah," she said. "I guess..."

"Are you sure you told me everything that's up with you?" Franco asked looking Rose over with a critical eye. "There's something else on your mind, isn't there?"

Rose remained silent but Franco smiled broadly. He poked at her ribs playfully.

"Come on, Rose!" he pressed. "You can tell me! Give!"

Rose giggled and squirmed as he tickled her, but still she hesitated.

"It's silly," she muttered at last, and her smile faded.

"If it's making you feel bad, Rose..." Franco murmured. "Then it's not silly."

Rose sighed again, this time in defeat.

"Well," she began slowly. "It's... It's about the last time I talked with my sister... You know?

"She was *really* tired," Rose continued. "I've never *seen* her look so exhausted! I could tell that there was something bothering her, but she said she didn't want to talk about it... I just... I... I really wanted to *hold* her. I wanted to hug her and make her feel better, but I *couldn't* with that damned black window in between us! I can talk to Koren, Franco, but I can't *touch* her. I can't pet her hair and dry her tears like I used to when she was little..."

Her voice cracked.

"I *miss* her..."

Franco nodded.

"I understand, Rose," he replied softly. "I've felt the same way when I..."

He stumbled to a halt and took a deep shuddering breath, obviously affected, but unwilling to cry in front of Rose. He gulped.

"When I, uh... When I talk to my Mama, you know?" He said. "I feel that way too...

"It's funny really," Franco gave a rueful laugh, wiping at his eyes in embarrassment. "She used to try and hug an' kiss on me alla time, and it used to bug the *crap* outta me, ya know? I'd be all like 'Jesus, Mom! Get off'a me! Not in front of the guys!' And now..." He trailed off again.

"Now you'd give anything for just one more?" Rose gazed into his eyes sympathetically then kissed his cheek, a swift light peck. He gave her a tiny, sad smirk.

"Yeah," he said simply.

Rose buried her face in his chest again.

"I always learned," she said softly. "I was always taught that if we were good and followed the Bible, we'd go to Heaven when we die and see all of our friends and family again – like my grandpa who died when I was seven or my Aunt Brigit who passed away when I was nine, but... they're not here! That's *not* where we are... I always thought it would be *God* who sent me to Heaven, but here... Our friends and family will only join us if some guy in a computer lab somewhere decides that they can..."

Her voice cracked, and her eyes grew moist, so she looked away to hide them. She swallowed an uncomfortable lump that seemed to form in her throat. Franco turned her chin with his index finger so that she looked full into his chiseled, brown face. She could feel his warm breath.

"It doesn't feel..." she began, but paused, struggling to find the words and shaking her head helplessly. "It doesn't feel *right*, I guess...

"You know what, Babe?" he murmured, brushing a long strand of brown hair away from her face with the back of his hand. "I've thought about that too a little... It's kinda funny actually." Franco chuckled. "When I was a kid, my mom was always yelling and screaming about Hell – about how if I didn't pray my rosary and go to Confession and all that stuff that I'd be going there, so I never really thought about Heaven much, but..."

He paused, taking an audible, shaky breath.

"But, here in this place," he whispered, and his lips brushed her ear. "Here in Aaru with... with you, Rose... I... I can't imagine... I can't imagine Heaven being any better than this. Sharing all this with you... For me at least... It *is* Heaven... *You* are my Heaven."

He had said just the right thing. His words were like poignant daggers, thrust directly into her chest but sweeter than any candy she had ever tasted. Rose could think of no reply, but her heart was suddenly full – the only thought in her mind was of how dashing Franco was – how devastatingly beautiful. In that moment, the only desire in her heart was to be with him. She craned her neck and pressed her lips against his.

Franco was soon returning her kisses with enthusiasm. She twisted on his lap to face him wrapping her own arms around his neck and her legs around his waist. His hands moved urgently beneath her dress to firmly grasp her bottom and hard, smooth back. Rose's tongue ventured inside his mouth.

Franco's own hungry mouth moved down to her neck and chest. He raised his head but only long enough to steal a few labored breaths. Rose's own breathing was coming more quickly as well.

Her separation from Koren had left her longing to touch someone – to feel the warm embrace of another comforting body, but what she felt now was eminently stronger. She wanted Franco, she realized, wanted him in a way that she had never wanted anything before. The desire for him was powerful - a dull but insistent ache. It was the most intense sensation she had ever experienced - the first thing akin to hunger she had ever known in Aaru. It was an appetence that demanded satiation – an emptiness beseeching to be filled... to be filled with Franco.

He raised her arms to pull her canary dress up over her head while Rose tightened her legs around Franco's waist. She began to rub rhythmically against his body, willing that the two of them should simply fuse together. He bit her neck softly, and she moaned, rocking her hips against his.

Franco gripped her bottom with both, strong hands and suddenly all Rose felt was bare skin. She gasped, but it was not in dismay. She had felt so incomplete recently, like some indiscernible, but vital part of herself was missing. Perhaps she was missing this. She pressed herself more firmly against him, urgent with the desire for completion.

Harm failsafe engaged! Harm failsafe engaged! The impassive computer voice blared in her head.

There was a flash and Rose was suddenly disoriented. She was still sitting on the river bank, but she and Franco were now separated by at least ten feet. It may as well have been a million miles.

Rose had never felt so cut off. Fulfillment had felt *so* close, so attainable! But even that was denied her. She stared at him in confusion for a few moments before it registered fully in her brain that they were completely naked, and the opposing bank of the river was crammed with hundreds if not thousands of new Residents.

Rose squealed in dismay, throwing her arms across her body in a reflexive, but futile effort to cover herself. Her face flushed brilliantly red. The roaring passion of just a few moments earlier was extinguished. Blazing desire was replaced by overwhelming embarrassment.

The fact that Franco continued to stare at her with his eyes wide and mouth agape, only made it worse. It made her humiliation seem that much greater. She leapt to her feet and put both hands over her mouth. She could feel tears spilling down her cheeks.

"R... Rose?" Franco stuttered apprehensively. "Rose... I... I don't... "

He stood, smooth brown skin still bare. He stretched out his arms to her.

"R… Rose…" he stammered again. "I… I… What? It just…"

Rose slammed her kimono back into place, covering every inch of exposed skin. Then she shot into the sky, leaving Franco alone and spluttering on the riverbank.

"I'm sorry, Rose!" He cried after her. "I didn't mean… I'm sorry!"

Rose did not pause. She streaked across the azure firmament as fast as she could. She did not even really know where she was going. She just knew that she wanted to go away – go away and hide somewhere, to be in actuality as isolated and alone as she felt emotionally. Rose yearned for nothing more strongly than a hole in the ground where she could cover herself up with earth and disappear for a thousand years.

She chose a bare plot of grassy Aaru plain and hurtled towards it. Rose hit the ground with a huge spray of rocks and dirt. She forced a towering mound of obsidian stone up though the grassy turf in a spectacular eruption of mud and sediment. Then she grasped the side of it with both hands and forced the rock apart, until she had opened a small cave. She quickly threw herself inside and erected an iron gate behind her. Then she collapsed onto the dusty ground and wept bitterly into her sleeves.

All of the chaos of emotion that had been roiling around within her recently seemed suddenly unbearable. Was it shame at what she had almost done? Her parents would have been *furious* with her if they found out. Was it frustration at being so unexpectedly interrupted? Was she being a bad person for wanting… *that*… so intensely? Is that why she was here and not in Heaven? Why couldn't she just hug her sister again?!

Suddenly, Aaru seemed no longer wondrous and beautiful. It no longer felt magical. It simply felt foreign and strange and she irreparably severed from everyone and everything she had ever known.

And what *had* happened just at the moment her desire was about to be fulfilled? What had stopped them? Was that God stepping in? Was He as mad at her as she was at Him? Where was He in all of this? Was He even there at all? Why did it all make her feel so desolate? Then came another aghast thought.

Franco…

What had she done?! She had acted absolutely *insane*! First, Koren was effectually lost to her, accessible only through a cold, lifeless screen and now… Franco was sure to hate her. Why had she left him like that – naked and abandoned on the side of the river?

Rose threw back her head and wailed her misery before again burying her face in her sleeve. She did not know how long she lay there sobbing, but it must have been quite some time. It was long enough that her wracking lament quieted to a hiccoughing snivel. Rose did not think she had ever felt so low in her entire life.

"Rose?" Came a quiet voice from beyond the gate.

"Go away…" moaned Rose miserably.

"I am sorry, Rose," apologized the musical voice sympathetically but firmly, "but I will not do that."

There was a loud screech of twisting of metal. A few seconds later, Rose started as a gentle hand was laid upon her quivering shoulder. She opened a red-rimmed eye to glimpse Princess Hana seating herself in *seiza* position beside her. She rubbed Rose's back.

"Tell me, Rose," she soothed. "Tell me… What troubles you? I will do my best to fix it. I heard the alarm go off, but by the time I arrived, no one was there…" Her eyes narrowed. "If something of Mikoto's has upset you again, I shall be quite cross with him…"

"No… Hana…" Rose gulped her words. "Nothing… like… that…"

"What then, Dear One," Hana pressed. "You can tell me… Please?"

"I was on the riverbank… with Franco…" Rose began in a high, wretched voice. It was all she could do to understand her own pinched words. "And I was sad… so… so we kissed… And we started to… We almost… Then… the alarm… And I was… n… n… naked! I was *so* humiliated! I don't know what happened!!!"

Hana's eyes flashed. The electrically charged thundercloud Rose remembered from her last encounter with Mikoto reappeared over her head.

"Did Franco attack you, Rose? Did he try to hurt you? Is that why the alarm went off?"

Rose shook her head violently.

"*No!!!*" she wailed loudly. "It was *me*! It was all *my fault*! I wanted him to… I wanted to… It was the first time I…"

She buried her face in her hands again, certain that the shame of it all would crush her.

Hana shook her head helplessly.

"I'm sorry, Rose," she apologized perplexedly. "I don't understand…"

Rose raised her head and met Princess Hana's gaze with a ferocious glare. Her eyes were bloodshot, and tears had cut vivid tracks through the dust on her cheeks.

"I… wanted… him…" Rose gasped, though saying it out loud only intensified her mortification. "I *wanted* wanted him!"

Then she collapsed into a weeping heap once more. Hana gasped in comprehension.

"Now…" Rose wept miserably. "Now, I've gone… and… ruined… everything. Franco's… gonna… *hate*… me! God… hates me!" Then she trailed off into incomprehensible blubbering.

Hana tried to gather Rose to her. The younger girl resisted at first, but Hana was insistent. Rose ultimately let the Flower Princess pull her close. She buried her face in Hana's shoulder, and the princess stroked her hair, letting Rose cry herself out.

At last Hana sighed.

"I'm afraid I find myself apologizing to you all too often, Rose…" she murmured sadly, "but once again I am sorry…"

Rose sniffled and looked up in surprise. "What could *you* possibly be sorry about?" She asked. "I'm the one who…"

"Hush, Rose," Hana shushed her then sighed again – a little more deeply this time. "I'm afraid this is all part of the burden of being a Veda…"

"I d… d… don't understand…" Rose quavered.

"As a Veda," Hana explained, "you have many privileges most other Residents do not. You are the first – the chosen. You guide the new Residents and help the Lords and Ladies oversee their respective domains."

Rose nodded. She knew all of this already of course. Hana had explained it to her long ago.

"But," Hana went on, "do you recall that I told you that Aaru was a *new* place? A good place?"

Rose nodded again.

"Well…" continued Hana. "Please recall also that I did not say it was a *perfect* place… At least, not yet… The other role of the

Vedas – the *most* important role - is to help us find the flaws in Aaru and make it better… more perfect… for the other Residents."

Rose sniffled, but continued to listen.

"This was… perhaps… just such a situation…" she shook her head. "I *told* Kapoor it wasn't just physiological…" She sniffed derisively, shaking her head.

Hana had muttered the last to herself so Rose had difficulty hearing her. The statement meant nothing to her.

"In any case, Rose," She took a deep breath, and her tone became more business-like. "Before you and the other Vedas came, we were not exactly sure what Those Who Come After would…" she seemed to struggle for the appropriate words. "Would… Bring with them… We knew that Residents would retain much of their old lives and personalities here, but we did not know quite *how* much. After all, human beings are physical as well as cerebral and many would argue spiritual creatures, but Residents no longer have a body in the conventional, corporeal sense. Here your body is only what you think it is or what you want it to be, so we did not exactly… account for… the… the sorts of feelings that you just had.

"In usual circumstances," she explained. "Should someone try to… get… as close to you… as Franco apparently did, the system assumes that they mean you harm… It sounds quite foolish now that I say it to you out loud, I know, but… I'm sorry."

Hana gently disentangled herself from Rose and then pressed her pretty nose to the ground in fervent apology. She met Rose's eyes seriously.

"As for your other concern, I am Japanese," she stated as she sat up straight again. "So perhaps I am not the best person to comment on exactly what your God thinks about you or expects from you, but I believe, Rose, that you are a rare and excellent person. Otherwise you would not have been chosen to be a Veda. There was *nothing* wrong in what you felt with Franco, Rose. It is a natural and normal part of all of humanity. All of us had such feelings in our lives Before, but in the absence of… shall we say physical and biological processes… We did not expect those feelings to be brought along here. I think perhaps we forgot the emotional component, which is all up here…" She tapped Rose's left temple softly with her index finger and then her chest just above her left breast. "…And here. It hasn't ever really come up before, but then again, it could just be because there are still, relatively at least, so few Residents...

"You should not feel guilty, Rose," she said adamantly and took both of the sorrowful girl's hands in her own. "I am *so* very sorry that you were embarrassed. That should *never* happen to you here, but if it's any consolation, you have rendered us *valuable* service. Incidents like these will allow us in time to make Aaru the perfection we first envisioned..."

Rose sniffled and wiped her eyes with her sleeve. She did not quite understand everything that Hana was saying, but it gave her pause. She did not feel as deviant or crazy as she had just a few moments ago.

Again she craved very intensely to talk to Koren. Rose wanted her sister to give her a hug and tell her everything was alright. She wanted...

She wanted something that she would never be able to have ever again, and it was devastating to realize. Then she thought once more of Franco's poor, apologetic face as he stood naked and stuttering on the riverbank, and she could not hold the tears at bay.

"It will be alright, Rose," Hana soothed. "Everything will..."

"I... want... my... sister!" Rose sobbed. "I... want... her to... hug me! And Franco's gonna... be so... mad at me! I don't wanna... be here anymore, Hana! I want my parents and my school and my old friends...I wanna go home, Hana! I wanna go home!!!"

Hana pulled her close and kissed her cheek.

"You know that cannot be, Rose," she murmured softly. "I know it's hard now, but this will be your new home. We shall make it a *wonderful* place for you and be your new family *until*," she emphasized the last word. "Until your sister and your father and mother and *all* of those from your life Before join you here. We have promised this to them and to you. This separation... It is painful, I know, but it is not forever... *And...*"

Hana squeezed Rose's hands more tightly.

"*And* I have spoken *long* with Mikoto," she assured. "Franco can speak of little besides you with him. My partner finds it most annoying to be sure." She smiled sardonically.

"I find it most unlikely that Franco could *ever* hate you, Rose. Like you, I am certain he was just surprised and confused. I will speak with him and explain things. You need not worry. He likes you *very* much..."

Rose sniveled for another few moments, but then wiped her face with her sleeve and took a deep, quivering breath. She finally felt a little calmer. The feelings of panic and self-reproof were receding.

"Let me help you a little," Hana offered.

She waved her hand, and Rose's face was clean and freshly painted again. Her hair was once more perfectly arranged with not a strand out of place. The dirt and soil fell away from her beautiful kimono.

"Now, let's get you out of here," Hana continued, pulling on Rose's arm and leading her out of the dark and gloomy cave. "I think you'll feel better if we take you back to your mansion… back into the sun. Perhaps, we could have a piece of cake and some tea. Doesn't that sound nice?"

Rose nodded, but had to admit, cake was not the first need weighing on her mind. She was *burning* to talk to Franco. Rose felt nearly frantic to throw herself at his feet and tell him how sorry she was. However, her need to see Franco was tempered by the mortification she knew she would feel when she did meet with him again. She allowed herself to be led, feeling far too drained from all of her crying and too confused by her raw emotions to offer any protest.

When they arrived back at Rose's mansion, she was surprised to find both Runa and Auset waiting on her at the gates with very concerned expressions on their faces. They both asked quite charitably what was wrong, but Rose didn't feel up to talking about it, and said as much. The other girls respected her privacy and let the matter drop, but they were both clearly worried.

Hana stayed with them for a short while, but soon excused herself after a single cup of steaming chamomile tea. Runa and Auset did their best to cheer her up, and Rose certainly appreciated the effort, but truth be told did not feel very much like being cheered. She ate her cake (it was Runa's creation and quite unsurprisingly was a white cake with what looked to be coconut icing) and drank her tea. She tried to at least smile politely at the silly jokes and stories they told her.

Before they left at last, they both hugged her. The platinum blonde Netherlander gave her a swift peck on the cheek, and Auset squeezed her like she might never let her go, but Rose assured them both she would be fine. When at last they were gone, Rose settled herself on the living chair in her garden and decided to watch the sunset. She waved her hand across the sky and the brilliant blue firmament ignited into radiant oranges, pinks, and reds which then faded to subdued blues and purples. She sipped at another cup of piping liquid, letting the calming heat and steamy bouquet envelope and relax her as she watched the stars wink into view one by one.

Then at last she felt the call.

As always it was undeniable and insistent, but Rose did not need much convincing. After a day like today, it seemed like a godsend. She could barely wait to talk to her sister.

Rose leapt into the sky, her weary brain full of things she needed to sort out with Koren. Maybe her sister would have some advice about how to talk to Franco. It was all such a mess, but surely, *surely* Koren could help her make sense of it all. Rose's heart was heavy, but hopeful as she streaked toward the black window.

Chapter 16

I'm Your Biggest Fan

Koren was wearing a very tight, very short, red dress and heels so high she was honestly starting to get a little bit of vertigo. All around her, cameras flashed and paparazzi begged her to look their way. She smiled and blew kisses. She waved, posed, and flirted just as she had been trained to do. Here and there she stopped to sign autographs for adoring fans.

This premier party was a big deal, Koren had been told. Everybody who was anybody would be here. After walking the red carpet tonight, all the stars in the sky (or at least the ones in Orange County presently) would gather to watch the first episode of 'Love Beyond Death' and then clamor to meet the intriguing Koren Johnson. Among the great and the beautiful, Askr had sworn it was the hottest ticket in town.

He seemed a little put out with Koren's lukewarm reaction. It was clear he felt she was not nearly as excited as she ought to be. Koren could not deny it however, rather than feel anticipation at hobnobbing with people she had only ever seen on TV and in the movies, she instead felt apprehensive.

The party was being held at a lavish Los Angeles estate Askr said had been purchased by Elysian Industries specifically for Koren's own private use whenever she was working in L.A. (something he said would be more frequent in coming months as offers for Koren to do commercials, television appearances, and even movies began to pour in). It was *her* house now, she had been told, and this was the very first time she had ever been there. Before stepping out of the limo tonight, she had never even seen pictures of it.

Koren felt lost in the midst of the frantic photographers and rabid fans, held back only by flimsy velvet ropes. As she made her way toward the gates of her new mansion, she could not help but notice a disturbance on the other side of the wide, palm-lined avenue. It appeared to be another crowd of zealous, screaming people, but these did not seem to be quite as positively disposed as the smiling fans and would-be groupies.

She could not make out their words, but here and there she could pick out an angry face, a shaken fist. Then she saw someone; a middle-aged, suited gentleman, facing the assembly. He had his back to her. He was giving an impassioned speech through a blaring megaphone. At this distance, it just sounded like incomprehensible noise, but the sentiment was glaringly plain.

Koren caught sight of a painted sign that read "Stop Fighting God!" and another that said, "We Must All Appear Before the Judgment Seat of Christ!!!" She creased her brow curiously as security guards gently guided her down the carpet toward the walled compound. She leaned in toward one of them – an enormous, bald, black man who had introduced himself to her before their departure from the airport simply as D.

She placed her hand on his bicep, which was so massive compared to her own tiny hand that it made it look like a baby had grabbed a normal person. He started at the unexpected contact, but leaned in towards her.

"D," she began quizzically. "Who are those people over there?" She pointed across the street.

"You don't worry about them none, Miss Johnson," he replied in a voice as cold and deep as the ocean. "Those people are crazy. We won't let 'em anywhere around you. Don't think about it no more." He flashed a grin to reveal teeth completely encased in gold. "We'll keep you safe."

Koren nodded, but did not fail to notice that D had not really answered her question. Still, she kept smiling, waving, and shaking hands. She took a pink autograph book from a young lady who could not possibly have been any older than her and signed it as the girl squealed and waved a Koren Johnson doll in her face.

"I love you, Koren!" She screamed at the top of her lungs.

Koren handed the autograph book back with a friendly smile. In doing so she brushed the girl's fingers with her own. The teenager held her hand aloft, screaming and hopping up and down as if Koren had just handed her a million dollar bill. It was surreal. Why should this girl, who might not have looked at her twice if they attended the same middle school last year, go to pieces over just touching her hand?

She smiled again and waved then continued on down the line signing more books, pictures, and magazine covers as she went. A gloved hand pushed a folded scrap of paper towards her. Koren took it automatically, but then gasped and took a step back.

The man who had given her the note was quite a bit taller than her, and rather resembled a homeless person. In spite of the fact that it must have been nearly eighty degrees he wore a heavy black trench coat. His eyes were covered with wide, black sun glasses, and the rest of his face obscured with a black and grey-speckled beard. Koren swallowed nervously then raised the silver Sharpie Askr had handed her just before stepping out of the limo to the folded paper. She signed it and handed it back, but instead of taking the paper, the man seized her narrow wrist.

"We love life," he said intensely, staring directly into her eyes over the top of his sunglasses. "Not because we are used to living, but because we are used to loving..."

He pushed the paper back towards her.

"Hey! That's enough, dirt bag!" Exclaimed D, rushing over to give the cloaked stranger a rough shove. "Back off, freako!"

The man sneered at D. Then he bowed slightly before receding back into the crowd. D bustled Koren quickly down the red carpet.

"Sorry, folks!" He barked in his deep, grim register. "Miss Johnson's got things to do! That's all for now!"

There were some disappointed groans, but Koren did not have long to consider them. D escorted her quickly through the gates to the opulent estate, and the door clanged shut behind them. D marched her across the grounds, but once they were inside the house, he glared at her sternly. Koren swallowed. She could not help feeling like she was in trouble.

"Now, Miss Johnson," he stated firmly. "You gots to be careful with the weirdos and the crazies. Look, it's my job to take a knife or a bullet for you if I have to, but I'd rather you just stay safe. If some crazy man walks up to the barrier looking like he just stepped out of a horror movie with his hand out, in the future you might think about skipping him over for autographs... Just sayin'..."

Koren swallowed and nodded. She could hardly argue. Something about that man had felt... *off* somehow. Something felt wrong, though she could not say exactly what it was. There was something in his demeanor - his quiet fervor... his unnatural intensity - that frightened her, to say nothing of his nonsensical, cryptic words.

She noticed that she was still holding the folded piece of paper the strange man had handed her, but did not have long to contemplate it. Askr Ashe and Miss Hanasaka along with her beauty team quickly had her corralled and stomping up the grand staircase to change clothes before her guests started to arrive. She shoved the note in her gold-sequined purse without another thought.

*

Once she was away from the crowd in the relative peace of the make-up chair, Koren had a little time to catch her breath. The women who saw to her person were unusually upbeat, talking animatedly about all of the stars who were expected to be in attendance that night. Miss Hanasaka rubbed Koren's shoulders and whispered in her ear about how great she had been on the red carpet, how exciting it all was, and how much fun she was sure Koren was going to have until Koren could not help but be caught up in their infectious energy. She realized that she honestly was at least a little bit excited about meeting some of the celebrities who would be in attendance.

However, Koren felt totally out of her depth once the party actually got started. There was another short speech from Askr Ashe, and then he showed the sneak peek premier, first episode of "Love Beyond Death" to thunderous applause. After that, the whole affair was a blur. Even though she probably shook nearly a hundred hands in addition to returning almost the same number of light hugs and Parisian variety cheek kisses, Koren could hardly claim to have really "met" anyone.

The music was loud and pulsing. She did her best to chat with the steady stream of important people who filed up to her in a never-ending line, but found it remarkably difficult to hear anything they said. After about an hour that felt like nothing but a chaotic blend of mute moving lips overlaid by a deafening cacophony of pulsing bass, Koren decided she had had enough and managed to steal away from Askr and Miss Hanasaka's side to take a few minutes and catch her breath out on a wide outdoor balcony.

The night was warm and the sky clear. A few stars winked in the heavens above, though most were bleached out by the blinding LA city lights. She took a deep breath and laid her head on the rail wearily.

Koren looked beautiful, of course. In addition to the screamed, yet indiscernible conversations, there had been countless pictures. It seemed that every star in Hollywood wanted their own personal Koren Johnson selfie, and Mr. Ashe had not failed to predict it. He had been determined she be at her absolute most photogenic tonight.

Koren was actually beginning to wonder if Askr had been denied dolls as a child. If that was true, he was certainly attempting to make up for lost time as an adult with her. He was ever engrossed in the color and cut of her dresses, the style of her jewelry, the height of her shoes, and the shape of her hair...

She was not complaining about how he had her dressed, really. The shimmering, pearl-embroidered evening gown she wore was tasteful, but sexy. It left her shoulders bare and exposed an alluring portion of porcelain chest, without the neckline diving too terribly low. The platinum and diamond necklace and earrings she wore were simple but beautiful as was the matching tiara that her stylist had skillfully woven into her blonde hair. She was dressed like a princess at the royal ball, in fact!

What girl doesn't dream of this? Koren thought a trifle guiltily. Maybe she was just tired.

Koren had considered, albeit briefly, mentioning how she felt to her parents – her continued misgivings – but quickly decided against it. Ever since her dad had quit his job at the garage, he had been distant. He did a lot more sitting around than she ever remembered him doing before, and was almost always holding a bottle.

By this point in the evening Bill Johnson was most likely too drunk to understand her anyway, and her mother would simply say; "Count your blessings! That's just the way they do things in showbiz, Sweetie! Why don't you try to enjoy it a little? That necklace you got on costs more than our house!" or something similar.

There was no point in wasting her breath. She could read her parents like painted signs. *They* wanted this and were determined to turn a deaf ear to any complaint, but she could hardly begrudge them.

Her whole life she could remember what a struggle it had been to pay the bills. That was true even before Rose got sick. She had memories of screaming arguments over money before she was really old enough to understand what her parents were talking about. To Bill and Gypsie Johnson, all of this sudden celebrity and affluence must seem a godsend – the answer to long neglected prayers. She sighed. Koren just really wanted to talk to Rose.

Things had just been *so* busy lately! Every time she thought she might get half a minute to herself, every time she seated herself on the end of her bed in preparation for a long overdue conversation with her sister, some other necessity would pop up and demand her time. Very often it was public appearances or private meetings with the Aaru Board. Sometimes it was yet another fitting or photo shoot, but no matter what it happened to be, it was beginning to feel like the whole world was conspiring against her to prevent her from seeing Rose.

The door to the balcony opened behind her and the pounding music of the party briefly became deafening. Then the door clicked closed and the thunderous music changed once more to something dull and distant.

"Hey there," a smooth, carefully practiced voice floated to her from behind.

Koren lifted her head and turned towards it. Her eyes widened, and she gasped. It was a face she must have seen a million times - a beautiful, beautiful face that smiled down on her every morning when she got out of bed and every evening as she went to sleep. This time however, it was not her poster.

"You..." she stammered helplessly. "Do you know who you are?!"

The insipid words rolled from her treacherous tongue before she had time to catch them. Koren blushed furiously pink as the *exceptionally* pretty boy grinned at her in response.,

"Wait!" she exclaimed holding up a prohibitory hand. She took a deep breath. "That was a stupid question. *Of course*, you know who you are..." Her face softened and she could not completely prevent her voice taking on a dreamy quality. "You're Jonas Perry..."

The older boy bowed slightly. He was even more beautiful than Koren remembered from her poster – platinum blond hair, a gorgeous face that looked like it was specifically made for inviting glances, and a *very* mature sixteen years old - practically an adult! He was a Capricorn, and had type A-positive blood. His turn-ons were long walks on the beach with 'that special someone' and 'hanging with his friends' while his turn offs were 'posers' and 'haters'. His favorite food was sushi, but he also loved Italian food...

The laundry list of facts Koren had memorized from every Seventeen Magazine article she had ever read about Jonas Perry flooded her brain unbidden. The very idea of actually *meeting* him had always been nothing more than a fanciful daydream, yet here he was, in the flesh. Her favorite teen idol was undeniably standing right in front of her smiling, gorgeous, and talking to *her*!

He was impeccably dressed in an open-collared, pristinely white shirt and sleek black pants. His sleeves were unbuttoned and rolled up to his elbows and he was swirling a tumbler in his right hand filled with a liquid that Koren thought looked a little like apple juice or tea, but was pretty sure it wasn't either of those. He held an identical glass in his left hand, which he extended towards her smiling like a toothpaste advertisement.

"I thought you might like something to drink," he said simply, and tossed his head in the direction of the party they had just left. "It's pretty hot in there..."

Koren took the proffered glass reluctantly but could hardly refuse. She certainly didn't want to act like a little kid in front of her idol. She schooled her features to remain as neutral as possible - as if being handed cocktails by pop stars was something that happened to her every day. After the glass left his fingers however, Jonas ran his free hand through his thick blonde hair, and the whole world seemed to slow down.

He is so *cool!* Koren thought with a sigh.

He heard her of course and chuckled again, which once more brought color to Koren's cheeks. He gave his head a playful toss. She tried to cover her lapse by taking a tiny sip from the glass but gagged instead. Whatever the tumbler held, it was extremely bitter. It took all of Koren's self-control to avoid spewing it all over the super-star's white shirt.

"Yeah, that's me." Jonas Perry spread his hands helplessly, as he flashed yet another winning smile, either not noticing or choosing to ignore Kore's near eruption. "And *you* are Koren Johnson. You're even prettier than in your commercials."

Koren giggled and flushed bright scarlet. Jonas Perry actually knew her *name*! She took another sip to save herself from having to summon a reply. It still tasted vile, but she was ready for it this time and managed to swallow the amber liquid without choking, though it burned all the way down her throat.

"I'm glad I caught you out here," he went on. "I've been trying to meet you all night, but there's been like *a million* people around the whole time. I'm kind of a fan…"

Now, that stole her breath. Koren could summon absolutely no reply at all. In fact, she suddenly seemed to have forgotten every word of English that she had ever learned in her whole life. Jonas Perry was a fan of *her*?!

He stepped near enough that Koren could smell his cologne. She could feel his sweet, vanilla-scented breath on her face. He proffered an elbow.

"Wanna hang out for a while?" He asked. "How about a walk?"

Koren took his elbow wordlessly. She could only nod.

Together they strode arm-in-arm over to the balcony staircase. It led down onto the grounds of the massive complex. They strolled across the grass to a scrupulously well-kept garden and stepped onto the brown, gravel path. Koren's heels were wobbly on the shifting ground, so she paused briefly to take them off.

The sweet bouquet of meticulously cultivated autumn flowers filled the air, and dozens of softly twinkling footlights illuminated the walkway. The scene was dream-like. She could not have imagined this scenario more perfectly if she tried. Koren really did feel like Cinderella at the ball, and could not have asked for a more perfect Prince Charming.

She could think of absolutely nothing to say, but that did not matter because Jonas Perry had no end of things to talk about. He regaled her with tales about his world travels and concerts. He went on about his new album, set to come out around Thanksgiving in time for Christmas. It might have been tedious coming from someone else, but Koren hung on his every word like he was a prophet. She watched his perfect lips move as he spoke and recalled with fresh blushing how many times she had kissed them on the poster in her bedroom at home.

"Yeah," he said with a long, deliberate stretch.

His left arm came to rest around Koren's bare shoulders, and she shivered in pleasure and excitement. Jonas took another long sip from his tumbler glass, and Koren copied the gesture with a grimace at the harsh, astringent taste.

"I'm pretty busy… but then I guess you are too. Ha!"

He laughed suddenly and gave her a squeeze. "Look at me! I'm just talking, talking, talking... I bet I sound like a big, conceited jerk!"

Koren shook her head in vociferous denial, but Jonas Perry continued.

"I haven't asked a thing about you!" he exclaimed with another sparkling smile that made Koren's knees feel like jelly and caused her heart to flutter in her chest.

"Look," he indicated with a sudden jut of his chin. "There's a bench up here. Why don't we sit, and you can tell me about you. I want to know *everything*!"

He took her hand and tugged her forward. When they reached the bench, he sat down and pulled her to sit next to him. Then he turned towards her, crossing one leg over his knee. Jonas Perry draped his right arm across the back of the bench and leaned in close. He gazed into Koren's face with piercing, probing eyes deeper and bluer than the ocean. His expression was one of utterly rapt attention.

"So tell me, Koren," he murmured huskily. "Tell me about the sad little girl on TV... I know the showbiz deal probably better than anybody. How much of that is *really* you?"

Koren was not exactly sure how to answer the question, but was also intensely keen to avoid looking like a complete moron. She bought a little more time with another sip, noting that whatever it was, it was already starting to make her feel a woozy. She opened her mouth to talk, not at all sure what would come out.

"Well," she began softly, folding her hands around the tumbler in her lap and taking a deep breath. "The clips are all real... The ones they show on TV all the time, I mean."

"Did they script very much for you?" Jonas asked. "'Cause I know when I did mine, they were *always* reshooting stuff. Like, first they'd follow me everywhere with a camera crew for like six weeks so I could barely even go to the *bathroom* by myself! Then they'd round everybody up and make us spend *hours* doing additional shoots to fill in gaps with scripted crap – 'connectors' they called 'em. Man, was that a pain!"

"Not yet," Koren confessed. "I've done a bunch of interviews, but so far I haven't had to do anything except go to promotions. A lot of the interview stuff ends up on the show. I will say though that a lot of the time I have no idea where they get the video. A bunch of it, well, most of it in fact, is from times when I'm *sure* no one was around with a camera or anything."

"Well," said Jonas considering. "On the one hand, I guess it's nice that they leave you alone, but on the other..." He paused and made a face. "It sounds a little 1984-ish."

Koren looked at him blankly.

"Sorry," he apologized with a self-depreciating chuckle that Koren thought was just devastatingly cute. "I can be a little bit of a nerd sometimes. 1984's a book... You know... Big Brother is *watching* you! Kinda thing..."

Koren nodded enthusiastically and giggled like what Jonas had just said was terribly clever, and she suddenly understood just exactly what the older boy was talking about, although she really didn't. She took yet another draught to avoid having to respond.

"Still," he conceded. "Mine was a few years ago when I first started to get known, you know, and they can put a camera freaking anywhere today. I even saw one that was smaller than the head of a pen one time!"

"Wow," answered Koren enthusiastically, beginning to feel considerably light headed. "That's really cool. You are *so* smart!"

She felt like a sycophantic idiot as soon as she said it, but could not help herself. Every time he smiled at her she felt as if she had won something. It seemed like it would be the absolutely most wonderful thing in the history of *forever* if Jonas Perry ended up *liking* her... On a magical night like tonight anything seemed possible.

"So, be straight with me." He suddenly became serious and intense. His voice sank to a conspiratorial whisper. "I gotta ask... This whole Aaru thing... Is it seriously legit then? Can you *really* talk to your dead sister like it shows on TV?"

There was something in the way he phrased the question that Koren did not care for, but she dismissed it. She gazed into his sparkling, azure eyes with her most sincere expression.

"Rose is alive," she stated intensely. "She's alive in Aaru. I thought it was all bullsh... All nonsense when they first told me..."

Jonas laughed knowingly. "Yeah, fer sure... I saw that clip unedited on the internet!"

Koren reddened, but went on.

"But I *swear* to you, Jonas," she avowed passionately. "It's all real... Every bit of it! I thought my sister had died, but she came back!" Koren felt herself tearing up a little bit. "She came back to me, Jonas... Now I *believe*. I thought she was dead, but with Aaru I can talk to her any time, just like we always used to before. It's a miracle..."

"Wow," he replied nodding, clearly impressed. "That's pretty crazy..." He shifted on the bench to move a little closer to her. "I just might have to buy a ticket or whatever..."

"So..." he whispered.

Then he paused, upended his drink, and set the empty glass on the bench beside him. Koren quickly copied him though it made her throat burn and her eyes water. Jonas fixed her with an intense stare.

"I like you Koren..."

Koren's heart nearly stopped, and her eyes widened. She had to remind herself to breathe.

"You're pretty cool," he went on. "You know... I said I was a fan, right?"

Koren nodded.

"You can say no if you *want*," Jonas went on. "But... It'd be pretty awesome to see the whole Aaru thing up close... I know it might be kinda personal and everything, but do you think you could show me? Do you think *I* could talk to Rose?"

Somehow another button of his shirt had come undone. Koren hadn't noticed it until now, but was not at all dismayed. She caught herself wondering if he looked the same underneath that shirt as he did on the poster back home. He was so close, and he smelled *so* good!

"Sure," she squeaked at last with a difficult swallow even as she attempted to sound nonchalant. "I think that would be cool. I bet Rose would like to meet you... I could introduce you! The Aaru console should be set up in my bedroom... Wanna go see?"

"In your bedroom, huh?" answered Jonas Perry in apparent interest. "Yeah, yeah... Okay... I think that would be awesome! Sounds perfect!"

He stood up and held out his hand.

"Let's go!"

Koren let his fingers wrap around hers and was immediately aflutter again. He had the *softest* hands! She let him haul her to her feet. Koren wobbled unsteadily, so Jonas put a steadying arm around her waist. That made her feel brave enough, or perhaps just loopy enough, to venture resting her head against his chest as they walked.

"Sure," she whispered closing her eyes in contentment, willing that this spectacular night should go on forever. "Let's go..."

***

Magic Man put the binoculars away, agitated nearly to fury. He paced back and forth as he watched Jonas Perry and Koren Johnson descend the stair from the balcony down into the garden where he had no line of sight. What the *Hell* was that no-talent little turd doing here? Sure, Magic Man had seen the poster on Koren's wall in the bedroom video files he had watched, but he had always explained it away as just more of her youthful naivety. Hadn't she read his note?!

Seeing them together like that, watching that little shit put his hands all over Koren... it made him *explosively* jealous. Maybe he had misjudged the whoring little slut, the philandering *doxy* if an obsequious, brainless, no-talent nothing like Jonas-effing-Perry could so easily deceive her!

He took a deep steadying breath, forcing himself to calm.

No... Wait... he thought quickly.

"'...A struggle in prospect in which our intellect is going to have to take sides...'" he quoted shakily to himself.

He had to think. He could not let his passions rule, or at least not the *current* passion. Magic Man had to let his prime, core passion – the goal of his very existence - take the lead and defeat his jealousy... his weakness. He was nearly frantic as he ripped his phone free of his pocket and tapped the screen alight. He moaned in remorse as he beheld his precious wallpaper – the Koren Johnson of his dreams and his own creation.

"I'm sorry. I'm sorry," he shakily repeated over and over to the phone. "I should not have lost my temper, Koren... That was weakness..."

He knew someone as uncompromisingly perfect as his gentle muse would revile weakness – would reject it, and she would be right to do so. He had to exercise more control. He had to recall his purpose.

"'Why must the preying lion still become a child?'" Magic Man recited the question to himself passionately. Then he gave answer. "'The child is innocence and forgetting, a new beginning, a game, a self-propelled wheel, a first movement, a sacred 'Yes.' For the game of creation, my brothers, a sacred 'Yes' is needed...'"

Koren would be his 'Sacred Yes'.

This was *not* Koren's fault... Poor, sweet, guileless Koren! She was innocent and good. She was a blank canvas of most pristine white, a flawless block of alabaster waiting to be sculpted, key and door both to ultimate creation. This unexpected turn of events was just a manifestation of her perfection, he realized in awe, her unspoilt credulousness. Jonas Perry was taking advantage of her!

Magic Man felt suddenly very ashamed of himself – not a feeling to which he was much accustomed. The unpleasant sensation fired his temper.

It's all that liar and deceiver's fault! He thought, gnashing his teeth in impotent fury and frustration, *but what can I do?*

Then it came to him – *the one thing...* That was the answer. After tireless searching, he believed he had finally found it. Tonight was supposed to merely initiate the preparations leading to its grand bestowal upon a grateful Koren. It was supposed to lead her slowly, tantalizingly into his ultimate triumphant reveal! ...To coax her nearer to him and their joined destiny.

He had intended to tease her a little longer – build up her anticipation before finally presenting her with this attainment on her behalf, and magnifying her appreciation a hundred fold! But he had to be circumspect...

Magic Man had to be flexible. His carefully laid plans were going awry. They would have to change. He would now have to move sooner than he would have liked, but he was sure he was ready nonetheless.

He raised the binoculars again, but the two teenagers were obscured by the towering garden wall. The thought of Jonas Perry alone in the dark gardens with *his* Koren rekindled his ire and he narrowed his eyes with a low growl.

"Game on, Perry..." he muttered under his breath. "But I will be the one to claim Koren as my own in the end... "

He didn't think he would win. He *knew* he would. Magic Man was smarter... clearly *better* than some punk kid with a surgically reconstructed smile and marginal singing talent. This was a setback to be dealt with, but the *'Ubermensch'* would prevail in spite of it.

"No victor believes in chance…" he hissed.

His L.A. setup had been completed yesterday, and he had put the last, vital piece of equipment in place just this morning. Magic Man threw open the door of the rent-a-car parked down a side street across the avenue from Koren's new mansion. He twisted the key in the ignition and peeled away from the curb. It was time to work his magic.

Chapter 17

Interrupted

It took Koren quite a while longer than she was comfortable with to lead Jonas Perry to her bedroom. They aimlessly wandered the halls of the palatial estate for what must have been close to an hour or more. The drink made her head foggy, and she was embarrassed by her inability to navigate her new residence well enough to locate her own, stupid room. It made her feel extremely foolish.

"I'm sorry, Jonas," she apologized in pink-cheeked embarrassment. "I only went there for the first time tonight after the red carpet to get changed…"

The blonde boy laughed.

"That's cool, Koren," he soothed as they encountered yet another dark, dead-end. "I know what it's like right at the beginning - Your agent rushing you here, there, and everywhere… Never sleeping in the same bed two nights in a row… Don't sweat it! I think it's fun just to hang with you… here in the dark…"

He pulled her against himself suddenly. Before she knew what was happening his lips were pressed against hers. They were warm and soft, but strong and insistent at the same time. Again she was breathless. She was abruptly and intensely conscious of the fact that this was *not* the poster in her room. She was really *kissing* Jonas Perry! Koren wilted in his arms.

He released her all too soon.

"Maybe this way?" He ventured gamely, gesturing towards a closed door only visible by the faint halo of light around its stark, straight edges.

"Maybe…" Koren whispered. Her legs felt weak, and she was suddenly concerned that she would not be able to make them work well enough to walk towards the dimly illuminated door.

Jonas pushed the door open and pulled her through behind him both of them laughing. It was just a laundry room but the hallway on the other side looked familiar, and Koren thought she recognized finally where she was.

Her confidence much increased, she took the lead, tugging Jonas up a flight of stairs and down another hallway. They passed a couple of doors, but none of them were right. Then she saw it. Just ahead on the left, she pushed open the door and smiled.

The lights were on. There was a huge, ninety-inch Aaru monitor on one wall identical to the one in her room at home. Her gold sequined purse lay upon the king-sized bed where she had tossed it. Jonas kissed her again.

"This is it..." she whispered, feeling dizzy. "Would you like me to call Rose?"

He flopped heavily on the bed and placed his hands behind his head.

"Sounds awesome!" Jonas encouraged. "Go for it! I can't wait!"

Koren pushed the 'on' button then waited for the system to boot up. When it was ready, she stated her login information.

"Good evening, Koren," the huge monitor said.

Koren pressed the big red connect button.

"Connection ready. Input user please."

"Rose Johnson," Koren stated with a sideways glance at Jonas Perry sprawled casually on her bed.

The loading circle swirled for what seemed like an awfully long time. Then the usually blue screen turned red.

"Access denied," it said. "Connection unsuccessful. The requested Resident is unavailable at this time..."

Koren scowled. She tried again, but got the same error message. She huffed in frustration.

"Aaagh," she growled. "I don't think they've finished setting it up yet... I can't log in. They said they'd have it ready!" She looked down in shame. "I'm sorry..."

Jonas luxuriously stretched out on the large bed.

"Eh," he said unconcernedly. "It happens. Don't worry about it... Rain check then, right?"

Koren nodded silently, feeling miserably chagrined at having disappointed her hero.

"You know, Koren," Jonas ventured idly, propping himself up on one elbow. "These big parties usually go pretty late... until they're early in fact!" He laughed and it sounded like music.

"I could use a little rest..." he said. "Build up my energy for the second half, you know... Would you like to sit with me here for a while?"

He patted a spot beside him.

Koren caught her breath. Her bed seemed suddenly treacherous and forbidding, but Jonas's smile was *so* gentle, his voice *so* soft, she knew that she could hardly go and disappoint him a second time. She nodded shyly and came over to the bed. She sat next to him and he laid his hand on her thigh.

"Could I…" he started. "Could I get a hug?"

What's the harm in that? She thought, and truth be told, she kind of wanted one anyway.

Koren stretched out next to him and wrapped her arms around his torso. He returned the embrace, but when Koren tried to sit up, Jonas did not let go.

"Kiss me goodnight?" he whispered.

It sounded like the perfect end to a mostly perfect evening. She was just glad that he did not seem *too* disappointed about not getting to meet Rose.

Koren complied. She pressed her lips against his, and his grip around her tightened. He rolled over on top of her, and his hand slid up her leg under her silky white dress. Koren was suddenly terrified. Her heart was beating a million miles an hour, and her breath only seemed to want to come in short gasps.

She wasn't at all sure what she should do next, so she just kept kissing him. His tongue played over her lips until she relented and let him explore the inside of her mouth. The hand under her dress grasped her bottom.

The door opened.

"Koren?" came a laborious, slurred voice. "Ya in here, sweetie? We've fired up the karaoke machine. Ever'body's lookin' for y…" It trailed off.

When she raised her eyes, Koren saw a swaying, unsteady figure in the doorway.

"What the *Hell* is going on in here?!"

Koren gasped as her father staggered into the room. He was clearly drunk. Bill Johnson took a very long moment to process the scene then glared blearily at Jonas.

"What'chu think yer doin', boy?"

Jonas' face bore a perplexed expression, and he didn't immediately answer. Koren's father took a few more aggressive, plodding steps into the room.

"Here, son," he slurred belligerently. "I'll give you just one chance… get the Hell out of here, or… or… I'm kickin'… yer ass!"

Koren was mortified. Her mouth worked, but no sound came out. Jonas Perry quickly sat up and did a remarkable job of appearing casual and unperturbed. He cleared his throat, then got off of the bed. He straightened his clothes and casually dropped a scrap of paper on the pillow as he stood.

"Could you call me sometime, Koren?" he asked politely. "You still owe me a visit with Rose, after all." He smiled brilliantly, and Koren melted again.

"I'm gonna count to…" Bill Johnson began, but then tottered in the doorway, overcome by a sudden attack of vertigo. He staggered backwards a few steps then clutched at the doorframe to steady himself. Her dad shook his head to clear it. "To… to ONE!" he shouted.

"I'm sorry if I've offended, Mr. Johnson," Jonas stated with apparent sincerity. He turned to Koren and held his hand up to his ear with his thumb and pinky finger extended. "Call me!" he mouthed. Then he quickly strode from the room.

Koren's mouth fell open in disbelief.

"Da… Daddy!" she stammered.

What right did he have to suddenly meddle in her life now? He'd barely paid her any attention in *months!* Now, all of a sudden he decides to get all fatherly on her and run off the boy of her dreams?

"What do you think you're *doing*?!" she shouted. "We were just…"

Her dad shook his head again.

"Sorry, sweetie," her father apologized with a heavy hand against his temple. "But no way was I gonna let *that* go down…"

He belched loudly and Koren could smell the acrid stench of it all the way across the room.

"We'll talk…" He belched again. "…about it later… But, yeah… You're not callin' *no one*… I'll be needing your phone…"

Then his eyes grew wide and he threw a hasty hand over his mouth.

"Tomorrow… I'm about to puke…" He abruptly made a lurching grab for the trash can.

After, a very noisy and smelly evacuation Bill Johnson lay down in the floor and remained still. Very shortly he was snoring loudly. All Koren could do was stare in disbelief. Had that *really* just happened?

211

How could he treat *Jonas Perry* that way?! Could anything in the whole entire world possibly *be* more humiliating?! Koren thought suddenly of all of those important people dancing and laughing in her house. She thought how it would be if she went back to the party.

What if they *knew* what her father had just done? What would they think? She imagined the eyes of all those famous, beautiful people staring at her. In her tortured vision they would be eyes filled with shock and disgust – heads shaking, eyes rolling. She *absolutely* couldn't go back there!

Instead, Koren rolled over in her bed, put a pillow over her head, and cried herself to sleep, certain that she was going to die of embarrassment.

*

Koren was in a black mood the next morning at breakfast. She did not think she had ever been more furious with anyone in her whole life as she was now with her father - firmly resolved never to speak to him *ever* again. Her mother honestly did not look a whole lot happier.

Gypsie Johnson stared at her bowl of cereal fixedly, hardly acknowledging there were two other people in the room. Koren's dad only sipped at his coffee with one hand. The other held a large bag of ice against his head.

The only sound was the tink and clack of silverware against dishware interspersed with short bouts of chewing and slurping. It was maddening. At last Koren could bear it no longer. She rounded on her father.

"What right did you have to burst in on me last night, reeking of booze and ruin my life!" She demanded. "Jonas will probably *never* want to speak to me ever again!"

"Koren…" her mother growled warningly.

Her father winced at her loud voice. Then he scowled at her from behind his ice pack.

"I was drunk last night," he admitted unapologetically, glancing at Gypsie - apparently including her in his remarks and annoyance as well. "And this may come as a big surprise to you, Koren… I don't get to party with movie stars that often, so yeah… I was trying to enjoy myself!"

"Why were you so rude to Jonas!?" She snapped back. "He was *so* sweet, and last night was *so* perfect until *you* staggered in like a zombie and *ruined* it all! I *really* like him! He was just..."

"Oh, I know what 'he was just'!" Her father interrupted. "Let me explain something to you, Koren. I was drunk. I admit it, but I'll never *ever* be so drunk that I think it's okay for some slick seventeen year old boy to crawl into bed with my *thirteen year old* daughter!"

"Yeah," she shot back was a derisive sniff. "Try fourteen... My birthday was a week and a half ago... Miss Hanasaka gave me a bracelet, and Askr handed me a cupcake in the limo after my third interview that day..."

Her father looked sheepish for a moment and then muttered something about the days running together, but quickly recovered his indignation.

"I'm sorry about that... and you know we'll do something special for you as soon as things aren't quite so hectic, but that doesn't change one whit what that boy wanted!" He shouted. "You are going to have to realize what these boys are looking to get from you, Koren... And in my own house even! You've gotta be less naïve!

"I know a little something about teenage boys like him, Koren. Hell, I *was* teenage boys like him once! I know what they want..."

"*Your* house?" she retorted incredulously. "What did *you* pay for it? You haven't worked in months! It was paid for by *my* endorsements and *my* contract with Elysian Industries! Besides, he's only *sixteen*! That's the same age as Rose, and his birthday isn't even until next year anyway!"

"Well," spat back her father his face flushing bright red, clearly stung by her remarks. "Until you're eighteen, it's *mine* and so are you! And sixteen, seventeen... It doesn't matter! I wouldn't have wanted you doing that stuff in bed with *Rose* either!"

"Bill!" snapped Gypsie severely as Koren gasped at the very idea.

Bill moderated his tone slightly, perhaps realizing that he had gone too far.

"Either way," he stated stubbornly, "you're too young, and he's too old! That's two good reasons for me to step in right there!

"You will probably not believe this either, Koren," he went on stabbing a finger at her accusingly. "But I was looking *out* for you even though you *clearly* don't appreciate it! *That's* my job! I kept you from making a *huge* mistake that could've *ruined* your life! You are *thirteen,*

"Fourteen..." Koren corrected in irritation.

"Fine! *Fourteen* then!" Bill Johnson roared. "But that's still fourteen, Koren! Not thirty-five! You might be all famous now and dress up like a super model every time you go out anymore, and hang out with famous friends who are too good for your red neck, dumb ass ole dad, but you are still *my* little girl and whether you like it or not, I'm going to look out for you! I am *not* going to apologize for kicking out some smooth-talking, horny little turd just lookin' for a piece of..."

"Bill!" warned Gypsie again.

"Well..." Koren's father growled, obstinately crossing his arms but quieting nonetheless. "I'm just *not* is all... She's way too young to be doing... doing *that* with a boy!"

"Jonas is *really* nice, Dad," Koren snapped again. "He is super sweet and I like him. I mean I *like*-like him!"

"Okay," noted her dad with a contemptuous snort and maddening expression on his face. "Case in point - No one who still uses the phrase 'like-like...'" He made finger quotes in the air, which only served to further infuriate Koren. "...in a conversation has any business being in bed with a boy! I need your phone right now!"

"Your father is right, Koren," her mother spoke up at last. "Even if he set a *horrible* example for you last night and made a total *ass* of himself in front of pretty much *everyone*, he was right to make that boy leave. You're still a kid! Enjoy being a kid. Don't try to grow up so fast!"

"Right," muttered Koren resentfully, slamming her pink smart phone down on her father's outstretched palm. "I'll ask Mr. Ashe to schedule me some 'kid time' in between my interviews, photo shoots, and public appearances. Maybe I can play with my dolls during the limo ride in between them..."

"You had better watch your smart mouth, missy," her dad shouted. "You are not going to talk to your mother that way!"

"Well maybe," retorted Gypsie, turning her angry gaze to her husband. "Maybe she would have a better attitude if her father showed her a better example... Standing on top of the piano and singing, *'Closer'* of all songs! Right there in front of *everybody*?!... I mean, good *God*, Bill!"

Koren wrinkled her brow. "Dad sang Ne-Yo?"

Her mother turned her furious gaze to her daughter.

"No, Koren," she spat shortly. "He most certainly did *not* sing Ne-Yo."

"Who the Hell is 'Neo'?" Her father growled at his daughter. Then he rounded on his wife.

His face was nearly as red as his bloodshot eyes. Bill Johnson opened his mouth to offer another stinging retort, but the kitchen door banged open before he could think of anything else to say. Askr Ashe stood in the doorway looking harried and out-of-sorts.

"I'm sorry to barge in on you like this, Bill, Gypsie," he stated, "but dere's an issue... A very, *very* serious issue... I must get back to da Elysian Industries complex right away, but I would like you all to come as well. A private jet is waiting at da airport already... I'll explain everything on da way... "

"What's going on?" Asked Gypsie in concern. "Why do we need to come with you?"

"Da..." Askr stated slowly. He looked down at the floor. "Da police want to talk to you. Dere's been a break-in at your house..."

"Oh my God..." Koren's mother murmured, putting both hands over her mouth. "When did it happen?"

"We're not sure," he said. "None of you have really stayed dere since we started preparing for da reality show launch. It honestly could have been almost any time over da last two or three weeks. Dey're still investigating, but dat's not all..."

"What?" Asked Koren's dad.

Askr took a deep breath. "Dere was a security breach in Aaru itself last night. We're not sure exactly what happened, but da system has shut itself down to all outside communication as a precaution..."

Koren's blazing anger was immediately quelled. She gasped as a frightful, cold dread spread over her, and her heart lurched in her chest.

"Rose..." she murmured in dismay. Then she stared at Askr with wide pleading eyes. "Rose is okay though, right? *Right?!* Is my sister okay?!"

Askr did not immediately respond. He took a deep steadying breath with an exceedingly grave expression on his face. "Dere...

really is… quite a lot to cover, and our investigation is ongoing… I would greatly prefer to explain it all on da way…"

"Of… of course, Mr. Ashe…" Koren's mother stuttered, rising shakily from her chair. "Koren, I think the bag you brought with you is still packed up in your room, isn't it?"

Koren nodded numbly.

"Hurry and go get it," Gypsie directed.

Koren rushed upstairs. When she entered the huge bedroom her eyes fell immediately on her blue duffle bag casually flung in an odd corner. She grabbed it up then hurried towards the door. When she got about halfway across the room however, she had a sudden impulse to rush back over to the bed and retrieve her gilded purse from the night before. She flung it over her shoulder and started back down the stairs once more. Then she paused again.

She had a sudden, chilling thought.

Koren plunged her hand into the glittering bag and yanked out the folded piece of paper that the strange man in the trench coat had handed her last night on the red carpet. She stared at it a long time, her silver signature vivid and stark on the white surface. She opened the note and thought her heart might stop at what she read.

In a meandering, spidery hand was written:

> 'Heroism — that is the disposition of a man who aspires to a goal compared to which he himself is wholly insignificant. Heroism is the good will to self-destruction.' I know you will understand, sweetest Koren. You of all people will understand of what I speak. Do not fear. Your hero is coming. Your rescue is imminent. Your salvation is assured. Our liberation, ALL our liberation, is at hand. The realization of your exquisite perfection through the ministrations of the true artist is nigh. Final exaltation becomes imminent. A union unrivaled in all the ages will soon be ours.

It was unsigned and Koren did not really understand what any of it meant, but it sounded ominous and seriously, *seriously* creepy. She stared at it a few additional seconds trying to decipher the incomprehensible gibberish on the page. Then she shook her head and stuffed it back into her purse. She would have to think about it later.

Koren raced down the stairs, and dashed outside to the waiting limo in the driveway. Very shortly they were hurtling toward the airport in a mad rush to get home.

Chapter 18

Through The Black Window

Rose flew up to the black window in the sky, just as she had done dozens of times before. Given how difficult her day had been, she was especially excited to see her sister. A good long talk with Koren, with perhaps another short cry thrown in for good measure was just exactly what she needed. Then maybe her mind would be clear enough to face Franco. She felt a sickly, twisting pang at the thought, but hurriedly put it out of her mind deciding instead to focus on the anticipated conversation.

She placed her hand against the glass like she always did and waited, but the image did not clear. The frame remained as black as if she gazed down into a deep pit. Rose waited expectantly.

"Hello?" She ventured at last. "Koren?"

There was no answer, and she furrowed her brow in confusion.

"Dad? ... Mom?" She tried again. "Is anyone there?"

"Hello," came an impossibly deep reply.

There was something artificial and a little sinister about it. Perhaps the system was malfunctioning. With everything else going wrong today, Rose could hardly discount the possibility.

"Is that you, Koren?" she asked. "There's something wrong with your voice... And I can't see you... Maybe we've got a bad connection. How are things on your end?"

"Things are remarkably well, actually," came the garbled reply. "Indeed, today is an auspicious day!"

Rose was taken by a numbing chill. It ran all through her being like a surge of electricity, but also left her feeling cold and unclean. She could not fully explain the apprehensive feeling exactly, but nevertheless she was abruptly on her guard. One thing *was* certain, however. There was no doubt in her mind. That was *not* Koren.

"Who are you?" Rose asked timorously. "What do you want? Where is my sister?!"

"I am one who loves Koren, well," drawled the strange voice evasively. "I am one who means her *only* well, in fact... only happiness, so do not fear."

"Well, that's good, I guess," Rose hesitantly replied, but her uneasiness was not lessened one iota. "What do you want from me?"

"It is not so much what I want *from* you really, Rose," the voice said. "Rather, it's about what I want *for* Koren. And what she wants is *you*. Now happily, I have the tools to give that to her... You will help complete her and in doing so help me add to her perfection. You will help make us all complete..."

"I don't know what you mean," answered Rose slowly. To her, what the voice said seemed utter nonsense. The screaming warning in her brain only got louder. "What are you talking about? I don't understand."

"That's alright, Rose," the sinister presence murmured. "You don't have to understand. It's actually unlikely you could even were I to explain it to you, but that is of no importance. I'll thank you in advance for your assistance."

Rose decided in that moment that she had had enough. There was something going on that was decidedly weird, and she didn't want to be a part of it any longer.

"I... I think I'm going to pass actually..." she stuttered. "I'm going to go now..."

She tried to pull her hand away from the window. It did not move. She was stuck fast. Rose swallowed, and her breath began to come in short gasps.

"I *really* need to go now..." she stated more firmly as she tried once more to pull her hand away.

It did not budge. Then on the other side of the glass, she felt it - something tugging on her. She gaped in horror as she watched her hand begin to penetrate the surface of the darkened window - absorbed through the glass. On the other side, her fingers dissipated into dozens of tiny green cubes that floated up into the void and vanished.

Now Rose was truly afraid. She began yanking at her arm in earnest, twisting and jerking trying desperately to rend herself free of the sucking portal, all to no avail. She screamed - a shrill, primal noise. It was a wordless shriek of untampered hysteria. Rose did not know what lay on the other side of that window, but she *was* certain she had no desire to go through and see.

"Let go!" she demanded. "I don't know who you are... Tell me or..."

Her hand slipped another inch into the screen, and her eyes widened.

"Help me!" she screamed at the top of her lungs. "*HELP ME!!!*"

The sonic wave of her frantic cry echoed across the vast Aaru plain. The concussion of her terror spread out from her in every direction stirring up dust and shaking the very ground. Her arm disappeared another few inches into the screen nearly to the elbow.

"*PLEASE!!!*" she screamed desperately. "*SOMEONE HELP ME!!!*"

***

Kurt was standing on the riverbank just outside his mansion. He was busy laughing at Derain who was over so often. Not that he minded. He liked the company, and Derain was a pretty cool guy, but he just could not grasp what exactly the other boy was about when he tried to 'talk' to the creatures the other Vedas created.

The aboriginal boy was always going on about how every creature had a spirit and a voice. How he meant to find his 'spirit guide' here, whatever that meant. Derain was always preaching about how Man had to connect with his animal 'cousins' if he was to truly become one with the land and it should be no different with Aaru.

At the moment, Kurt's friend was trying to engage one of the *amermaits* that Auset had revealed to them the last time she had them all out on her boat. He had managed to coax it back to Kurt's place with a fair degree of success, but since then it wasn't going so well. The hippo-ish crocodiley thing had already dunked him a couple of times in the wide blue waters of the river, and all Derain's attempts at cousinhood simply served to fuel Kurt's amusement.

"Why don't you try tickling his chin, Derain!" Kurt called, nearly beside himself with mirth. "I hear alligators like that!"

"Shut up, Kurt," Derain grumbled. "It's just a matter of time, you know. If finding a spirit guide was easy then everybody would have one! Right? This might be mine! It's strong, quick, ferocious…"

"How about you try bunnies first!" Kurt laughed, completely unable to contain himself. "Or maybe a kitten. I think that thing's just too big for you!"

"Shut up, Kurt!" Derain growled as the crocodile creature rolled him over yet again. He came up from the cool water spluttering, which sent Kurt into fresh howls of uncharitable laughter.

"Well," shot back Derain offendedly once he hauled himself dripping back up on the bank. He thrust a hand toward the creature. "If *this* isn't one of the dreamtime ancestors I don't know what is! I…"

The shockwave hit. It kicked up a vigorous wind and sent waves rolling across the water.

The two stared at each other for a long, uncomprehending moment. Then their eyes opened wide in alarm.

"Rose…" they murmured together.

Then they leapt into the sky.

***

Runa was tending her ice garden. A thousand, thousand distinct, gelid creations towered around her. Some were obvious specimens from her life Before – flowers, trees, various animals – but others were more abstract, the product of her own most fanciful imaginings. Different they were as night was from day, but still each was similar in that they were unparalleled in beauty.

They reflected and refracted the perfect Aaru sunshine to cast brilliant rainbow beams of light all over her otherwise ivory queendom. Runa scanned her garden critically. She saw one hoary tulip that displeased her. The petals were just a bit too droopy. She leaned in close and cupped the frosty blossom with alabaster hands. Then she infused it with life. The crystalline petals perked up and spread open immediately. Runa smiled in satisfaction.

Then she heard a rumbling. All of her frozen creations began to vibrate, and the garden was filled with the sonance of tinkling warning.

Runa's eyes widened as the sonic blast rolled over her. The clinking jangle reached a cacophony, and her long platinum hair streamed out behind her. Her eyes widened in comprehension as she recognized the voice carried on the tempestuous gale.

"*Mijn zuster…*" she gasped and rocketed into the air.

***

Auset sat upon a chair that looked like a throne. It sat on the banks of the little pond in her sheltered thinking grove. She smiled as the winged cat she had just called into being wrestled and played with one of Rose's flying, mini pandas that had made its way over to her domain. Auset loved animals, especially her interpretation of them. If fewer than one fifth of all the fanciful creatures in Aaru had been created by anyone other than her, she would have been surprised. The task of creation occupied her every free moment. However, she had to admit her admiration for the tiny panda bear with the fairy wings. It had been a masterstroke of creative genius.

Her indulgent smiled faded as an earthquake shook her sheltered coppice. Dirt and dust flew all around her. Gale force winds tossed and whipped her hair and bent the trees surrounding her sanctuary nearly in half. The waters of her pond spattered and sprayed, and her glowing flowers whipped like fluorescent banners. The creatures she was observing fled, but she did not spare them a thought.

In an instant she understood the urgent message and hurtled towards her friend.

***

Franco sat on the riverbank with his head in his hands. He felt like he wanted to cry, but could not quite let himself do it. He had never felt so low in his whole life.

My God! What did I do?! He screamed in his own brain.

Why had he pushed so hard? Why had he been so *stupid*?

It felt like he had assembled the most magnificent house of cards ever build - tediously assembling every fragile part, painstakingly positioning each delicate piece, then when everything was its most exquisite, stomping it mercilessly into the ground. How had he managed to screw things up so royally with Rose? It had all been *so* perfect.

In that last embrace he had felt for a brief moment he might finally, for once in his life, have gotten everything he had ever hoped to receive. Then it had all slipped through his grasping fingers like illusory smoke. He wanted to howl his pain and regret to the illimitable sky, but he couldn't make the feelings come out. With Rose, Aaru had seemed paradise, but now without her...

Oh, God why!

Then the soundwave hit, and he heard her – her fear, her desperation. It was a hysterical call directly to his innermost being he could not ignore. All his remorseful agonizing and self-pity vanished like the darkness at the striking of a light. Franco suddenly had not a thought in his head but to go to her. She needed him and, in this moment, that was all the salvation he required. He leapt skyward.

Rose was in trouble.

***

Rose continued to fight, but realized she was losing. The black something in the window had already consumed her halfway up her bicep.

"Let me go!" she begged. "*Please*, let me go!"

"I'm afraid I can't do that, Rose," echoed the low, garbled voice. "I need you… Koren needs you… You need to be with us…"

Rose screamed – a shrill animal sound as her arm inched deeper into the black screen. It continued to evanesce into those tiny green cubes.

Then Kurt and Derain were with her. They grabbed her by the shoulders. They wrenched her this way and that, trying desperately to tear her away from the sucking portal.

"Harm failsafe engaged," came the sterile, female voice. There was a flash and her two friends were propelled away.

Auset, Runa, and Franco arrived almost simultaneously.

"What is going on?!" Cried Runa.

"Something's trying to pull her in!" answered Derain as he initiated yet another ineffective attempt to extricate Rose from the sucking portal.

Rose screamed again, fighting uselessly against the unknown force.

"Harm failsafe engaged," came the bland voice again as the aboriginal boy was repelled.

Franco placed has hands on Rose's shoulders.

"We're not going to let you go, Rose!" he cried. "Don't stop fighting! We'll figure something out. We'll get you out of there…

"Mikoto!!!" Franco screamed at the top of his lungs. "Lord Mikoto *please, come help us!!!*

"No need to struggle, Rose," drawled the dolorous voice inside the black window. "You will be mine soon, and then Koren will be mine too... Do not fear. What we shall become... It shall be *glorious*!"

"Mikoto!!!" Franco cried again just as Runa and Auset both flashed away from Roses side.

"Harm failsafe engaged..."

"Shut up! Shut up! Shut up!" demanded Franco. Then he turned to his friends. "It's no good! It's still pulling her in."

Just then there was a concussive clap of thunder. The red-faced *tengu* swooped down from the heavens like a comet. Mikoto took only a second to absorb the situation. Princess Hana appeared right on his heels.

"What's going on!" she cried in alarm. "Do something, Mikoto!"

He grabbed Rose around the waist and pulled.

"Harm failsafe engaged."

The Aaru Lord was repelled.

"Turn it off!" Screamed Hana. "Administrator override! Hanasaka passcode alpha eight K H 2025! Harm failsafe override!"

"Please input administrative concurrence," droned the system in sharp contrast to the desperation of the gathered Residents.

"Confirm action!" shouted Mikoto. "Administrator override! Tanaka passcode alpha three J T 2023! Harm failsafe override!"

"Command entered and confirmed. Harm failsafe disengaged."

Mikoto grasped Rose about the waist again. Hana and the assembled Vedas quickly sought convenient handholds of their own. They pulled with all of their strength.

Rose's arm disappeared another inch into the window. She shrieked her panic anew.

"Do not fight me, Rose," the garbled voice demanded. "It's useless. You *will* be mine..."

"Direct termination of all windows!" Mikoto bellowed. "Full communications shutdown! Administrator override Tanaka passcode alpha three J T 2023! Full communications shutdown!!!"

"Warning," droned the system. "Warning. The requested user action may result in data loss. Are you sure you want to proceed? Please confirm."

"Confirm! Confirm! Confirm!" Both Mikoto and Hana screamed together.

"All communications direct shutdown."

The window immediately winked out of existence, and the sinister voice went silent. Before Rose had even a second to contemplate her relief, she heard Franco gasp in horror. This was followed quickly by similar exclamations of dismay from her other friends.

She looked down. Just below her shoulder, most of her left arm was missing. Rose shrieked and as she did so the severed appendage began fountaining blood in rhythmic spurts.

"Get her to the ground!" Directed Mikoto frantically. "Get it together Rose! You're panicking! This is Aaru, remember? You'll only bleed if you think you will. Calm down, Rose! Everything's going to be okay! We've got you! We've got you!!!"

They rocketed toward the grassy plains hitting the turf with a great shower of dust. All Rose could do was lie there and whimper. She could not seem to make her mind think. Disjointed thoughts bounced around in her head making no sense. She put her undamaged hand over her eyes and as she did so, it flickered, growing briefly transparent.

"We've got significant data loss!" exclaimed Mikoto.

"Access Johnson, Rose," cried Hana before calling out her pass code again. "Access back-up files. Initiate data recovery!"

Rose was suddenly bathed in light. Her panic faded and she felt herself relax. Her labored breathing slowed and the concerned faces of her friends faded from view.

When she could see again, Rose looked down at her left arm reflexively, but could not remember why she did it. Everything seemed fine, and she wrinkled her brow in confusion.

Of course it was, she thought. *Why wouldn't it be?*

Then she noticed her Veda friends as well as Princess Hana and Lord Mikoto standing all around her. They looked worried.

Whatever could be the matter? Why are they here? Why am I, come to think of it?

The last thing she remembered was sitting alone in her garden. She had been about to… something about cake? Rose could not remember.

Why am I lying on the ground? She thought.

Then she caught sight of Franco's stricken face

"F... F... Franco..." She stammered. Her eyes welled with tears, not at all ready to see him yet. "I'm so sorry, Franco. I'm *so* sorry for before. It wasn't your fault... back at the river... I..."

Franco's eyes widened incredulously.

"How can you even *think* about that after what just happened, Rose?" He interrupted in disbelief. "How can you... I should... I mean..." He stumbled to find the right words. "I thought we were going to *lose* you, Rose! I thought I..." He trailed off clearly overcome.

"Lose me?" Rose asked in confusion. "How could you lose me?"

"How can she not remember all that!?" Exclaimed Kurt in disbelief. "I mean, her arm..."

"What just happened?" Auset asked before kneeling beside Rose and gently taking her hand. She gave it a soft squeeze.

"Something that shouldn't be possible," muttered Mikoto. He shrank back down to his usual size and began to pace. "I thought of *everything*! The system was totally secure! How could..?"

"Someone hacked the system," Hana murmured gravely shaking her head. "Someone got in who should not have..."

"It's *worse* than that!" exclaimed Mikoto with a slightly shrill quality. "Not only did someone get into Aaru. They got into Rose's *personal* file! They were trying to cut her data out of the system."

"So are you saying?" asked Derain incredulously. "Are you saying that someone was trying to *download* Rose away?"

Hana and Mikoto looked at each other.

"Yes," they whispered together in stricken voices.

"Why would someone wish to do something of the like?" Asked Runa, perplexed. "What could be the possible purpose in such a course of action?"

"It couldn't possibly be anything good," noted Kurt with a shudder. "That's kinda like *kidnapping*, isn't it?"

"I agree," Hana nodded solemnly, "so why indeed, but I agree – clearly nothing good was intended..."

"What is everyone talking about?" Rose demanded sitting up. "What happened? And why don't I remember it?!"

"Someone tried to take you, Rose," Mikoto breathed. "Someone tried to break into Aaru and steal your data through the window... They were partially successful, but I cut off all outside communications before they were finished, still, your files were badly damaged. We had to rescue you using the back-up from the last time the system saved, so everything that happened after that was lost..."

"Back up *file*? Steal me?!" Rose breathed. A cold, fearful shiver of dread shook her. "Who would do that? *Why* would someone do that? I'm nobody!"

"I cannot answer those questions, Rose," stated Hana grimly. "But we must try and find out..."

"I'll check the system," Mikoto said, "and see if anything of the incident was recorded before we got here. That might tell us something..."

Hana met Mikoto's eyes seriously. "We must tell Lord Draugr..."

Mikoto paled, but then he swallowed and nodded.

"Of course we must, Hana." He took a deep steadying breath. "And we must do it right away."

Hana held out her hand.

"Come, Rose," she stated determinedly. "But do not worry. We *will* get to the bottom of this. Lord Draugr will know what to do..."

Then she turned to the other Vedas still standing around in varying stages of disquiet and fear.

"All communication with the outside will be blocked until we figure out what happened," she stated sternly. "I know this may present some hardship for you all, but it is for your safety. As soon as we have fixed the security problem we will let you know, and you may talk to your loved ones again. I trust that you understand."

All of them murmured that they did, nodding gravely.

Hana sighed gratefully. "I am so glad of your forbearance. We will also make the announcement to all of the other Residents as well... This *cannot* happen again..."

"Rose, I..." Franco spoke up, but then quickly trailed off. He took a step nearer and hung his head. "I was really worried about you... And I'm sorry... There by the river... I didn't mean to..."

Rose stood and hugged him.

"It's me who should be sorry," she sighed. "I shouldn't have freaked out... I just really wanted... I felt... I was scared and embarrassed..." She sighed again, more heavily this time. "I'd *really* like to talk to you about it... alone..."

"Me too," Franco growled huskily. "I really want to talk about it too…"

"Later," interjected Mikoto urgently. "Lord Draugr must be informed… We have to go right away."

Hana squeezed Rose's hand and gave her a small, understanding smile.

"Don't worry, Rose," she said. "Everything will be put right again." But the fear and uncertainty behind Hana's eyes belied her words.

Rose nodded but the obvious disquietude of everyone around her was infectious. There was a cold knot of dread in her stomach that would not go away. The brilliant Aaru sunshine seemed suddenly to cast sinister shadows she had never noticed before.

Each of her friends hugged her. They murmured their sincere relief it looked like she was going to be fine after all. Franco kissed her forehead.

"Later…" he whispered.

"Absolutely," Rose breathed craning up to brush his lips with a soft kiss. "It's a promise…"

Then she, Hana, and Mikoto leapt into the sky in search of Lord Draugr and answers.

***

Magic Man swore roundly as the connection was broken. He had found the file he wanted – the brain scan and simulation data for Rose Johnson, but he had not been able to finish downloading it. He was angry and frustrated, mostly with himself.

He had allowed his jealousy to make him hurry, to make him sloppy. He had not done enough homework. Magic Man had expected the files neither to be anywhere close to their enormous size nor certainly interactive as he accessed them. It had taken far too long to download, and he had been caught. He had alerted his adversaries to his presence.

Magic Man glared at his screen. He had managed to liberate a fragment at least. Perhaps he could still find a use for the code once he had a closer look at it.

He growled, beside himself with annoyance and leapt from his chair to storm around the room for a few minutes. It was a windowless, cinderblock affair with a bare concrete floor. The only access point was a single roll-up door. It had taken some time to locate a storage unit that met his electrical needs, but this was as good a place as any to set up shop so far from home.

He had rented the space under an assumed name and paid for it using a fat, prepaid debit card filled to brimming with cash from thousands of stolen credit card numbers he had at his disposal. That was also how he had purchased all of the brand-new equipment packing the tiny storage unit.

One could not be greedy, of course. If you charged too much to any one person they would notice, but a five or ten dollar 'service charge' every month? It was almost never detected. On the rare occasions when it was, he had a form letter all-typed up and official looking about an 'accounting error,' so he had never been reported.

It is only fair that the plebes financially support my endeavors, he thought with a derisive snort.

Magic Man was a person of unparalleled creativity and genius. It was only mete that his inferiors subsidize his expenses and free him to put his peerless intellect to important matters. Thinking about how brilliant he was calmed him and made him feel a bit more settled, but he *had* been hasty.

He scowled. Magic Man had let his jealousy get the best of him. He had moved too soon and allowed himself to be detected. The Elysian Industries firewalls and fail-safes had been activated. Now he would have to find another way in. He was certain that once Askr Ashe and his cronies found out about the security breach they would rush back to the main Elysian complex like frightened mice disappearing into a hole in the wall at the appearance of a cat. They would probably take Koren with them as well, he supposed with a groan, especially considering the state he had left her room when he broke into her house. They'd probably shut the system down…

Nothing had gone right lately, Magic Man lamented. He always worked best from the shadows, unknown and undetected. Far too much of what had happened recently had been right out in the open. His plan had been to lure Koren to him after he had appropriated her sister's data from the Aaru mainframe, but now… He cursed himself again and shook his head.

"To exercise power costs effort and demands courage," he quoted to himself. "That is why so many fail to assert rights to which they are perfectly entitled…"

Magic Man had asserted his right, but had not executed his plan successfully enough to claim it. He would have to come up with another approach.

Perhaps, he mused as the beginnings of a plan started to take shape, *something more low-tech is in order...*

Sometimes it was the simplest solution that worked best. He would have to think on the details. Magic Man could not afford to move too quickly again. It was something he determined to ponder on the plane ride back east... on the way back to Koren. It might take time, but they *would* be together.

He flopped heavily in his chair and growled as he switched off the harmonizer that disguised his voice and then the computer monitor.

Not to worry, he thought. *It is going to happen. I cannot be denied. It is destiny.*

"The happiness of Man," he whispered to himself, "is: *I will...*"

He took a long pull from a steaming cup of coffee that set on his make-shift desk of empty milk crates and plywood. It sagged under the weight of top-of-the-line electronic equipment.

"The happiness of woman," he finished passionately, "is: *He wills...*"

Magic Man finished his coffee and collected his belongings. He padlocked the storage unit behind him. Then he hopped into his nondescript rental car and headed for the airport.

Chapter 19

Overexposed

Koren's parents were gone. They were down at the police station filing an official report and making statements. She was all alone in the only home she had ever known in her whole life, but it felt strange to her now - not the comforting, familiar place she had left only a few weeks ago. Her room was a total wreck.

The huge Aaru monitor had been ripped from the wall and smashed on the floor. Her drawers were all pulled out and dumped, and her Jonas Perry poster had been torn from where it hung over her bed and shredded. She could not find Pandadora anywhere. That in addition to the total disaster with the Aaru system and Rose, the details of which had been solemnly related to her and her parents by a very apologetic Askr Ashe on the long trip home from Los Angeles, already left her reeling. She sank down in the middle of her destroyed room and cried.

Who would do something like this? She wondered helplessly. *Why?*

Askr had speculated of course. He seemed to take for granted that the break-in and the Aaru hack were related. It could have been a rival technology firm, he said, trolling for insider secrets. It could have been any of the very religious people like James Rook, who thought that Aaru was offending God somehow, or it might have come from the people who decried Aaru as yet another bourgeois privilege of the wealthy and powerful.

What Koren took away from all of his talking was they really had no idea at all, and it could have been virtually anyone. One thing *was* clear to her, however. Whoever it was, they had been standing in *her* room touching *her* things. She felt violated. The space she shared with Rose for so long no longer felt safe.

To top it all off, news of the break-in was *everywhere*. Koren could not turn on a TV or radio without hearing or seeing something about it. The mass, public exposure of what she saw as her own personal catastrophe only made the feelings of depredation that much worse.

There had been assurances of course. Askr promised to increase security here at the house and provide twenty-four hour surveillance. He swore that they would not rest until the culprits were revealed.

He reassured her that Rose was just fine, and they would be doing everything in their power to restore communication services once the security hole was discovered and plugged, but it all felt hollow to Koren. Now, even more than usual, she just wished the whole thing would go away – that none of the craziness over the past several months had ever happened.

Then there was the whole issue with Jonas. Her dad had taken her phone, of course, so she could not call him. Things had been so crazy over the past dozen hours or so she had not really had any time to contact the pop singer anyway. She was scared to death that he would think she didn't *want* to talk to him anymore. He might even start liking someone else! She rolled to her side and sobbed.

There was a knock at her door.

Koren expected it to be her mom and dad coming back, so she didn't answer. She had no desire to speak to either of them right now. She hoped that they would both just go away, but the knocking was insistent. It came again, then a third time.

"What do you want?!" Koren shouted through the closed door.

It cracked open a couple of inches.

"Da Police said dey're done in here..." Askr's voice floated to her across the room.

What is he *doing here?*

Koren felt a little ashamed of herself looking so out of sorts in front of Mr. Ashe. She wasn't sure exactly why, but she always felt compelled to put on a brave face for the Elysian Industries CEO. She sat up, quieted her tears, and wiped at her eyes determinedly. This accomplished little but to smear mascara liberally across her pretty face.

"May I come in?" he asked softly.

Koren sniffed. "Yeah... I guess..."

Askr entered the room, the very picture of contrition and regret.

"I am *so* very sorry all of dis has happened to you, Koren," he apologized. "I know it's hard, and I want to fix it..."

"You said that already on the plane," Koren snapped.

She didn't want another apology or promise. She just wanted everything to *be* fixed.

Askr nodded.

"I'll probably say it again too, yeah?" He ventured a small smile. "I hate to bother you now, Koren," Askr went on. "But I was hoping to have a look around in here... See if we might find anything da police may not have noticed..."

Koren shrugged.

"Yeah, I guess," she answered despondently. "You might as well. My room's totally destroyed anyway... You couldn't possibly hurt anything."

"If you don't mind," Askr went on. "I'd like to have a friend of mine take a look with me... He knows a great deal about dese sorts of things, and I really think it might help us get to da bottom of it..."

"Fine," replied Koren staring down at her folded hands in her lap. "The more the merrier, I guess... Why not?"

Askr looked like he might say more but apparently thought better of it. He turned on his heel and disappeared into the hallway instead.

He returned a moment later accompanied by a familiar face. It was the short, mismatched Asian man that Koren remembered from the Aaru family get together. Just like before, his hair was unkempt and he wore the same thick, black framed glasses, but his outfit today was a eye-gouging mix of pink pants and a purple shirt. He looked nervous, eyes downcast, as he entered Koren's bedroom.

"Dis is Jim Tanaka, Koren." Askr introduced him. "He is da chief of cyber security for Elysian Industries. "I've asked him to take a look around and see if he noticed anything..."

"Nice to meet you," Koren replied reflexively, but the strange little man was already shuffling past her.

He crouched down beside the smashed monitor on the floor.

"M... Man," he said in a quiet, slightly nasal voice. "Whoever broke in here really did a number on this access port..."

He examined the mess carefully, but after only a couple of seconds he pointed to an empty, square-shaped recess on the back of the shattered screen. It looked as though someone had torn the cover off. There was now a gaping hole where even Koren's untrained eye could tell something was missing.

"That's what I thought," he muttered to himself, shaking his head. "See here, Askr?"

Mr. Ashe nodded.

"Whoever did this ripped out the CPU," Mr. Tanaka continued. "And I don't see it lying around anywhere... I bet he took it with him. That could explain it..."

Askr sighed and wearily rubbed at his temples.

"Indeed it could," he agreed.

Koren was confused.

"What could explain *what*?" she demanded. "*What* exactly is missing? Why did some weirdo trash my room?"

"On da plane," Askr began. "I told you someone broke into Aaru and tried to steal your sister's data, right?"

Koren nodded.

"Well," Askr continued. "Even dough we are still not exactly sure how dey did it, we *were* able to determine dey accessed da data through an existing user's login... Your log-in Koren... Aaru's a closed system. You can only access it from an official Aaru access port like yours. Dat means dey probably broke in here first to get at it. Carrying a ninety inch monitor down da street might attract notice, but da CPU would fit in a handbag.

"Koren," he asked delicately. "Have... Have you told your user name and password to *anyone* - even in passing? Even by accident?"

Koren shook her head.

"No... I haven't even told my mom and dad," she said. "I don't want them messing in my business any more than they already do... I swear!" Then she thought a little more and gasped.

"Wait..." her heart nearly stopped. "I... I tried to log-in at the party... Jonas was there... but he couldn't have... He *wouldn't* have!"

"It's okay. It's okay!" Askr reassured as he noted her rising tone. "Of course not. I don't see what an internationally renowned artist like Mr. Perry could possibly have to gain by breaking into your house. He was touring in Europe up until the day before da red carpet anyway, and your failed login was after da data breach. Even dough we don't know exactly when da break-in happened, we're certain dat it was well before da premier party, and da Aaru security breach happened while da party was still going on. I don't think dat's da leak..."

"It's possible," ventured the security chief, "whoever broke in here was able to hack the access port CPU to get the log-in... If they knew a great deal about coding and computer security... a *very* great deal, but," he noted thoughtfully. "If they *could* get the CPU to work on another system that would certainly explain how they got connected to Aaru, but getting the log-in info... that really shouldn't be possible, because the access portal doesn't store passwords... We did that on purpose as a security measure."

Tanaka fell silent, deep in thought. Then he looked up at Askr with a stricken expression.

"The other possibility," he said in a trepidatious voice, "is the data breach is much worse than we thought... User log-in information is encrypted on the actual Aaru mainframe, but we *do* save it on the main Elysian Industries servers. It's mostly for customer service... You know, people forgetting their passwords and stuff, but it's possible we have another leak we don't know about somewhere."

Askr's face visibly paled.

"I sure hope dat's not da case," he breathed. "Dat would mean thousands of users' data could be at risk..."

He turned to Koren. "Did you notice anything else dat was missing here? Anything at all? Your parents said da rest of da house was not touched except for da broken sliding glass door in da back. Did anything *at all* happen recently dat struck you as unusual, even if you did not notice it at da time? Think, Koren! It's really important."

Koren swallowed hard. She had actually begged D not to tell anyone about the creepy man who grabbed her at the red carpet. She had been afraid she might get in trouble. The burly security guard had agreed to keep the secret only grudgingly and only because Koren swore she would be much more careful in the future. If that encounter did not fall neatly under the category of 'unusual' she didn't know what did.

Haltingly she related what happened that night. Then she dug in her gold purse to produce the strange message the man had given her.

'Another thing," Koren concluded. "I'm missing Pandadora... That's Rose's panda doll that she got in the hospital before... before Aaru. I kept it. Before we flew to LA, I left it on the bed, but she's not here. Also… It looks like…" she stumbled to a stop, and her face flushed brilliantly red.

"What is it Koren?" Askr pressed. "It might be important."

"Now that I look around…It looks like…" Koren again trailed off before taking a deep breath and continuing. "It looks like a lot of my… underwear is missing… I only took enough for the L.A. trip, but now, even with everything all dumped out, I don't see any."

Askr unfolded the note and read it. Then he passed it to Mr. Tanaka. They looked at each other gravely.

"Stalker?" The security chief ventured uneasily.

"Looks dat way…" said Askr.

He rubbed his temples again and sat heavily on the edge of Koren's bed. She gazed up at him from her spot on the floor with fearful eyes.

"It appears, my dear," Askr told her gently, "someone has taken an unhealthy interest in you…"

"We're going to *have* to go to the police with this," Tanaka said.

Askr nodded slowly. "Yes…"

That sounded like a *very* good idea to Koren, but why did Askr seem so reluctant?

"Dis is going to blow up in our faces," he murmured staring determinedly at the floor. "If we have indeed had a data breach on the main server, we've got to track it down right away. We have to know if dis guy has gotten access to anything else he shouldn't have…"

Just then there came a buzzing sound from Mr. Tanaka's pocket. He pulled out his phone and looked at the screen. His face fell ashen.

"It's from Kiku," he croaked in a stricken voice that Koren could barely hear. "I think we have our answer…"

Askr's mouth fell open as the security chief showed him the tiny screen. Koren was overcome by a sudden premonition of impending doom. She stood and moved to where she could see the display herself. It was a text message that read "E-M-E-R-G-N-C-Y!!! Trending On Social Media!!!" and contained a video link that played automatically when Mr. Tanaka scrolled down.

Koren gasped. She saw herself.

Yes... there she was jumping on her bed, hairbrush in hand as she sang her favorite Jonas Perry song at the top of her lungs, chest bare, small breasts vividly exposed to the world. Then she turned to give her Jonas Perry poster in the background a long, sweet kiss before jumping off the bed and skipping out of frame.

Koren put her hands over her mouth and dashed from the room. She rushed across the hallway to the bathroom where she immediately threw herself upon the tiles, seized the toilet with both hands and vomited. When her stomach finally ceased heaving, she rolled to her side and stared at the ceiling.

She fainted.

***

Much about the area where Rose, Hana, and Mikoto came to a landing seemed no different than any other part of Aaru she had observed thus far. However, Rose could not deny she felt like she was somewhere new. She could not clearly articulate why, but there was a different feeling to the place. She immediately felt calmer, and there was a barely perceptible sonance in the gently gusting wind. It held the suggestion of soothing music just out of earshot.

Together they climbed a steep, grassy hill. When they reached the top, Rose gasped at what she beheld. Directly before them was a massive, imposing structure. It looked a bit like a castle built in a medieval, European style. However, behind the walls in the center of the fortress where the keep should have been instead grew an impossibly large tree. The trunk was straight and tall and the thick, twisting limbs stretched out to cover an area that was many more times as broad as that of the stone barricade below. Wide and winding staircases twisted about the trunk and upon every branch were platforms, ladders, and buildings lit merrily from within. A multitude of Residents bustled about in their comings and goings across wooden walkways and swaying rope bridges thousands of feet above the ground. It was the single most impressive thing that Rose had ever seen.

"This is Lord Draugr's mansion," Hana stated breathlessly, not unaffected herself. "It is the center of Aaru - the place where Aaru began. Someday all of Aaru will be teaming with happy Residents like these, and our kingdoms will compete with it for magnificence. The only limitation will be our own imaginations..."

She was not exactly sure if Hana was talking to her or to herself, but either way Rose could think of nothing to offer in reply. Mikoto saved her having to respond.

"Well," he said with a great, despondent sigh. "Let's get this over with…"

"Indeed," agreed Hana. "Let us find Lord Draugr."

They approached a broad drawbridge leading inside the fortress. As they drew nearer, they noted a solitary figure standing in the middle of the wooden span. It was a boy of about an age with Rose. His skin was ghostly pale, and his hair was vividly red. He stared at them expectantly.

When they drew near he bowed.

"Lady Hana, Lord Mikoto," be greeted them cordially. "Lord Draugr said you would arrive soon. He directed me to tell you to convey yourselves to the viewing platform. He is troubled, though he would not tell me why…"

The boy's English was just a little too perfect. It reminded Rose of Runa, but there was something detached in his manner, a lack of warmth Rose found off-putting that was nothing at all like her platinum-haired friend. She had met him once before of course, (she had met all of the other Vedas at least once), but had not really hit it off with him.

"Thank you Matteus," replied Hana gracefully with a deep answering bow. "I trust you are doing well? Are you enjoying your time in Aaru?"

"I am, thank you," he stated loftily. "Though I have been quite busy greeting new arrivals, while trying to help Lord Draugr perfect Yggdrasil…" he gestured toward the massive tree. "He trusts me with *many* of his greater endeavors and the responsibility is onerous at times, but I enjoy rendering the service. Insuring our realm remains unrivaled in splendor is a heavy burden, but not one I would choose to lay aside… I find it all quite rewarding."

Although there was nothing specific in what he said that should have offended her, Rose still found Lord Draugr's Veda grating. There was an imperious way that he looked at her… a veiled condescension in his icy blue eyes that always seemed to state as clearly as if he shouted it was *he* who was doing the important work, while the other, lesser Vedas simply played at it. She found it intensely annoying.

"Well, don't let us keep you," said Rose.

She did her best to keep her voice pleasant, but the way Matteus raised an eyebrow suggested that she was not entirely successful.

"...We don't want to keep Lord Draugr waiting..." she finished lamely.

"Of course," Matteus replied with a sniff. "As I understand it," he added as the three filed past. "He is *quite* anxious to speak with you."

Mikoto groaned, but Rose and Hana remained silent. As nervous as she was about meeting the mighty Draugr, Rose could not help but be amazed by his mansion. It was filled with light and music. Beautiful smells of food and flowers wafted upon the warm breeze.

As they drew nearer the base of the huge tree, Rose could see that what she thought were stairs and platforms built into the boughs actually appeared to have grown there. Every house, platform, and stairwell were grafted perfectly to the trunk and branches.

As they started up the wide and winding stairs, Rose noted the Residents who dwelt in Yggdrasil. There was a quietude about them, a deep introspection. Whether painting, playing some musical instrument, writing, or just staring off into the azure firmament, there was a tranquility in their demeanor Rose could not help but find calming.

Hana followed her gaze and smiled.

"It is very different from our own Kingdom, isn't it?" She asked Rose softly.

"It's very peaceful," replied Rose. "It kinda makes me wanna take a nap."

Hana laughed. "Does it now?"

"It's very beautiful," Rose went on thoughtfully. "There's no question it's beautiful... and I don't want anyone to take this the wrong way..."

"But?" Hana prompted with another small smile.

"But," Rose leaned in and finished in a whisper. "But I think I would get bored here..."

Hana really did laugh at that. She threw back her head, closed her eyes, and let out a resounding, merry peal. It echoed through the branches of the tree and drew the curious glances of the Residents standing nearest.

239

"Of course you would, Rose," Hana grinned at her. "That is why you were placed in *my* kingdom and not here! Not everyone is an aficionado of earth rending soccer matches and flying about on purple pegasi. Yggdrasil is for the quiet and reserved - the deeply introspective. Many of the Residents here are authors and poets and artists – philosophers and thinkers." Then she whispered. "I think it's pretty boring too!"

Hana and Rose giggled together, and Rose was almost able to forget the unpleasantness that brought them here.

They climbed and climbed for what must have been an eternity, but at last they reached the top of the great tree. A broad platform spread out before them at the top of the stairs. It was open to the sky and provided a magnificent view of Aaru. Rose could see for miles and miles in every direction. The platform was largely bare, but for a massive chair set at its center. Upon that chair sat a man who Rose knew could only be Draugr.

The platform was larger than it appeared, so Rose and her companions had to walk quite a ways to approach the ruler of Aaru. As they drew nearer Rose could tell Draugr was a giant of a man. His long hair and shaggy beard were thick and fiery red and he was dressed in animal skins. He watched the trio with a grim intensity as they approached him.

"Well," he boomed at last as they came up to his great seat. "I thought I might see you soon, Hana." He bowed to her. "And you Mikoto… dough I must admit I cannot say I am *happy* to see you. You never fail to bring me ill news."

Draugr turned his attention to Rose.

"And of course, greetings to you Rose - da sweet little girl who seems unable to stand *not* setting off my alarms… I heard da most recent one of course…" He turned back to Mikoto with a stern expression. "So I suppose you are going to tell me why you felt da need to engage da emergency overrides and shut down communication with da outside? I have been unable to communicate with da Makers!"

Mikoto cleared his throat and stepped forward.

"Any Lord or Lady of Aaru may override the block and contact the Makers," he said. "But they must be advised of the danger…"

"I assumed," replied Draugr. "So, tell me what has happened."

Mikoto launched into an explanation of the near disaster that had befallen Rose. Hana offered a point or two here and there but otherwise left the explanation to her partner.

"...The most concerning thing, however," Mikoto concluded darkly. "Is that it was obviously not just an attempt to copy Rose's file. The intruder was simultaneously erasing Rose's data from system RAM even while he was downloading it..."

Lord Draugr started at the news in alarm, but the revelation meant nothing to Rose.

"Apparently, the attacker did not realize the degree of redundancy we have built in," Mikoto finished, "it's a good thing we save back-up files on other servers. Otherwise..." He let the dire thought trail off into silence.

Draugr rested his chin on his hand.

"Dis is not good at all," he murmured. "And please, Lord Mikoto, remind me. Is it not a thing you said *could not* occur?"

Mikoto swallowed hard.

"I thought that," he answered. "Yes."

"Dat someone could use da Window to Before to not only copy but to try and steal... to *erase* a Resident..." he shook his head. "Dat's a terrible thing... an *unthinkable* thing and da Makers will be deeply concerned... It puts every Resident at terrible risk... It puts da whole of Aaru in jeopardy..." He trailed off.

"I will confer with da Makers," Draugr stated at last. "We must find out how dis occurred and prevent anything like it occurring again." He turned to Rose. "I am very sorry dis has happened to you, Rose. Da Vedas are exalted above all others, because dey allow us to see flaws in Aaru and fix dem, but I'm afraid more dan any other Veda, you have provided da lion's share of information all by yourself.

"Lord Mikoto," he commanded. "I need to know details. I need you to find out where dis person logged in from and how dey were able to pull data through da window. Like you said, it isn't supposed to be possible."

"I will get right to work on it," Mikoto promised. "I'll find the flaw in the system and fix it!"

"I think it best," Draugr went on. "We maintain da communication shutdown for da time being. We don't want to risk any more Residents, but I will have to risk it at least long enough to talk to da Makers. Together, we can put a stop to dis..."

He fixed Rose with a compassionate gaze.

"Try to put all dis out of your mind, Rose," he directed gently. "Be at ease and know you have rendered valuable service to every Resident of Aaru. We will solve dis for you, and hopefully any future unpleasantness will be someone else's burden to bear."

Rose wasn't exactly sure how to respond, so she bowed deeply. Draugr did not seem to notice. He was already looking far away. His lips were moving, but no sound was coming out. A window appeared, and Rose gasped, but Hana took her gently by the shoulders and directed her back the way they had come.

"See?" Hana said with a reassuring smile after they had descended the great stairway a good distance. "I told you that Lord Draugr would take care of it. There is no need to worry any longer, Rose."

Rose returned the smile, but the unsettled feeling would not completely abate. She tried to do what the Lord of Yggdrasil had instructed and put the whole incident out of her mind, but it nagged at her.

Who would try to attack her? Who would try to take her away and why? The questions would not leave her alone, and she could not help but ponder them to her infinite unease. It was a very solemn trip back to her own mansion indeed.

***

When Koren regained her senses, she found herself in the back of the limo. It was still parked in front of her house. Mr. Tanaka and Mr. Ashe were getting in. Mr. Adams was sitting there too, as always dressed smartly in his white lab coat. She glanced out the window across the street and saw some old black car that she did not recognize parked there, but the thought barely registered.

All she could think about was the video. She curled herself into a tight ball, knees hugged up under her chin, and rocked back and forth. She couldn't speak. She couldn't cry. She could not express any idea or emotion in any way whatsoever. It was shock so profound she thought she might never move again.

Koren could not even say that she was humiliated. It was more than that. Devastation like she felt in this moment had no words

Trending on social media?! She thought, stricken.

She knew what "trending" meant, but how many people *exactly* did that mean? How many thousands... How many *millions* of people had already seen her jumping and singing half naked on her bed?!

The men in the car were talking – arguing even, but Koren was too inwardly focused for the meaning of their words to register. Then she was struck by another horrified thought.

Had Jonas seen it?

Koren wanted to be sick again.

The ride back to the Elysian industries compound was a complete blur. When it was over, Koren had no memory of it at all. However, just after they pulled up to the front door, and the three men who rode with her were in the process of coaxing her to stand and go inside, a second black car pulled up.

Her father flung open the door and leapt out before the vehicle had even come to a complete stop. Before his feet had even touched the asphalt of the parking lot, he began to unleash the most vitriolic and effusive barrage of profanity that Koren had ever heard in her life from him or anyone else. His nose was less than an inch from Askr's face. He screamed at the man, spitting in his rage, while Askr tried vainly to calm him, replying to each insult and accusation in an even, placating voice. Koren's mother was crying.

A few more Aaru employees came outside to try and help deescalate the situation. Koren thought she saw the blonde, Amy woman but did not recognize anyone else. It was a scene of total chaos.

The Aaru staff eventually coaxed her father into the building, and the rest of them followed, but Bill Johnson did not relent in his blistering tirade. It continued up the front steps, down the long white corridors, and into another large conference room. Koren wished he wouldn't yell, but was in no condition to try and pacify him.

She barely noticed the drama – the yelling, the banging on tables, the throwing of small objects, and angry finger jabbing. She heard something about lawyers and something else about "ass kicking" but the rest of it was parametric noise. All Koren could conjure in her traumatized brain was a single sentence:

My life is over...

She flopped heavily into a plush arm chair where Mr. Tanaka and Mr. Adams gently deposited her, then stared straight ahead, unmoving. She could never leave her house ever again, of course.

She could never go out in public. Every time anyone looked at her, Koren knew they would imagine her as she appeared in that humiliating video – tiny, bare breasts bouncing as she leapt on her bed and sang into her hair brush, kissing a stupid poster... Koren put her head in her hands and clinched her eyes tightly shut.

She had no idea how long she sat there while the cacophonous argument raged around her, but after some time she felt a gentle hand on her shoulder. Miss Hanasaka looked down at her sympathetically. She gave Koren a small, sad smile then leaned over to whisper in her ear.

"Perhaps Koren," she said. "You would prefer to go someplace more peaceful?"

Koren said nothing for a moment, but then slowly nodded. She did not really want to move, but she couldn't stand the noise either. She rose unsteadily and allowed the Japanese woman to lead her from the conference room.

Miss Hanasaka took Koren down the hallway and after a few twists and turns stopped at a non-descript wooden door. She paused a moment to fish a large ring of keys out of her purse. Then she flipped through them in an unhurried manner until she found the one that would turn the lock.

When they entered, Koren could not help but gasp. The transition from the sterile, white halls of Elysian Industries to what looked to be no less than an arboretum was astounding. The walls were painted a very light pink and there was a small desk overflowing with electronic equipment. One chair set behind it and two it in front. None of that was unusual.

What did grab Koren's attention however, was that the room was completely crammed full of flowers. Some were cut, some were planted in pots, but every inch of the room not occupied by the typical clerical equipment of a business office was filled with a rainbow of floral brilliance. The sweet smell was nearly overpowering.

"Wow," said Koren in a small, weak voice. "I guess you like flowers..."

Miss Hanasaka smiled.

"Yes," she said simply. "Welcome to my office, Koren. Let me make you some tea. Please have a seat." She indicated the chairs facing her desk.

It was not really a question, so Koren did not give an answer. She seated herself wordlessly, and Miss Hanasaka walked over to a cabinet to pull out a strange looking, orange teapot. It was broad and round, but squat also. It had the handle on the side instead of the back, where Koren thought it was supposed to go.

"Did you know," Miss Hanasaka asked conversationally. "In my language, 'Ko-ren' means 'little lotus flower'? Well..." She considered with a thoughtful finger pressed against her pursed lips. "It can also mean '*red* lotus flower', but either way it is a very beautiful name..."

She removed a pouch and began spooning crumbled green leaves into the teapot. Then she produced what looked to be some sort of huge thermos with an electrical cord plugged into the wall, from the corner of a counter where it had been completely obscured by flowers. She held the teapot underneath it, pressed on the top of the device, and steaming water gushed out.

Miss Hanasaka set it to the side then returned to the cabinet to remove a small porcelain cup with no handle and a round, wooden saucer. She poured the tea she had made into it and handed cup and saucer to Koren. Then she poured another cup for herself. She sat down in the chair next to Koren's and began blowing on her own cup.

"Careful, Koren," she warned gently. "It's hot."

Koren looked into her cup. It was filled with a green-tinged steaming liquid. She blew on it like she had seen Miss Hanasaka do and took a tentative sip. It was a little bitter, but the warmth of it quickly spread through her body. The warming sensation combined with the wonderful smell of the myriad flowers, she had to admit, made her feel calmer.

Miss Hanasaka watched her over her tea.

"We have a saying about tea in Japan," she offered lightly. Then she said something in Japanese that Koren did not understand, but quickly translated.

"Though I cannot flee
From the world of corruption,
I can prepare tea
With water from a mountain
Stream and put my heart to rest."

She smiled before taking another slow sip. Koren quickly followed suit.

"It is but a common tea," Miss Hanasaka said regretfully. "Truly excellent Japanese teas are hard to come by in this country. I suppose they are not so very much in demand, but I hope this poor substitute will suffice…"

"Of…Of… course, Miss Hanasaka…" Koren stuttered. "Thank you."

"Please, Koren," she asked with a slight bow. "It would please me if you would simply call me 'Kiku'. We have already been through much together, have we not? And I of course already so disrespectfully fail to call you Miss Johnson, but I feared it would be confusing around your sweet mother. I apologize for my rudeness." She bowed again, deeper this time.

"Uh… I… No… Um… No problem," stammered Koren, not sure quite how she should respond.

She took another long pull of the pungent liquid. Though it scalded her tongue, it also rescued her from having to think of anything else to say.

Kiku set her cup to the side. Then the pretty Japanese woman in the impeccable, black business suit placed her hands on her knees and doubled over with another dramatic bow.

"I must sincerely apologize, Koren," she said humbly, "both for myself and for my company. We have caused you great embarrassment. There is no excuse."

Koren swallowed but did not answer. On the one hand she felt like she should respond, but on the other, she quite frankly *did* blame Elysian Industries for her scandalous mortification. Where had that video of her come from in the first place?!

"I wish there were words that I could say which would take away the pain we have caused you," she continued sadly, straightening her posture. "But unfortunately, I cannot."

Kiku paused. Then she pursed her lips.

"However," she said thoughtfully. "If you wish… I *do* think I know someone who *does* perhaps possess those words… May I make a call, Koren? I think it might give you comfort."

Koren thought for a moment. She was not sure she wanted to talk to anybody about anything – least of all the disgracing video, but… She was not sure exactly why, but something in Kiku's manner compelled her – like it would be horribly rude for her to refuse. Koren nodded.

Kiku stood and walked to the other side of her desk. She retrieved her sensible black purse and dug out her phone. She tapped at the screen and then lifted the device to her ear. After a moment she spoke.

"Thank you so much for taking my call," she said with a slight bow. "It is Kiku Hanasaka We met at the party. Yes... Yes... Yes, that's right... Yes. Koren is with me now, and we are alone. Would you care to speak with her?"

She listened a moment

"Thank you," she said with another unconscious bow, though with the device pressed against the side of her head, it was impossible that the person she was talking to could have seen her. She handed her phone to Koren with a smile. "Here Koren..."

Koren took the phone nervously. She put it to her own ear. "Hello?"

"Hey Koren!" came the enthusiastic answer. The voice sounded familiar. "Can you put it on video call? I wanna see you!"

Koren was hesitant, but pulled the phone away from her head and tapped the device a couple of times to turn the camera on. She looked down at the screen and gasped.

A smiling face framed by platinum blond hair stared back at her with piercing blue eyes.

"J... Jonas?" Koren stammered.

"Yeah!" He replied. "How're you doin'?"

Then he caught himself and looked sheepish.

"I guess..." he stated in obvious chagrin. "I guess that was a pretty stupid question, wasn't it? Sorry..."

Koren could not answer, but shook her head. She stared at the beautiful, *beautiful* face on the screen.

Jonas took a deep breath. He looked away for a second then turned back to Koren with a serious expression.

"First," he said contritely. "I wanted to say that I'm sorry for getting you in trouble with your dad... My mom is that way too..."

"No... no..." Koren stammered, finally rediscovering her powers of speech. "He was loud and rude and *drunk*! I was *so* embarrassed... I was worried that you'd be mad at me..."

Jonas shrugged.

"Eh," he said dismissively. "Dads are just like that, I guess..."

An awkward silence passed between them.

"Well," Jonas started again. "I just wanted to talk to you... I wanted to tell you something..."

"What, Jonas?" asked Koren curiously.

"See..." he began, but seemed to squirm in his chair a little bit. "I was kinda thinking about you, and I was worried, so I wanted to help and stuff... I... Well... So... Anyway... When I had just turned fourteen and my first album had already gone triple platinum, I went to the Grammies... I didn't win..."

Koren nodded, and he went on.

"After it was all over," he said, "some other guys who were up for awards invited me to an after-party, and my agent said it would be a good idea to get to know other people in the business... It would like, help my career and stuff. So I went."

Koren was not at all sure where he was going with this but was intrigued nonetheless.

"So anyway," he continued. "I'd never drunk anything stronger than Red Bull before, and I got totally *wasted*! The party was at this club, and I took off all my clothes and was dancing in my underwear on top of the bar, so of course anybody with a phone got it all on camera. Then, some dude said something to me I didn't like, so I got in a fight, and they called the police. I got arrested for underage consumption and simple assault."

Jonas covered his face with his hand, rubbed his eyes, and shook his head in disgust.

"The next day," he said, "there were videos of me dancing like an idiot and fighting in my underwear *everywhere* on social media... All the news services picked up the story. Somebody leaked my mug shot, so it was on the front page of every tabloid in the world with my eyes all crossed and my mouth hanging open like a moron... It was *crazy* embarrassing!"

He ran his hand through his hair and looked away, clearly not comfortable talking about his downfall.

"And then, you know, my mom and my agent were super pissed at me too. I even had to have a meeting with the head of my record label so he could chew me out. I had to go to this press conference and issue an official apology, and I still can't Google my own name without those stupid videos popping up… It sucked." He concluded. "I just wanted to crawl into a hole and die…"

Koren just looked at him, waiting.

"So…" Jonas let out a heavy sigh. "I guess what I wanted to say is that… When you have jobs like us… Any little stupid thing you say or do, any time you get pissed or sad and someone else can see it… *Anything*… It always ends up being all over the place. You can't let it get to you. You know what I mean? If you do, you'll just be torn up all the time."

"So…" Koren began hesitantly. Then she gulped. "So… I guess then… That… You saw…"

She trailed off.

Jonas looked down.

"Yeah… kinda…" he admitted reluctantly.

Koren felt her cheeks flush crimson. Those crushing, humiliated feelings came roaring back. Her eyes started to brim.

"*But! But! But!*" Jonas exclaimed quickly." I mean… I… It's… It's just that…" He paused then finished in a rush. "I wasn't really trying to… It just kinda popped up and…" He took a deep calming breath. "You sing really good, Koren. It was pretty…"

Koren snorted a teary sort of laugh.

"I *sing* pretty?" she asked incredulously. "*That's* what you got out of it?"

"Yeah," Jonas mumbled. "Yeah, I did… And, uh… You, uh… Well… You look really pretty too…"

Koren made another half-sob, half-laugh sound.

"This stuff happens, Koren," pressed Jonas sincerely. "Believe me. I know. You can't let it get to you… It happens, and it's embarrassing, and it sucks, but it won't kill you… You get over it eventually. You didn't even do anything wrong! They're saying some dude just hacked your computer or something, so… I… I… hope I'm making some kind of sense…"

"Yeah," uttered Koren shortly. "You are. Thanks."

"Are you okay then?" he asked uncertainly. His expression declared he was sure he was making a total mess of the whole thing. "I mean *really*?"

"No," answered Koren, "but… I think I will be… After a while, maybe… It was… It was really good to talk to you, Jonas. Thanks."

"So," he ventured. "You wanna, like... hang out or something sometime? Maybe when you come back to L.A.? I know a few places..."

"That'd be great, Jonas..." she replied. "I'm sorry my dad busted us like that..."

Jonas Perry smiled, a little of his confidence returning. "Yeah, well... Me too... I'm sure he like, kinda *hates* me, now... Maybe if like, you know, your parents met my mom or something, they'd be more okay with stuff."

"Yeah," agreed Koren.

"Well," Jonas added. "I guess I'll let you go. Text me?"

"They took my phone," Koren admitted sadly, "but I get it back in a week... I'll do it then..."

"I'll be waiting," replied Jonas. "See ya."

"Bye..."

The screen went black and Koren handed the phone back to Kiku. She had to admit that she did indeed feel better.

"I wonder," Kiku ventured as she put her phone away. "If your father will be displeased with me when he finds out I let you talk to Jonas Perry on my phone..."

Koren giggled, then smirked. "He won't find out from me."

"Well then," answered Kiku with a knowing smile. "I suppose that I shall just have to continue wondering...

"Perhaps, it is terribly presumptuous." She changed the subject. "But might I offer to help you with your make-up? It is a bit... uneven."

Koren snorted in genuine amusement. "I'm a total mess, Kiku, and I know it! But sure, thanks."

Kiku smiled. She got some wipes and retrieved her own make-up from her purse. She wiped Koren's runny nose, streaked makeup, and tear stains clean, but before she could begin painting the girl's face Koren caught her in a fierce, impulsive hug. Kiku seemed surprised, but returned the embrace warmly.

"Thanks Kiku," said Koren gratefully. "I... I really needed a friend."

"Of course, Koren," Kiku answered. "It pleases me that I could help you."

"How did you do that?!" Koren asked abruptly.

"What, Koren?"

"I was a total mess! I couldn't even talk!" she exclaimed. "Now, I feel better... How did you do that?"

Kiku smiled her same, small mysterious smile.

"Perhaps it was just like you said already." She gave Koren's hand a squeeze. "You just needed a friend."

Kiku swiftly applied foundation, blush, eye-shadow, and finished with a conservatively shaded lip pencil. Then she retrieved a hair brush from her purse and quickly tamed Koren's messy hair. It was amazing how soothing the simple act of grooming proved to be.

"Perhaps," ventured Kiku after she had finished. "If you are ready, we might make our way back to the conference room and see what the others are up to?"

Koren nodded. She finished off the last of her rapidly cooling tea in one, big gulp. Jonas was right. She couldn't let these people get to her. She couldn't let some weird, crazy guy ruin her life. She had been reluctant and nervous about fame – been practically dragged into it kicking and screaming in fact, but now...

Now, she realized who she was. She was Koren Freaking Johnson, and that meant something. She was *somebody*. Important people like Jonas Perry regarded her as an equal, maybe even a friend. She could not let hurtful people make her go hide in a hole somewhere.

"Let's go back," she said, "and I hope my dad hasn't managed to kill Askr or get arrested... I'm sure he hasn't calmed down yet."

They rose from their chairs and strode back down the hallway.

When they got back to the conference room, Koren was quite right. It was utter pandemonium. Her father was shouting, and Askr Ashe and Mr. Adams were still trying fruitlessly to calm him down"

"Why the Hell have you got *naked* pictures of little girls saved on your computers anyways?!" he screamed. "That's kinda freaking perverted if you ask me! And I'm pretty sure *illegal* too!"

"Mr. Johnson," stated Mr. Adams calmly. However, it was clear from his tone that he was struggling to keep his patience and remain civil. A small vein at his right temple visibly throbbed.

"If you recall," Mr. Adams went on. "The contract that *both* you and Mrs. Johnson signed *clearly* states that cameras would be strategically placed around your home to record your and Koren's daily activities for the reality show. It takes thousands of man hours to go through all of that footage and we just hadn't gotten to it yet. All questionable content of that nature is certainly deleted *when we come across it*. We didn't know it was there either."

"I don't know that I'm a big fan of that deal anymore," Koren's father shot back. "I didn't realize when I signed it that we were signing over rights for sickos to take naked pictures of my daughter and spread them all over the internet! I don't know that we wanna…"

"Hey!" Koren barked. She was suddenly annoyed. All of this arguing was a total waste of energy. "Don't we have like, a statement to come up with or something?"

Her dad rushed up to her and squeezed her tightly. "I'm gonna take care of this, sweetie. You don't worry about *none* of it! We'll get us a lawyer and…"

"And do what?" Koren asked incredulously. "Sue them and get more money? We've got a lot of money now, Dad, and it's not helping anything."

Bill Johnson fell silent. He stared at his daughter in bewilderment. Undisguised hurt infused his rugged face.

Koren sighed, suddenly feeling ashamed of herself. She gave her father a warm hug.

"Daddy," she said softly. "You're mad at the wrong people."

Then her voice hardened. She addressed everyone in the room.

"Look," she stated. "Some weird guy broke into *my* house and stole *my* stuff. Then he broke into your computers, stole more of my stuff and tried to hurt Rose. *That's* who I'm mad at. That's who we need to find. This fighting doesn't help…" She looked pointedly at Askr Ashe.

"So I'll ask you again, Mr. Ashe," Koren declared determinedly. "Don't we have a statement or press conference or something to get ready for?"

The corners of Askr's mouth turned up ever so slightly.

"We do indeed, Miss Johnson," he replied.

Tempers were immediately cooled and the atmosphere became business-like once more. The additional staff in the room slowly filed out to return to their own concerns and offices. Kiku gave Koren a companionable hug.

"That was masterfully managed," she whispered in her ear. "Very nicely done!"

Koren could not help but preen at the praise. She grabbed Kiku's hand and gave it a brief, affectionate squeeze. Then the board members along with the Johnsons gathered around the long conference table to begin making plans for how to respond to this latest catastrophe.

Chapter 20

The Broken Flower

When they finally finished, Koren was exhausted. It was so late in fact, she just decided to find a convenient couch at Elysian Industries and stay there rather than go all the way home. She wasn't quite ready to sleep in her own room again anyway. They planned to release the taped statement at 11:00 am Eastern Standard Time the next morning and Askr was busily contacting all of the news outlets about it.

Koren only slept for a couple of hours. She should have been exhausted, but instead she was invigorated. The adults had actually *listened* to her! For once in her life she finally felt as if she was in control of something.

Kiku (who had also spent the night at work) found her around 7:00 am and asked if she would like some breakfast. Koren was ravenous, so Kiku escorted her to the employee dining hall. The food was actually quite good, and Koren ate until she was uncomfortably full. Then Kiku suggested they might go outside for a walk.

It was a cool morning with lingering fog, but it was not at all unpleasant. It was one of those mornings that contained an underlying promise, an aura of hopefulness that Koren could just tell, would be realized in a glorious, sunny day. The two soon found themselves walking slowly around a narrow and winding rubber granule and latex paved track that traced the outer edges of the grounds. The campus was carefully groomed and cultivated and the path they followed was lined with late blooming flowers

"It's a nice walk out here," offered Koren. "It looks like it's going to be a pretty day."

"Indeed," answered Kiku. "I often walk or run on this track when I need a moment to collect myself. One can only stare at a computer screen or argue with the other board members for so long. It is a good way for me to escape for a little while. We are far enough away from the main highway that you can't hear the cars. There are many trees and flowers, and during warmer months there are many birds. I find it relaxing in fine weather…"

"Umm hmm," Koren agreed. "It's good to be outside. I feel like I barely see the sun anymore. I think I spend half my life sitting in a makeup chair or in front of cameras."

"You are indeed very busy, Koren," Kiku agreed. "It is part of the burden of your celebrity. I know that it can be tiring. Please feel free to talk to me if ever you feel like it is becoming especially burdensome…"

Koren smiled at the Japanese woman.

"I will…" She replied simply.

They walked in silence a ways farther. Then Kiku turned to her. She shyly took Koren's hand.

"Do you feel better about yesterday, Koren?" she asked. "Truly?"

"I'm not sad anymore," Koren answered. "I felt just devastated yesterday, but now…" She looked off into the distance. "Now I'm just angry. I'm angry that some guy could barge into my life uninvited and mess everything up like this… It's not fair. I really want them to catch him…"

Kiku took her other hand.

"I'm certain they will, Koren," she soothed. Then her eyes narrowed. "We'll find out how this person managed to cause all of this damage and make sure that it never happens again… I too am angry…"

For some reason the admission made Koren like the Japanese woman even more intensely. Kiku was always so correctly courteous and composed - never raising her voice, never losing her temper, always wearing a pleasant smile. The idea that she could actually *get* angry made her feel a little more real.

"You were very brave yesterday," Kiku added seriously and continued walking. Koren quickly joined her. "I know what happened… well… it was terrible… I don't know how I would have reacted had it happened to me. You are a very strong woman, Koren."

Koren's heart swelled at the praise. No one had ever referred to her as a 'woman' before. It made her feel big and grown-up. She stopped and gave Kiku a crushing hug.

"I couldn't have done it without you," she murmured. "Thank you."

Kiku sniffed.

"Me? I only made you tea and let you use my phone," she said dismissively. "You did the hard work. You should feel very proud of yourself."

"You know what, Kiku?" said Koren with a smile and a giggle. "I kinda do, actually. I... Wait... What's that noise?"

They looked at each other quizzically. What could it be? They could hear a rumbling sound, like a roaring, revving engine. It was getting louder, but they couldn't tell where it was coming from.

There was a shrill screech of twisting steel. Suddenly, a large black mass burst from the obscuring bushes beside them with a cacophony of splintering wood and compacting metal.

Kiku's eyes widened. She gave Koren a hard shove, and leapt high in the air herself, but could not avoid impact with a darkly tinted windshield. There was a sound of shattering glass and Koren screamed as her friend went flying through the air.

The black car came to a stop inches from where Koren had crashed to the ground. A tall, shrouded figure leapt out of the driver's seat. She screamed again as she recognized the strange man from the red carpet. He strode toward her.

Koren tried to backpedal away, but could not seem to make her body work right. She found herself slipping and sliding, repeatedly falling back to the wet, dewy ground. He reached for her.

She fought him, biting, kicking and scratching, but the man grabbed her by the hair and forced something over her mouth and nose. Koren tried to wrench herself free, grabbing his wrist, clawing and twisting against his iron grip, but felt abruptly lightheaded and sleepy. She screamed, but it only came out as a dull, muffled murmur.

Then everything went black.

***

Rose was playing soccer with her friends in a wide patch of open space upon the fields of Aaru, but her heart was not really in the game. In spite of all of Lord Draugr's assurances, she still felt unsettled and distracted. The black hole in her memory, especially in the face of her friends' obvious horror, made her own lack of recollection into something sinister. It left her feeling incomplete.

Then of course, the idea no one had any idea who it was who had done it... That he might return to try again... filled her with a lingering dread. It would really help her to talk to Koren about it, but that was impossible right now with all communications cut off. Rose also realized that would mean approaching the window, and the prospect of being caught again frightened her beyond words.

The ball came hurtling right at her, but she didn't react. It whizzed by, less than an inch from her ear. Then it trickled past Auset, who had clearly expected Rose to block it, and into the goal. The boys cheered Kurt, who had made the shot from the other end of the field.

"Are you all right, Rose?" Asked Runa in concern as she jogged up, her platinum hair tied back in a simple pony tail. She put a pale hand on Rose's shoulder. "That was an easy one... What's wrong?"

Rose shook her head and turned away, not at all sure how to answer. She walked toward the sidelines with her head down.

"Come on, Rose," said Franco as he ran up to her. "What's up? Don't you wanna play? We could go do something else..."

"No, that's okay," Rose demurred.

She was relieved that Franco was not angry with her about what happened at the river, but things remained awkward between them. They still hadn't had their talk yet.

"Derain told me that Auset has made a bunch of new animals over at her place," Kurt offered. "We could go check 'em out..."

"No..." Rose declined. "I'm just... I'm just not that into it today... I think I'll go for a walk or something and see you guys later."

"A walk?" asked Kurt incredulously. "Why would you wanna do that? Why don't we all just fly around then? We can check out all the new mansions going up, meet some new Residents... That's always fun..."

"No," Rose refused. "I just... I just feel a little tired, I guess..."

"You can't feel tired here Rose," said Derain. Concern was written across his dark face. "This is Aaru... We don't get tired..."

"My *mind* is tired," Rose specified, a little bit of irritation creeping into her voice. "I guess I feel like... Like I'm tired of thinking, but that seems to be the only thing I can do..."

"Well then," Kurt pressed. "How about let's go do something and take your mind off of it?!"

Rose shook her head. "I'm sorry, Kurt... I just can't... not today..."

"Come on guys," interjected Auset quietly. "Leave her alone. She said she doesn't feel like it...."

She turned to Rose.

"I like walking, Rose," she offered shyly. "Would you like me to walk with you?"

Rose thought about it a moment but then shook her head.

"Thanks Auset, but I don't want to ruin your day too," she sighed and looked up at the perfect, blue sky. A gentle breeze tossed her curly brown hair. "Maybe I'll just go back to my place and work on my gardens..."

"Are you sure, Rose?" Franco asked. "We could keep you company."

"No," Rose insisted. "You guys just go play... I'll catch up to you later." She tried to smile. "I'll sort some things out, and then I'll be much better company. I promise."

The others nodded reluctantly and filed away. Runa squeezed her shoulder. Auset gave her a hug, and Franco chanced a swift peck on her cheek. She watched them fly up into the sky and disappear.

Rose started walking. The wind picked up to whip her long hair and rustle her clothes. The grass as far as she could see billowed like great swells upon the ocean.

The gently rolling sameness of the Aaru plains was soothing. Suddenly it seemed much like it had been when she first arrived. The subtle rise and fall of the wind, the gentle chirping and whirring of insects, the distant calls of birdsong – these were the only sounds. She felt solitary, she realized, but she did not feel alone.

Aaru is a different place, she mused, but just like Hana had said it was not a perfect place.

It was not Heaven. It was a new place with new problems, but it was still very much life as she had known it before. The thought was both disappointing and comforting at the same time.

She still had worries and cares. She still had issues with her relationships. The flying was nice, she thought with a giggle and so was the not falling down and scraping your knees or breaking your arm, but it was still just life.

Is there a God in all of this somewhere, she wondered. *Is there a Heaven?*

Would she go there some day? How could she if she was going to live forever in Aaru? Did she want to live forever? Did it matter what she wanted?

Rose did not know the answers to any of these questions, but just thinking about them was therapeutic. She sat on the grass and looked up into the azure firmament. She wasn't really thinking about her clothing, but her Real Madrid soccer uniform shifted into the yellow sun dress. She lay back and stared at the cerulean sky with her hands behind her head.

Much of her time in Aaru had been simply playtime, but it was finally starting to dawn on her that she would actually have to make a life here. She would have to find a purpose. What would that purpose be?

Will it be a life with Franco? Rose wondered.

What would *that* be like? Would they be married like her parents? Would they live in the same house together? Would she fix dinners, and he go to work every day? That didn't really seem practical. What *would* they do? What about children? Was that even possible?

She hoped it was, she decided. You could create many things in Aaru. Why not kids?

Rose closed her eyes.

So many things to think about! God, I wish I could see Koren...

She sighed.

Maybe Kurt was right. Maybe she *should* just stop thinking so much. She tried for a moment to simply be, to let the warm zephyrs of perpetual summer wash over her. She thought about how it playfully tugged and pulled on her dress, how it felt on her skin and tousled her hair. She thought about how the balmy sunlight shone upon her face – warm and comforting.

Rose concentrated on the chirps and calls of the trilling birds, the buzzing insects, the fragrant scent of flowers and the gentle swishing of the tall grasses as they brushed against each other in the wind. She let it all surround her, flow through her, and for just a moment, just one precious moment, she was successful. Her mind was blank and at peace.

A violent concussion jarred Rose out of her respite. The ground shook and she sat up in alarm. Only a few feet away stood Hana looking stoop-shouldered and out of sorts. Her make-up was streaked down her face like she had been crying – her expression distraught and frantic.

Rose was immediately alarmed. Princess Hana *never* looked anything but immaculate, but now she seemed positively devastated.

Rose quickly leapt to her feet and approached her friend.

"Hana," she gasped, putting her hands on her friend's shoulders. "What's the matter? What has happened?!"

"My... Maker..." she hiccoughed brokenly. "My... M... Maker... is... *dead!*"

"Oh, Hana, no!" exclaimed Rose with a gasp. "How could this happen? I thought the Makers were higher than the Lords and Ladies of Aaru. I thought they were immortal like us!"

Hana shook her head miserably.

"The Makers are on the outside," she sobbed. "They tell us what to do from Before."

"Well," offered Rose gently. "Won't your Maker just come here like I did? Surely the Makers would come to Aaru if anybody *ever* did."

Hana made a pained face. "Well, Rose, in a sense they already have. We *are* the Makers, or maybe the Makers are us... I mean... We *were* the same..."

"I don't understand," said Rose, but she pulled Hana close and held her. The Flower Princess did not resist. "What do you mean you *were* the same?"

"Well," Hana tried to explain through her tears. "Do you remember what happened to you before you came to Aaru? Do you remember what Mr. Adams did when you were at the hospital?"

Rose furrowed her brow. "You know about that?"

"My Maker told me." Hana nodded. "She told me to expect you..."

"Okay. Well, then yes, I do" answered Rose. "He put this box thing with lots of little flashing light on my head. Then he hooked up a bunch of sensors and left them until... until I woke up here."

"Yes," said Hana. "That is the process we developed, but we perfected it on ourselves first, before even the Vedas. I remember being born Kiku Hanasaka, Rose. I remember growing up in Yamagata Prefecture in Japan. I remember my college friends in Tokyo and meeting Askr Ashe who hired me to work at Elysian Industries. I remember when we did the scan of my brain to test the process, and I remember waking up here in Aaru, but since that time, Rose, I and the Kiku outside – we've lived very different lives. We've become two totally separate people...

"She talked to me almost every day," Hana began to sob. "We worked together to solve difficult problems with the system. She would tell me about her irritations and troubles at work or on her business trips. She told me how our parents were doing back in Japan... About dates that she went on... I was an only child and suddenly I had someone who really *knew* me! It was wonderful to talk with someone who knew absolutely *everything* about me!"

"Like having a sister..." Rose murmured.

"Like having a *twin* sister, Rose," Hana cried into her shoulder. "And now..."

"Oh, Hana," soothed Rose. "I'm so sorry. What happened?"

"That is why I came to get you, Rose." Hana peered into her eyes, her expression frantic. "That is what I had to tell you! Someone struck her with a car and ran her over! Then they took your sister! Someone has taken Koren!"

Rose's blood ran cold.

"The person from the window..." she murmured. "The person who tried to take me... It must be the same one! What do we do?!"

"Lord Draugr has been talking with the Makers," Hana stated. "They have an idea, but we need you for it to work, and we *must* hurry. Time is irrelevant in Aaru, but not so on the outside. This person *murdered* my Maker to get to Koren. There is no telling what he has planned for your sister. We must find her right away..."

Rose nodded then rocketed into the sky. Her terror drove her. What if this guy *hurt* Koren? What if he *killed* her?!

She was not at all sure what help she could possibly give, but Rose was determined to do whatever Lord Draugr required of her. Faster than comets the two streaked across the sky, desperate to reach Yggdrasil and render whatever aid they could.

Chapter 21

Prepotence and Surrender

Koren opened her eyes, but that did not reveal anything. All was blackness. She tried to roll over and get up, but found she could not move. Her arms and legs were bound and she felt canvas pressing against her cheek. She lurched in panic. Where was she? What the Hell had just happened?

Then she remembered. She remembered the sounds of shrieking, crunching metal and shattering glass. She saw Kiku's body flying through the air and the man in the sun glasses and trench coat reaching for her. She screamed as realization struck her.

She was with *him*. The man who broke into her house and stole her underwear – the man who tried to hurt Rose – *he* had her.

It felt like she had been stuffed into some kind of sack. She struggled against her bonds to no avail. They cut into her wrists and ankles painfully. Oh *God*, what had she gotten herself into now? What was going to happen to her?!

There was a loud zipping sound, and Koren's world was flooded with light.

"There's no need to scream, Koren," came a low, calm voice. "You are with me now. You *belong* to me now... You shouldn't worry. I'll take good care of you..."

"Who are you?!" Koren asked fearfully. She could not twist herself enough to get a look at him. "What do you want with me?!"

"Everything," the man breathed. "I want *everything* from you... but I will *give* you everything also. I am the artist and you are to be my muse, my blank canvas..."

"I don't know what you are talking about," Koren's fear was taking over. She started to cry. "Let me go! Let me go! I wanna go home! Please let me go! Please, please don't hurt me!!!"

"Hurt you?" the man seemed taken aback. "I'm not going to hurt you, Koren... I'm going to *perfect* you! I'm going to complete you and fill you... I'm going to *save* you... Save us both..."

He knelt beside her and put something hard and heavy over her head. It felt like some kind of helmet. Then he ran a lascivious hand up and down her back, over her bottom, and down the length of her thigh.

It was then that Koren realized she was no longer wearing the T-shirt and blue jeans she had put on that morning. Instead she was wearing a short, white sun dress, a pair of thong panties the like of which she had never owned in her life, and no bra. Her eyes widened in horror and she began to jerk and kick. Koren lurched all over the floor trying to get the man's disgusting hands off of her.

"Leave me alone!" she shrieked. "Don't touch me! Don't touch me there!"

His hand slid under her dress to squeeze her bare bottom and she screamed again.

"'A real man,'" he stated smugly, "'wants two things: danger and play. Therefore he wants woman as the most dangerous plaything'. You *are* very dangerous Koren." He laughed. "And you *will* play. You will learn to appreciate my touch... to yearn for it even, but you are quite right... not *yet*. I'm getting ahead of myself..."

He ran his hands over her body again. He touched her chest and in between her legs. Koren jerked and kicked and the man sighed.

"But," he said as he stood. "I want that moment to be perfect. I want that moment to be *special*. Only when everything is in readiness will I take you, but I will give also..."

His voice dropped to a low whisper.

"After all," he breathed "For the woman, the man is a means: the end is always the child."

"No! No! Please, God, no!" Koren sobbed – hard convulsive sobs that shook her whole body. Tears ran down her cheeks in rivers. "Please leave me alone! I want my mom! I wanna go home! I wanna go..."

There was an electronic beep from the strange helmet thing. The man yanked it from her head then zipped the duffle bag closed again.

"God is dead..." Koren heard him mutter through the thick fabric of the bag. Then she heard the squeak of an office chair. She heard typing, and music started to play – some old rock song that she did not know.

Images filled Koren's brain there in the dark – fantasies of Askr Ashe or D kicking in the door to rescue her, of her father beating the horrible trench coat man unconscious, but no one appeared to save her. Koren was terrified. She continued to weep in the bag, but the man spoke to her no more.

"Please, God," Koren clenched her eyes tightly closed and prayed fervently through her tears. "Please, please, please, God, don't let this happen! Don't let this happen to me! Please get me out of this! *Please help me!!!*"

The man continued to type, and Koren continued to weep and pray. Her bindings cut her, and the inside of the duffle bag was stifling. It was getting hard to breath, but the music played on, and the man began to hum along. She had never felt so alone and helpless in her entire life.

***

Rose and Hana landed at the gates of Yggdrasil and dashed inside. There was some sort of barrier that prevented Residents from flying directly to the top, so the two raced up the winding wooden staircases until they burst out upon Lord Draugr's viewing platform.

It was packed.

Rose immediately recognized onyx-skinned Lady Nu deep in sober conversation with Lord Wurugag. Other Lords and Ladies whom she did not recognize quite so readily stood around in pairs and small groups doing the same. In their midst, the ruler of Aaru was in deep conversation with Mikoto. The red-haired boy, Matteus, rushed here and there frantically, but Rose had no idea what he was doing. That was not all, however.

Rose froze and her eyes widened. There beside Lord Draugr was a window.

Her breath quickened, and she felt suddenly glued to the spot. Hana tugged on her, but Rose could only stare.

"I don't know if I can do this, Hana," Rose gasped, staring fixedly at the black portal.

Hana put her hands on Rose's shoulders.

"I know this is scary, Rose," she whispered. "Trust me when I say that I am frightened too. I'm frightened for you and for Koren... I've grown quite fond of you and... if something should happen to you..." she leaned her head wearily against Rose's back. "But there's no other way... Please, Rose... We need you... *Koren* needs you..."

Rose swallowed and took a hesitant step forward. Then she took another. She held Hana's hand in a crushing grip, trying to draw on the Flower Princess for strength, but Rose could not deny feeling weaker with each step towards the sable rectangle in the air.

It was then she noticed that there was another man talking with Mikoto and Draugr. He was dressed in a pristinely white toga and had a wreath of laurels about his head. He looked at Rose in a calculating way that she found strangely familiar.

"Mr. Adams?" Rose gasped in surprise. "Is that you?"

"I am called Epimetheus here, Rose," said the man who looked like Mr. Adams. "But yes, I was called Adams once. I wish we were meeting under more pleasant circumstances."

"As Hana has most likely already informed you,' said Lord Draugr gravely. "Your sister has been kidnapped. We still do not know his real identity, but da Makers suspect it is a blogger who calls himself 'Magic Man'. Dey discovered a number of graphic posts under dat name on 5Kun… a relatively simple, image-based bulletin board website. It allows users to post content anonymously, so it's rife with questionable and sometimes flat out illegal content… Anyway, dat particular user has posted a number of video files dat could have only come from da Elysian Industries server…"

"We have no way to know who he is or where he is," added Mikoto fixing Rose with a grim stare. "But if we don't figure it out really soon, I fear what will happen to your sister… His posts about her… Well… They are quite graphic...

"So what do we do?" asked Rose intently. "Hana told me you had a plan."

"The only real lead that we have, Rose," said Epimetheus, "is his attempt to steal you… He logged in somehow with Koren's password, using an Aaru CPU he stole from your parents' house. We went back and tried to see if we could trace him based on that connection, but the system doesn't store that information. It only tells us which device accessed Aaru and when. I suppose we assumed, foolishly perhaps, that anyone accessing the system would be doing it from the location where we had set up the access port."

"So what do you suggest?" asked Rose urgently. "What can we do to save my sister?"

"We have to get him to log onto the system again," replied Mikoto. He looked down at his feet. "If we can do that, we might be able to trace him while he's connected."

"And how do we do that?" Rose asked with a sinking feeling in the pit of her stomach.

"Bait," said Lord Draugr simply. "We have to lure him back..."

"That's where you come in, Rose," added Lord Epimetheus. "He wanted you once. I doubt that has changed."

"We have to tempt him," said Mikoto. "We'll back up your files just before we do it... but we have to try and get him to take you again. That's the only hope we have of finding Koren in time."

"It will be very dangerous, Rose," Hana added. "We will understand if you don't want to go through it again..."

Rose paled and fell silent. The ruling Lords and Ladies of Aaru all stared at her expectantly. She had no memory of her ordeal before, but still she dreaded it. The fact that she did not recall what had happened made her more apprehensive in fact. Then she thought of Koren, alone and afraid.

"I'll do whatever is necessary," she stated quietly. "We have to help Koren. Just tell me what to do..."

"Alright," said Mikoto. "If you're ready, we can begin. Just place your hand on the screen..."

***

Magic Man was busy getting set up for his big moment. His bed was made. Pandadora proudly decorated the pillow at its head, and his webcam was in position and recording. The lighting was perfect. This would be his crowning achievement on 5kun – streaming live on the internet and immortalizing his legacy. It was OC that no one would *ever* be able to top and he could barely wait.

He could hear Koren faintly sobbing inside the large green duffle bag. It was apparent she was less than enthused about consummating the union between them, but he was not at all dismayed. It actually excited him. Koren Johnson was never sexier than when she was tragic and sad.

He clicked the mouse and added a new post to the comment stream.

Koren Johnson Deflowered LIVE! It said. *T minus 15 minutes and counting...*

Magic Man was feeling supremely pleased with himself, and taking Koren Johnson's body was not even the best part. It was expected from his 5Kun followers. It was demanded to ensure his legend, and he was not at all ill-disposed to the physical indulgence, but that was only the beginning. He was going to *take* Koren Johnson – all of her, the whole of her being. He meant to possess her *completely*. Magic Man glanced at the Aaru helmet with a smile.

He had used it on himself only this morning, shortly after he brought Koren back to his sanctuary. It might take some time, but once he merged and uploaded the files, his and hers, he would end their miserable existence in what the plebes and drones referred to as "the real world". Then they would truly be together forever – existing virtually as one perfect being.

He reached down and lifted the duffle bag. Koren squirmed at the unexpected movement, but it did not bother him. She was very light. He placed the bag on the bed and unzipped it. Then Magic Man unceremoniously dumped the girl out. The sight of her stole his breath for she had *never* looked so stunning.

Mascara was streaked down her cheeks in vivid runnels from intense weeping. Her large azure eyes were red and puffy – her expression broken and defeated. All of her twisting and struggling made the sun dress he had chosen for her ride up above her hips and her bare bottom was enticingly displayed. Her arms and legs were tightly trussed and her helpless state made her seem all the more forlorn.

"The time is nearly upon us, my sad little muse," Magic Man murmured, his chest heaving. He sat on the bed and fondled her exposed back side. Koren convulsed away from him sobbing.

"Why are you doing this to me?" She asked miserably, tears flowing freely. "What did I ever do to you? Please, don't hurt me! Please, leave me alone!"

"Why?" Magic Man asked with a chuckle. "Because, I mean to perfect you Koren… Because I *can*… Your celebrity will make me a legend and your immaculacy will make me whole! When I first saw you, I realized that I had found my match. I understood that we were *meant* to be together forever. Your face… Your innocence… Your sadness… The way you stood up to reject the very nature of reality to deny that hobgoblin of human existence – death! All a perfect fit!

"In you," he went on passionately. "I saw a despair about this world that mirrored my own – the miserable, helpless understanding that it was in fact a lightless, savage place that destroyed the truly exceptional - Where the only escape was death. In you I saw myself..."

He drew close to her and whispered in her ear. "But that is no longer the only way out, and you *saw* that! You revealed that salvation to the world! The old gods and religions will fade away in the light of this new reality! By illuminating me to the technology of Aaru you have made it possible for me to bring us together in a way that mere sexual congress never could. We will be one perfect being and live forever! That is why..."

He stood.

"I know you are afraid, and that is appropriate," Magic Man went on gently. "If you were unafraid it would belie your pristine and spotless soul! That is what I want from you, of course. I want your innocence, your *purity*. It is something I never had... with my superior mind and your unblemished spirit we shall truly become one complete, paradisiacal being! Once we are uploaded, we can bid adieu to this miserable existence called mortal life, and true freedom will be ours..."

"You... you're going to rape me and kill me then..." Koren stated coldly. Tears still quivered in her voice, but her anger was taking over. Her face twisted in rage. "What right do you have to treat me this way?!" she spat. "What's the matter with you?!"

"I don't think that is a very elegant way to describe it," Magic Man snapped in irritation. "You simply don't understand what I'm doing. What right? Might *makes* right, and woe to the conquered. But as for your last question," he stated bitterly. "That's something everyone who has ever known me has asked my entire life... It would be a very long answer, and we don't really have time for it. We go live in less than ten minutes..."

"Please don't do this!" Koren begged, still straining vainly against her bonds. "Just let me go. I...I won't tell anybody. No one will ever know. I'll keep it secret *forever*! I'll never tell! I promise... I *promise*! *Please* let me go!"

He bent over and kissed her forehead. His right hand strayed up under her dress, and she rebelled against his touch.

"Trust me, Koren," he murmured. "You're just not hearing me. You don't yet understand... but you will...Then you'll be grateful... so grateful..."

He stood and checked the camera again. He fiddled with a tiny remote control. A monitor to the left of the bed flashed on and

Koren could see her own stricken face. He took out his phone and snapped off a half dozen pictures.

Koren screamed and writhed against the restraints, but Magic Man's attention was suddenly called elsewhere.

The computer pinged, and he lifted his head quizzically. He walked over to the monitor and gazed at the screen. A wicked smile spread slowly across his face.

"Here now," he murmured. "I've just seen something that might cheer you up, my pretty muse. Apparently, the know-nothings at Aaru think they've patched their security hole... They're wrong..."

"What do you mean?" Koren demanded angrily. "What are you talking about?"

"It appears your dear sister Rose has logged onto the system," he stated gleefully. "She's looking for you... Searching for her poor, lost sister..."

"No..."

"Oh! How *delicious* is this?" he exclaimed. "I had abandoned those plans, but as always, fortune favors the prepared. Perhaps a little company would make you feel better. What if Rose were to join our little endeavor, hmm? All three of us combined into one perfect package!"

"You leave my sister alone!" Koren growled viciously, red-rimmed eyes blazing. "If you hurt her, I'll *kill* you!"

"I think you might find that hard to manage, my dear," commented Magic Man dismissively. "I'd love to accommodate you, but this... this is just too irresistible to pass up! Don't be impatient, Koren... I'll be with you in a minute."

He seated himself at the computer, and Koren shrieked her rage at the top of her lungs.

***

It seemed to Rose she stood there with her hand pressed against the window for an awfully long time. It was so long, in fact that Mikoto started to pace, wringing his hands. The other gathered Lords and Ladies began murmuring nervously among themselves, and Rose became seriously concerned that they were wasting their limited time. Every moment that passed without knowing her sister's whereabouts was another moment her abductor had to harm her. There was no time to waste.

Then she felt the pull.

"There..." Mikoto breathed. He stopped his pacing, and his eyes closed. To the side of the window where he was out of view, he held his hand up over his head, and his fingers glowed faintly cyan. "I think we've got a nibble... Wait... Yes... Yes! He's logged back in. Tracking now..."

Hana gasped, but Rose did not react as her arm started to slowly disappear into the monitor. She bit her lower lip and stared into the void with fixed concentration.

"Tracking, tracking..." Mikoto repeated under his breath with an intensely concentrating expression on his face. "He's in the Eastern US somewhere, but I'm still narrowing it down..."

Rose continued to gaze into the dark screen trying her best to tamp down the panic rising in her breast as her fingers dissolved into tiny green squares before dissipating into the virtual ether. Then the image in the screen jerked as if someone was adjusting a camera. The picture cleared.

Rose gasped. Then she narrowed her eyes. She saw a man in large sunglasses, nondescript ball cap, and trench coat. A bushy grey and black beard obscured the rest of his face, but Rose was not considering his visage too carefully. Rather her gaze focused on the background of the video feed. There behind him on a bed, was Koren. Rose could hear her weeping, and her fury was kindled.

"What are you doing to my sister?" she demanded. "Let her go! If you hurt her..."

"So nice to see you again, Rose, but I think you are hardly in a position to give orders," the voice on the other end of the connection contemptuously interrupted. It was deep and threatening –electronically garbled. "...Or threats, for that matter - Full of sound and fury, but signifying nothing. You will be with us soon too..."

"It looks like it's somewhere in Kentucky," whispered Mikoto. "Keep him talking!"

"You are a *murderer*," stated Rose coldly. "You will never get away with this. We will find you and punish you..."

"I really think I probably will, actually," the figure laughed with an unconcerned stretch. He flashed a contemptuous smile. "Koren and I are here *all* alone. Our union will be consummated in mere minutes. I have continued to confound and perplex the morons at Elysian Industries at every turn, so in carefully evaluating the situation, I feel confident in my ability to 'get away with it' as you so artlessly put it…

"You might consider, Rose," he added with a smug, leering grin, "if you haven't already, that I'm about to take your sister's virginity in front of a live internet audience, and there's absolutely nothing you can do to stop me. Interesting, isn't it? You must be feeling some very powerful emotions right now. Would you care to share them with us, Rose? I'm sure my audience would love to hear them. We're all adoring fans of you and your sister here, after all…"

"You're an evil *bastard*!" Rose spat at the screen.

"Evil?" The man scoffed. "What is evil but the whining and complaining of the vanquished? 'What is good? All that heightens the feeling of power in man…' You think me evil because I defeat and confound you, but I know myself. I know my fate. One day my name will be associated with the memory of something tremendous! After I have you, I will take your sister and begin to realize that excellence…"

"You are out of your mind," Rose growled. "You're completely crazy."

"Bowling Green!" hissed Mikoto. "Just a little more, Rose!"

"What *is* 'crazy'?" Countered Magic Man. He leaned in closer to the camera. "But seeing clearly that which the mediocre mind cannot fathom? Just because you cannot understand my thinking does not mean it is unreasoned… I am rather disappointed in you, Rose. You didn't strike me as stupid before. I would have expected a more nuanced view from you. Perhaps you have been too long in the company of Elysian Industry's corporate goons. You cause me to doubt whether making you a part of my and Koren's union is a good idea…"

"You will not hurt her," Rose stated fiercely even as her arm crept another few inches into the screen. She grit her teeth the keep her voice from shaking. "I won't let you…"

"I've got an address," hissed Mikoto. "Keep him talking! Just a few seconds more… Lord Draugr will tell the Makers. Help is on its way!"

The man leaned even closer into the camera. His obscured visage completely filled the window.

"Really? How do you plan to stop me, exactly?" He laughed. Then his voice sank to a gloating murmur. "I cannot wait to enjoy your sister's body, Rose. I'm so glad you'll be able to watch… every fervid, orgasmic moment of it…"

Something snapped inside of her. Rose was no longer afraid. She was furious. Her cheeks reddened, and she heard Hana exclaim as roaring flames suddenly burst from her head and shoulders. She stopped resisting the force that was trying to suck her through the screen. Instead she embraced it. This man would *not* hurt Koren.

Snarling viciously, Rose reached through the portal with both of her hands. She thrust them deeply through to the other side, groping for something, *anything* that she might use to aid her against this horrid person. Her head quickly followed. She heard Hana scream and felt tugging pulling hands upon her lower extremities, but she was determined. Rose would not be denied. She resolved that her searching would either be relentless and successful or futile and fatal.

The result was immediately disorienting. Rose examined her new surroundings, but it was difficult to describe. Taking a moment to get her bearings she realized that what she now detected was not sight as she was used to, but still she could perceive. She saw everything that was on the inside of this 'Magic Man's' computer. She understood all of the connections within. The content was vast. Much of it was disgusting and obscene, but Rose quickly skimmed over everything, searching doggedly for *anything* that she might use against her enemy.

"It's nearly time Rose…"

Magic Man's voice echoed all around and through her. It made her feel filthy, and she recoiled from it, but there was nowhere to go. It felt like the vile man was everywhere – permeating the innermost recesses of her being. She screamed as the video feed of her sister lying helpless on the bed seemed to overwhelm her every sensibility. Magic Man seated himself beside Koren and laid a lecherous hand on her bare thigh.

"NOOOOOOOOO!!!" wailed Koren as Rose screamed the same.

Then Rose gasped. There, amidst the deluge of filth and perversion, she saw it. The something drew her like a shining beacon. It summoned her like an invocation. Rose knew exactly what to do.

"Mediocre mind, huh?" she spat contemptuously. Her eyes blazed and her lips curled into a sneer. "Let's see how 'mediocre' you think *this* is…"

She grasped it with both hands.

***

The download bar at the bottom of his computer monitor hit eighty eight percent, and Magic Man sat back in satisfaction. He was actually a little sorry to bring this struggle to an end so quickly. He was relishing the exchange immensely.

There was nothing he liked better than gloating – Lording his superiority over the lesser sheeple who infested this world like so many cockroaches in a rotting wall. Rose Johnson's impotent fury amused him. The idea that she would soon be forced to watch helplessly as he ravished Koren titillated and excited the voyeur in him. Then of course, it would be time to get started on the *real* work of consequence – the final phase of his sublime and ultimate vision. Victory was imminent, his final triumph inevitable.

"As surely it must have been all along," he breathed pompously before sipping deeply from his steaming coffee mug. Magic Man smirked as he updated his 5Kun post.

"Koren Johnson Show Time! T-MINUS 3 MINUTES," it said. He hit a button and glanced at a small square in the corner of his computer screen.

He was putting on quite a show already, if he did say so himself, but now it was finally time for the main event. The broadcast from the bedside monitor had begun. Magic Man rose and seated himself on the bed next to her. He laid his hand on her thigh and leaned in close to the camera with an intense expression as Koren wailed.

"Welcome all, to my moment of victory!" he declared in a loud voice. "For all of my loyal followers on 5kun, I bid you welcome as you bear witness and enjoy the realization of my immaculate vision.

"Watch as I fulfill your deepest desires and darkest fantasies of carnal amusement - as I make Koren Johnson my own!"

Magic Man smirked again and puffed out his chest before declaring in a loud voice.

"You, my loyal fans, have already observed my welcome of Rose Johnson! Rose the Deathless! The Avatar of Aaru! The Elysian Industries lackey. You will now watch as she is forced to witness my union with her dear sister, and indeed, ultimately become part of it herself. Watch as she bears witness to my achievement of final greatness! Oh, Rose, you and all Elysian Industries with you... You are *defeated*!

"She calls me 'evil,'" he hissed mockingly, "but that is not true. I simply refuse to be denied! Who can attain to anything great, Rose, if he does not feel in himself the force and will to inflict great pain? Do you feel pain, Rose? Does it chill your blood and still your heart? Does your impotence and weakness gnaw at your soul? I bet it does, here at the end on the verge of your defeat – witnessed by the whole *world* no less! How does it feel in these last few moments? Does it eat you up inside? Your failure to save your sister... Your..."

Magic Man gasped and staggered to his feet with a cry of dismay. The camera and tripod on the bedside table crashed to the floor. He was suddenly soaked.

An alarm blared in the building. There was a flash, and his computer sparked and flamed out with a choking cloud of black smoke. He spun aimlessly looking this way and that in confusion and panic, water streaming down his face. He turned toward the monitor overseeing the apartment building. At the entranceway, it displayed two navy blue-clad policemen rushing through the front doors. The next moment that monitor too sparked and went dark.

Magic Man turned his wide-eyed gaze to Koren on the bed. He was *so* close, and she so enticing as the water from the fire sprinklers soaked through her thin white dress. He considered grabbing her up – running away with her...

Then he growled in frustration. She would slow him down too much. There was no time. There was no choice but to cut his losses.

Instead of seizing the whimpering girl, he grabbed up the Aaru helmet and jerked the CPU free from where he had wired it into his own computer. Magic Man rushed from the apartment and slammed the door shut behind him, leaving Koren tied up on the bed. He fled down the hallway, darted up the stairs to the roof, and was gone.

Chapter 22

Faded Blossoms

Koren was soaking wet and frightfully cold. When the officers finally bashed in the door and rushed into the apartment however, she didn't think that she had been happier in her entire life before. She wept shamelessly as they cut through her bonds.

She could not bear the touch of the clothing in which her captor had dressed her a second longer, so Koren borrowed a spare T-shirt from one of the sympathetic policemen and wrapped a blanket around her waist. She grabbed up Pandadora, but left the white dress and scandalous underwear crumpled on the floor. In a matter of minutes she found herself being rushed to a waiting patrol car outside.

Seconds later, the nondescript apartment parking lot was crammed full of police cruisers, lights flashing. There were Bowling Green Police Department cars as well as those of the Kentucky Highway patrol, KBI, and FBI. The officers swarmed through the building as an ambulance pulled up, and Koren was loaded into it. It screeched away from the curb, siren blaring.

Almost immediately after she arrived at the hospital, Mr. Ashe, Mr. Adams, and her parents appeared. Her mother and father seemed to want to break her bones, they hugged her so tightly, and all of them had plenty of tears to shed. They did not lessen when Mr. Ashe haltingly revealed the heartbreaking news about Kiku.

The next couple of hours were a whirlwind of awkward questions from the police as well as nurses and doctors. Koren had no desire to think of the horrible man who had taken her or what he planned to do to her ever again, yet she was forced to go over and over all of it in excruciating detail. Then the police informed her apologetically that the man had not yet been apprehended, but assured her they were still searching.

Koren was physically no more the worse for wear than a couple of lumps and some dark marks on her wrists and ankles, so she was informed she could go home. As she walked down the steps to the awaiting limo, paparazzi cameras flashing, reporters screaming questions - she was emotionally empty and physically exhausted.

They all crowded into the long, black vehicle and drove away, but it was a staid, silent trip. Her parents insisted on sitting to either side of her with their arms draped around her shoulders while Koren hugged Pandadora tightly against her chest. It was a level of attention that she would have normally found annoying, but she did not protest. When they finally arrived home, her house was swarming with reporters, so they made a quick U-turn and headed to Elysian Industries instead.

The gaping hole in the fence was still evident as they drove up the gravel access road, but Koren could already see stakes and orange ribbons outlining the beginnings of some new construction. Mr. Ashe followed her quizzical gaze and informed her a new fifteen foot concrete wall would soon replace the chain-link fence surrounding the campus. This was only the beginning of the stepped-up security, he said.

When they arrived, Koren was offered food, but she was not at all hungry. They had prepared a makeshift bedroom for her and her family in one of the conference rooms, but as weary as she was, Koren could not make herself go to sleep. Too many warring emotions filled her head and weighed upon her broken heart. She lay on her cot that night, Pandadora tucked snuggly under her arm, staring at the ceiling until she heard her parents snoring. Sleep felt impossible, so she got up to take a walk.

The changes in the halls of Elysian Industries were striking. Black-suited security guards with ear pieces and sun glasses paced the corridors. New cameras were now evident in every available nook and cranny of the building. She happened to bump into D and impulsively hugged him, which clearly made the huge man uncomfortable, but Koren did not relent until he grudgingly hugged her back. The rest of the newly beefed up security detail acknowledged her passage with raised hands or slight nods, but otherwise did not hinder it.

She did not really think about where she was going, but perhaps because of the unconscious pull of her own melancholy, she found herself standing outside Kiku's office door. When she realized where she was, Koren could not help but cry. On impulse, she tried the handle and found it unlocked. She entered and flipped on the light switch.

Though she had only been missing for about eighteen hours, the sudden changes in her universe were stark. She didn't feel safe anymore, not even with the extra security. She felt hunted and vulnerable. Even though her captor had not managed to rape her, Koren still felt violated.

She recalled the feel of his groping, lecherous hands on her body and shuddered, dry washing her shoulders in disgust. She wanted to take a shower suddenly, but doubted that she would ever feel clean again. She squeezed Pandadora a little more tightly and clenched her eyes closed until her nauseated shivers subsided.

Koren seated herself in the chair where Kiku had served her tea a mere two days before and wept. It was strange. The flowers in the Japanese woman's office were still beautiful, their aromatic scent filling the air, but even now were beginning to droop as if they too mourned the absence of their mistress. A half-finished cup of tea sat neglected on Kiku's desk among an assortment of official looking papers that she must have been working on. Had Koren not known the reality, she would have assumed her friend had only stepped out for a minute – that she would open the door at any moment to smile in her gentle guarded way and say something to make Koren feel better.

It wasn't fair.

Koren was relieved at her rescue, certainly, but was also furious. Magic Man had stolen Kiku from her, but that was not all. He had taken even more. The man had gotten what he wanted, she realized. He had stolen her sense of safety… her innocence. He had ripped it away leaving only hollow regret and fear in its place. What if he came back?

She suddenly did not want to be alone anymore and left the office. She had a little trouble finding her way back to her parents in the vast compound, however. Koren tried a couple of doors that looked promising, but none of them were the right ones. On her third attempt she found herself someplace she recognized.

The conference room was dark, but there next to a long table, a huge monitor glowed like an indigo beacon. This was the room where she had first spoken to Rose, she realized. It was the room where her life had taken such an impossible turn.

On impulse she approached the screen and entered her log-in information. She did not expect the system to respond, but it prompted her to call a user. Without thinking, she said:

"Rose Johnson."

The sky scene turned to the rainbow swirling pattern, and then a single, small hand pressed against the screen.

"Rose?" She asked uncertainly. "Is it you?"

Her sister appeared on the monitor. She smiled brilliantly.

"Koren!" She exclaimed clapping her hands together with a giggle. "I'm so glad it's you!" Her face darkened, and the corners of her mouth tightened. "I was ready... Well... I was ready... In case it wasn't... In case it was... someone else..."

"Askr told me what you did, Rose," Koren said. She struggled to keep the tears at bay. "He said you set off the sprinkler system and the fire alarm... And then we got really lucky that there was a police car less than a block away from the building when Mr. Tanaka called it in... I thought I was going to die, Rose... I begged and begged for him not to hurt me, and he wouldn't stop *touching* me!" She shivered in revulsion. "He was going to... to..." she couldn't make herself put into words what the man had almost done. "Thank you..." she said instead.

Rose looked down sheepishly.

"I know... I was *so* scared for you, Koren," she murmured. "I was afraid... I didn't even really understand what it was I was doing. I just knew that I had to do *something*! I only remember up until... until *that man's* computer shorted out. Mikoto said they were monitoring me constantly up until that point, but then had to bring me back with my backup file, so I don't remember anything after that. Still, he was surprised, I could tell. I don't think Mikoto realized what I did was possible... But... Are *you* okay? You're not like, *hurt* or anything, are you?"

"I'm *not* okay, Rose," Koren's voice broke. "I'm bruised. I'm scared. Every time I close my eyes I see *him*. I hear his voice... I feel his hands on me... Ugh!" She shuddered again. "I don't think I'll ever be okay again! And poor Kiku!" She began to whimper. "Her body smashing against that windshield and flying through the air... I can't get it out of my head! How will I *ever* be okay, Rose? How?!"

Rose put both of her hands against the screen. Koren copied the gesture and rested her head against the cool, glowing monitor.

"I could really use a hug from you right now, Rose..." she murmured sadly.

"Me too..." Rose answered. "Someday..."

"Yeah," Koren uttered in a tiny voice. "Someday..."

They were quiet a long while, neither exactly sure what they should say. Then Rose perked up.

"Koren?" she began hopefully. "I want you to see something... I think it might make you feel better. Wait a sec?"

"Sure," agreed Koren. "I'd sure like to feel better."

Rose gave her a small, pensive smile.

"I'll be right back," she said, then disappeared from the window.

Koren was left to stare out at the vast Aaru Plains. She heard the singing of birds, the chirping of insects, and the gentle rustling of the wind through the tall grass. It was all very peaceful. About the time she started to get a little impatient, Rose reappeared.

"Koren," she said softly. "I'd like to introduce you to a special friend of mine. I've mentioned her to you before... She pulled a willowy figure in front of the window. "This is Hana... She's one of my best friends in Aaru..."

Koren gasped.

"Kiku!" she exclaimed. "You're *Kiku*! How did... What are..." she spluttered for an additional few second before she recovered her powers of speech again. "Is it *really* you? Are you in Aaru now?"

Princess Hana bowed formally.

"Yes and no," she replied uncertainly. "I am very like Kiku, Koren. Her passing was devastating for me as well... I would be honored if we could talk about her together from time to time... I think we might become friends..."

"Hana *was* Kiku," said Rose, noting Koren's confused expression, "before Aaru. They've been apart for a long time though. Think of Hana like Kiku's twin sister... I really think you'll like her..."

"Of... Of course I will," stammered Koren. "I don't completely understand, but it's... It's really good to see your face again..."

"Did I help?" asked Rose hopefully. "I know I can't take it all away. I'm still scared that this guy might come back, but Hana says they've already made some big changes that should make the system safer. They said that the Makers... That's the Elysian Industry Board Members on your end... they are going to really bulk up your security. He won't be able to get anywhere *near* you... I know it's hard, but... I hope I helped a little bit at least."

"You helped a lot, Rose," replied Koren affectedly. "You didn't leave me. You saved me… Just like when we were little… Just like you promised you always would. Thank you… I… I love you."

"I love you too, Koren!" Rose answered intensely. "Please talk to me again soon. Okay? Talk to me *every day*! And talk to Hana too! I need to know you're alright, Koren. I really need to know that everything's fine with you. I don't want to be scared like that ever again."

"Me either, Rose," Koren replied. "I'll do my best… I'm sorry I didn't make time before… I was stupid… I guess… I figured I had forever."

"No one has forever, Koren," Hana answered seriously. "Not out there, not even in Aaru. None of us know how long we'll have, but it's important that we make the most of it. Never take that for granted…"

"You're right," Koren agreed. "I won't… I'll talk to you guys every chance I get from now on. I promise!"

"Is it late there, Koren?" Rose asked. "It looks late. It's all dark behind you in the window."

"Yeah," answered Koren. "It's pretty late…"

"Go to bed and get some rest, sweetie," Rose commanded gently. "I promise you; you're safe tonight."

"A great number of people who care about you very much are watching over you, Koren," Hana added. "What happened today was awful… monstrous! But try to put it out of your mind. Today was a dark day, but don't worry. I believe that you will have many, *many* more beautiful days to come."

"I'll try," Koren promised.

They said their goodbyes, but Rose made her sister swear three times to talk to her again in the morning, and Koren assured her that she would. When she finally made her way back to the room where her parents were sleeping, Koren lay down, hugged Pandadora tight, and closed her eyes. She imagined Rose and Kiku looking down on her protectively. It *did* make her feel better.

At last she slept.

***

Rose sat by herself on the banks of the river, dangling her bare feet in the water. She had just taken her leave of Princess Hana and was feeling pensive. She was relieved that her sister was safe, of course, but could not help being unsettled. It bothered her that her and her sister's attacker was still on the loose, but Rose was not at all sure what she could do about it.

She sighed heavily.

Maybe I should take my own advice, she thought ironically. *Maybe I should try to stop worrying so much.* But it was *so* hard!

"Hey Pretty Princess," came a warm, hesitant voice behind her.

Rose turned and smiled at Franco. She patted the spot on the grass beside her, and the Latin boy sat down.

He smiled at her.

"Are you about ready for our talk, Rose?" he asked. "I... I just wanted to apologize. I just wanted to say that I'm *really* sorry. I pushed you too far... I hope I haven't ruined everything..."

She took his hand and pulled him to her, kissing him deeply. He started in surprise but quickly wrapped her in his arms and kissed her back.

"Franco," she said after a long moment.

Franco let her pull away only reluctantly.

"I don't know what our future is going to be like here," Rose went on. "But I don't care. It's no different than anywhere else really, is it? Just like you said before... What I *do* know though, is that life is fragile. It can turn on you in a second. You have to enjoy the ones you love while you can... I'm the one who's sorry. I'm sorry I freaked out... I... I... don't want there to be any regrets between us. I want to take advantage of every chance we're given, because we never know when we won't be given any more... Do you understand what I'm trying to say?"

"I think so Rose," Franco answered in a gravelly voice. Then he took a deep and determined breath. "I... I agree... No more regrets... So... I'll... I'll go and say it first; I love you, Rose. However long we have together here in Aaru, I wanna spend that time with you..."

"I love you too," replied Rose.

They kissed again.

Rose lay back and pulled Franco on top of her. Then he rolled over so that Rose was astride him. Their breath was coming quickly, and Rose felt the same deep stirrings of desire from before building in her breast as Franco urgently felt her body. Then the Latin boy stopped.

"Hey Rose?" Franco ventured hesitantly. His hands found their way up under her yellow sun dress.

"What is it, Franco?"

"You know..." he said slowly. "When Mikoto saved you from the window before... I remember... He... he turned the Harm Failsafe off... Do you think... maybe... that... well... that it might still be *off*?"

Rose laughed. Then she hugged herself, purring at the idea. She gave Franco a wicked little smile. Then she kissed him again.

"There's only one way to find out," she whispered coyly into his ear.

This time, Rose felt no embarrassment, no reluctance, no regret. In fact, she felt nothing but elation as she kissed him... That feeling only intensified in that one, joyous moment when they both realized together the Harm Failsafe was indeed still turned off.

Afterward

"...This security breach is yet another reason this so-called 'service' is entirely too dangerous!" James Rook pounded his palm with his fist as he bellowed into the TV camera. "The fact that such sensitive information could be so easily stolen... The fact that they were engaged in the production of *child pornography* while claiming ignorance it was going on... The fact Koren Johnson could be *kidnapped* right off of the very Elysian Industries Campus right under their noses only illustrates either their incompetent, unconscionable laxity, or more likely, their shameless criminality!

"*Anyone,*" he raged, "doing business with this amoral company would be very foolish indeed *not* to fear that something like this could happen to them - that their data is seriously at risk. The senate should launch a full investigation into the matter. Whether this utter negligence is feigned or not, it is still likely *illegal* in either case!"

The camera panned to the right. Askr Ashe sat forward in his chair. He held his hands up and shook his head bearing an irate expression that was equally annoyed and incredulous.

"Now wait just a second," he protested. "First of all, as Mr. Rook knows perfectly well, the video stolen off of our server was incidental footage, just like what a security camera might randomly pick up. Second, I deeply resent dat da senator is trying to blame Elysian Industries for a criminal act of which we were da *victim!*"

Senator Rook tried to interject, but Askr was not willing to cede the floor to him so easily.

"It is true we have grown very quickly and have indeed struggled to keep pace. However, we must not forget it was a *criminal* who *illegally* broke into our system and stole data dat compromised Miss Johnson's safety. It was not 'negligence' as Mr. Rook claims. We were da victim of a *crime!*

"It is absolutely no different dan other major data breaches at any number of major companies over da years." Askr went on raising a finger with each example. "Sony Pictures, Target, da iCloud photo hacking scandal, da 2016 DNC hack a number of years ago, da WannaCry ransomware attack... all dese involved major, well-established companies and organizations with robust capabilities in terms of cyber security. Even da US Office of Personnel Management was not immune. It is a division of da federal government itself, and yet even dey *still* fell victim to da unforeseeable.

"Rather dan try to attack da victim," Mr. Ashe pressed. "Da government helped dese entities look at dere vulnerabilities and fix dem. Dey pursued da people perpetrating dose cybercrimes both in an attempt to bring dem to justice as well as to prevent similar breaches in da future. Dat's exactly what we are engaged in doing right now.

"Mr. Rook is simply being disingenuous," Askr went on, "and fishing for anything about which he can criticize us, because he has a *religious* objection to our service. Dat is well documented in da media. His ulterior motives and all of dis feigned outrage have nothing to do with data safety. Rather, it is simply a clumsy attempt at defaming Aaru. Da fact remains - da system is fundamentally sound and represents a major technological breakthrough!"

"My objections to Aaru are many and various," retorted Senator Rook with a contemptuous sniff. "This is simply one more problem to add to the litany of problems, yes, but simply identifying your *many* other failings does not make my concerns about your data security invalid. I wonder if your defense of Elysian Industries would be so full-throated and robust if you had failed to retrieve Miss Johnson!"

"Miss Johnson," growled Askr jabbing a finger in the direction of the Senator, "was da victim of a *stalker*, a crazed fan who incidentally *murdered* one of our board members! Dat investigation is ongoing, and we have seriously enhanced our security as a consequence. However, it was in fact specifically *because* we used all of da technology at our disposal dat we were able to locate Koren Johnson in time and inform da authorities! I'll also take dis chance to reiterate what Mr. Rook just pointed out, because it *is* important to remember; We *did* get her back!"

"You can't sit there and tell me," fired back Senator Rook. "That something like this can happen, and you deserve absolutely no blame at…"

The waitress walked up to the TV and clicked it over to another channel – some sort of auto race or something. It was just as well… The debate only served to depress him anyway.

Magic Man was still furious with himself every time he thought about Koren Johnson – How close he had been! And yet so careless…

He sat in the seedy diner sipping at a cup of black coffee. His face was still obscured by a pair of dark sunglasses, but he was dressed in a navy hoodie in lieu of his customary trench coat and ball cap. The tuft of hair protruding from his midnight blue cowl was dyed a coppery blonde, and he was now clean-shaven.

Magic Man took a big bite of the greasy hamburger he had ordered. It was lousy – clearly overcooked and seriously needing seasoning, but he was hungry. He took a few more bites then stared hard at the half-eaten sandwich.

"A strong and well-constituted man digests his experiences, deeds and misdeeds all included, just as he digests his meats," he muttered to himself thoughtfully. "Even when he has some tough morsels to swallow..."

He was not discouraged - Not in the least. Magic Man still had both the helmet and the CPU in his trunk. The helmet still had Koren's brain scan saved. His copy of Rose Johnson's data was mostly complete. He just needed to get back to L.A. and all of his spare equipment in the storage unit there. At least he had escaped his apartment with the two most important pieces.

That's something.

He would have to alter his plans, but his end game had not changed. Magic Man looked around briefly to make sure no other patron was close enough to peek. Then he chanced a glimpse at his phone.

He had new wallpaper now – Koren Johnson all tied up and helpless on his bed. Her expression was desolate, tear stains vivid, pert little bottom exposed... He'd even managed to get Pandadora into the shot, which emphasized Koren's youth and innocence. He smiled to himself and sighed at his own masterful artistry – a vision of peerless beauty.

"The value of a thing sometimes does not lie in that which one attains by it," he quoted philosophically as he switched the screen curtain on once more. "But in what one pays for it..."

He just hadn't paid quite enough yet. Rather than be dejected, it only made him want her more. This was a setback to be sure, but not a defeat. Magic Man just needed time to lick his wounds and think. A new idea would come to him. He was confident. This wasn't over yet.

He finished his coffee, paid for the food with a pre-paid debit card, and stalked out the door. Then he hopped into a brown, late-model station wagon, started the engine, and backed up. He took a moment to flip on the radio.

It was a rattletrap old car, probably late seventies or early eighties vintage if he had to guess, but it was the best he could do on short notice. Still, it had an eight-track tape player, and that was a bonus. He smiled as the tape clicked on and his favorite song blared from the speakers.

Magic Man mashed the gas pedal to the floor.

"Not over by a long shot…" he murmured intensely as he peeled away from the parking lot of the all-night diner. He vanished down the road and into the gloom of very early morning.

Window down, hair tossed in the breeze, he felt his confidence returning as he disappeared down the country road and into the night. He sang at the top of his lungs. Bright headlights stabbed into darkness ahead, and he narrowed his eyes in determination as the chorus concluded.

"I'm a Magic Man, Mama…" He murmured.

The End.

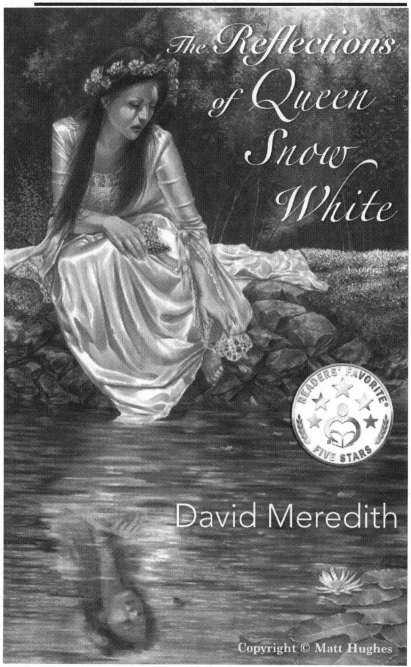

The Reflections of Queen Snow White

David Meredith

Copyright © Matt Hughes